THE BOY IN THE RED DRESS

THE
BOY
IN THE
RED
DRESS

by

KRISTIN LAMBERT

VIKING

VIKING

An imprint of Penguin Random House LLC, New York

First published in the United States of America by Viking,
an imprint of Penguin Random House LLC, 2020

Visit us online at penguinrandomhouse.com

LIBRARY OF CONGRESS CATALOGING-IN-PUBLICATION DATA IS AVAILABLE
ISBN 9780593113684

Printed in the United States of America

1   3   5   7   9   10   8   6   4   2

Book design by Nancy Brennan

Text set in Baskerville

For Shannon, who took me to my
first drag show. And for my sister Kelly.
I'd solve a murder with you anytime.

CHAPTER

1

MY STORY BELONGS on the front page next to a photograph the size of the Saint Louis Cathedral. That's what the reporter told me. She said I should picture my name and hers in capital letters, and imagine showing her editor and the whole city of New Orleans that girls can be the heroes of stories and write them, too. But I know the truth—newspapers only care about girls who are rich and pretty and blonde, especially when they're dead.

The real story is one the paper would never print.

The real story isn't about me or that dolled-up debutante either. It's about my best friend, Marion, undisputed queen of the Cloak and Dagger and definitely *not* a murderer, no matter what the cops and the papers said.

It started on the last night of 1929 with a knock on a door. That night, my aunt Cal had run off to Baton Rouge for a last-minute vaudeville engagement and left me in charge of her speakeasy, the Cloak and Dagger. In all the four years since my mother ditched me with her sister, Aunt Cal had never trusted anyone else with the club, so I thought something might be about to change for the better. Maybe I wouldn't be stuck mopping floors, busing tables, and cooking Cal's books forever. Maybe if this night went well, she'd let me quit school early and run the place on weeknights.

New Year's Eve is second only to Mardi Gras in the French Quarter, but Cal said I shouldn't expect any more than the usual amount of trouble. The beat cops were bribed extra, the hidey-holes were stocked with double the hooch, Marion was getting beautiful in his dressing room, and while Frank the bouncer broke up a fight over a boy between two sailors, I was running the door.

So, when the girl knocked, I was the lucky one who slid back the slot in the club's front door.

"*Jittersauce*," she said confidently through the sandwich-size opening. All I could see of her were long-lashed eyes and one bright curl plastered to the middle of her forehead. She wasn't a regular, but she was pretty and about my age and, most important, she had the password. I lifted the latch and let her in.

Right away, I regretted it. She swept inside the club, leading a conspicuously wealthy pack, all of the kids except her sweating in oversize raccoon-fur coats. Even in dead winter most nights in New Orleans produced no worse than a clammy chill, but the girl was the only one with the sense (or the vanity) to leave the fur at home. She wore a slinky dress covered with an angular pattern of gold beads, and enough jewelry to fuel the fencing trade in the French Quarter for a month—a gold necklace with translucent green dragonfly wings spread across her collarbone, an emerald ring, and nickel-size emerald earrings that sparked light under her helmet of silvery-blonde curls.

I tried not to roll my eyes as the Uptowners stopped just inside the door and gaped at the scene before them, tugging their fur collars away from their necks. The sign hanging over our door said we were a soda shop, but everybody who made it this far knew the truth. Including the cops we bribed to keep the feds off our backs and overlook some of the less-than-lawful things going on inside. My aunt's club was a risky joint to be seen in, for lots of reasons, but we still got our share of looky-loos, mostly kids my age or so, who came purely for the sensation of being somewhere scandalous once in their strait-laced lives.

Oftentimes, folks like these wandered in, took one look at the boys dancing with boys, girls with girls, and wandered themselves right back out again. This bunch looked like they were about to do the same, but their blonde ringleader jabbed an elbow in her date's ribs, and he skittered forward like an agitated crab.

"Go find a table," she told him imperiously. His hair was equally platinum and looked like it was molded out of porcelain. "Please," she said a little nicer. "I'll be right there."

"You got it, peach," he said agreeably, and the others followed after him into the smoke-hazed belly of the club.

The girl, though, stayed put and turned to me. She opened her handbag, all covered in gold beads to match her dress. For a second, I thought she was going to give me a tip, and I'll admit, I wasn't going to turn it down.

"Hello, Miss . . . ?" she said, like she was waiting for me to fork over a last name.

I leaned forward on my stool, fingering the collar of the tuxedo jacket Aunt Cal didn't know I'd borrowed. "Call me Millie."

"Okay. Millie." She looked flustered all of a sudden, different from when her friends were around. It made her seem younger, less like a queen. She held out a small photograph. "Have you ever seen"—she edged closer, as if afraid of being overheard, though the jazz band's blasting made it unlikely—"a boy who looked like this? In here?"

"Can't say that I have." I adjusted Cal's top hat over my chin-length black hair to avoid taking a closer look at the picture. It was one of Cal's rules for all of us working at the Cloak and Dagger club; you didn't give out names and you didn't confirm you'd seen anybody here. We'd had wives and husbands come looking, fiancées, boyfriends, mothers. They didn't get far with us.

The girl's tidy penciled brows came together in a frown, and she stamped her little gold-clad foot. "But you didn't even look!"

Two knocks sounded on the door, and I held up a finger to silence her. I flipped up the panel in the door. Three of the Red Feather Boys, which is what Marion and I call his most devoted fans, waited outside. I didn't bother to ask them for the password and jerked open the door on its squealing hinges.

"Welcome! Welcome!" I said, sweeping off the top hat with a flourish. The boys grinned, and I waved the hat toward the bar. "Drinks are thataway, fellas!"

"Lookin' swell, Millie," one of them said, nudging me with an elbow. "Is that lipstick I see?"

"Nah," I lied. "Just ate half a jar of maraschino cherries."

Truth was, I'd found a tube of stage lipstick in the flotsam on Aunt Cal's dresser and swiped it on, then quickly rubbed it back off with a handkerchief. It'd felt too waxy, too red, and false as a three-dollar bill.

Not that I minded a good lie. It just had to be one that suited me. And red lipstick didn't. That was Marion's affair.

When I turned back, the rich girl was still standing there. I sighed and stuck my hands in my trousers pockets, touching the pearl-handled switchblade in one and a brass money clip in the other.

"Please look again." She caught her bottom lip between her teeth and looked up at me through those unreasonably long lashes. She was a number, all right. Too flashy for me, but maybe our waitress Olive would like her. Might even steal her away from that porcelain-doll date for a smooch at midnight. Not that I particularly liked the thought of that either.

I rolled my eyes heavenward, but I plucked the photograph from Blondie's hand, only to make a show of taking a closer look.

But once my eyes were really on the picture, I couldn't even blink. The boy in it was handsome, with shining hair and dramatic cheekbones like a movie star's. It was Marion. *Our* Marion.

His brows were thicker instead of plucked into fashionably skinny arches like they were now, but his smile was the same, showing all his million white teeth. He looked happy in this picture, at least for this moment. It didn't exactly fit what I knew of Marion's past.

"You've seen him," the rich girl said, the words sucking in on a breath.

I forced myself to blink, to look up at her, away from the picture, and stretch my lips into a languid smile. "Nah. Handsome fella, though." I tipped back in my chair. "Your date know you're on the prowl for another guy?"

The girl's lashes fluttered. Her lips pursed into a high-hatty expression, little nose pointed up, eyes narrow. She snatched the photograph out of my fingertips.

"I know you recognized him. So I'm not leaving. Not until I find him."

"Be my guest, sis." I spread out my hands, grin broadening. "Buy all the liquor you want while you wait."

"Thanks for nothing," she said, and whirled away so forcefully the strands of beads on her dress whipped against my trousers.

"You're welcome!" I called after her.

I half turned to let another group in the door, but I kept one eye on Blondie. She sashayed her way through the maze of crumbling red-brick columns and tightly packed round tables, dodging around a pair of women leaning their heads so close together I knew they'd probably sneak out to the balcony later for some privacy. This building had been a cigar factory in its less-sordid past, and Blondie passed all eight of the tall windows we'd boarded over to dampen the sounds of our music and block the view from nosy cops and neighbors. The girl's bright hair and dress subdued in the warm, smoky cave, she sat down at the table her group had chosen, right near the stage under one of the electric candelabras hanging on the walls. I had a perfect view of her, and *she* had a perfect view of Marion's next show.

A shiver of misgiving traveled up my spine. Marion rarely talked about his past. All I knew was he'd been from the rich part of town once, too, but something had happened with his family and he took off.

If this girl thought she could drag him back into that world, she had another think coming.

"Frank," I said, tapping the bouncer on his oversize shoulder.

He held up a hand to hush me while he finished dealing with the sailors, whose friends had showed up and joined the argument.

"You fellas will have to leave if you can't get along."

"It's a free country," yelled one of the sailors, jabbing a finger toward Frank's face. "We can go where we want!"

I knew what was coming next and took a step backward to give Frank room. He snatched up the sailor by the collar, so that his toes barely scraped the floor. I held open the door, and Frank tossed him out, right onto the concrete banquette bordering Toulouse Street. His friends quickly followed.

I let the door slam shut behind them and brushed off my hands like I'd done the dirty work.

Frank grinned and cuffed me gently on the shoulder, his teddy-bear side breaking through the tough demeanor he put on for the customers. "What'd you need, Mill?"

"If you're still in the mood to throw somebody out . . ." I pointed to the rich kids' table. "There's an Uptowner here looking for Marion."

Frank smirked. "The fella with the yellow hair?"

"The girl next to him."

Frank gave me a skeptical look. "I'm not in the business of knocking around little girls."

"C'mon, you don't have to punch her in the teeth. Just escort her out. Ladylike."

Frank snorted, crossing his muscled arms over his broad chest. "What would your aunt say? They look like big spenders."

"She'd say kick 'em to the curb," I lied.

But Frank's known Cal almost as long as I have, and his dubious expression only deepened. "Go tell Marion they're here. If he says throw 'em out, I'll throw 'em out. But not until then."

"Fine. I'll ask him." I held up both hands in surrender. "But keep an eye on 'em, okay?"

Frank nodded, the lamps shining yellow on his pale bald head. "Count on it." He hitched a thumb toward the front door. "First sign of trouble, and they're out."

———·———

"It's me," I said after a three-beat knock, though he'd already know. I was the only one allowed in his dressing room before a show. No one else bothered to try anymore, even the Red Feathers, who could be a tad overeager in their admiration.

Marion slid the latch, and his eyes went wide. "God, is it ten thirty already?"

He dashed back to his vanity table before I had the door full open, his silky red dressing gown trailing behind him. He jerked pins out of his hair and tossed them in a little bowl on the table, *clink-clink-clink.* In the mirror, his fine collarbone peeked above the lacy edge of his slip; the smooth slope of his thigh stretched out below it.

I shut the door behind me and propped against it. "Ten. You got plenty of time."

"Easy for you to say." Marion waved a hand impatiently behind him. "Pass me those stockings."

The stockings were draped over the edge of the Chinese screen in the corner. I snatched them down, balled them up, and tossed them to Marion.

"Watch it!" he cried, shooting me a horrified look and examining the stockings for snags.

"How much those things set you back?"

"You don't want to know." He rolled them up his legs one by one, letting his dressing gown fall open. When it was just the two of us, he never bothered to hide the tight undergarment he'd sewn to disguise the parts of his body that spoiled his sleek silhouette in a dress.

"Big crowd tonight," I said. "Even for New Year's. All your Red Feathers are here."

Marion swiveled on his stool toward the mirror and began laying out his makeup in an orderly row on the dressing table, trying not to look excessively pleased.

"There's . . . something else I need to tell you." I fiddled with the pins on his dressing table and slid my gaze sideways toward his face. "There's a bunch of raccoon coats out there. Look like they're from over in your old stomping grounds."

Marion smiled at my reflection as he selected a pencil from his collection. "Pretending they're at the Pansy Club tonight, are they? New York City entertainment for New Year's Eve?"

I didn't smile back or even smirk. "I don't know. But one of them is showing around a photograph. Looking for somebody."

"Who?"

"A boy." I bit my lip. Hesitated. "A boy who looks an awful lot like you."

Marion's face froze into a mask as he traced his plucked brows in dark brown pencil with long, confident strokes. "Oh? And which one of them was doing the asking?" His tone was casual, flippant, but I detected a catch in his voice, a higher pitch even than the one he feigned onstage.

"Some girl," I said. "A real ritzy kitten. Blonde hair. Emeralds. The works."

Marion dipped his finger in Vaseline and rubbed it across each gracefully arched brow to make them shine. If I wasn't mistaken, his finger trembled.

"You know anybody like that, Mar?" I said.

"Can't say that I do." He took his time filling his lips with Siren Red, his eyes not meeting mine in the mirror. "Must've been some other kid in that picture."

"Marion," I said, laying a hand on his shoulder.

But he abruptly rose and went to the clothes rack, dropping the dressing gown from his shoulders. He took his favorite red dress off its hanger and carefully stepped into it.

"Come be a doll and button me up?" He smiled at me over his shoulder, as if nothing was amiss, but he wasn't fooling me.

Six tiny red buttons at the small of his back held the flimsy contraption together. He could do them up himself, but it took some contortion. He might break a sweat.

"Marion," I said quietly to the center of his back as I finished the last button. "They're sitting right near the front. If that girl—"

"Don't worry, Millie." He tugged on a pair of long white gloves and turned, smoothing his dress in the full-length mirror on the open door of the armoire. Side by side, our reflections were almost the same height, with the same lanky arms and angular hips. With him in a red dress and me in a black tailcoat and wide-legged trousers, there wasn't much to say which of us was born a girl and which a boy.

He smiled too brightly, already transforming from my

friend into his stage self, Marion-the-glamorous, the one who was never afraid and never doubted herself. Her shoulder rose in the slightest, most casual shrug.

"It wasn't me in that picture," she said lightly, tweaking my chin with one satin-gloved hand. "It couldn't be."

I have to give credit where it's due. Marion's almost as good a liar as I am.

CHAPTER

I LEFT MARION-THE-GLAMOROUS to put the finishing touches on her ensemble and went back downstairs. Marion clearly didn't want to face facts, but I could still keep an eye on that girl and make sure she didn't cause any trouble.

The flaw in that plan became apparent pretty quick. Duke, the bartender, who is no fan of mine even when Cal hasn't left me in charge instead of him, yelled, "Where you been? I'm swamped here!" The customers were three deep at the bar and looking cranky. So, I hung up Cal's top hat, slipped in next to Duke, and helped slosh hooch into our motley collection of glass tumblers, demitasse cups, and shot glasses inscribed with such slogans as VOTE DRY and BERTOLINI'S NATURAL HEALTH TONIC.

A steady succession of humanity arrived in front of me, eyes eager and money in hand. There were fellas posturing in their fresh clothes and combed hair, girls cutting their eyes at each other from behind veils of chatter and laughter and smoke. Most of the early crowd had gone home to their wives and mothers, and the dandier folks had trickled in till the whole place was full up with the laughter and chatter of old friends meeting again and new friends just getting acquainted. By this time of night, they were beginning to look like stage-actor versions of themselves— voices too loud, expressions too big—and the hooch became a cloak to keep their duller selves carefully hidden.

Close to the stage, Marion's Red Feathers clustered around the little tables, clasping each other's arms or drumming fingers in anticipation of her entrance. They'd fallen in a dizzy sort of love with Marion's stage persona and came back to see her so often, I knew them all by name. One clerked at the bank a few blocks away; one was the son of a well-to-do jeweler; one made his money entertaining sailors in town for a night. All were members of an exclusive club that had no rules or fees, only an understanding, a wink, a red feather in a hat band to say "I'm one of you. We can be ourselves together."

The band started up a song that had played on the radio every other minute since Thanksgiving. The cornet called sharp and bright, and soon dancers followed, customers tossing their hats on tables and joining hands to wind their way to the open floor. Not that rich girl, though. I spotted her leaning over talking to people at the next table, that photograph in one hand and a drink in the other.

Bennie Altobello, whose father supplied our bootleg hooch, and his friend Eddie Dwyer pushed their way through the current of dancers and bellied up to the bar in front of me, blocking my view of the girl. They were a mismatched pair: Bennie, dark-haired and solid and steady, and Eddie, freckled and wiry and probably voted Most Likely to Pick Your Pocket in school.

"Hear you're the boss tonight," Bennie said, smiling his easy smile that always caught me off guard these days. I'd known him since that summer my mother first left me here, when we were both skinny thirteen-year-olds running around, getting in fights in the streets. But he wasn't skinny anymore, and I hadn't had to punch anyone for him in ages.

I straightened my shoulders. "That's right."

Eddie bumped Bennie out of the way, smoothing back his vivid red hair. "Does that mean you're dishing out freebies to your old pals?"

I glared at him. "There's free water dripping off the roof."

"Aw, c'mon. Don't be such a wet blanket, Mill."

"Don't be such a pocket twister."

Eddie staggered around, pretending I'd shot him with an arrow straight through the chest.

Bennie rolled his eyes and shoved him aside. "I'll have a whiskey. And one for this bozo, too."

"What a guy!" Eddie clapped Bennie on the shoulder. "What a chief! What a solid gold—"

"That'll be a dollar," I interrupted, so Bennie knew he wasn't getting any special treatment either. He started fishing in his pocket, and I set out two glasses and started to pour.

A familiar fake laugh from nearby caught my attention, and I glanced up to see our waitress Olive dodging away from a sweaty male customer's grasping hands. Her lips were smiling, but her eyes looked ready to kill. My fingers tightened on the whiskey bottle, itching to smash that customer with it, but Olive met my gaze and gave her head a little shake. As she'd told me before, she didn't need a white girl to fight her battles.

"You ever dance, Millie?" Bennie said as he reached for his drink, bringing my focus back to him. His fingertips brushed against mine on the damp glass, and I quickly withdrew my hand, pretending his touch hadn't sent an electric zing straight through me. He wasn't the only one to make me feel that way, after all, and Olive was still looking in our direction, her deep bronze shoulders held straight as a queen's.

"Why you want to know?" I said, shoving Eddie's drink across the bar without looking at him. "Your date taking too long in the john?"

Bennie laughed, making his warm brown eyes spark. "Maybe I just want to find out if you got two left feet."

"From what I've seen, you might want to worry about yourself."

Bennie splayed a hand flat against his chest and lifted his chin. "*I'm* an excellent dancer."

"Oh, really?" I raised my brows. "Is *that* what the ladies tell you?"

Eddie guffawed. Bennie's grin faltered a fraction. "Maybe you should judge for yourself."

I blew a strand of black hair out of my face and saw Olive moving on to another table, turning her back to us. I rotated my dish towel inside a damp glass and let a smile slide across my lips. "Maybe I already have."

Bennie angled closer. "And what did you decide?"

My smile expanded slowly. "That I'm glad I'm not your date."

Bennie blinked. I gestured over his shoulder with the glass. A girl with red hair as fake as my mother's used to be stood behind him, arms crossed under an ample chest. I recognized her from the school I went to before Ursuline; we had not been friends.

"I *came* here to dance," she said in a pouty baby voice. That much hadn't changed since primary. "When you gonna spin me, Bennie?"

Bennie gave me a sheepish look and led his girl away toward the dance floor, with Eddie and his own date close behind. Miss Buxom shot daggers at me over his shoulder, and I offered her a toast with the empty glass in my hand.

I glanced at my new wristwatch Marion had given me for Christmas and carefully rubbed a spot of water off the face. Two more minutes until the show. The band blared a final note, and a bright light shone on the stage. Only then did I realize I'd forgotten an important detail. I shot a black look toward Duke, who studiously avoided my eye. I'd bet anything he'd remembered and neglected to tell me on purpose.

With Cal gone, it fell to me to announce Marion.

I caught a glimpse of Marion's red dress beyond the doorway to the back hall. She needed an audience primed to receive her. I couldn't let her down.

I adjusted Cal's jacket on my shoulders and plopped her top hat back on my head. I'd heard her spiel enough times to know it by heart. I just had to *be* her for a few seconds. I just had to lie.

—·—

Talking on the stage felt like a train was rushing by me, and I had to jump into the boxcar and grab hold or die. I said Cal's words and winked where I was supposed to wink. People laughed where they were supposed to laugh. Maybe not as loud as for Cal, but nobody slunk out the back of the club either.

Right on cue, I swept my arm toward stage left. "I give you the beautiful, the enchanting, the *in*-com-parable . . . Miss Marion Leslie!"

Applause burst from the audience as our star performer stepped out of the shadow and into the silvery spotlight. We passed each other, trading places, and Marion squeezed my hand before I disappeared back down the steps into the dark.

Marion posed in the center of the light against Lewis's piano, like a statue of a Roman goddess if statues wore red-sequined gowns. Somebody let out a wolf whistle, and Marion wagged one white-gloved finger at the crowd, teasing, chastising. More whistles came from around the room. Marion tossed her head back and beamed, soaking it in.

I propped myself against the wall beside Frank, who always stayed close to protect Marion during her show in case her adoring fans—or a rare drunken heckler—got any funny ideas. Marion held up her hand, palm to the crowd, and they hushed. Every movement was routine; I'd seen each one before, both onstage and when Marion practiced them in the mirror, but the crowd ate up the performance like it was the last olive in the jar. They tilted and pushed forward, chairs scraping on the floor.

Marion turned her head sideways, toward the piano, and lowered her gaze to a spot on the floor, as if she was almost too shy to continue. But when Lewis played the opening notes on the piano, Marion looked up suddenly at the audience again, turquoise eyes sparkling wetly in the spotlight, red lips parted. There was a soft gasp across the room.

Then she began to sing, soft and sure and sultry.

Someday he'll come along
The man I love
And he'll be big and strong
The man I love

She dragged out the notes, putting a catlike growl on the word *big*, and winked at someone at the Red Feather Boys' table.

And when he comes my way
I'll do my best to make . . . him . . . stay

Some in the crowd giggled. Some sighed dreamily. Others looked at their friends with big goofy grins on their faces, like they couldn't believe what they were seeing.

He'll look at me and smile
I'll understand
Then in a little while
He'll take my hand

Marion stretched out a graceful arm, this time toward Lewis at the piano. Marion's lashes flashed. Her breath caught, and her eyes locked on Lewis as she sang. A blush crept up the back of Lewis's pale neck into the neatly trimmed line of brown hair, and his long fingers fumbled a note. He bent over the piano and quickly found the thread again. I glanced at Frank, and we both suppressed a laugh. How much longer was it going to take for those two to figure out they liked each other?

Marion released her hold on Lewis and turned back to the rest of the audience, and I looked for Blondie's table near the front. It was easy to spot, with the way the Uptowners spread out their chairs, cocky enough to take up every inch of space they could. Their fur coats hung on the back of the chairs and pooled on the floor. As the person who mopped the floors every night, I could say with certainty those coats were getting wrecked. One of the girls was even doodling something on a piece of paper instead of watching the show. Then she shifted to the side, and I saw Blondie perched so close to the edge of her chair she was in danger of falling off. Her mouth was open, her ring-bedecked fingers curled against her lips as if to stop herself from crying out.

My stomach tensed. Was this girl about to cause a scene? We didn't have hecklers often, and when we did, Frank's retribution was swift. But such scenes ruined the show for Marion. No matter how much applause she got afterward, and no matter how she pretended nothing rattled her, I'd seen her tears in the dressing room after. And in my experience, cruel words stung whether you wanted them to or not.

I edged closer, fists clenched, and Frank looked over, a question in his eyes. Was there something he needed to handle? I shook my head. *Not yet.*

I turned my gaze to Marion. The song was almost over. The seduction in her eyes didn't waver. Her voice didn't falter. Had she seen the girl?

And so all else above
I'm dreaming of
The man I love

The moment the applause began, Blondie stood up, wobbled a bit, and grabbed the table with one hand to steady herself. The drink in her other hand sloshed, and some of it splashed onto the floor.

Marion bowed her head, seeming to soak up the admiration, but her gaze darted to the right, toward the rich kids' table.

Blondie's date touched her arm, but she shrugged him off. She stood there, staring, and for one long moment, Marion stood still and stared back.

I thought I knew all of Marion's expressions, thought I'd seen them all so often I knew what she was feeling just by looking. But I had never seen this particular expression on her face before. It was like love and longing all tangled up with hate and pain.

The piano launched into the next song in her set, but Marion was still frozen and missed her cue, something that almost never happened. Lewis looped to the beginning of the verse again, and this time Marion blinked and shook her head, trilling a laugh.

"Lewis, honey, play it just one more time, and I promise I'll get it right. This *crowd*! You're so *distracting*! Look at you, all dressed up for New Year's Eve!"

The crowd tittered as if she'd spoken to each of them individually. Blondie, as if freed from a spell, turned and shoved her way through the people filling the long, narrow room. From my spot on the floor, I lost sight of her, but when I looked back at Marion on the stage, her eyes still traced the girl's path.

CHAPTER

I SLIPPED BETWEEN the tables in the same direction the blonde interloper had fled. Olive grabbed my wrist as she passed me with a tray of empty glasses. I felt that same zing from her fingers against my skin as I had with Bennie, making me pause.

"What was that about?" She gestured toward the stage with her precarious tray. Nobody in the crowd seemed to guess anything was amiss, but Olive's golden-brown eyes noticed everything. She could always tell which customer would try to skip out on his tab and which needed to be rushed to the bathroom before he heaved up a mess on the floor, and she always appeared with a fresh handkerchief the moment anyone shed the slightest tear.

But now wasn't the time to explain. "That's just what I'm gonna find out."

I spun away out of her grasp and found Blondie right where I figured she'd be—nursing a drink at the bar. Wasn't that where they all went? Home base for the sad and discouraged.

I elbowed my way into the space next to her and propped against the bar. "Rough night?"

Her gaze swept over me, taking in my tailcoat, my white shirt, my top hat as if really seeing me for the first time. No matter what she'd known about this place before she got here, she hadn't been prepared . . . or hadn't believed. She turned back to her drink and took a slug of it. "What business is it of yours?"

"Gotta keep the customers happy." I winked, turning so I was parallel with her, my wrists on the bar next to hers.

Her face in the smoky mirror behind the bar went all high-hatty again, nose in the air. "You didn't care about that before." She swiveled toward me, drink tilting. "*You* said you didn't recognize him. You said he wasn't here. Obviously you were lying." Her words slurred a bit as she waved her glass toward the stage. Marion was barely visible from this angle, but her voice purred another song over us.

"I don't owe you information," I said. "A lot of people in here have secrets. We don't go around handing them out to strangers."

"Strangers!" Blondie gave a sharp, bitter laugh and knocked back another large swallow of her drink. Her eyes met mine over the rim. "He was still in New Orleans the *whole time.*" She jabbed her finger down on the bar. "Right here. And not one word."

So she'd definitely known Marion in a past life, in a place with richer blood and fatter pocketbooks than here. A surge of jealousy rose up in my chest. She'd known him before I did, knew a whole side of him I didn't. Even if I got his true self, that other part was still inside him somewhere. I'd seen it when Marion looked at her from the stage.

"Why are you looking for him anyway?" I narrowed my eyes and clenched my fist against the bar. "What do you want with him?"

"I just—" She looked down at her handbag and picked at a loose bead. "I thought . . . maybe . . . if I talk to him . . ."

She looked so lost and sad all of a sudden, I almost felt sorry for her. But Marion didn't want to talk to her. He'd made that much clear.

"Listen," I said, making an effort to gentle my voice, "if he's gone all this time without getting in touch, he has his reasons, don't you think? Maybe you should let him be."

The girl curled into herself, hugging the drink against her chest. "I wouldn't blame him if he doesn't want to see me." Her eyes blazed with anguish, with regret. Who was she and what had happened between her and Marion?

The questions hovered on my tongue. Marion had only told me the barest information about his life before he came to the Cloak and Dagger a year and a half ago. He was sixteen then and had been sleeping on a bench until Cal caught him nodding off in one of our booths and asked him if he needed a bed. When he told us his name was Marion Leslie, it came out trembling and new, a wobbly colt of a name. We didn't ask him about his old one.

Cal, who knew a thing or two about runaways, had given him a job busing tables and found him a place to rent at Bennie's grandmother's rooming house. Marion and I had become fast friends, especially once I gave in to his wheedling to try on dresses for him at the Maison Blanche department store, since he couldn't do it himself. He'd treated me to coffee and a slice of pie in the store's restaurant, and not long after that, he'd given up mopping with me and started singing on our stage.

I'd always been deeply curious about the life he'd led before us, and what terrible event had sent him running away from home, but I also knew Marion's history was something I should hear from him, not a stranger. I pressed my lips together, trying to keep my curiosity from taking over for once.

Then the girl's date barged between us and clapped a hand on her shoulder.

"Arimentha, darling!" he said. "Getting us another round?"

"Fitzroy! You scared the daylights out of me!" She surreptitiously wiped a tear from the corner of her eye.

Arimentha and Fitzroy? These couldn't be real people. Those names belonged to porcelain dolls or racehorses.

Fitzroy laughed heartily and looked from her face to mine and back. His lips curled upward. "Making friends with the locals?"

"No," she said, not even sparing a glance my way. "She's some kind of *employee* here."

My face hardened. I regretted feeling even a moment's pity for her.

"Then let's have a dance," Fitzroy said. "What do you say, darling?"

Arimentha glanced toward the stage, where Marion was still singing. "Maybe later."

"Millie!" Duke barked from down the bar. "Icebox sprang a leak. Get back here!"

I wanted to tell him to fix it himself. Or to go to hell. But it was New Year's Eve, and he was too busy with the customers to visit with the devil tonight.

I straightened, and my eyes met Arimentha's in the mirror. She smirked and made a shooing motion with one hand. "Go on, do what you're paid to do."

Rage bloomed hot in my chest. I rose from my barstool, fists curling at my sides.

"Want another round then?" Fitzroy said, ignoring me entirely, and Arimentha's gaze flickered away from mine, too.

"I've had enough," she said. "Get yourself one." She fished a dollar out of her beaded purse and stuffed it into his hand. She turned to me. "Do you have a ladies' room in this . . . *place*?"

Her tone made me want to push her into the john myself, but I grinned back like a shark. "We have an *everybody's* room," I said brightly, and pointed the way. "But I'm warning you—it ain't that clean."

Arimentha shoved herself away from the bar. "*That* doesn't surprise me in the least."

—·—

Marion finished his set while I was on my hands and knees fixing the icebox before the leak could spread out onto the dance floor. When I finally stood up, a streak of black sullied my clean shirt, and Duke told me I looked like a shoeshine boy. I resisted punching him in the nose, for now, and climbed up on a barstool on my knees to scan the crowd for Arimentha's fair hair. There were other blondes in the club, but none with hair quite so pale as hers, and few that hadn't obviously paid for the color.

I finally spotted her in the back corner, near the hallway that led to the stairs and the john. Her date, Fitzroy, was there, too, hovering behind her elbow. And right in front of them sparked the red of Marion's dress.

Marion and Arimentha stood close, shoulders curving inward so they almost touched, like friends or even lovers. Then Marion shifted, and I glimpsed his face, wrenched into an ugly mask, his red lips twisting around ugly words. He was *angry*. My mouth fell open. Marion and I had fought our share of battles, but never like this.

Arimentha's shoulders hunched up toward her ears, like a turtle trying to retreat into its shell. She didn't look like the haughty girl I'd spoken to minutes before. She looked crushed and beaten.

I slid off the stool, shoved aside a big oaf blocking my way, and started toward the corner. I called out Marion's name, but my voice drowned in a blare of sound from the cornet. A girl in gray trousers and a matching vest grabbed my hand and yelled, "Wanna dance?" over the music, but I didn't have time for that now. I mimed *maybe later* and kept moving.

I emerged from a knot of Red Feather Boys to see Fitzroy take Arimentha by the elbow and begin tugging her away. Her powdered face was streaked with tears, and she kept looking back over her shoulder toward Marion as he whirled and, hiding his own face with one gloved hand, skirted around the edge of the room in the opposite direction.

I pivoted and shoved through the crowd that had closed up in his wake, but he'd still made it all the way up the stairs and into his dressing room before I got there. The door was shut tight, and no sound came from the other side.

"Marion?" I said. "You all right?"

No answer. I tried the knob, but it was locked. I pressed my forehead against the door. He'd never locked me out before. Not me.

"C'mon," I said. "Let me in. Tell me what that girl said, so I can go smack her for you."

"She's not worth it." His voice sounded muffled, dense. Like he'd been crying.

"That was the same girl who was showing around your picture," I said, my lips almost touching the door. "You know her."

"It doesn't matter."

"Yes, it does. Who is she?"

His voice hardened. "Don't worry about her. She's gone now, and she won't be back."

"What'd you say to her?"

There was a long moment of silence.

"Mar?"

"Nothing. I said nothing."

"Then how—"

"You better get back out there. Duke'll be needing you."

I hesitated, scratching at the loose paint on the door with my thumbnail. Should I tell him I'd spoken to her? That I knew her name?

"Will you be okay for your next set?" I said, stalling, hoping he'd let me in once the storm had passed. "The Red Feathers'll cry a river if you don't come back out."

A sound filtered through the door, either a sniffle or a laugh.

"And Lewis—" I said, "oh boy, he'll be out there looking like somebody stole his lollipop."

This time it was definitely a laugh. A small one. Then a sigh.

"I'll be okay, Millie." Another sigh. "I'm always okay."

"O'course," I said, trying to sound cheery. "Never doubted you."

There was another pause. Then, "Love you," he said, his voice close to the door. It sounded so weary, so sad.

"Love you, too, kid." I laid my hand flat against the wood, wishing I could put my arm around his shoulders. Something was definitely wrong, and it was all that rich girl's fault.

CHAPTER

4

WHEN I GOT back to the bar, Duke and I kept up the steady flow of alcohol into the hands of our increasingly sloppy customers. Every time I got a second to spare, I peeked at the hallway, waiting for Marion to return, trying to gauge what each minute that passed signaled about his state of mind.

I checked the stock of clean glasses stacked under the bar—we were getting low, but I thought we'd probably make it. The flow of customers would slow once Marion's second set started and most folks settled into their seats. After midnight, a stream of people would start trickling out of the club, though there were always stragglers hanging on until the very end when we closed at two. But by then, business at the bar would be slow enough that we could wash glasses if we had to and catch our breath.

I glanced up at the hallway again, and this time, Marion was there. According to my watch, it had been exactly twenty-nine minutes since I talked to him through the dressing room door, and now he looked exactly as glamorous as he had at the beginning of the night. No puffy eyes or red blotches on his cheeks to show he'd been crying, but then he was an expert at makeup. You couldn't tell he had a spray of freckles across his nose either, or that he'd over-plucked his left eyebrow the other day.

I started to put down my bar rag and grab my top hat, but this time Marion didn't wait for my announcement. She strode right up onto the stage, swished her red skirt, and kicked out one silk-clad leg. Hoots and whistles went up from the crowd. Marion leaned over the piano and gave an instruction to Lewis, who deftly changed dircction mid-song. The band followed behind a beat later.

Marion led with a splashy song she usually saved for last and performed the second set even more fiercely than the first. Her voice was always throatier by now from the heavy smoke in the room, her body always looser from the single shot of honey-and-whiskey she'd sneak between sets in her dressing room. But tonight, every smile was a little too intense; every word she sang teetered on the brink of too much. Something was off, and I knew it had to do with that girl.

I slipped away from the bar when Duke wasn't looking and braced my shoulder against a brick column in the middle of the room to watch the show, and the audience. A nervous energy built in my stomach, like I was waiting, though I didn't know for what.

"Marion copacetic?" Olive slouched against the column beside me, with one hand in the pocket of her dress and another propping a tray against her waist.

Anyone else, and I would've lied and said Marion was aces. But Olive's eyes said she already saw the truth.

"I don't know," I said. "He's putting on a good show, but I think he's rattled."

Olive jerked her chin toward the piano. "Look at Lewis. He sees it, too."

Olive was right. She usually was.

Lewis's fingers played the piano, but even from across the room, it was plain his mind was on Marion. And not in the usual way. His thin shoulders were tense, and he wasn't just watching—he was *watchful*. Protective. I knew that feeling, and I was glad someone else shared it. Two someones, or else Olive wouldn't be over here.

"He knew that blonde girl asking around with the picture," I said. "But the stubborn fool won't tell me how."

Olive laughed. "I think Cal made that rule about secrets just for you."

"Hey!" I made a face at her and folded my arms across my chest. "I was right next to that girl, could've asked her anything I wanted to know, and she would've spilled it all. But I didn't say a word."

"You're a real saint, Millie Coleman." Olive's gaze slid sideways, her mouth curving upward. "You should see if Ursuline is looking for any new nuns."

I nudged her shoulder with mine. "I do hear there are some perks to the nunnery."

"Oh, really? What sort of perks?" Her body moved closer, and I wasn't inclined to get out of her way.

But over her shoulder, I saw Frank let Fitzroy return through the front door, without Arimentha, his hair no longer perfect, and an irritated expression on his face. He weaved through the crowd, smoothing his stray hairs back in place, and sat down with the rest of the Uptowners, who gave him odd looks. He'd probably stuck Arimentha in a cab and come back to watch the last minutes of 1929 drain away without her. Clearly, owning a tuxedo did not make him a gentleman.

The two girls at the table abruptly stood up, clutching their little handbags, and navigated single file between the tables toward the back of the club.

Olive thumped my arm. "You see someone you'd rather be talking to?" Her eyebrows were raised in neat, incredulous arches.

"Than you?" I forced my attention back to her face. "Hardly."

"Then what're you looking at?"

"That rich girl's date is back."

Olive cast a surreptitious glance at their table. "But *she's* not back, is she?"

"No."

"Then I don't see why you should care. A table's waving for drinks. Talk to you later."

"Later," I mumbled. I looked at my watch. Eight minutes till midnight.

Marion and the band were performing the final bars of a slow song. Next up, they'd do a real toe-tapper to draw everybody out on the dance floor ahead of the big countdown, and at midnight, Marion might lean down and give Lewis a kiss, and they'd both pretend it was for show. I'd get a bottle of terrible champagne from the bar and pour it in glasses, while the band started up "Auld Lang Syne," and people would hug and cry like they even knew what those words meant.

That's how it was supposed to happen. But between the slow song and what was supposed to be a fast one, there came a three-second breath of silence.

And in that silence came the scream.

Long and shrill and terrible, too strangled with emotion and fear to be a joke.

My head shot up. Every head shot up. More screams pierced the air from the same direction as the first. My eyes darted toward the back hallway, where those two raccoon-coat girls had gone.

The screams were coming from there.

I looked back at the Uptowners' table. Fitzroy and the two other boys stared at one another with wide eyes and leaped to their feet. They'd obviously come to the same conclusion. Fitzroy grabbed his coat off the back of his chair, knocking it over in the process, but the other two left theirs and started weaving through the crowd.

Some of the customers stayed in their seats and craned their necks to see what was going on, but a good many downed their drinks and surged toward the exits in case this was a raid. Marion stood stock-still on the stage, mouth open in an O. The band members froze in place, too, embracing their instruments protectively. Olive and the other waitress, Zuzu, were in the middle of the crowd, holding on tight to their trays as overly excited customers jostled around them.

Instinctively, I looked around for Aunt Cal and then remembered she wasn't here. I caught Lewis's eye and gestured for him to start up the music again, and he played the first notes of "Auld Lang Syne," even though midnight was still at least five minutes away. The cornetist lifted his instrument to his lips and joined in a beat later, and someone popped premature confetti into the air.

I spotted Frank pushing his way through the crowd toward the back hall, and I fell in beside him.

"I'm going with you," I shouted over the din, and he nodded, his face solemn.

Whatever trouble was happening with those two girls, it was my responsibility tonight.

——.——

Frank's shoulders were wider than a lot of doorways in the French Quarter, and the skin of his neck bore a fine horizontal scar from a past knife fight. Just looking at him was enough to deter many a potential troublemaker.

But this time the trouble had already been made.

We went through the doorway into the back hallway, Frank first and then me. The door to the john was shut, and a line of women snaked around the corner waiting to use it. One wide-eyed girl stretched out a long thin arm and pointed.

"That way."

Frank and I turned left past the stairs that led to Marion's dressing room, past the alcove underneath where I stored the mop and bucket. At the end of the hallway, a door opened onto a small, weedy courtyard between the Cloak and the building behind it, where I lived in an apartment with Aunt Cal. Usually, we kept this door locked, and only Cal and I used it when we were coming to work from home. But now it stood open, letting in a gust of cool, damp air, like breath from a tomb.

One of the rich boys—probably named Vanderbilt or Rockefeller—stood there, propping it open with his shoulder and blocking my view of what was beyond him in the dark alley.

The two girls weren't visible and weren't screaming anymore. But I heard crying, one voice soft and gulping, the other shrill and continuous.

Dread curled in my belly like smoke. Frank and I shared a look, his mouth set in a grim line.

"What's going on here?" I called out, and Vanderbilt turned to stare at me, his face pale in the light of the two naked bulbs hanging from the hallway ceiling. His mouth opened, but no sound came out, and he pressed a fist against it as if he might be sick.

He turned away again, doubling over and retching. And then I saw the bright shape under the silvery moonlight, motionless on the damp gray cobblestones.

My footsteps slowed. The night enveloped me like a giant clammy fist. A cacophony of champagne pops, happy shouts, and jazz rose up to meet midnight in the crowded streets all around us, but here in this sheltered courtyard, no one acknowledged the time. The air smelled sharply of vomit, thanks to Vanderbilt, and something else underneath it I couldn't place and didn't want to name.

I knew this courtyard at night. It was the place where rats skittered when I dumped the mop water or took out trash to the burn barrel. It was the place I trudged through to get home after closing, when my feet were tired and my eyes barely open. The place we were supposed to escape through if Prohibition agents or cops came through the front.

Beyond the slanted rectangle of yellow light from the open door, just past the dark shadow of the balcony above, Fitzroy and Rockefeller crouched over the shape on the ground, two black hulks in their dark suits. Rockefeller was touching the shape gently and murmuring something.

It was a person. A body.

"Who . . . ?" I said, my voice catching in my throat, coming out small.

No one heard me except Frank, who touched my arm as if to stop me moving forward, stop me getting involved, make me let him go first. None of which I was going to do.

"Who is she?" I said, louder. The body, it was obvious now that my eyes were adjusting to the dark, was a woman's. A girl's. Her beaded gold dress and brilliant hair spread out across the cobblestones beside the dry fountain like a shining puddle. A beaded handbag lay a few feet away.

No one answered me. I looked to my right at the two girls, clinging to each other and crying, both studiously not looking at the body.

I didn't want to look either. At least I didn't *think* I wanted to look, knew I *shouldn't* want to look, but my eyes were drawn back to it. My feet carried me closer.

Rockefeller picked up her hand, white and luminous in a ray of moonlight, and felt for a pulse in her wrist.

"Is she . . . all right?" I said, feeling a fool even as I said it. There was no way she was all right.

"She's dead!" wailed one of the girls. "Her eyes! Just look at her eyes!"

They were open, staring upward as if into the shadowed

face of the dark-haired boy hovering over her. Her head lay at a strange angle against the foot of the fountain. A fine mist beaded and glistened on her pale brow, her beautifully rounded cheekbones, her pink lips, her bright hair.

It was Arimentha. The girl who'd known Marion. The girl who'd wronged him terribly once, somehow, by her own admission.

But whatever she'd done, she hadn't deserved *this*. To die here on the cold ground, her body left to grow damp with mist and mop water while seventeen versions of "Auld Lang Syne" played around her and the whole Quarter celebrated.

No one deserved this.

My eyes pricked with tears I wasn't expecting. Why should I cry for this girl? Why should I feel bile in the back of my own throat at the sight of her blank eyes, her wasted life? "Do you know what happened to her?" Frank asked, looking around at the rich kids. "Did you see anything?"

They shook their heads, their eyes wide and staring.

"I think . . ." Rockefeller spoke up, his voice choked. "I think she fell off the balcony."

"Or someone pushed her," one of the girls whimpered, the brunette who until recently had been screaming continuously.

"What was she doing up there?" the other girl said. She was almost my height with auburn hair, though everything was washed strange and blue in the moonlight. "Look there in her hand—what's that?"

A folded paper lay in Arimentha's softly curled hand. In two strides, I'd reached her and plucked the paper up into my own hand.

"You shouldn't do that," Rockefeller said, straightening out of his crouch. "The police will want the crime scene to stay as it is."

"If it's a crime at all," I said. "Like you said, she could've fallen."

Whether this was a murder or an accident, it had happened at Aunt Cal's club—my club tonight—and I would decide what we did about it.

I held the paper up to the moonlight and saw it was a playbill for a circus that had already left town the week before. We had a stack of them still sitting on the end of the bar.

"What is it?" Fitzroy said, standing, too.

I ignored him and unfolded the paper. There was writing inside, a brief penciled letter, in a hand that looked like it would've been pretty if it wasn't scrawled in such a hurry. I didn't have the light or patience to interpret all the words, but I didn't have to.

The letter began with "Dear Marion."

CHAPTER

"WHAT DOES IT say?" Rockefeller said.

"Nothing," I lied, trying to push down the panic so it didn't show in my eyes or my voice. "It's just an old circus playbill."

"But why would she—"

"There's a pile of them inside. Maybe she didn't notice the date was old."

The girl with the auburn hair stepped forward and thrust out her hand, palm open. "Let me see that."

I folded it back in quarters and stuffed it in my trousers pocket. "Think I'll keep it safe for the police instead."

"You can't do that."

"I just did."

"We all saw you." She crossed her arms over her chest and thrust out her chin. "We'll tell the police you stole evidence."

I licked my lips and thought fast. "You should probably be considering your alibis instead." I narrowed my eyes and looked at each of them in turn, so they wouldn't miss the implication.

The brunette girl gasped. "Are you saying . . . one of *us* did *this*?"

I could almost laugh. I doubted anyone in this bunch had ever been accused of anything in their lives. Guilty, maybe, but never accused.

"It wasn't one of us." Fitzroy thrust his pointer finger in my direction. "It was one of *your* people."

I stared at him, struggling to keep my expression smooth. My grip tightened on the letter with Marion's name on it in my pocket.

"Who do you think it was?" Rockefeller said, touching Fitzroy's sleeve.

"Yeah, who?" I said. Frank moved closer beside me.

"It was that . . . that boy singer in there!" Fitzroy said, his gaze hopping from face to face. "That boy in the dress! He killed her, I know it!"

Shit. Fitzroy had seen Marion argue with Arimentha half an hour—or less—before she died, and he wasn't going to forget it.

"How do you know it was him?" Rockefeller said.

"The only reason she came back in the club was to talk to him." Fitzroy rocked up on his toes, looking agitated. "I tried to tell her not to go. I saw his face when he threatened her! I knew he was dangerous, and I told her—"

"He threatened her?" Rockefeller said. "What did he say?"

"He told her to never come back here." Fitzroy hugged his raccoon coat tighter around him. "Or he'd make her regret it."

I tried not to show the shock on my face. I'd seen Marion's anger for myself, had heard him say through the dressing room door that she was never returning to the club. But Marion couldn't have done this to her, not even if he threatened it. He couldn't have *killed* someone and left her out in this courtyard in the cold, with the damp already settling on her skin. *No.*

"If you thought he was so dangerous," I said, crossing my arms over my chest, "then why didn't you come back inside with her?"

Fitzroy ran a hand through his hair, mussing it. "I . . . I was looking for a cab. I thought she'd give up on this silly errand and come back out."

"But she never returned," Rockefeller said, looking soberly down at the girl's body. "Someone, maybe this female impersonator, brought her out on that balcony and pushed her over."

Fitzroy looked stricken. "I should've taken her home. This whole night is a mistake. I should've—"

"Don't cast blame where it doesn't belong, old bean." Rockefeller reached an arm around Fitzroy's quaking shoulders and gave him a manly embrace. "We'll call the police now. They'll sort everything out."

I looked at Frank, my heart beating fast and my thoughts spinning faster. I didn't even have time to make a joke about Rockefeller saying "old bean." What happened if we let them call the police now? Fitzroy's story looked bad for Marion—the whole scenario did—and that auburn-haired girl wasn't going to let the note thing drop. Others in the club could've heard Marion threaten that girl, and the whole place had seen Marion disappear for half an hour between sets. Plenty of time to shove a girl off a balcony, especially one conveniently located right down the hall from his dressing room.

Shit, shit, shit. The cops would arrest him for sure. Not to mention what would happen to the rest of us. Cal's hefty bribes kept the cops out of our hair most of the time, but the presence of a potential murder victim—especially a rich one—might make them feel obliged to arrest everybody who'd served alcohol, plus any of the customers they could lay their hands on. I was supposed to keep this place and these people safe while Cal was gone. Letting them get beaten up or thrown in jail was the dead opposite of that.

I looked down at Arimentha's eyes, at her face that had been beautiful and alive an hour before. I certainly didn't keep *her* safe.

But I'd be damned if I let Marion meet the same fate.

"You're right," I said, standing taller, hoping I looked and sounded authoritative enough to keep the Uptowners in line. "I'll call the cops now. There's a telephone inside. You five stay here with the—with, um . . ."

"Arimentha," the auburn-haired girl said through clenched teeth.

"Yeah. Her. And no funny business out here." I pointed at each of the rich kids. "Don't touch her."

"But—" the brunette said.

"Don't touch her, I said! And don't go anywhere. The cops will need to talk to you when they get here." I bent and scooped up Arimentha's beaded handbag in one swift motion. Marion's photograph was in there. The last thing we needed was the cops finding that. "And I'll take this inside so you don't get any funny ideas about tampering with the evidence."

"Hey!" Fitzroy said.

"I don't know about that," Rockefeller said.

"Don't worry." I was already backing away. "I'll put it in

the lockbox until the police arrive. Just wait here."

I grabbed Frank's sleeve and tugged him with me back into the club.

"I don't trust her," the auburn-haired girl hissed to her friends as we turned away.

"And you shouldn't," I muttered under my breath.

If I had anything to do with it, these swells would be waiting on the cops for a long time.

— . —

Sure, I was going to call the cops. But first, I had to get Marion out of there. And second, I had to protect my people.

I sent Frank to the front door to start quietly shuttling out the customers nearest to it. Marion stood by the piano, slightly out of the spotlight, with Lewis's gray suit jacket draped across his shoulders. The band behind him half-heartedly played a dance tune, but nobody was dancing. Everybody was murmuring, waiting for news.

I paused behind a brick column and opened Arimentha's handbag. The corner of the photograph poked up, and I snatched it and stuffed it in the back pocket of my trousers with the note written on the playbill. What else might Arimentha have that could incriminate Marion? Quickly, I glanced around, but no one seemed to be watching me, so I rifled through the rest of the bag's contents. A small brass key, a compact, ten dollars folding money, and a fancy enameled tube of lipstick—nothing that looked immediately interesting, so I clicked the handbag shut.

Now for Marion. I took a breath and tried to smooth out my face as I approached him. It didn't work.

"What's wrong?" he said as soon as he saw me. "What happened back there?"

Lewis rose to stand beside Marion, abruptly cutting off the music. I turned my back to the audience so they couldn't read my lips and angled my head closer to the boys. "A girl has died in the courtyard."

"Died? No! How?" Marion's fingers gripped my arm. "Who was it?"

I studied his eyes for signs of guilt, malice, fear. What I saw there was unclear. "She fell—or was pushed—off the balcony. Looks like she hit her head on the edge of the fountain on the way down."

"Oh God, that's terrible." Marion wrapped his arms around his middle. "And Cal's not here! What are we gonna do?"

"*You're* going to leave. Now. And take this with you." I slid out the photograph and the note on the folded playbill and pressed them into his palm. He stared at them, uncomprehending.

"But—"

"Marion, the girl who died was *the* girl. Arimentha."

He flinched at the sound of her name. His fingertips rose slowly to his mouth, and his eyes widened and widened until the whites showed above the dark blue irises.

"No." His head swung back and forth, and he sagged into Lewis.

That was when I noticed the necklace. The dragonfly trimmed in gold, spreading its translucent green wings across Marion's collarbone. I'd never seen it before on Marion—only on Arimentha.

An image of the girl's dead face rose in front of me, her hair darkened with blood, her white throat silver in the moonlight. Her *bare* white throat.

The necklace had been missing. Someone had taken it.

"Marion," I said, barely breath left in me to say it. My stomach swirled. "Tell me . . . tell me you didn't."

Marion swiped away tears with his thumbs and saw where my eyes were focused. He flung up a hand to cover the necklace, or protect it. I couldn't tell. Maybe I'd never really known anything about him. Maybe everything had been a lie. The note, the balcony, the argument, the necklace—all of it added up to Marion.

His eyes went glassy, panicked. "She gave me the necklace, I swear!"

"When?"

"When we were . . ." He trailed off, swiping at his eyes again, more roughly.

"When you argued?" I said.

He swallowed hard. "I . . . Oh, Millie. I told her . . . I told her to never come back or . . . or . . ."

The expression on his face was anguished, guilty. But not in the way of a murderer, or at least I didn't think so. I shook myself. This was Marion, *my* Marion, trembling under a suit coat and Lewis's long skinny arm, his eyes big and wet and innocent, red lipstick chewed ragged on his bottom lip. No matter how bad things looked, there was a reason I'd stolen that note, hidden that photograph, and handed them both over to Marion. I believed him. Of course, I did.

"I know what you told her." My fingers found my now-empty jacket pocket. "You said she'd better not come back or else. Her date, Fitzroy, already told everybody outside, and he'll tell the same to the cops. That's why you've got to leave. Now. Before I even call them."

Marion hugged his arms around himself. His eyes were on my face, but they looked uncomprehending, far away. Maybe they were still seeing Arimentha's crumpled expression when he'd spat those words at her. I had so many questions to ask him—why seeing that girl had upset him so much, why she gave him her necklace, how he knew her before—but there was no time for that now.

My gaze shifted to Lewis over Marion's head. His focus was sharp, like mine. His arm tightened around Marion's shoulders. "I'll get him out."

I didn't like trusting Marion to anyone else, but if it had to be someone—and Aunt Cal wasn't there—I figured Lewis was the next best thing. At least he cared about Marion. He'd keep him safe the best he could.

I grabbed Marion's wrist and made him look at me. "Go with Lewis now. I'll take care of everything here. We'll figure out the rest tomorrow."

Marion's eyes filled. "Okay," he whispered. For once, he didn't joke or argue about me bossing him around. I almost wished he would.

Finally, he heeded the pressure of Lewis's guiding hand on his arm. I watched them slip through the crowd and past Frank through the front door. I had to hope Lewis would keep my best friend safe tonight.

It was up to me to handle the rest.

Even if he killed her? a voice whispered in my mind.

He didn't, I whispered back firmly.

It was true I had no idea what had happened for the half hour between when I left his dressing room and when he came back out onto the stage. It was true he'd had motive and opportunity.

There was nothing but my gut to tell me Marion wasn't the killer.

And I'd still chosen to help him slip through the door.

—·—

The band hightailed it out behind Lewis and Marion, and a steady trickle of customers followed them, though there were still a good many waiting around to find out what had happened. Before I told the rest of them to run for it, I had to deal with Cal's other employees. They were the ones most at risk if federal Prohibition agents showed up with the cops; it was a bigger crime to serve alcohol than to drink it.

I gathered them up in a small knot behind the bar—Frank, Duke, Olive, and Zuzu—and explained that a girl had died in the courtyard.

"Who *was* it?" Duke said, eyes bugging.

"A girl. No one we know." Frank remained silent; he was loyal to a fault to Aunt Cal and the club, and I knew he wouldn't speak up and spill more than I wanted him to.

I looked around at the others. Zuzu had gasped at the news and was now hugging her plump arms around her middle. Olive touched her mouth with her fingertips, her eyes unfocused. A girl our age was dead twenty yards away.

"How did she—" Olive started to ask.

"We can't worry about that now," I said, blinking away the images of Arimentha's face that were crowding into my head. "Our problem is if we don't call the cops soon, one of those rats outside will. So our first priority is getting everybody out of here."

"Then I should take the cash box with me," Duke said, recovering quickly from his shock about the death. "You know, for safekeeping."

"I don't think so," I said. "Frank, you take it."

"Aren't you leaving with us?" Olive said.

I shook my head. "I've got to stay here this time. Duke, you dump the booze."

"What?" He looked appalled. "Why?"

"Just do it."

"But you said the cops were coming, not the Prohibition agents." Duke crossed his arms over his chest. "What's the point of all those bribes if we still gotta be scared of the cops?"

"Cal bribes beat cops and captains, not murder detectives. They could report us to the feds without even blinking."

"So we give the detectives some cash now."

"This might be a *murder*, Duke. A girl is *dead*. This isn't like breaking a law nobody cares about. Somebody could hang for this, and I don't want it to be one of us."

Duke blew out a frustrated breath. "Cal's not gonna like this."

"You let me worry about Cal."

Duke shook his head but finally moved to slide the liquor bottles down the old coal chute. They'd smash against the cobblestones in the alley, eliminating most of the evidence of our illegal business—and at least a hundred dollars' worth of hooch.

Olive took my arm and pulled me aside behind the same column we'd leaned against what felt like hours ago. "I know there's something you didn't tell us."

I tried to extract myself gently from her grasp and snatched one of the old circus playbills from the bar. "I'll tell you later. Promise."

"But you said it might be a murder. Who was killed? You said we don't know her, but then Marion—"

"We don't know her." I said it more sharply than I'd meant to, and Olive leaned back, her eyes flashing to the color of whiskey. I sighed. I didn't want to make Olive mad, but I didn't have time to explain it, and more than that, I didn't *want* to. Not till I sorted it all out in my own head. Not till I talked to Marion again.

"Look, Olive," I said, softening my voice, touching her arm. "I need you to get yourself home safe. There could be a killer out there. Let Frank walk you, just this once?"

Olive's eyes were still narrowed, but she nodded, finally, grudgingly. "All right."

"I have to go," I said, already turning toward the stage and folding the playbill into my pocket. The customers deserved a warning, too. Police could get billy-club-happy in bars with reputations like ours. I had to get them out of here, especially the Red Feather Boys, who would attract the most attention from the cops.

"Millie!" Olive's voice called after me, a few beats late. I turned and walked back, brows raised in question. "Get yourself home safe, too." Her hand rested on my arm, ever so lightly.

I forced a smile. "Always."

———·———

I stood onstage in the same spot I had earlier, but this time a sparser audience stared back. Now their eyes were wide, anxious, and above all, curious. Was it possible a murderer was still here among them? Most of them were liars. All were criminals, if you counted the ones who'd broken laws that shouldn't be laws. Maybe even one or two had killed someone before, in the name of love or war or bootlegging.

"Good evening again, folks." I cleared my throat. What could I say that wouldn't set off a panic? The smoke haze was thinner now, and I could see all the familiar faces in the room—Bennie looking around at the crowd as if counting them, the Red Feathers at their tables, Zuzu hastily putting on her purple coat and hat, Olive scrambling to gather abandoned glasses from the tables and empty them of their incriminating contents. What would happen to them if I got this wrong?

"As you might've noticed," I said, trying to keep my voice light, "we've had . . . an incident. And it's the kind of thing the cops can't overlook. So—"

The sharply rising tide of voices drowned mine out.

"Wait, wait—hold still." I raised both hands. Faked a grin. "Here's the thing. We don't like the cops around here, do we?"

A few in the crowd tittered. A few jeered, their eyes shining from drink and the fake orange glow of our electric candelabras.

"In the Quarter, we like to sort things out for ourselves, don't we?"

Some murmured agreement. Some snorted.

"There's no getting around calling the cops *eventually*. But it doesn't have to be right this second. If you want to leave before they get here, I can't stop you."

Chair legs squealed against the floor, and the hum of voices doubled. Everywhere, customers knocked back drinks and flooded toward the front door. Olive piled glasses on her tray as quickly as people set them down, and Zuzu chased after her with her coat, trying to get her to quit and put it on. Duke shoved open the tall windows we normally kept shuttered to protect our customers' privacy and started waving folks through them into the alley.

"What happened out there?" Bennie's loudmouth friend, Eddie, called out over the noise.

I waved a hand. "You'll read about it in the paper tomorrow."

Arimentha's blank eyes and slack face hovered at the back of my vision, and I rubbed a hand across my own eyes. What if someone here had seen what happened to her? What if I was shooing away our best chance to find out?

It was too late to fix that now, even if I wanted to. Everyone was busy draining out of the club like whiskey out of a jug. A woman stumbled, and the people behind her would've trampled her if Duke hadn't grabbed her arm and helped her up. So much for an organized evacuation.

"Wait a goddamn minute!" I yelled into the microphone. "Don't jam up at the doors!"

Maybe on another night they would've listened. But tonight was not my night.

"Cops!" someone yelled. "They're here!"

Over the heads of the crowd at the front door, I saw a half dozen white hats shoving their way into the club, their billy sticks raised.

Run fast, Marion, I thought, and then the real hell broke loose.

CHAPTER

6

SHOUTS AND DUST and drinks flew as customers pushed and scrambled, knocking over tables and one another. Frank leaped out of the way, clutching the cash box under his arm like a football, and let the crowd shove and punch to get past the cops. The rest veered, shrieking madly, toward the windows Duke had opened, the one exit the cops weren't blocking.

At least, the one exit the customers knew about. There was still the courtyard, the escape route the Cloak employees used when Aunt Cal rang the alarm bell and made us practice what to do in the event of a raid. But it wasn't ideal, considering there was a potential crime scene out there.

"Stop where you are!" the cop in front bellowed, but nobody listened or stopped. "It's not a raid, you fools! Stop!"

Frank met my eyes where I stood on the stage, above the fray. I pointed him toward Olive and Zuzu, so he could gather them up on his way out. He nodded and started barreling through the crowd toward them.

"Millie!"

I looked down and saw Bennie Altobello on the first step, holding up a hand to me.

"Come on!" he said, his dark eyes urgent. "Let's go! We can get out through the courtyard!"

The hand was tempting, and not just because it belonged to Bennie. I wanted nothing more than to run away into the night, to reach the safety of my apartment and ring the bell to say we'd made it, then double over laughing, with a stitch in my side and friends all around me, like we had after all the times Cal made us practice.

But this wasn't a raid. This was life and death. I had to stay and listen to what Fitzroy and the other Uptowners told the cops. Had to tell them something to counter that tainted testimony, as soon as I made up what that something was.

"Sorry, Bennie," I said. "I have to go down with the ship."

"What—why?" He took another insistent step toward me.

"C'mon, Bennie," whined his buxom date, tugging on his sleeve. "Just leave her."

"Yeah, we gotta get out of here, Ben," Eddie said, already dancing away. "Your pop'll kill you if you get busted in a speak."

Eddie was a jackass, but he was right. If Bennie got arrested, the cops could use him to get to his dad and blow their whole bootlegging operation.

"Go on," I said, hopping down the steps past him. "I'm all right. But watch out in the courtyard. That's where—"

Something crashed to the ground, breaking glass and sending up a fresh wave of shrill screams. Bennie's date yanked at his arm in earnest now, and I gave his chest a gentle shove.

"Just go, fast as you can. Don't look at the fountain."

He looked puzzled, but Eddie and their dates were already

pulling him away toward the arched entrance to the back hall. Frank was close behind them, his massive arms managing to protect the cash box and Olive and Zuzu.

Olive glanced back over her shoulder at me, and I smiled and waved, pretending not to be afraid.

Even Duke was slipping out a window into the alley now.

I was the only one left to defend the club. The only one left to defend Marion.

I wished hard for one moment that Aunt Cal was there. Then I pasted on a smile and marched over to face the cops.

—·—

I'd seen cops beat up and haul off a homeless man who was raving on a corner. I'd seen them look the other way when white men turned over a black man's fruit cart and set the oranges and apples rolling into the street. I'd seen cops do good things, too, but I didn't like my odds.

As a rule, I crossed the street if I saw a white hat coming. But now I planted myself in front of the two cops who looked to be overseeing this operation. Unlike the white-hatted uniformed officers, these two wore black fedoras and trench coats over cheap suits.

"Hello, Officers," I said, smiling and leaning an elbow on the bar. "Would you fellas care for a soft drink? The cherry cola is our best seller, but me personally—I think the vanilla is the bee's."

"Save it," said the older cop with the craggy face. "We're not here about your small-time speakeasy."

I batted my lashes. "Don't know what you mean, sir. This is a soda shop, as you can plainly see."

The bitter fumes of spilled liquor wafted around us. Behind

me were the chaotic remnants of the fleeing crowd and the other cops being ignored as they yelled at everyone to stop.

"Sure it is," the cop said. "And I'm a tightrope walker."

"So was my granny."

The cop glowered at me. His younger cohort suppressed a smile under the whisk broom of a mustache on his face.

"Cut the comedy, kid," Craggy said. "Don't you know there's a dead body out in your courtyard?"

I hopped up on a barstool. "You don't say."

"If you knew, why didn't you call the police?" Whisk Broom said.

"If I didn't call, what're you doing here?"

The downward-curving lines around Craggy's mouth creased deeper. "A young man called us from the coin phone down the street. Said something about not trusting the girl in charge of this joint to do it."

I pressed a hand to my chest. "He couldn't have meant *me*?"

Whisk Broom took off his fedora and ran a hand through hair the color of a well-used penny. "Are you really in charge of this establishment, Miss . . . ?"

I didn't want to tell him my name, but I couldn't think of a way to avoid it long enough to make it worth my while. "Millie Coleman. And I am for tonight."

Craggy jabbed a finger at me. "Look here, girlie. It's in your interest to cooperate with us. We got a witness says your fairy threatened that girl right before she turned up dead."

I narrowed my eyes at him, bristling at the slur. "Looks like *you* scared off all the so-called witnesses."

"Not all of them," he said, showing a row of yellow teeth. He turned and called over his shoulder. "Bring 'em in here!"

In trooped the rich kids, looking chilled and puffy-eyed. Fitzroy and the auburn-haired girl both glowered at me.

"All we need," Whisk Broom said, drawing back my attention, "is for you to tell us where Mr. Marion Leslie is right now. We want to have a little chat with him. That's all. Get his side of the story."

I reclined against the bar on my elbows. "He left a while ago. This was his farewell performance. He's been planning for ages to go to New York City, and he finally did it. I expect a letter from him any day telling us all how well it's going. Hell, I might take off and join him someday."

Craggy looked at me impatiently. "You expect me to believe that booshwash?"

"Did you ever see Marion's show? He's gonna be a big star. Wouldn't doubt if he's in pictures one day."

Craggy whipped off his hat and looked like he'd dearly love to hit me with it. Instead, he pointed it at me. "Look, girlie. Selling liquor is one thing. Harboring a murder suspect is another. You don't want to get on our bad side, understand? We could make this business dry up real quick."

"I don't know what you mean, Officer. We just sell soft drinks here."

"It's *Detective*. And you won't be selling nothing if you don't tell us where that boy is."

I smiled sweetly. "I *did* tell you. Aren't you listening? He's on his way to *New York City*." I said it slowly, as if to a three-year-old child.

Craggy's face turned the color of an overripe tomato, and his teeth clenched so hard he looked apt to chip one.

Whisk Broom stepped forward, a little black notebook in his

hand. "The kids outside told us you took the victim's handbag and some kind of paper found in her hand, possibly a letter? Is that so?"

I hesitated only a beat. "Sure, I got it right here." I pulled the handbag out of the back waistband of my trousers. Craggy's eyes got keen, and he snatched it out of my hand.

"Why did you take it?" Whisk Broom said, keeping his eyes on me, as Craggy rifled through the handbag's contents.

"Figured it was important evidence. Thought I'd keep it safe for you." I faked an expression of wide-eyed innocence. "After all, who knows what those friends of hers might be capable of?"

"There's ten dollars in here," Craggy said. "Was there more?"

"Don't know. Didn't even open it."

"So, you're not worried your fingerprints'll be all over it?" Whisk Broom said.

"I might be if your pal here wasn't rubbing his mitts on it right now and covering them up."

Craggy started to sputter, but Whisk Broom cut across him. "What about the paper?"

"Oh, sure." I whipped a fresh playbill out of my back pocket and tossed it on the bar.

Craggy snatched it up before Whisk Broom got the chance and unfolded it. "Thing's blank inside." He showed it to Whisk Broom.

"Why wouldn't it be?" I said. "It's just a playbill. Maybe the poor kid liked the circus."

"One of the witnesses seems to think there was a note of some kind written on it."

"Not that I ever saw." I shoved my hands in my pockets and rocked back on my heels. "But it *was* dark out there."

"Look there," Whisk Broom said, pointing. "There's a stack of these at the end of the bar."

"Must be where she got it from," I said lightly. "Too bad the circus already left town. We should've tossed those already, but our soda jerk can be a little lackadaisical."

Whisk Broom studied me carefully, eyebrows raised. It looked a little too much like he saw straight through me, so I fished a maraschino cherry out of the jar on the counter for some misdirection.

"What about the necklace?" Craggy said. "Girl over there says Miss McDonough was wearing a necklace. Some kind of butterfly thing."

"Dragonfly," Whisk Broom corrected, checking his notebook.

"Whatever." Craggy waved a beefy hand. "Was it in this bag? Have you seen it?"

I chomped the cherry to delay answering the question. "Nowhere except on that girl's neck when she came in the door."

"You met the deceased before she died?" Whisk Broom leaned forward, eyes widening.

I twisted the cherry stem around my fingertip. " 'Met' might be too strong a word, but I saw her. I was running the door."

Whisk Broom glanced significantly at Craggy, but the other detective was walking in a circle now, staring at the ceiling.

"Maybe the necklace came off up on the balcony," Craggy said abruptly. "Show us."

I didn't care for his tone, but I didn't want to let these cops see anything they did bothered me. So I hopped off the stool and said, "Right this way, fellas."

I led Craggy and Whisk Broom past Fitzroy and his pals being interviewed by the other cops. The auburn-haired girl was still staring at me, but I pretended not to see her. I had enough on my plate without piling her on it, too.

The detectives snagged a couple of extra officers and followed me up the narrow staircase, all of them clomping and breathing loudly behind me. At the top, I breezed past Marion's closed dressing-room door and turned right, toward the storage room. Its door was half open.

"Dust that doorknob," Craggy ordered, and one of the uniformed cops squeezed past me to do the job.

I watched with some curiosity as the officer dusted white powder on the age-darkened brass knob and all along the edge of the wood door. I held my breath as he straightened, but then he shook his head.

"Nothing usable."

"Figures." Craggy slapped his hat against his thigh and turned to me. "You, girl, what's in there? Any surprises?"

"No birthday parties, if that's what you mean." I slipped past the uniformed man to pull the chain on the light bulb, revealing piles of extra chairs, crates of dusty glasses, a cracked mirror. The door that led to the balcony was shut, and after a moment of staring around at the flotsam in the room, Craggy sent his underling to check that one for fingerprints, too.

I sighed loudly. At this rate, I wasn't getting to bed anytime soon.

The cops strongly suggested I stay in the storage room while they looked around on the balcony. But they left the door hanging open, so I crept closer and closer while they were busy talking about trajectories and dusting the wooden railings and the arms of the two metal chairs. Whisk Broom took a flashlight from one of the uniformed cops and shone it in slow arcs across the floorboards, looking for the necklace, I guessed. I knew he wouldn't find it because it was on Marion's neck somewhere, hopefully far away and safe. But Whisk Broom stopped, crouched, and pinched something out of a crack in a board. He held it up, and it winked in the dull light.

"What is it?" I said before I could help myself, rushing forward the rest of the way to the door.

Whisk Broom cocked his head as if debating whether to tell me, but it didn't matter anyway. In the light of his flashlight were more of the same objects scattered across the boards—tiny gold beads the exact color of Arimentha's dress.

"There was a struggle," Whisk Broom said slowly, looking back at the floor. "These beads popped off Miss McDonough's dress. And that chair—see how the dust is disturbed in streaks around the legs? Someone shoved that chair back hard, like they were leaping out of it. Knocked the chair over and later straightened it back up hastily, not quite in the same place."

I leaned forward, squinting at the marks in the dust. He was right. So that meant . . .

"Someone pushed her," Whisk Broom said, staring at me now, as if reading the words off my face. His mouth hardened.

This was no accident. It was a murder. And the cops wanted to pin it on Marion.

—·—

I froze where I was, suddenly afraid that even breathing would give away how scared I was for Marion.

Whisk Broom straightened, his eyes never leaving my face.

"Miss Coleman, you're going to have to show us your friend's dressing room now."

"Says who?" I said, but with only half the bravado. "You got a warrant?"

"We don't need a warrant. It's legal to search the premises if we have reasonable suspicion that a suspect is inside."

"I told you he's not—"

"Get out of the way then," Craggy said, barreling past me. "We'll bust down all the doors till we find the right one."

"Wait." The last thing we needed was them searching Cal's office, too. We kept the real books at home and a sham copy here at the club for just such an occasion, but I couldn't be one hundred percent certain Cal hadn't left something incriminating in a locked drawer. I shut my eyes for a moment so I didn't have to look at the cops' stupid faces. "It's the first door on the right, top of the stairs." My eyes popped open again. "But I'm coming with you."

Craggy just laughed, and I scrambled to stay with them as they shoved past me out of the storage room and flung open the door to Marion's dressing room. Normally, he would've locked it before he left for the night, but he hadn't known he was going to be leaving so early. The door swung open to reveal the usual casual disarray. The smell of his spicy Shalimar perfume wafted out, and Whisk Broom sneezed.

"Ugh, what is all this?" Craggy started pawing through the drawers of Marion's dressing table. A uniformed cop opened the armoire doors and raked aside Marion's dresses, while another poked at his sewing machine in the corner.

I didn't answer. I stood in the doorway with my arms across my chest and teeth clenched, watching them open his drawers, shove aside his bowl of hairpins, toss a white feather boa on the floor. His second-favorite silver-beaded dress slithered off its hanger and puddled in the bottom of the armoire. A spool of black thread rolled across the floor and bumped against my foot.

I ground my teeth, and my hand twitched toward the pocket where I kept my switchblade, as if I could chop off every finger that touched Marion's things.

"You don't think this is right, Miss Coleman?" Whisk Broom said curiously.

I turned to look at him. I hadn't realized he was still beside me. He hadn't joined in the ransacking of Marion's dressing room, at least not yet.

"No." I'd intended to say more, but I found the rest choking in my throat.

"It's necessary, Miss Coleman. If he is innocent, as you seem to believe, this will only help prove that."

"Unless one of you tries to plant something. I'm watching you."

Craggy laughed, a sound as harsh as the lines on his face. "We don't need to plant evidence. This one sounds pretty open and shut to me."

"Open and shut? Open and shut!" I clenched my fists against my sides. "Aren't you even going to look for anyone else before you decide it's Marion? Aren't you going to explore all the evidence?"

"Listen to this kid." Craggy grinned maliciously. "Thinks she can do it better than us." He took a book off the stack piled precariously on a chair and showed the cover to the other officers. "These yours, kid?"

I stiffened. "Ours." Marion and I shared detective novels

back and forth. We'd read them each half a dozen times. Marion liked the Hardy Boys, but I thought they were stupid. Too many boys.

Craggy and his cronies laughed, but I noticed Whisk Broom didn't join in.

"Girlie, this ain't a storybook," Craggy said. "You leave the investigating to us. And rest assured—we'll catch this killer." He snatched down a photograph of Marion tucked into the mirror frame and jabbed his finger at it, just in case I had any doubt who he thought that killer was. "I'm taking this," he said, and stuffed the photograph into his jacket pocket, then shoved past me out of the door, stomping on the feather boa as he went.

My face flamed with rage and hate. I bent and snatched up the feather boa and clutched it to my chest as the other officers marched out after Craggy. Only Whisk Broom remained, on the opposite side of the doorway from me.

"Marion didn't do this," I choked out.

He took a card out of his pocket. "We all want to believe loved ones are innocent, but I've seen things go south before. You have to consider the possibility your friend is the killer, Miss Coleman. And if he is, you're in more danger than you realize. If you need me, here's my card."

I found my hand reaching for the card automatically.

Detective Laurence Sabatier
New Orleans Police Department
Tel. Main 3579

Sabatier, huh? I still liked Whisk Broom better.

He didn't wait for me to answer; maybe he knew I had

nothing good to say to him. My eyes bored into the back of his head as he followed the others back down the stairs.

All these cops wanted was a simple answer. Blame it on the boy in the dress. Maybe they thought he was weak and couldn't fight back against the police. Maybe they thought he had no one with power on his side.

But they didn't know Marion.

And they didn't know me either.

The words jerked loose from my throat before I even realized I'd thought them. "I'm going to find that killer, Detective Sabatier. And it's not going to be Marion."

The cop paused at the bottom of the stairs and looked back up at me. His face was mild. "I would tell you to stay out of it, but I have a feeling my words won't mean a lot to you."

I lifted my chin.

"Please just be careful, Miss Coleman." Concern showed in his brow. "A killer who doesn't want to be found is a dangerous thing."

I suppressed a shiver and folded my arms over my chest to hide it. "Don't worry about me, Detective. I'm always careful."

That was another lie.

CHAPTER

7

THE PLATINUM-HAIRED GIRL winked at me. Her emerald earrings flashed. We were dancing the tango, she and I. The golden dragonfly stretched its wings across her collarbone as if it might take flight. Behind us, Marion sang onstage about flying.

I spun the girl out into a turn, and she came spinning back to me, throwing back her head and laughing. But something was wrong. Blood trickled from her hair, down across her face. Her laugh turned into a scream of rage. She stared in disgust at my hands on her and shoved me back.

You, she said, eyes blazing. *You let him go.*

Who? I said, and looked at Marion, but he'd turned his back to us.

It's your fault, the girl said, and lunged for me, and I was falling, the wind knocked out of me, down, down, down.

I couldn't breathe. I tried to call for Marion, but he was retreating, out of the spotlight and into blackness. He didn't turn around.

My scream went silent. No one heard.

Someone took hold of my arm and shook me once, again. I swam upward out of sleep and broke the surface gasping and flailing.

Aunt Cal's laugh washed over me. "That must've been some dream."

I opened one eye a crack to find my face was directly in a shaft of sunlight. I threw an arm over my face. "You don't want to know."

Cal slapped me on the hip. "Get up. I got something to tell you."

I chanced another peek through my eyelids. Still too bright, the morning light a wash of white. It couldn't have been later than ten o'clock, and I hadn't crawled into bed until the sky was lightening to pale gray in the east.

"Move over about a foot to your left," I grumbled. School was out for New Year's Day, so there was no reason to be awake.

Cal obliged, and the shadow of her solid, rectangular body fell across my face. I opened my eyes a little more. She nudged my mattress with her knee and smirked. "How'd it go at the club last night? Frank have to throw anybody out?"

My stomach sank. The fear from my dream sang again in my blood.

Someone was murdered in our courtyard.

The cops think Marion did it.

He didn't do it. Probably.

I helped him run away.

I wasn't awake enough yet for that conversation. I'd have to think of the right way to tell her, and I needed coffee for that. "Thought you had something to tell *me*," I said, rubbing my face with both hands to coax it back to life.

"I do," Cal said, but then fell silent again. There was something odd in her voice that sounded almost like a lie.

"What is it?" I pushed myself up and studied her. With the sun at her back, her square-jawed face was softened with shadow. Between that and my own bleary eyes, I couldn't read her expression.

She hesitated, chewing her lip. Something was definitely wrong. Cal believed in drinking whiskey straight and pulling out splinters before they got infected. What could make her hesitate?

"Did something happen in Baton Rouge?" I said, kicking my legs over the side of the bed. "How was the show?"

Cal's eyes steadied on mine. The muscles in her jaws worked. "There was no show."

I glanced at the chair in the corner, where I'd tossed her tailcoat and top hat when I got home. This explained why she'd left them behind. A feeling close to anger began to build in my chest. We were lawbreakers. We were liars. But we didn't lie to each other.

"What was so important in Baton Rouge that you left me alone to run the club on a night like that? I had to—and Marion—and that girl—" I shut my eyes against the pictures of her dead face, but they didn't go away.

"Now, Millie," Cal said, sounding baffled, "you're always saying you want to take charge more. I know it was New Year's Eve and a little hectic . . ."

I pushed off the bed and past Cal to the dresser, where my glass of water from last night stood half full. I took a long drink and slammed it back down. The contents of my pockets were spread across the scarred surface of the dresser where

I'd dumped them—my switchblade, my money clip with two dollars in it, and the business card from Detective Sabatier.

I'd told that cop I was going to find Arimentha's killer. I'd told myself I would.

But I hadn't thought about what that meant. How I would go about proving my best friend wasn't a liar. And now my aunt had been lying to me, too.

She came up beside me and tried to catch my eye in the mirror over the dresser, but I stared down at the matchbook instead.

"What were you doing in Baton Rouge?" I said.

"I was . . . helping someone." She shoved her fingers through her short, pomaded hair, tracking streaks in it. She usually kept it meticulously smooth. "I was bringing someone back home. Here."

Alarm bells clanged in my head. *Back home*. Like this person belonged here, was a part of us already. Cal and her girlfriend, Rhoda, had been together six years now; could this be about her? But no—Rhoda had a nicer apartment than this and a so-called better address, too. Why would she move to a place with a shared bathroom down the hall? And she certainly wasn't hiding out in Baton Rouge. . . .

There was only one other person she could mean.

"Please tell me it's a goldfish," I said, and Cal rolled her eyes. That was somewhat comforting. Maybe I was wrong. She wouldn't be rolling her eyes if this was the terrible news I was anticipating, would she?

But then she reached out and squeezed my shoulder, her mouth pinched small and grim. "Millie."

I didn't want her to tell me any more. I wanted to go back

to sleep. To wake up in two hours and find out this conversation was just another nightmare.

"She's downstairs now," Cal said, her eyes drifting away from mine, as if they, like me, wanted no part of this news. "She's going to stay here awhile."

My stomach felt like someone had wrenched a knot in it. I wrapped my arms around my waist and hunched against the side of the bed, staring at the old newspapers pasted over the cracks in the wall.

"Who?" I rasped, my voice barely forcing its way up my throat.

But I already knew before she formed the words. I didn't hear the sound of them—only saw them on her lips as a rushing sound came up in my ears like a hurricane.

"It's Gladys, Millie. It's your mother."

"Why?" I gritted out through my teeth. "Why did you bring her here?"

Cal heaved a heavy sigh.

"She's my sister, Mill. She needed me. I know she's made—"

"Don't you dare say 'mistakes.'"

Cal held up her hands, like someone trying to calm a skittish horse. "I know how you feel, babe. Truly I do. I know what it's like to have parents who shove you out to fend for yourself. But that doesn't change who Gladys is to me. She isn't *only* what she did to you."

I stiffened, wanting to cover my ears with my hands like a kid pitching a tantrum. The last thing I wanted to hear was anything about Mama's so-called redeeming qualities.

"No," I said, shaking my head hard. "She can't come here."

"You don't get to decide that!" Cal snapped, a familiar flinty edge in her voice. It was her take-shit-from-no-one voice.

Her I-am-the-boss-and-don't-you-forget-it voice.

She blew out a breath and swiped a hand over her face, and when she spoke again, all trace of hardness was gone, replaced with a note that was almost pleading. Not for my permission, but for my understanding, my forgiveness.

"This is why I told her to wait downstairs. I wanted to prepare you first. She's in bad shape, bruised up. That man she was with—"

"I already know this story," I said, getting to my feet. "You forget I was with her for almost thirteen years. You forget I've seen this before."

Cal looked at her hands. "I didn't forget." Her voice was quiet now, her eyes drooping with exhaustion and sadness and—I hoped—guilt. I pushed my advantage.

"She can't *stay* here, Cal." I let my voice break on her name. "She can't. *I* can't—"

"It's just for a little while." Cal tried to plunk a hand on my shoulder, but I dodged out of the way. Her mouth hardened into a flat line. "It's *happening*, so you might as well get used to it."

She turned on her heel.

"Where will she sleep?" I called after her. "Not with me, I guaran-damn-tee."

Cal answered without turning around, her hand on the doorknob. "She'll sleep with me."

"And just how long is this torture supposed to last?"

"I don't know." Cal sounded bone-weary, like the long night spent on buses and bus station benches was catching up with her. If I were a kind and dutiful niece, I would cease the ruckus, let her bring Mama up, tiptoe around the apartment while they got some much-needed shut-eye.

But I was tired, too, goddammit. And I wasn't kind and dutiful. Who would have taught me? Not Mama. Not Cal. They'd taught me how to skirt around the edges of the law, how to get what I wanted without giving anything in return. They'd made me exactly who I was. Now they could reap what they'd sown.

"Shouldn't be long," I spat. "She'll split the second she finds another lowlife."

Cal's hands curled into tight fists at her sides. "I'm going down to fetch her now. Get yourself sorted."

She banged the apartment door shut behind her, and I started grabbing clothes out of my dresser drawer. "I'll get sorted all right," I muttered, yanking off my pajamas. "I'll sort *you*."

I stuffed my legs into fresh underwear, undershirt, and trousers. I threw on a shirt, but my fingers were shaking too hard to button it. None of my socks seemed to be where they were supposed to be, and I didn't have time to find them. I shoved bare feet into my oxfords and snatched my newsboy cap off the hook on the wall, grateful boys' clothes were so much faster to put on than girls'. These were the clothes I'd begun to wear after Mama was gone and I was free to do what I wanted, to be the opposite of her in every way that mattered, without hearing her pointed comments.

Last, I stuck my money clip in my side pocket and Sabatier's card in my back pocket and my wristwatch in my side pocket to put on later. My fingers hesitated over the pearl-handled switchblade. Mama had given it to me, told me it was my father's, even taught me how to use it. I'd named it Pearl, like it was a friend, and it had been a better one than her. Maybe I should leave it on the dresser. But then she might see it here and know I still had it, and I wouldn't give her that satisfaction, so into my pocket it went.

I yanked open the apartment door, and there she was.

Mama. Gladys.

My body stopped still, like she'd turned me to stone. The punch to my chest made it hard to breathe. The ache in my throat hurt worse than I'd remembered.

Mama's eyes met mine for the first time in fifty-four months. Her hair was brown now instead of dyed red, the waves hanging limp under her felt hat, and a bruise was already turning green and purple under one eye. She had a split lip that quivered at the sight of me.

But my eyes flicked quickly away from that. I didn't want to see her weak and sorry. I didn't want to see her at all.

"Welcome home, *Mother*," I said with as much venom as I could muster.

Then I shoved past her and Cal, and ran down the stairs.

"Millie!" Cal called after me in her exasperated voice. I didn't want to hear it. Didn't want to look at her anymore after she'd lied to me and left me alone to deal with a dead girl and the cops and a best friend accused of murder.

I stopped at the bottom of the stairs, my hand on the doorknob. I didn't look back. "You might want to pick up a newspaper. See what you missed last night."

"What do you m——" Cal started to ask, but I jerked open the door and burst through it and was gone.

Out into the streets, where no one owed me anything, and no one trusted me. So I was free to do the same.

CHAPTER

8

I WALKED FAST, head down, past shoe shiners and fruit sellers and grubby boys sword-fighting with sticks. Past knobby-shouldered girls carrying lumpy burlap sacks, grannies in kerchiefs selling pralines on the steps of Saint Louis Cathedral to all the extra New Year's Day parishioners, and tired-looking mothers pushing babies in prams, while crying toddlers clung to their skirts.

How many of those mothers would give up one day and leave?

I imagined Arimentha McDonough had a devoted mother somewhere, weeping behind the door of her gilded mansion. If I died, would my mother even cry? Or would she feel a terrible, guilty relief?

Eventually, the morning's blinding sun disappeared behind a gray blanket of cloud, and rain pattered against my cheeks. I'd walked so long my shoes had rubbed my sockless ankles raw. The whole world deserved a swift punch in the gut.

I stopped and leaned both hands against the nearest building. The clapboards swam in my vision, chalky gray where the paint wasn't flaking off, and I realized where my feet had taken me. Marion's rooming house loomed, shabby and listing to one side like a drunk elephant. Relief flooded my chest, cooling the hot coil of pain in my throat. Marion would understand why this was disastrous, why it couldn't be happening. Why I would rather stand in the rain in no socks than spend one second in the apartment with my mother.

I jerked open the shutter with a squeal of the hinges and pounded on the front door. I recalled Marion had problems of his own right now, but we'd deal with that, too. I'd warn him the cops were looking for him and for the necklace. We'd figure out what to do together.

Finally, I heard Mrs. Altobello grumbling and cursing in Italian. The door opened a crack, and Mrs. A glared around it, clutching at the pocket of her dress like she thought I would mug her for her pipe tobacco.

Marion had lived at Bennie's grandmother's rooming house for more than a year now. Plenty of time for her to decide she hated me and for me to decide the feeling was mutual.

"You!" she said. "What you want?"

"Sorry to bother you, Mrs. A," I said, forcing a smile. "Is Marion home?"

Her scowl deepened. "No! He don't come home!"

"You mean he didn't come home last night at *all*, or he came home and then left again this morning?"

She hesitated. "I don't see him. You find him, you tell him come home. Now go!"

A thin blade of fear jabbed at my heart. I'd told Lewis to

bring Marion straight home, to keep him safe. Where had they gone? Had the cops caught them somehow?

"Wait, can I—"

But Mrs. A shoved the door shut, knocking me off balance. I stumbled backward, missed the step, and fell, smashing my hip against the wet banquette.

"Thanks for nothing!" I yelled, waving my fist at the door.

The rain was picking up steam now, pinging off the concrete and my skin like little daggers. I climbed to my feet and tucked the rest of my hair inside my cap, contemplating what to do next. My rain-spattered wristwatch read just past eleven o'clock. Six hours till I had to be at work. I'd be damned if I'd spend it in the apartment with Gladys and the Traitor.

"Millie? Is that you?"

I shut my eyes a moment, then turned slowly, remembering whose store was next door to Mrs. A's boarding house. I didn't want to see Bennie, not now, cursing his grandmother with my shirt half buttoned, the side of my pants wet, and rain leaking into my shoes and dripping off my nose.

But it was too late. Bennie had already seen me. He stood there in his crisp white grocer's apron, looking as warm as a fresh croissant and holding a black umbrella over his head.

"Heard you yelling at my nonna."

"So?"

"So, you usually at least pretend to be polite to her."

I crossed my arms over my chest to hide the buttons I'd missed. "I'm not in the mood to be polite."

His gaze swept over me, taking in my hastily assembled ensemble, and settled on my face again. He crept closer, bringing me under the umbrella's protection with him, and reached out a hand as if to touch me but stopped short, like I was a dog who might bite.

"Millie, did something else happen after I left last night? You weren't arrested, were you? I saw in the paper about Marion and . . . and what happened to that girl. They printed her picture . . . and Marion's. I saw . . ."

He trailed off and looked away at the rainy sky. I hadn't slowed down long enough to read the paper yet. But I doubted there was anything in it I hadn't seen or overheard for myself last night.

"Everything's copacetic," I said, though the rain was sluicing across the banquette and drenching the hems of my trousers.

Bennie's thick black brows rose gently, and his eyes drifted toward the buttons of my shirt again. I cinched my arms tighter around myself.

"You sure you're okay?" he said. "You want to come in the store and get warmed up? Wait out the rain?"

I could feel the ache coming back in my throat, the hollowness in my chest. If I stood there much longer, I would cry, and if I cried, Gladys won. That had always been the way.

But I also couldn't go into Bennie Altobello's warm, dry store, sit on a barrel of pickles as the whole neighborhood passed through, and pretend everything in the world wasn't exploding all at once.

I swiped at my nose with the back of my hand and straightened my shoulders.

"I'm going to the club," I said. "To wait for Marion to come back."

Like me, the club was the only other place he had to go. It

was home as much as the apartments we lived in, maybe more.

"Then let me go with you." Bennie spun the umbrella over our heads. "I'll even drive you."

"No. It's only a few blocks, and I'm already soaked. You don't have to do that for me."

Bennie's lips quirked upward. "Who says it's for you? I got deliveries to make. You can help me carry the crates."

I smiled back, unexpectedly relieved. "Then what are we waiting for?"

———·———

As Bennie parked his delivery truck at the curb in front of the Cloak two hours and six deliveries later, I crossed my fingers that Cal and Mama wouldn't be there yet, and that Marion would. I wanted to talk to him before they got hold of him, wanted to hear his side of the story—*all* of it, not just the half version he'd told me last night.

The rain dripped into my eyes as I followed behind Bennie, toting one of his crates of hooch. Mine was stamped SO-DA-LICIOUS on the side, which usually made me chuckle, but today my stomach bubbled with too many nerves.

He held the door open, and almost instantly I heard voices. One carried above the others, and I knew whose it was without laying eyes on her. I almost turned back. Only the weight of Bennie's crate in my arms stopped me. I arranged my face so Mama would see nothing to give me away: no tears; no guilt; no love; and definitely no forgiveness. I resolutely slipped into the club, expecting every head to turn. They'd have wondered where I was, wondered if I'd even show up. They'd watch to see the expression on my face.

But nobody even looked up. Olive and Zuzu were across the room setting knocked-over chairs back on their feet. Aunt Cal and Frank sat at a table, heads bent together as they counted cash from the lockbox. And Mama perched high on a barstool reading aloud—really loud—from the afternoon newspaper, as if she was performing a dramatic monologue. I braced myself, expecting it to be an article about Arimentha and Marion, but after a moment I realized it was a review of a movie about some prisoner falling in love with the warden's daughter.

Mama caught Frank's eye over the edge of the paper and wiggled her brows at him. The bruises on her face were almost concealed under a heavy layer of makeup, and her hair was so freshly dyed it looked like the inside of a rare steak. My stomach wrenched tight.

I set down the case of hooch none too gently, sending the bottles clinking together, then stalked across the room and snatched the paper out of Mama's hands.

"Hey!" she screeched. "You cut me!"

I rattled the paper in her face. "This is no time for *movie reviews*. Someone is *dead*." I spun on my heel to find Cal standing two feet in front of me, hands balled in fists on her hips and scowling like a concrete gargoyle.

"Oh! The prodigal niece returns!"

I set my hands on my hips, too. "So?"

"*So . . . ?* All of *this* happened . . ." She waved a hand, mouth working but no sound coming out, as if blocked by a logjam of too many angry words fighting to get out all at once. "And *you . . .* you ran off this morning without even *telling* me? There were *cops* in my club, and I had to find it out from the goddamn *paper?*"

I said nothing. Kept my chin up and my gaze steady on hers, the paper crumpling in my hands.

"I see this *disaster* in the afternoon edition," she continued, no longer logjammed in the least, "and I come here and spend an hour on the phone, reassuring my vendors and the electric company that the club isn't padlocked. And *you*? Where've you been? Off having a sulk like a five-year-old child."

"I'm not a child," I said in a low voice, less than thrilled to have an audience for this conversation. Tears pricked behind my eyes, but I'd be damned if I shed a single one. "I stopped being a child a long time ago. Thanks to *her*."

I didn't spare a glance back at Mama, but Cal's gaze flickered over my shoulder.

"That's no excuse," she said, but a bit of the heat in her voice had cooled.

I knew an opening for a truce when I saw one. I swallowed over the lump in my throat and tossed the crumpled paper on the bar. "Has Marion been here?"

Cal narrowed her eyes at me. Marion was one thing we always agreed on. She knew what I was doing, changing the subject, but after a beat, she sighed and ran her hands through her hair, mussing its smoothness for the second time that day.

"No, we haven't seen him yet. Where'd you send him?"

"Lewis was supposed to take him home to Mrs. A's, but he hasn't been there."

"So *that's* where you went."

I ignored that. "And now his picture is right here in the paper." I flipped back to the front page and jabbed at it with my finger, under the big, bold headline FEDERAL JUDGE'S DAUGHTER FOUND SLAIN IN VIEUX CARRÉ. A photograph of Arimentha in debutante white glowed above the one of Marion that Craggy snatched from his dressing room. She was smiling, showing the perfect little pearls of her teeth. I shut my eyes to stop that other image of her from coming into my mind—Arimentha's face in the courtyard, in my dream—but it came anyway. My gut felt hollow, scooped out.

Cal rubbed a hand over her face. "If he's out there wandering around, the cops are bound to find him."

"And then what?" I said. "They throw him in jail? Or worse?"

A little cry made my head pop up. Cal and I both turned toward the back hall.

Marion and Lewis stood shoulder to shoulder, just inside the doorway. Marion's face was pale and his curls disheveled. He swayed, and Lewis grabbed his arms and steadied him. Together, they took another step into the room.

Everyone else stopped moving. I felt Olive's eyes on me from across the room, but I kept my face forward, focused on Marion as he moved slowly toward me and Cal.

"What's going to happen to me?" he said, his gaze shooting from my face to Cal's and back again. "Are they going to . . ." He swallowed hard and touched the collar of his shirt.

Against my will, my mind conjured up an image of Marion shivering in a windowless room. Marion with a rope around his neck.

"No," I said firmly, banishing the worst thoughts back to the shadows.

"Don't worry about that yet," Cal said. "But this girl was a federal judge's daughter. Bribes won't work for this, at least not the kind of bribes I can muster."

I crossed the room to Marion and took his hand in mine.

"I told the cops you were gone on the train to New York to find your fortune."

Marion's chin quivered. "And they believed you?"

I bit my lip. "Not exactly."

"I can't go to jail, Millie." Marion clutched my hand. "I won't. It would be just like—" He bit his lip and shook his head, eyes brimming.

"Just like what?" I said.

But Marion didn't answer. He buried his face in his hands. Lewis met my eyes across Marion's bent back, and his expression matched mine—worried, curious, itching to do something to help.

"If you didn't do it," I said soothingly, "they can't prove you did."

"Yeah, don't worry, kid," Cal said. She straightened and paced the floor with one arm set firmly behind her back and the other rubbing her chin, like the Napoleon Bonaparte of the Cloak and Dagger club. "You just have to ride this thing out, wait for them to find the real killer. You'll lay low for now. Can't be seen at the club—especially not in drag. At least not while the cops think you're a suspect."

Marion's shoulders trembled. "Maybe I should leave town," he murmured. "Go away."

"To where?" Cal said gently.

"New York, like Millie said? Don't you know some people there? At the Pansy Club? You could get me a job."

"No," Lewis said, and I looked at him, surprised to hear his voice.

"No," I agreed. "They'll already have an eye out for you there because of what I told them."

Marion's shoulders sagged. "Then what do I do?"

"Lay low, like Cal said. They'll never pin this on you. I won't let them."

"But what can you do to stop them, Millie?" Marion said in an anguished voice. "What can any of us do?"

I set my hands on my hips. "I'm gonna find the killer myself is what."

Mama snorted behind us.

Cal's brow creased. "No." She shook her head and waved her hands in the air. "Absolutely not. I don't want you mixed up in this."

"I'm already mixed up in it," I said. "We all are."

Cal studied me. "What makes you think you can do a better job than the police?"

I lifted my chin. "What makes you think I can't? I got eyes and ears, same as them. And people might talk to me who'd clam up around the police."

"What people?" Cal said.

"The customers who were here last night. The people who work here." I flicked a hand toward Olive, Zuzu, and Bennie. "Somebody might've seen something that could help Marion. Plus, unlike the cops, I don't have to put on a show of following procedure."

"Yeah, but—"

"No buts!" I said, slapping my hand on the bar. I wasn't in the mood for Cal's warnings and rules. Not after she'd lied to me and brought Mama back. Not after she'd left me to handle a murder and the cops on my own, then yelled at me in front of everybody. "Those police detectives want somebody convenient to blame it on, so they can tell the papers the case is solved.

They don't care what really happened. They don't care if they ruin Marion's life."

"Not all cops are bad," Mama piped up. "I used to—"

"Nobody asked for *your* opinion," I said, and Mama's jaws clamped together so hard I heard her teeth click. I felt the others shifting their eyes toward each other, felt them silently asking each other, *What's the story there?*

Cal squeezed the back of my neck. A warning and a comfort in one. *Give your mother a break*, it said. But also, *I understand*. I dodged away from her touch.

"Maybe Millie's right about the cops," Cal said in her conciliator voice, the one she used for breaking up bar fights and talking Bennie's father into a cheaper price on a case of whiskey. "They'll want to solve this case quick for Judge McDonough, but they might not care about solving it the way *we* want it done."

"The way *we* want it?" Mama's eyes glittered. "Some girl is dead, and nobody is asking the most important question."

I curled my hands into fists and glittered right back. "Yeah, what's that?"

She smirked and took her time striking a match and lighting a cigarette. When she looked up, it wasn't at me but at Marion. Her brows curved upward.

"So, kid, did you kill that girl or what?"

ALL HEADS TURNED to Marion. He looked around at us, eyes wet and full of sadness and fear.

I put my hand on his shoulder. Bennie shifted from foot to foot beside the bar, as if he couldn't decide whether to stay or go. Frank rubbed a hand across his bald head, back and forth and back. Olive edged closer, the tension obvious in her posture.

Marion sucked in a long breath, eyes flicking to Lewis's face and back to mine. "I didn't kill her, I swear. I—"

"You don't have to talk about it right now," I said, glancing sharply at Mama. She didn't need to know all the specifics. Didn't need a story to tell the cops. "Let's go to your dressing room and fix it up. The cops were in there last night."

Marion stood up straighter, looking alarmed. "Can I?" he said uncertainly, glancing at Cal.

"Go ahead, kid," she said.

I took Marion's elbow and dragged him out of the room. We didn't speak again until we were upstairs.

"It's . . . I tried to clean it up, but I couldn't remember where everything went . . ."

Marion jerked open the door. The room was definitely not as bad as it had been when the cops left, but it still looked like a child had picked the whole thing up and shaken it. Marion paused for a moment, his teeth set, then started to reorganize the mess without a word.

I shut the door behind us. "I'm sorry this is happening, Mar."

He made a small sound. "Me too."

"But also . . . I need you to tell me the whole truth now."

Marion sniffed, his fingers deftly winding thread around a spool that had been knocked off his sewing machine. "I told you last night."

"But what you told me doesn't make sense. How did you know Arimentha McDonough? Why did you get so upset when you talked to her?"

"I didn't."

"Marion. What did that note say?"

He turned his back to me and began to steadily rearrange his makeup. "I haven't read it yet."

I blew out a sigh, my frustration rising. "Then what *did* you do last night? I went to Mrs. A's and you weren't there. She said you hadn't come home yet."

To my surprise, a bright red blush crept up Marion's neck, and in the mirror, I saw a shy smile pull at the corners of his mouth. "Lewis . . . took me to *his* place."

I punched him in the shoulder. "You dirty dog! What happened?"

Marion's blush deepened. "We just talked."

"The color of your neck says different. Spill it."

Marion ducked his head. "I . . . I was upset about Arimentha. I wanted to forget." He peeped at me guiltily. "I took a bottle of gin on the way out. I'm going to pay Cal back, I swear."

"Oh." It was nothing I hadn't done before myself. Nothing we hadn't done before together. But a sharp tweak of jealousy pinched me under the ribs. The whole year and a half since he'd come to us, it had been me and him. He was the first best friend I'd ever had, and I liked being the only one allowed into his dressing room and into his heart. "So, you went to Lewis's apartment?" I said, pushing my jealousy down.

Marion bit his lip to hide his expanding smile.

"And drank too much?"

He covered his face and peeked from between his fingers.

I raised my brows and gave him a hard look, a trick from Cal's interrogation playbook. "But you just talked?"

He dropped his hands back to his lap. "That's all, I swear!"

I laughed, unexpected relief flooding my chest. Marion, who turned pink at the mere thought of kissing the boy he liked, never could have killed someone in cold blood and left her to rot in a damp courtyard. The truth was, I couldn't stand here two feet away from him, looking into his eyes for more than a few moments, and believe he'd done it. One high-hatty girl couldn't change everything about who he was.

But I also needed to know the whole story of how he knew her if I was going to find out who'd done her in. I had never pressed him for details about his past before, but I couldn't solve this mystery without them.

"Marion," I said, and he froze as if he heard the question coming in my voice. "I need you to tell me about Arimentha."

Now Marion whipped around, eyes narrowed. "What are you asking me?"

"You know what."

"I didn't kill her. She was—" His face crumpled, and he abruptly whirled back around.

"She was what, Mar? You said you weren't close, but the way you're acting . . . Was she an old girlfriend or something?"

Marion snorted. "You know better than that."

"Then a friend."

Marion sighed heavily, and his hands stopped moving. "Yes."

"A close friend?"

He sank into the chair that had held our detective books before the cops knocked them to the floor. "Yes, my best friend . . . once."

"Best friend." I tried to take that in, tried not to sound envious. "But you didn't exactly look happy to see her. Did something happen between you two before you came here to the Cloak? Was she part of why you left home?"

Marion nodded slowly. "But it's a long story."

I pulled my armchair next to his stool and propped my elbows on my knees. "Okay, I'm listening."

Marion shifted in his chair and sighed heavily. "We were friends a long time, since we were little. I loved her, but eventually we grew up and Arimentha wasn't content to be only my friend. I tried to pretend it wasn't happening. I hoped it would pass. But it was her debutante year, and she asked me to be her escort to the ball, so of course, I said yes. But she must've thought it meant more than it did."

"Eek. Did she try anything?"

He gave me a *be patient* look. "There was bootleg champagne, and we'd never had any before. Arimentha said she was getting overheated in the ball and asked if I'd come with her for a stroll in the garden."

"A walk alone in the moonlight, huh?" I said.

"I know." He shook his head. "If the champagne wasn't making me giddy, I might've known what she was up to. But I'd been making eyes at this waiter all evening across the room, and I felt as if I might fly off the edge of the world." The lilt in his voice dropped. "Then Arimentha invited me to sit with her on a bench. She pointed out the full moon, said what a beautiful night it was, a perfect night for romance, and I agreed that it was. I was daydreaming about that waiter. Then she said she was cold and snuggled up against me."

"I thought she said it was too hot," I said with a smirk.

Marion ignored me. "I was about to offer her my jacket when she grabbed me and planted a kiss right on my lips. I tried to move away, but my back was against the bench, so I stayed put, waiting for her to stop."

"Ack, nightmare!"

"Yes. When she realized I wasn't kissing her back, she pulled back, looking confused . . . hurt. 'What's wrong?' she said. I shook my head, horrified that things would change between us, horrified that she would discover what this meant about me.

"She leaped to her feet, her face twisting into this ugly mask, and yelled, 'Something must be wrong with you. Every boy at this party would love to kiss me.' She tossed her head and flounced off into the house."

Marion's eyes focused on his thumbnail, where he was scraping it against the edge of the dressing table.

"She'd never spoken to me that way before. Never. I was upset. I wandered to the back of the house, and then I saw him—the waiter, leaning against the wall by the kitchen door, sipping from a flask."

"Holy smokes," I said, and a small smile flashed across Marion's face.

"The waiter grinned and offered me a drink. I leaned against the wall beside him, much closer than I would've normally been bold enough to do, and sipped, my lips where his lips had been. And the next thing I knew, we were behind a hedge kissing, our bodies touching from shoulder to toe, and my God, it was the most fantastic thing that had ever happened to me in my entire life at that point."

The glimmer of excitement in Marion's eyes dulled, and his shoulders sagged.

"Then Arimentha came back, maybe to say sorry, maybe to yell at me some more, I don't know. She was calling my name, but I was so entangled with the waiter I didn't hear her until she burst through the hedge and saw us. The two of us broke apart, and he made things worse by smirking at her. The shock on her face turned to rage and disgust, worse than before. She held my life in her hands, and she knew it.

"I left the waiter and chased after her. I grabbed her arm. Said 'Arimentha, please.' But she said, 'Don't say my name. Don't touch me.' Then she shook free and ran into the house."

"Oh, Marion," I said. "That must've been awful."

He nodded. "But it got worse. I watched her through the window as she made a beeline for my older brother and dragged him away. I was afraid they were coming after me right then, afraid they would make a scene and everyone—*everyone*—would know. I didn't wait for the car. I ran home alone and hid in my room, afraid of what would happen when my brother returned. He was always cold as ice until he'd suddenly explode.

"But when he came home, he didn't come to my room at all. I lay awake all night, waiting and hoping that somehow Arimentha had changed her mind at the last minute and kept my secret."

"But she hadn't?" I said quietly.

"No, she'd told him exactly what she'd seen. Every minute detail, down to the fact the buttons were broken loose from the top of my shirt. In the morning, my brother came and told me I wasn't returning to school. That he had made other arrangements for me. I was stunned. For a moment, hope flared again—perhaps he was sending me to Europe with the other wayward sons sowing their wild oats—but he had other plans."

My belly filled with dread. My mouth went dry. "What did he do?"

"He sent me away to . . ." Marion stared at his lap. Swallowed hard. "To the Louisiana Retreat for the Insane."

For once, I had nothing to say. I reached for Marion's hand, my heart aching.

"Everything was stolen from me," he said without taking his eyes off his lap. "My books, my friends, my schoolwork, my life. I'd thought to be a lawyer someday. Can you believe it?" He laughed, but the sound was bitter, broken. "Instead, I spent seven months of my sixteenth year in an asylum, being treated as if everything about me was a disease to be cured."

Rage rose in my throat, suffocating me.

"The doctor and nuns thought they could persuade me out of my 'deviance' by telling me night and day how wrong and disgusting my 'proclivities' were." Marion's voice and face grew harder, angrier. "They told me how much *richer* and *fuller* my life would be if I quit these abnormal ways and married a nice woman and had children."

"But they failed," I choked out. "They didn't convince you."

Marion shook his head fiercely. "The only thing they convinced me was that I could live without luxury or family. That I wanted nothing more than to be free, no matter the cost."

"So you escaped?" I said. "What did you do, carve yourself a weapon out of soap?"

"No." He smiled faintly. "I lied. I convinced the doctor I'd seen the error of my ways, that I could never look upon another man with lust in my heart, that I was disgusted by everything I had been before and would never return to it. They were so proud. They believed their methods had changed me."

"And they let you out?"

Marion nodded. "My brother came to get me, pleased as punch, absolutely convinced of his own rightness in sending me. He said Arimentha was eager to see me again, and I pretended to feel the same. He took me to my room, and I stood there in the space that was once mine, and for a moment—just one moment—my resolve shook. If I left, all of it would be gone. No soft bed, no fine shirts with my initials embroidered on the cuffs. I didn't know where I was running to or where I would sleep that night."

"But you ran anyway," I said, remembering the vague story I knew of Cal and Mama running away from home to do vaudeville years ago. The inside of my nose stung with tears, and I wished hard that I'd been there to run away with Marion, so he wouldn't have been alone for even one night.

He took a deep breath and let it out. "Yes, I ran anyway. I didn't want their money, not if I had to be someone else to get it. I stole a little jewelry and money from my mother's dresser, shimmied down the lattice, and left with the same suitcase I'd brought home from the asylum." Marion looked at me and squeezed my hand. "It was entirely worth it."

I squeezed back, tears stinging my eyes. "But what about your mother?" I said gently. "Do you miss her?"

His back straightened. "She let him put me in there." He shrugged as if it didn't matter, but I knew something about mothers who did nothing but disappoint you. I knew how they stuck under your skin like splinters.

"But why did you keep the asylum a secret?" I said. "Even from me? Did you really believe I would judge you?"

"I don't know." Marion bit his lower lip. "When people hear something like that about you—that you've been to an asylum— even if they know you, even if they think they love you, can they help wondering if there *is* something wrong with you?"

"I already know who you are, Marion," I said, wrapping an arm around him. "I know you're not insane or deviant or whatever they called you in that place. I'm just sorry your own family didn't. And that awful Arimentha."

Marion nodded slowly. "I think she was trying to apologize to me last night, but I didn't listen. I was angry, because of the past and because she was wearing my grandmother's necklace. She gave it to me, but then my anger turned to panic. The only way she could have that necklace was if my brother had given it to her. I was so afraid she'd run back and tell him about me, just like she did the last time. I was afraid I was going to have to run again, go back to being alone." He looked urgently into my eyes. "That's why I tried to scare her into going away and never coming back. But I *didn't* kill her. I would never have harmed her. I would've run away if I thought she was coming back. That's all."

The thought of him leaving sent a bolt of fear through my chest. He was beautiful, generous, funny. Never cruel, not the way I could be when I was riled. He was better than me, kinder than me. He could never have pushed Arimentha off that balcony.

"I believe you, Marion."

Tears filled his eyes, and he flung his arms around me, making me feel guilty that I'd ever doubted him even a little. "Thank you, Millie. I knew you'd stick by me, if anyone did."

"Of course. Of course, I would." My heart ached as I patted his back.

Once, not long ago, this boy had been lost and alone. We'd found him—*I'd* found him—and by God, I wouldn't let him go. Now I'd do more than stick by him, more than hope for the best. I wouldn't rest until I found out who the real killer was, until I proved it and cleared Marion's name.

I released him and leaped out of my chair.

"What is it?" he said.

I paced back and forth across the small space, mind whirring. There were so many loose ends dangling, so many paths I could take next. Which was the right one? Which was the easiest? I'd have to talk to all the regulars at the club, try to find out what they'd seen. But what about Arimentha's Uptown crowd? How would I find out the dirt on them?

I rubbed my temple, chewing over the possibilities. "Who would know all the gossip about Arimentha?" I said aloud.

Marion looked up, a light in his eyes. "I know exactly who!"

He fished through a stack of old magazines and newspapers on the floor and thrust a copy of the paper into my hand. It was folded to the society page, a page I never read if I could help it. It was nothing but articles about debutante balls and pink teas, whatever those were.

Marion jabbed at an article. "Kitty Sharpe."

"Who?"

"She's the best gossip columnist in the city! I don't think that's her real name, because she keeps herself absolutely anonymous, but she knows *everything!*"

"If she's anonymous, how do I find her? And how do I get her to tell me anything?"

Marion grinned. "You're Millie Coleman. You'll figure it out."

A shrill whistle blew down the street at the fish-packing plant, signaling the end of the afternoon shift, and we both jumped. The first wave of customers would come straggling in soon. We needed to get Marion out of here.

I folded the paper and stuffed it in the waistband of my trousers. Hurriedly, I helped Marion pack an old carpetbag with everything he'd need for a long stay in hiding, including three detective novels to keep him occupied. I glanced at his face as he concentrated on rolling up a set of silk stockings. Without his makeup and dress, with the freckles on his nose showing, he didn't look like a star; he was just my friend, a kid like me.

I *would* save him. I had to.

CHAPTER

BUSINESS WAS USUALLY respectable on Wednesday nights, but this night the crowd was thin. Maybe all the regulars were hungover from a mid-week New Year's Eve, but just as likely, the winning combo of a police raid and an unsolved murder had scared them off.

On top of that, our star performer was out of commission. In his place, Cal had hired a singer at the last minute who was caterwauling like a drunken circus tiger. Cal leaned against a column with her girlfriend, Rhoda, watching the singer with a disgusted expression and a whiskey glass held halfway to her lips.

I nudged her with an elbow, sloshing her drink. "Could be worse. You could've hired Mama."

Cal licked the spilled whiskey off her hand and gave me a careful look. We hadn't exactly apologized for our harsh words to each other, but then, we never did. We had dustups, then pretended nothing happened. That was the Coleman way.

Cal took a sizable swallow from her drink. "Gladys is *miles* better than this gal."

I barked a laugh. "Her head is miles bigger, too."

Cal spluttered in her drink, and Rhoda hid a smile in her own glass and said nothing. She'd been around me and Cal long enough to know it was best to keep quiet and wait for the fuss to blow over.

I took advantage of the coughing to get in another dig at Mama. "Where has your ward slipped off to? There's plenty of mopping to be done if she plans to earn her keep."

Cal narrowed her eyes at me. "Worry about your own keep, kiddo."

I batted my lashes. "You planning to fire me, boss?"

"Not if I don't have to." The look she gave me was part joke, part warning.

"So, it's like that?" I said, gritting out a smile. "Mama's back, and you're ready to shove me off the boat?"

Cal's jaw softened. "You know that's not how it is."

"How do I know? Blood's thicker than water, they say."

"You're my blood, too. And you know blood don't matter around here anyway. We choose our own family."

"Then I'd like to *un*-choose her."

Cal looked exasperated. "Millie, you could give her a chance. You don't know everything—"

"I know enough." I saluted Cal and dipped my head at Rhoda. "See you around, ladies. *I* got work to do."

I didn't mention that most of the "work" I had planned was on Marion's case. I sneaked up to Cal's office and rummaged in her desk until I found a little red notebook and a pencil. While I was there, I cut Arimentha's debutante picture out of the newspaper and pasted it inside the notebook's cover.

I'd already spotted some of the regulars that had been there on New Year's Eve, and I needed to talk to them and find out if they'd seen or heard anything that might lead me toward a suspect other than Marion.

But the first interview on my agenda was Duke. Sometimes customers got chatty with bartenders and told all their business, like who they were meeting upstairs on the balcony. I raced downstairs, planted myself on a stool at the mostly empty bar, and waited for him to stop pretending not to see me.

"Duke," I said.

"Mildred," he said silkily.

He was trying to get under my skin, but I refused to show any reaction. I opened my red notebook and tapped the pencil against the bar. "I gotta ask you some questions about last night."

Duke wiped a rag in a circle on the already-clean bar, looking far too pleased with himself. "Well, kid, as you can see I'm pretty busy right now."

I folded my arms across my chest, like that cop Sabatier had. "Where were you when that girl was murdered?"

Duke snorted. "Right here, chained to this bar, like always."

"Someone said they saw that girl talking to you awhile," I lied. "Did you see her?"

"I'm the bartender. I see everybody."

"That doesn't answer my question."

Duke finally stopped wiping the clean bar and crossed his arms, too, so now we were both elbows out. "Why *should* I?"

"Because not answering makes you look like you've got something to hide. Did you talk to her or not? It's a simple question."

Duke studied me with narrowed eyes for a long moment. "She came up here with that cake-eating date a couple of times."

"You hear what they said?"

"Nah." Duke's shoulders lifted in a shrug. "Her date always wandered off right when it was time to pay. Pretended to see somebody he knew. But I know the type."

I knew the type, too. I remembered how Arimentha had given him a dollar out of her own handbag to pay for his drink. Maybe he wasn't as rich as the raccoon fur coat and the company made him look.

"You think he could've killed her?" I said. "Based on what you saw?"

"I didn't see nothing."

"*Between* them, I mean. Were they arguing? Tense?"

"Nope," Duke said unhelpfully.

I blew out a sigh. "What happened when the date wasn't around? Did she show you a picture of Marion?"

Duke shrugged again. "Yeah. So? I didn't tell her anything. She saw him with her own eyes on the stage about five minutes after that."

"Did you ever see her other friends with her? There were two girls and two other guys."

"Not sure. Saw a couple of different ladies trying to make nice with her, but they were ones I'd seen in here before."

"Who?" I said eagerly.

"Nobody I'd peg as a killer." Duke glanced down the bar at his customers. One of the Red Feathers pointed to his empty glass and raised a finger. My leg jiggled under the bar as Duke took his time pouring another whiskey and delivering it to his customer.

"Duke, who was flirting with that girl?" I said the moment he returned.

He opened the cash box and stuck the customer's dollar in it. "I don't know their names."

"Then what did they look like?"

He hesitated. I thought at first he was still just enjoying the power of withholding information from me, but he surprised me by looking me in the eye with sincerity instead of antagonism. "These are our customers, Millie. Our people. You don't need to give them a hard time."

"Do you really think I would?"

"I think you'd do whatever you had to for Marion. But he's not the only one that matters in here. Remember that."

Duke had a point, and I didn't like it. I clenched my fists in my lap below the bar where he couldn't see them. "I'll remember. Now, please—tell me what those ladies looked like."

Duke let out a long sigh. "Okay. But for Marion, not you. One was a kid with brownish-red hair, I guess. Maybe five foot eight and pretty femme. Hadn't seen her for a while before last night. The other is in here all the time. Dark brown curly hair and big brown eyes, short, always wears a pink flower in her lapel. Cute as a button . . . Too bad for me, she only likes girls."

I scribbled everything down in my notebook. Though Duke's descriptions were vague, I was pretty sure I knew at least who the second woman was, a regular named Lo who'd tried to get friendly with me a time or two.

When I looked up, Duke was watching me, eyebrows raised.

"You really think that deb went off upstairs with one of those girls?"

I slapped my notebook shut. "I don't know, but I'm going to find out."

—·—

Much as I hated to admit Duke was right, I kept his advice in mind as I made my way around the club, asking the regulars every question I could think of about last night. Had they seen this girl? When was the last time they remembered seeing her inside the club? Had they talked to her, even just in line for the john?

I asked them, too, about the ladies Duke had seen talking to Arimentha. There were a few possibilities who the first girl might've been, but everyone knew Lo. Someone had even heard her talking about that table of rich girls; Lo had reportedly said at least one of them must be interested in women, or they wouldn't be here, and she'd bet she could prove it. But no one knew if she'd been successful in that bet, and she wasn't there tonight.

In between, I served drinks and mopped a little, too, so I looked busy for Cal's benefit. One of the Red Feathers said he saw Arimentha come back into the club at about eleven thirty, but then he said it could've been another blonde girl. Two women nearly Cal's age said they'd slipped out onto the balcony themselves and it had been empty as a gin jug, but that was earlier in the night, more like eleven.

I talked to Olive, too, following her around while she served her tables. She already knew most of the regulars' names and drinks by heart, and she'd only been at the club a few months. If anybody'd noticed a girl mooning over Arimentha it was her.

"The Uptowners definitely attracted some attention from the regulars," Olive said as she cleared glasses from a vacated table. "New blood always does. And they were a flashy bunch, especially the blonde one. I'd guess every girl in here was giving her the eye."

She passed me the tray of glasses to hold while she wiped off the table.

"Even you?" I tried to sound teasing, but it came out stiff.

"I didn't have time for that," she said without looking up from the table, but I thought I saw a hint of a smile sneak up the side of her mouth.

"Did you see anyone have a confrontation with Arimentha?" I said, adjusting my grip on the tray. "Even a small one? Like maybe someone tried to flirt with her, and she was rude? Or someone flirted with her, and that someone's girlfriend or boyfriend saw and got mad?"

Olive shook her head. "I didn't notice if they did. But once the murder happened and everything went pear-shaped, I didn't notice anything except what you were doing and if you were getting out safe."

I stared at her. The faintest hint of pink tinted her light brown cheeks, and she wiped the table more vigorously.

"Did . . . um . . . did you hear Lo talking about her at all?"

"Yeah, I heard her boasting." Olive straightened and pressed a hand against the small of her back. "But that's just Lo."

"I know. But will you talk to her for me, if you see her? Ask her about last night?"

"Sure."

Duke was shooting me dirty looks from the bar, so I said see you later to Olive and went back to serving drinks. I interviewed a few more customers across the bar before the night was over, but none of them had seen or heard anything useful.

That night when I got home, I lay in bed with the lamp on studying everything I'd written in my notebook. Much as I hated to admit it, I only had two pieces of evidence that might lead me anywhere: the fact that Lo had been trying to pick up Arimentha, and the fact that Fitzroy might be a lot broker than he appeared.

What I wanted to do the next morning was go track down Kitty Sharpe, the gossip columnist Marion had told me about. She might know what skeletons were in Arimentha's closet—and in Fitzroy's, for that matter. The trouble was, it was a school day, the first one back since Christmas.

Over a breakfast of dry toast in the morning (dry because Mama had used up the last of the butter), I tried to convince Cal I shouldn't go to school with a murderer on the loose, but she didn't buy it. She never bought any of my excuses. She always said some variation of "I didn't get to finish school, but you're going to, by God, if I have to chain you to the desk."

This time, we had an extra audience of one to our familiar argument.

"I didn't graduate," Mama said, stifling a yawn and wrapping her floaty seafoam dressing gown tighter around her middle. "And it hasn't done me a bit of harm. I don't see why she has to go. Doesn't the law say she can quit at sixteen?"

Maybe she was trying to make me less angry about her living with us; maybe she was throwing me a bone. But I didn't want her lousy bones.

"You're the last person who should be giving out life advice," I said, shooting her a pointed look. "And you gave up the right to comment on mine a long time ago."

Mama looked affronted. "I was just trying—"

I pushed my chair back across the linoleum with a loud squeal, spun on my heel, and left to put on my school uniform. At least if I went to school, I wouldn't have to come up with creative ways to avoid Mama all day.

Instead, I suffered the indignity of a scratchy wool jumper, a Peter Pan–collared blouse, and a lumpy navy-blue cardigan. Navy blue might just be the worst color ever invented. Even worse than pastel pink.

I took the St. Charles streetcar uptown toward the finer parts of the city and walked the six blocks of Nashville Avenue to dear old Ursuline Academy, a highbrow Catholic school Rhoda somehow pulled strings to get me into. All the girls were buzzing about the murder when I slid into my desk at the last possible second. I caught an extra few glances aimed my way, some curious, some sneering. They all knew about my aunt's speakeasy, and most of them called me Dagger behind my back, only partly because of the club's name.

The putty-faced nun rapped on her desk for silence, and half the girls complied.

"Hey, *Dagger*," Virginia Baines hissed from behind me. "You sure that killer wasn't looking for *you*?"

Her cohorts giggled.

I turned in my seat and cocked an eyebrow. "How do you know *I'm* not the killer?"

"You probably *are*," Virginia said after a beat. "Since criminals run in your *family*."

I smirked. "Looks like mules run in yours."

Virginia's pretty mouth dropped open.

"Girls!" cried the nun sharply. "Miss Coleman! Face front, please!"

I gave Virginia one last up-and-down and turned around, pleased with myself. Until a few minutes later when she "accidentally" spilled ink down my back. These were the times a navy-blue cardigan wasn't so terrible.

The rest of the day was more of the same. Conjugating pointless Latin verbs, teachers yelling at me when I fell asleep in class, girls trying to verbally take me down a peg, and me trying to cut them back. I ate lunch alone out back by the trash bins. The smell of dead fish wafted up out of the nearest one, so I ate fast.

By the end of the day, I was even more relieved than usual to get the hell out of school and out of my stained cardigan. I practically ran home from the streetcar stop on Canal Street and was happy to see Marion standing outside my apartment, tucked inside the little porch to shelter from the wind, like any other day. For a moment, I forgot he was accused of murder. For a moment, my heart lifted. But only a moment. Because when he tipped up his fedora, I saw the panic and worry in his red-rimmed eyes.

"What is it?" I said, touching his sleeve. I realized he wasn't even wearing a jacket and was shivering in the chill.

"The cops." He swiped a tear off his cheek. "They found me."

CHAPTER

11

"WHAT?" I SAID, looking him over for bruises or injuries. "And they let you go?"

He shook his head. "They knocked on the door at Mrs. A's, but I heard them talking and climbed out the window. I didn't have time to grab anything except my hat and this." He held out a small paper-wrapped package.

"You can tell me about that in a minute." I hustled him through the front door, glancing around to see if we were being observed. No one appeared to be paying attention to us, and I didn't spot anyone that looked like a cop.

When we were upstairs and had safely slammed the apartment door behind us, Cal and Mama came out of the kitchen with matching looks of irritation on their faces.

Mama took one look at Marion and cinched the belt of her dressing gown around her waist. "I'm not dressed for visitors," she sniffed, even though it was four o'clock in the afternoon.

But Cal, who was already wearing her work clothes, took in Marion's harried appearance and beckoned him to sit down and tell the whole story. She parked herself across from him in her favorite green armchair and listened with her elbows on her knees.

"What'd Mrs. Altobello say to the cops?" Cal said after she'd heard the basics.

"That I'd moved out last month."

"Ha!" I said, propping myself on the arm of Cal's chair. "Didn't know the old bird had it in her."

Cal slapped my arm with the back of her hand. "Who do you think started that bootlegging business?"

"The cops didn't get in then?" Mama said, draping herself across the sofa. Smoke from her cigarette curled around her head.

Marion took off his hat and ran a hand through his disheveled curls. "They said they didn't need a warrant if there was 'imminent danger' or something, and they shoved past Mrs. A."

Cal's brow furrowed. "They're only supposed to do that if they think someone inside is about to be killed or hurt."

"Big shocker, they didn't follow the rules," I said. "The real question is how they found out where he lives."

"Mrs. A knows all the tricks to keep the city out of our business," Cal said. "She won't have put your name down anywhere."

"How many people know where you live?" Mama said.

Marion chewed the corner of his thumbnail. "Everybody who works at the club, except Zuzu. She's the newest. But I know they wouldn't tell."

"Did you ever take any Red Feathers home?" Cal said.

Marion's pale neck burned pink. "Never."

"Not that they didn't want him to," I said. "Maybe one followed him some time."

Marion shook his head. "The Red Feathers wouldn't hand me over to the cops either."

"Whoever it was," Cal said, "you can't go back to your place for a while."

Marion's head popped up, eyes wide. "Where am I supposed to go then?"

I slapped him on the shoulder. "Here, o'course."

Mama blew out smoke and an exasperated sigh. "Why don't you just turn yourself in? Let the cops ask their silly questions, and then you'll be free to go."

Cal's lips curled in a sneer. "They're not just gonna *believe* him, Gladys. You've been off in vaudeville-land, but here the cops only turn a blind eye when they feel like it, bribes or not. Last month they roughed up some boys who were picking up sailors on the dock."

"And remember that kid whose teeth got busted out when they raided that club in the back of the fur factory?" I said.

Marion shuddered and hugged himself tighter.

Mama tapped her cigarette on an ashtray. "Not all cops are bad eggs. I used to know that Larry Sabatier—I saw his card on the table. He's a good man . . . or at least he was . . ."

Of course, Mama would know one of the cops on the case. She probably knew every man of a certain age in town.

Cal snorted. "Even if they did believe him, they'd still toss him in jail until they found better evidence on somebody else— which might not be ever if they think they've caught the killer."

Marion's shoulders stiffened, and his back straightened. "I *won't* go to jail," he said, with a determined set to his chin.

"You won't have to." I reached across the coffee table and gripped his hand. "You can stay here with us. Hide out until the real killer gets caught. Can't he, Cal?"

I looked at her and raised my eyebrows in challenge. If she could bring my no-count mother back here, then by God, I could bring Marion.

Cal met my eyes for a long moment. Then she set her jaw and nodded. "It'll be tight here with four people, but we can do it. Or I could go stay with Rhoda awhile, and Millie could sleep with Gladys . . ."

"No!" I said quickly, almost falling off the arm of the chair in my dismay. Cal couldn't leave me here with Mama, and I definitely could not share a bed with her. A flash of memory surfaced—Mama's body curled around mine, her tears wetting my hair because some man had left her, me holding her hand and whispering, "It's all right, Mama. You still got me."

The memory tasted bitter as bile. Not a year after that, she'd left *me* for some man. And now she was back here because of another one. Nothing she did was ever because of me or about me.

Cal studied my face. She reached up and patted my leg.

"Okay, we'll make do," she said, agreeing without making a fuss about it for once. "Millie and Marion can sleep together." She winked at Marion. "I trust you."

He cracked a shaky smile.

"But wait a minute," Mama said. "That girl's a judge's daughter. They won't let up. Eventually someone will crack, and they'll find him. And *us*. Isn't it a crime to . . . to harbor fugitives?"

"We don't have a choice," Cal said. "We're all stuck together until the cops find the killer. Or Millie does."

"That means our lips better be sealed," I said, looking pointedly at Mama.

"What about my stuff?" Marion glanced at me, his eyes bright with worry. "What if they figure out how me and Arimentha were connected? I have to go back." He rose to his feet. "I have to get—"

"No," Cal said firmly. "You have to lay even lower. You shouldn't leave our apartment for any reason, barring fire, flood, or bedbug infestation."

"But what if the police find me here?"

"Then you run for it again, or if you can't, ring the emergency bell, and we'll come help." Cal reached over to the wall and pushed the button she'd had installed when she bought the club and we moved in here. Down in the empty club, a hideously shrill bell would be ringing. It was supposed to be both a warning system and a safety signal, but we'd never had to use it except when Cal made us run drills.

"And I'll go get your things tomorrow," I said. "You won't last long without at least a coat and a change of underwear."

Marion blushed and wrapped his arms around himself.

"But the cops are probably still watching the place," Cal said. "They could follow you back here if you're not careful."

"We could ask Bennie to do it," Marion said. "It won't look suspicious if he goes to his own grandmother's house."

There was a thought.

"Still, he should probably wait a couple days," Cal said. "And go after dark."

"You talking about that Italian boy?" Mama said, lighting another cigarette. "I'd be happy to talk to him for you. I can be *very* persuasive."

"Absolutely not," I said.

"Why not?" Mama looked affronted.

"Because you don't even know him," I said. "*I'll* ask him."

A sly smile tugged at the corners of Marion's mouth, the first time he'd looked properly himself since he'd arrived. "And I just bet he'll say yes."

—·—

Once we were alone in my room, ostensibly to find Marion some pajamas and get him settled in, I shut the door and asked about the paper package.

Marion bit his lip and handed it over, and my fingers traced hard lines and rustling chain through the paper.

"Is this the necklace?"

"I couldn't let the police find it."

"Good thinking. I know a place we can hide it, in case the cops come here." I scavenged in the bottom of my armoire for an empty cigar box I'd been saving and settled the wrapped necklace gently inside it, with an old sock as extra cushion to keep it from sliding around. The necklace was heavier than it looked, weighted with all those milky greenish stones. "How much is this thing worth anyway?"

"Quite a lot, I suppose." Marion touched the paper one last time before we shut the lid. "It was my grandmother's, and her side is where all the money came from . . . also, the fashion sense."

I smirked. "Sounds like some lady." I patted the box lid. "But for now her necklace is going for a little nap."

I stuffed the box in one of my best hiding spots—up the old chimney of the no-longer-functioning fireplace in my room, behind the gas heater that now stood on the hearth.

I dusted off my hands. "Now I've got to go find Kitty Sharpe."

"Not wearing that, I hope?" Marion looked appalled.

I glanced down at my school uniform and laughed. "God, no."

But when I started changing into my usual trousers and less-than-white blouse under a gray-checked vest, Marion looked just as unimpressed.

"Really, Millie? You're going to see the most vicious gossip columnist in New Orleans wearing that?"

"Why not?"

Marion shook his head. "At least comb your hair, please. And wash your face."

I sighed heavily. "Yes, *Gladys*."

But Marion didn't look offended and instead of handing me the comb, attacked me with it himself.

"Be careful with Kitty Sharpe," he said, curving my hair neatly around my ear. "She knows everything about everyone. If you give her half a chance, she'll find out who I am, where I'm from, and what rock you've got me hiding under."

"Don't worry," I said, dodging away from the comb. "Kitty Sharpe is about to meet her match."

Marion pursed his lips. "Or Millie Coleman is about to meet hers."

CHAPTER

12

THE *NEW ORLEANS ITEM* came out in the afternoon, so I figured all its reporters worked late to get every last scrap of news before it went to the presses. I strolled into the downtown office at five o'clock, hoping their gossip columnist was still there.

The front desk was about as helpful as a dead fish. The receptionist looked over my trousers and vest with a disdainful air and said, "Miss Sharpe doesn't take visitors."

"I'm not a visitor," I lied. "I'm her cousin."

The lady cocked one eyebrow impressively. "You don't look like her."

"I said I was her cousin, not her twin."

"Nevertheless, Miss Sharpe has a strict policy that no one should be allowed up to see her. Period."

"I bet if you call her and ask, she'll say to send me up. Tell her Millie McDonough is here to see her. And tell her it's about a murder."

The woman looked shocked, but she picked up the telephone. She turned her back to me to murmur into it, but I still heard most of what she said. She called me a hoodlum. I suppressed a laugh, feeling the teeniest bit proud of the label.

When she swiveled back around and set the phone down, her lips pressed together in a false, pinched smile. "Miss Sharpe says she will see you."

I pretended not to be surprised that had actually worked.

The woman pointed toward the elevator. "Go up to the third floor. Her desk is on the far left by the windows."

I touched the brim of my cap. "Thanks, ma'am."

She shook her head and flicked a newspaper open in front of her face, dismissing me.

The elevator man said nothing as he took me up to the third floor. He opened the gate, and I walked out into a big open room full of the clatter of typewriters and the swish of paper, punctuated by low curses from the half dozen reporters scattered around. They were all men, so I weaved my way through the desks toward the left, as the front desk lady had instructed. And there, in the last shaft of late-day orange sunlight, sat a woman, leaning over a sheaf of papers. A girl, I realized as I moved closer, not far from my age. She wore a white blouse tucked into a neat red skirt with a ruffle that touched her calves and matching red shoes with gold buckles. A red hat perched on the corner of her desk. Her chestnut hair shone with a hint of copper in the sun, but her face was bent too close over what she was reading for me to see it.

"Miss Sharpe?" I said.

"Mmm." She held up one finger. "A moment."

Her eyes scanned over the page. She crossed out a word with a red pencil and scribbled a new one above it.

"There," she said, finally lifting her head. "Done."

"Done with what?" I said.

She looked up at me, blinking blearily, and then her gaze cleared and she took me in slowly from head to toe with sharp gray eyes behind a pair of gold-framed spectacles. I was glad after all that Marion had made me comb my hair.

She didn't answer my question, but that didn't matter. It had only been a question to get her attention. "Miss Sharpe, I presume?" I said in my best imitation of a posh accent.

She didn't rise from her chair. Her eyes narrowed. "Your last name isn't really McDonough, is it?"

"My name isn't important." I propped my hip against her desk. "I need some information, and I hear you're the gal to give it to me."

"Oh, really?" she said. "From whom?"

"Never mind about that. Did you know Arimentha McDonough?"

Miss Sharpe sighed, took off her spectacles, and rubbed them with a handkerchief embroidered with an elaborate letter *S*. "I know *about* her. And what happened to her."

"You know what the cops told your paper. That's not everything."

Miss Sharpe's angular brown eyebrows rose. "According to the police, the evidence is clear. The singer at the speakeasy where she was found killed her. Case closed." She replaced her spectacles and watched my face carefully through them.

"That's just it." I leaned forward and jabbed a finger on her desk. "He didn't do it."

Miss Sharpe shifted back in her chair, pretending to be casual, but I'd seen the spark kindle in her eyes. "You know him, don't you? The killer?"

"He's not—" I stopped myself, realizing she was trying to bait me into revealing too much. I settled back onto my heels and tried to cool the angry heat that had been rising to the top of my head. "I'm investigating what happened. I'm going to find the truth."

Miss Sharpe still had that inquisitive light in her eyes. "Investigating for another paper? Hoping to make a name for yourself as a reporter?"

"What? No. I don't care about anything except this case. This murder." I jabbed the desk again, ruffling the pages she'd been working on.

She didn't even look down at them. Her eyes stayed on me. "Why?"

I swallowed and considered what I had to lose if I told her. The cops already knew I was Marion's best friend. They already knew how to find me. Even if this society reporter wrote about my investigation, or told the cops, what difference would it make?

I forced my eyes to stare steadily into her piercing gray ones. "That singer, the one you're so sure murdered Arimentha? He's my best friend. That's why I have to find out the truth. The cops think the case is open and shut, like you said, but I know they've got the wrong guy."

Miss Sharpe sat up a little straighter. "Do you know who really did it?"

"If I did, I wouldn't be here. That's what I need you for."

Miss Sharpe sagged a bit, looking disappointed, and shook her head. "I can't tell you who killed her. I don't know."

"But you know other things—like who her friends were, who she went out with, if you ever heard about any arguments or shady stuff any of them might've been up to. Romantic dalliances, financial troubles, that sort of—"

Miss Sharpe held up her small white hands to stop me. "That's a lot of information." She eyed me closely. "My question is—why should I give it to *you?* What makes you think you can find this killer when the police can't?"

"It's not that they *can't.*" I gave her desk a little kick, and my voice rose. "It's that they *won't.* Marion's a boy who likes boys and dresses up in drag and sings, and people love him for it—did you know that? He's a star. And those cops—especially that one in charge of this investigation—they don't like that. Marion is proof everybody doesn't have to fit into the same mold. Proof everybody can be happy if the world just gives them half a chance."

Miss Sharpe glanced over my shoulder, for the first time looking less than fully composed. She cleared her throat and reached out to straighten the papers I'd shifted on her desk.

"So, are you going to help me or not, Miss Sharpe?"

She didn't look up at me yet. "Do you at least have any suspects?"

"Her friends. Her date. I already know he's lying about some things. And I'll know more when you cough up some answers."

Miss Sharpe looked up finally, one side of her mouth curving in a bemused smile. "I think you've seen too many gangster pictures, Miss . . . it isn't McDonough, so what is your name?"

"Coleman," I said grudgingly. "What do you mean?"

"I mean when you want information, it's best not to launch into an attack right out the gate. Especially when the source is inclined to give you that information anyway. You don't want to scare them off."

I scowled, then realized what she'd said. "You—you're in-clined to give it to me?"

Miss Sharpe leaned back. "Of course, I couldn't share it without considerable risk to myself. You go around asking people about the things I tell you, and my sources would know the information came from me. Then they'd dry up and tell their friends to dry up. I'm already in hot water with these debs, and if it gets much hotter, I'm burned."

I cocked an eyebrow. How much trouble could a debutante give a person, I wondered. Then I remembered one of them had ended up dead in my courtyard. That was pretty troublesome. So why would Miss Sharpe want to give me the information? There had to be a catch.

"What do you want from me in exchange?" I said, regard-ing her with suspicion.

Miss Sharpe grinned as if I'd said just what she wanted me to. "I want to make a deal with you." She leaned forward and glanced around at the rest of the room. All the male reporters were busy clacking away on their typewriters or smoking cigars and laughing together. None were paying attention to us at the society desk. "If I give you the information to help you catch Arimentha's killer—"

"Sounds good so far."

She looked as if she was barely resisting rolling her eyes. "Then you come back here after you do and give me an exclu-sive interview with the girl who solved the murder."

"Wait . . . you mean *me*?"

"Who else?"

"Why would you want to interview me?"

She did roll her eyes now. "What I want is to get off this

wretched society desk and write real news. I want to see my by-line on the front page. No woman has ever done it at this paper. But I'm going to."

"So, my story could do that for you?" I looked smug. "*You* need *my* help."

"There you're wrong, Miss Coleman. I'll do it with or without you, someday. And I have a suspicion you feel the same about your murder case. But this way, we both get what we want a little faster. What do you say?"

I narrowed my eyes. "Why are you so sure I'll solve this case?"

She pressed her lips together, her eyes locked on mine for several moments. She seemed to be debating something. "Because I think we're alike, Miss Coleman," she said finally. "And because I happen to agree with you—everybody deserves the same chances in this world, no matter whom they love or how they dress or what they've got in their underpants."

I let out a laugh, surprised this prim-looking girl talked so frankly. I looked her over once more, searching for hints there was some other angle with this deal. If there was, I couldn't see it. Marion had been right about her.

I stuck out my hand, and Kitty Sharpe shook it firmly. We both squeezed too hard. I was pretty sure I understood her, and that she understood me. We were both doing things the world told us we shouldn't, but we weren't going to let that stop us.

I grinned. "Call me Millie."

She smiled back as smugly as a cat in a sunny windowsill. "You can call me Kitty."

—·—

Kitty said the newsroom was too full of nosy men who might try to steal her scoop, so she suggested we go to a coffee shop down the street to talk. The lady at the front desk looked surprised to see us leaving together, me in my trousers and scuffed oxfords, Kitty in her smart head-to-toe crimson ensemble. Kitty waved at her brightly, and she just stared. Kitty never accepted visitors, she'd said. I wondered why that was.

"Why are the debs all riled up against you?" I said, as the bell jingled over the coffee shop door.

Kitty waved a hand dismissively, sliding into one of the spindly chairs at a little round table near the window. Outside, night was falling and the streetlights were coming on. "They're always mad at me for one thing or another. Or their mothers are. Another one called up the paper last week to complain to the editor about how 'vicious' and 'cruel' my column was."

"And it's not?" I said.

She gave me a prim smile. "I prefer the word 'honest.'"

I laughed. The most honest girl in New Orleans sharing a table with the biggest liar. We made some pair.

"What does your editor think about all the grand dames complaining?"

Kitty's eyes rolled dramatically, but before she could answer, a waiter came and took our order—coffee for us both. As soon as he went away, Kitty leaned forward, her gray eyes sparking.

"Do you know what that great buffoon of an editor said to me?" She stiffened her shoulders and put on a deep voice. "'*Truth* is outside your purview, Miss Sharpe. Leave truth to the news.'" She dropped her shoulders and sighed. "He said I'm on the society page, not the front page. He said give the society folks what they want."

"So that's why you want off the society desk?"

"That and a million reasons. Who wants to write about pink teas forever?"

"But at least you've got all the good gossip," I said, trying to guide the conversation back on track.

She looked at me sharply. She'd chosen her pen name well. "I suppose that's my hint to start spilling the dirt."

I grinned and took out my red notebook. "Spill away."

The waiter returned and deposited cups of coffee in front of us. Kitty waited until he left to speak. "It's really a shame about Arimentha McDonough." She dropped one sugar cube after another into her cup. "She was good for business."

I paused in the middle of adding my own single cube of sugar. "How so?"

"She kept the gossip mill running. She was serious for a while with this future politician type, Philip Leveque. But then they split up all of a sudden about a year ago, for some reason even I could never discover. Ever since, she's been different. Running off to speakeasies all the time, drinking too much, dallying around, they say, though I haven't discovered with whom."

"What about her date that night, Fitzroy?"

"I don't think they were really 'dating' per se. Fitzroy DeCoursey is an odd case. He started showing up at every event about a year ago, and he's 'friends' with everyone, but few people seem to actually like him."

"Any idea why?"

"No one will utter a peep against him, so I haven't managed to figure it out. Yet."

"Then how do you know they don't like him?"

Kitty shrugged. "Ask about him sometime and watch what their faces do. It's obvious."

I jotted that down in my notebook and considered. The Uptowners obviously weren't put off by people who looked like department store mannequins, so that wasn't why they disliked him. Maybe this was another hint he didn't have as much money as the others?

"Have you heard anything about him having money troubles?"

"No . . . not exactly." Kitty bit her lip. "But there was a rumor going around that he and Jerome Rosenthal had some sort of financial arrangement between the two of them."

My brows rose. "What kind of 'arrangement'?"

A pair of well-dressed women walked by our table, and Kitty clammed up until they were past, then leaned closer and lowered her voice. "No confirmation, but I assumed Mr. Rosenthal was paying him for his company, if you know what I mean."

"So, both Rosenthal and Fitzie have something to hide."

Kitty arched an eyebrow. "Don't we all?"

I met her gaze steadily over my notebook. "Not me."

"How fortunate for you." Kitty glanced away at an older couple sitting two tables away from us, holding hands. "And unfortunate for Mr. Rosenthal and Mr. DeCoursey that having secrets makes them suspects in a murder."

I stirred my coffee slowly. If Arimentha had found out about Fitzroy and Rosenthal's "arrangement," one or both of them could've pushed her off the balcony to silence her. Fitzroy seemed broke at the bar, so Rosenthal probably had the most to lose. Then again, enough money could be instant insulation from trouble.

"Okay, what else?" I said, picking up my pencil again. "What do you know about the other three who were there with them that night?"

Kitty took a delicate sip of her coffee, made a face, and added yet another cube of sugar and a hefty pour of cream from the little pitcher on the table. "The other three were Symphony Cornice, Daphne Holiday, and Daphne's brother, Claude. Symphony is most recently Minty's best friend—"

"Wait . . . did you say—"

"What? Oh . . . *Minty*, yes. That's really her nickname."

"Oh." I suppressed a laugh. The girl was dead after all. But I would have to have a conversation with Marion about leaving out this important detail. "Please continue."

"So, *Minty*," Kitty said, with a small guilty smile, "was best friends with Symphony for the last year or so. They're both seniors at Sacred Heart and neither have siblings, so maybe that's why they bonded? They seemed very different in personality otherwise. Symphony lives with her parents a block away from Minty in the Garden District."

Of course, they went to Sacred Heart, the only school more ritzy than Ursuline. I paused with my pencil over my notebook. "What does Symphony look like?"

"Tall, auburn hair?"

I drew a line underneath her name. "That's the one who gave me a hard time the night of the murder."

Kitty tasted another tiny sip of her coffee. "I'm not surprised. Her mother is one of those who called the editor about me."

I wrinkled my nose. "What about Daphne Holiday? What's she like?"

"Brunette and small. Ambitious. Graduated from Sacred Heart last year. She's a tennis player, plays obsessively three hours every day from eight until eleven in hopes of going on the professional circuit, or possibly just killing time until she gets a marriage proposal. She is currently involved with Minty's former boyfriend, Philip."

"The politician?"

She made a moue of distaste. "He's going places, that one. When he donated a thousand dollars to the Children's Toy Fund this Christmas, he made sure the paper knew about it so we'd send someone out to get a photograph. He's good-looking and never a hair out of place, but to me, there's something cold and false about him."

"Like he wouldn't actually want to come too close to those poor kids?"

"Precisely."

"So why was Daphne with Minty on New Year's Eve and not him?"

Kitty shook her head and picked up her coffee but didn't drink it. "That I don't know."

"What about Daphne's brother?"

"Claude used to have a crush on Minty, but then he's had a crush on every girl in the Garden District at some point. I don't think he's a serious contender." She leaned forward like she was telling a secret. "Weak stomach."

I tapped my spoon on the table, remembering the boy who'd vomited on the cobblestones of our courtyard that night. "If not him, who do you think *is* a contender?"

Kitty propped her chin on her fist and looked around at the other customers, as if she might find the answer right there in the coffee shop. "I'd wager it was someone with a romantic connection . . . Money doesn't motivate these people enough. They've never even had to think about it."

"But what about Fitzroy? He was the one so eager to blame Marion for everything. And he was the last one to see her alive."

Kitty pointed her spoon at me. "That you know of."

"Okay, true." I sighed. "So now what? I need to talk to these people, right? How do you do it?"

"I don't." She rotated her coffee cup, looking smug.

"What do you mean you don't talk to them?"

"I talk to everyone else. I talk around them. And I listen. I stand out now"—she touched her bright red hat with the nine-inch black plume sticking up—"but when I go to one of their events, I blend into the woodwork. They hardly even notice I'm there. None of them even know Kitty Sharpe's face."

I was a little impressed but tried not to show it. "Then I need to go to an event. And I need to blend in. But what kind of event?"

"Just so happens . . ." Kitty looked pleased with herself again. She slipped a folded newspaper out of her red handbag and slid it across the table.

First Debutante Ball of the Season to Be Held at Roosevelt Hotel

Carnival season is here again, and with it come the debutantes in their angelic white finery. A glittering

gala marking the opening of the debutante season
will be held in the Blue Room of the Roosevelt Hotel
on Saturday, January 4, at 8 o'clock in the evening.

"That's in two days!" I said, not bothering to read the rest.

"Indeed."

"So, you're saying that if I somehow manage to get into this
ball, I'll be able to overhear all the gossip I need?"

Kitty stirred her full cup of coffee again. "Precisely."

"Will they really be talking dirt about Minty when she was
just murdered?"

"Of course they will." Kitty laughed as if I were impossibly
naive, which made angry heat rise up my neck. "Everyone will
have a theory about who killed her, and you can hear them all."

I looked at her warily. "Will you be there?"

"I will." Kitty patted her hair. "But don't expect to see me.
I'm good at blending in, remember?" She looked me over appraisingly again. "Do you think you can get in?"

I scowled at her across the little table. "I can get in."

I didn't mention I had no idea how.

CHAPTER

13

IT WAS THURSDAY night, our third busiest of the week, so I went straight from the coffee shop to work at the Cloak, my mind buzzing with all the things Kitty had told me.

"Hey, Millie!"

I turned on the banquette outside the club and saw Bennie, carrying a crate with bottles tinkling together inside it. "Hold the door for me!"

I propped the door open with the heel of my shoe. Bennie flashed me a smile as he brushed past me, and an idea came to me.

I caught up with him at the bar, where he was unloading bottles into one of our hideaways, a secret opening behind a panel of the wall. A piece of the hay the Altobellos used to cushion the bottles had floated up and landed in Bennie's black hair. I plucked it out and slid onto a stool, twirling it.

"Why, Bennie Altobello, you're just the man I wanted to see."

Bennie looked over his shoulder, his mouth quirking to one side. "Let me guess. You need a favor."

"Actually, two. Sit and talk to me a minute," I said, gesturing broadly to the stool beside mine.

Bennie brushed the hay off his hands and sat, his smile cautious.

"The first one's really a favor for Marion. Can you get his stuff from your grandmother's place for him? He'd hiding out at my apartment."

Bennie sobered. "I saw the cops over there. Nonna is furious!"

"So you'll help?"

"Of course." He nudged me with an elbow. "What's the other thing? I know you started with the easy one."

I grinned. "Depends on how you define 'easy.' Doesn't your friend Eddie work at the Roosevelt Hotel?"

"Yes."

"And haven't you filled in for him a couple of times?"

His answer was slower this time. "Yeah."

I scooted closer, touching his knees with mine. "Here's the thing—I need a way to get into the party there Saturday night."

His brows drew together in a frown. "Why?"

"Someone there might have dirt on Arimentha McDonough's friends."

Bennie leaned back, his eyes widening. "I don't know if that's a great idea."

"Sure it is. This gossip columnist girl told me it's the best way to—"

Olive appeared beside our barstools, her tray laden with fresh-washed glasses. She glanced at our touching knees, then started unloading the glasses onto the bar right between us, so we had to scoot back to give her room.

"You two look like you're plotting something," she said with a sly look at me, her hip bumping against my thigh.

"Bank robbery," I said. "Don't tell the cops."

"Only if you promise to split the take."

The jasmine scent floating from Olive's smoothly sculptured hair was distracting. "Ten percent. Take it or leave it."

Bennie cleared his throat. "Actually, Millie is trying to talk me into sneaking into the Roosevelt Hotel with her."

Olive's brows rose, her gaze flickering sideways toward me. "That so?" She plunked a glass on the bar with a little too much force.

"Yes," Bennie answered, though I was pretty sure the question had been for me.

"It's not how it sounds." I shot a glare at Bennie. "I need to crash the debutante ball there Saturday night. And Bennie has been a waiter there before, so all he has to do is dress me up as a waiter, too."

"But they only hire male waiters," Bennie said.

I set my fists on my hips and sat up straighter on my barstool. "Don't you think I can pull it off?"

Olive plunked down another glass, this time brushing my arm with her elbow. Her gaze flickered over my body, and a coy smile curved up the corner of her lips. "You look like a woman to me."

Heat fluttered at the back of my neck. Bennie looked from Olive's face to mine and scowled. "Well," he said, "Eddie still works there and could probably get us a couple of uniforms."

"Perfect. Then where should we meet?"

But Bennie was still glowering. "Eddie needs that job. We can't get him in trouble. If we do this, you need to be discreet."

I pretended to fluff my hair like Marion. "Who, me?"

Bennie didn't look reassured, but Olive coughed to hide a laugh. She made a show of setting down the last glass and whisking a dish towel over the lot. She tweaked my elbow and met my eyes again. Then she winked and murmured near my ear, "Discretion is overrated."

———·———

Back at home after work, I crawled into bed beside Marion, who wanted to hear everything that had happened at the club tonight and especially everything I'd learned from Kitty Sharpe. He listened carefully, making only minor interjections, until I got to the part about Minty being formerly involved with Philip Leveque. Marion spluttered and sat up straight, dragging the quilt with him.

"Hey!" I cried, but he ignored me. His eyes were urgent and shining in the dark.

"Philip Leveque? You're sure?"

I sat up, too. "Of course. Who is he?"

Marion's gaze flickered away from mine. He turned and propped his elbows on his knees, facing the foot of the bed. He blew out a heavy breath. "He's my brother."

It was my turn to splutter. "Your . . . what . . . ? The one who sent you—"

"That's the one. And then Arimentha went and *dated* him?" Marion shook his head. "She sure didn't mention *that* in her letter."

"Her letter . . . ?" I said, confused, but instantly remembered the note Minty had scrawled on the back of the circus playbill. The last time I'd asked him about it, he'd said he hadn't read it yet. I clapped my hand over my mouth, suddenly remembering the cops had been in his room this afternoon. "Please tell me you burned it."

Marion shook his head miserably. "I should've."

Dread filled my chest. "Where is it?"

"Inside the sleeve of my Bessie Smith record."

I'd given him that record for Christmas. So now a letter from his ex–best friend was hanging out in a gift from his new one. Perfect.

"Maybe the cops didn't think to look there." I nudged Marion's shoulder gently. "How bad is it if they find it? What does it say?"

Marion twirled a curl tightly around his finger. "It doesn't matter. The only thing that matters is it has her name on it, and mine."

I hated to hear the despair in his voice. "I bet they didn't find it. And I'll get Bennie to bring it when he gets your stuff."

Marion was silent.

"Now that you know about Philip and Minty," I said, "do you think he could be the killer? He did throw you in an asylum, so that makes him capable of just about anything in my book."

"If it threatens his reputation and ambitions, yes," Marion said glumly, twisting another curl. "But I doubt if he would ever set foot in a 'low-class' French Quarter speakeasy. He barely deigns to cross Canal Street except to go to Galatoire's. Besides, you said now he's seeing that Daphne girl."

"Don't you remember any of these people? Weren't some of them your friends, too, once?"

Marion puckered his lips as if tasting pickle juice. "I stuck with Arimentha mostly, and she with me. I went to an all-boys' school, so she was the only girl I knew, really."

"What about Symphony Cornice then? Kitty said she was Minty's best friend."

"Not when I was around, of course. But I remember her, I think. Reddish hair? Personality like a block of ice?"

"That's her. Apparently, once you were out of the picture, she moved in fast. Wanted a piece of Minty."

Marion's nose wrinkled. "I hated that place, you know," he said, his voice softer. "I'm so glad I'm out of there."

We were both quiet for a moment, the only sounds the wind whistling through the shutters and Aunt Cal and Mama climbing into their creaking bed next door. I could almost feel Marion thinking, remembering. I wanted to drag him back to me, to the present.

"So, who do you peg for the murder?" I said.

Marion paused momentarily in the darkness. "Her date maybe? What was his name?"

"Fitzroy DeCoursey."

"That sounds like a stage name."

"Maybe he's got a future in drag."

Marion looked contemplative. "He was sort of pretty."

We both giggled, until Cal banged on the wall and threatened to make us sleep in the bathtub if we didn't cut it out. We threw the quilt over our heads and laughed under there instead, until Marion abruptly stopped. It was pitch-dark under the quilt, and I couldn't see his face.

"She apologized, you know."

"Who?" I asked, but I knew.

"In that letter. That's what it was—an apology."

"Oh."

We both fell silent, our breaths mingling quietly together under the quilt. I wanted to see his face, but I didn't need to really. I'd heard everything in his voice. He was forgiving her, slowly. Maybe her being dead made it harder to hold a grudge.

Again in the blackness, I saw her blank eyes staring, the crooked angle of her head, her mouth dark and open.

"We'll catch the guy who did it," I whispered into the dark. I scrabbled for Marion's hand until I found it and squeezed. "I promise you that."

The promise was for Marion, but it was for Arimentha, too.

Marion squeezed back, firmly. "Yes, we will."

—.—

Bennie arrived after dark on Saturday night, laden with Marion's suitcases and boxes like an overworked bellhop in a movie. It was a good thing there were no banana peels for him to slip on.

"I made it," Bennie said breathlessly, and I rushed to start unloading him.

"Good thing you're so strong," Marion said, coming to help, too. He slid a sly look at me. "Don't you think so, Millie?"

I shot him a glare. "We're all very glad he didn't drop your stuff all over Royal Street." I glanced at Bennie and tried to soften my voice. "Thank you."

Bennie smiled and mopped his brow with a handkerchief now that he had one free hand. "Anything to help."

I picked up a brown leather suitcase. "I didn't know you had so much stuff, Marion," I said, eager to change the subject. "When you got here, you had just this one little suitcase." My thumb ran across a brass plate near the handle I'd never noticed before. The letters *R. L.* were engraved into it. I knew now that his last name had been Leveque, but he hadn't mentioned the R. So there was still a piece of Marion's old life he hadn't forked over. In a way, I was glad. He should keep whatever he wanted for himself, now that he was being forced to hand over so much. When I looked up at him, he was looking back at me apprehensively, as if waiting for the question, but I didn't ask it.

He smiled to himself and turned to Bennie. "Did you get my Bessie Smith record?"

"Sure did!" With some effort, he slid it out of the middle of a stack and handed it over.

Marion peeked inside and shut his eyes a moment in relief. The note was still there and untouched by the police. I breathed a little easier, too.

Marion carried his record and suitcase and an armload of other stuff into my room.

"Are you ready to go to the ball, my lady?" Bennie said to me, smoothing back a strand of hair that had gotten mussed.

"Almost. Marion's got to fix me up." I gestured to my hair, which still hung down in a sharp curtain around my cheeks. I turned to Marion, who was returning from the bedroom. "I could just cut it off."

"Not necessary." Marion grabbed my arm, hauled me into Cal's room, and plopped me down on the stool in front of her mirrored dresser. "I'll comb it back, and no one will be the wiser."

I wrinkled up my nose at my reflection. "If you say so."

"Is that all it takes?" Bennie asked.

"You'll see," Marion said. His roguish smile made my knee start jiggling.

Bennie looked anxious, too, as he watched Marion open the red makeup case Bennie had brought for him. When Marion started spreading makeup out on the dresser top, I sat up straighter.

"Now wait a minute!" I cried. "I didn't agree to makeup!"

Marion rolled his eyes. "I'm a master of illusion. Let me work."

I buttoned my mouth and dug my nails into the fabric of my trousers, but quickly I relaxed as I watched myself transform under Marion's skillful fingers. He shadowed my jaw and throat so I looked almost like I'd have to shave later, and even shaded in a fake Adam's apple. He added shading to my upper lip, too, and somehow even made my brow bone look more prominent. When he'd finished all that, he rubbed my hair with a dollop of pomade and combed it neatly back.

Bennie stood behind us, looking stunned. "You really are a magician!"

I had to admit the illusion was pretty good and would be even better in a dimly lit hotel ballroom. I stood and grinned, turning this way and that and enjoying the novelty of watching my transformed face in the mirror.

"All right, Benzo." I deepened my voice and clapped him roughly on the shoulder. "Time to go do some manly stuff."

Marion laughed. Bennie swallowed, eyes still on my face in the mirror. "Is it strange that I'm kind of attracted to you right now?"

Marion smirked. "Not strange to me."

I laughed to hide a blush and grabbed my jacket. I winked at Marion. "Me neither."

—·—

We walked to the Roosevelt so Bennie wouldn't have to find a place to park his delivery truck. The front of the hotel was all elaborate stone, and an awning arched over the wide quadruple front doors to protect the posh guests from New Orleans weather. But Bennie took me around to the back, to a door that was small and plain and unsheltered.

Eddie answered Bennie's knock quickly, as if he'd been hovering behind it waiting for us.

"Come in, quick," he said, waving us inside. He did a double take, eyes widening at the sight of me. A grin started at the corner of his mouth.

I held up a hand. "Don't say a word."

Eddie scowled. "You oughta be more polite. I'm risking my job for this escapade."

"Then maybe quit gawking and hurry it along before we get caught."

"She's right," Bennie said quickly, stepping between me and Eddie. "Let's go."

Eddie shook his head, but he turned and led us down a dim hallway lined with doors. Women in maid uniforms and men in waiter tuxedos rushed by us, barely glancing at us. No one seemed to notice I wasn't a boy, yet.

Eddie took us into an empty room filled with lockers. Apparently, all the others were already dressed and gone. He thrust two freshly laundered uniforms on hangers at me and Bennie.

"You got any pointers?" I said, already shrugging out of my jacket.

Eddie folded his arms over his chest. "Don't look the guests in the eye unless they talk right to you. And don't hand them a drink directly. Just hold out the tray and let them take it."

"That's an odd rule."

Eddie sneered, but for once, it wasn't directed at me. "They want to pretend we haven't touched it with our dirty peasant hands."

I pulled a grimace. Bennie looked down and studied his tan hands and fastidiously neat nails, as if contemplating their ability to offend with their very touch.

"I have to go back out or they'll be looking for me," Eddie said. "The party is in the Blue Room on the lobby level." He looked at Bennie. "Make sure she doesn't do anything to get me fired." He gave me one last sharp glance, looked as if he was considering saying something, then changed his mind, turned, and left.

"You're making him nervous," Bennie said.

I rolled my eyes. "He's always like that. Where do we get dressed?"

Bennie flushed and pointed toward a closet. "You . . . you go in there, in case somebody comes in."

I pulled the chain to turn on the closet light and saw the little room was crammed full of brooms and mop buckets. It was a struggle getting out of my clothes and into the stiff uniform without knocking anything over or dropping the pristine white shirt and jacket on the floor. I was sure Bennie could hear me cursing through the door and slamming into things.

"You okay in there?" Bennie said after a few minutes. I swear I could hear the laughter in his voice.

"I'm fine," I said through clenched teeth. "But . . ." I opened the door and flapped the bow tie uselessly. "I can't tie this ridiculous thing."

Bennie tried and failed to suppress a grin. "Come here then."

I stomped out of the broom closet like a toddler, feeling hot and flustered. I pulled at my starched white collar so I could breathe easier. Bennie moved closer to me and started working on the tie.

"You shouldn't fuss with your uniform when we're out there," he said mildly. "Just watch what the other waiters are doing and do it."

I sighed. I didn't see how anybody could work a job in this buttoned-up monstrosity. Whose genius idea had it been to put waiters in white jackets and white gloves anyway? Didn't they know waiters got stuff spilled on them?

I had to admit Bennie looked handsome in his getup, though, with his black hair and dark olive skin contrasting sharply with the white. But I could also see he had sweat beaded at his temples, and his shoulders shifted under the white jacket.

"You don't have to do this job with me," I said. "You can stay here and wait, or even go home. I won't blame you."

He gestured toward the door where Eddie had exited. "My friend does me a favor this big, I got to stay here to make sure it goes right."

"It'll go right," I said soberly, feeling the slightest twinge of guilt that Bennie didn't trust me not to blow our cover. I nudged the toe of his shoe with mine. "What's taking so long anyway?"

"I've never done this before on someone else."

His face was only a foot in front of mine. His eyes were busy studying my tie, so I was free to stare at his face. At the hint of stubble at his jaw. At the lower lip that was fuller than the top. At the line that formed between his brows when he was concentrating.

"Hold still," he said.

I held still. Held my breath. I'd never been this close to him before, especially not alone. I could lean forward and kiss him if I wanted to. *Did* I want to?

Before I could decide, he finished tying the bow tie, stood back, cocked his head to one side, and studied it. "I guess that will do."

I set my hands on my hips and stuck out my chin. "Do I look handsome?"

"Don't you always?"

Something about his voice made me pause. Something that sounded a lot like honesty. "You think I'm handsome?"

Bennie's shoulders lifted. "You are."

I stared at him. I considered returning the compliment, but then he cleared his throat.

"You ready to go get some dirt?" he said.

I dismissed whatever had just happened between us and smoothed my lapels. "Ready when you are."

CHAPTER

14

MY FINGERS JITTERED against the side of my leg as Bennie and I pushed through a swinging door and entered the public part of the hotel. Minty's killer might be here, or the person who could lead me to that killer. And finding them depended on me pulling this off.

"Just watch what I do," Bennie said. "Stay in the shadows so no one will look too closely at you—not that many of them ever think to look at us."

"Got it," I said, resisting the urge to tug at my stiff white collar again. Bennie led me to the famous Blue Room, where those with enough cash could dine and dance and see big-name jazz performers who used to live in New Orleans but now just passed through town. I'd heard about the place a million times but was still stunned enough to stop in the doorway a moment and stare. The ceiling and walls were all blue, with two huge chandeliers and massive columns painted in a swirling floral pattern of green and gold. Tables covered in crisp white cloth glittered with silver and crystal. Beyond a parquet dance floor

was a shallow platform, on which a small orchestra sat playing something dull in front of a massive plaster seashell. The
combined effect was tacky as hell, and my first thought was my
mother would love it. And Marion, too.

"Come on," Bennie said, gesturing for me to join him in the
back corner of the room.

The wall directly across the room from us was one giant
mirror, and the corner of my eye caught Bennie's reflection.
I looked at the waiter next to him, and it took half a second
before I realized it was me. My breath caught in my throat. My
own black hair, pomaded and neatly combed back, looked just
as fine contrasted with the white jacket as Bennie's. I *did* look
handsome.

"Told you," Bennie whispered, as if he'd read my face, and
bumped his shoulder against mine.

I wanted to grin, to giggle even, but I focused on Bennie's
reflection and copied his stance, legs a bit farther apart, shoulders back.

Dirt on Arimentha. That's what we were here for. Not to stare
at ourselves in the mirror.

"Okay," Bennie said, still facing out into the room, "serving
food is beyond your skills, so don't even try. But you can circu-
late with a pitcher of water or tray of champagne."

"Lucky me."

"This was your idea, remember."

"I know," I groaned. The idea of mingling with all these
fancy people with their fancy rules made my skin itch, but I had
to do it. It was clear how little attention they paid to the waiters
serving their food and wiping up their spills. They would surely

talk about their private business—and the private business of their friends—as if I wasn't even there. Kitty Sharpe had been right.

I scanned the room to see if I could spot her, lurking somewhere like a gossip-gathering spider, but I couldn't see her. Then I realized I was keeping an eye out for bright red, but she wouldn't be wearing that. Without it, a girl with her white skin, brown hair, and small stature would be easy to miss in this crowd, filled with more of the same.

"You!" someone said beside us, and Bennie and I both turned our heads. It was another waiter, this one with a blue pocket square, which Bennie had told me meant he was a head waiter. He gestured with an impatient flick of his fingers. "Come help me with this tray of hors d'oeuvres."

Bennie looked back at me, eyes wide. "Are you going to be all right on your own?"

"Course I am," I whispered. "Go."

"*Lay low*," he said.

"The lowest."

"Now!" the head waiter said imperiously.

"Sorry. Coming." Bennie scurried off after him, casting me one last anxious look. He was worried I couldn't handle it alone. Butterflies tickled the inside of my belly for the first time. What if he was right?

I couldn't think about that. I had a job to do. I approached another waiter who was carrying a pitcher of water.

"Let me have that one," I said. "Eddie said they need you for something in the kitchen."

The waiter sighed. "What else is new?" He handed over the

pitcher, which was surprisingly heavy. "Table's over that way."

He pointed toward the long row of tables on the left side of the dance floor.

"Got it."

I took my time strolling toward the tables with my pitcher, taking in every face as I passed. There were a lot of people in this room, and I needed to find my primary targets soon. All of Minty's friends from the night of the murder—Jerome Rosenthal, Fitzroy DeCoursey, Daphne Holiday, her brother, Claude, and Symphony Cornice, not to mention Marion's horrible older brother, Philip Leveque—would be here tonight, according to Kitty Sharpe.

I figured it would be pretty easy to spot Symphony, at least, with her auburn hair, and blond Fitzroy with his film-star sleekness, but the rest of the room was a sea of brunette white people, as easy to miss as Kitty herself.

I approached the table and started pouring water, ears pricked for names I recognized, though it was hard to pick out anything in the general rumble of voices and music.

Then I heard it—somebody said "McDonough." I poured slower, easing closer to the older woman who'd been talking. She had about twelve strings of pearls around her neck and a mountain of gray hair coiled on top of her head.

"It's horrid what happened to that poor child," she said in a genteel, nasal voice to the old gentleman next to her, who was wearing an actual monocle. "I heard she will be buried in the family tomb with her mother."

"Lafayette Cemetery number one, if I'm not mistaken?" the gentleman said.

"Indeed. It's a shame. Judge McDonough is devastated, I heard. Wife and child both gone, and now he is alone in that big house."

"Do you think he will sell it?"

"The house?"

"Yes, it has a rather nice garden."

"He may. You should ask Sanders, the attorney. He may know."

"I will."

They moved on to discussing their own various health ailments, and I moved on with my water pitcher, feeling a little sick. Kitty had been right about how quickly people would be ready to discuss Minty with callous detachment. I was no better, of course, but then I hadn't known her. I hadn't even liked her. These people were supposed to have been her friends.

My pitcher emptied into the last glass on the row, and I turned, still stuck on the image of Minty buried with her mother in a cold tomb in the Garden District. My gaze immediately landed on the familiar face of Symphony Cornice, not ten feet away. She was looking down at her plate, and I whirled around quickly before she could glance up, in case she recognized me in my disguise. I hurried down the row and traded in my empty pitcher for a full one at a table near the swinging kitchen door. Then, from that safe distance, I chanced another peek at Symphony. She was sitting next to a dark-haired boy who, after a moment, I recognized as Jerome Rosenthal, the one I'd thought of as Rockefeller the night of the murder. They were leaning close together, talking intently.

My heart picked up its pace. This was it. I needed to get over there quickly and listen without being seen. I hefted my pitcher and aimed for the row of tables behind theirs, but just before I got there, the pair of them stood up. I turned and poured water into a man's glass, keeping my back carefully angled toward Symphony and Jerome.

"Excuse me!" the man said, and I realized I'd overflowed his glass. Water was spilling out onto the white tablecloth.

"Oops . . . I mean, um, beg your pardon?" I snatched a napkin off a lady's lap and tossed it on the spreading puddle.

"Well, I never!" the lady cried.

"I'll just . . . I'll get you a fresh napkin." I backed away rapidly, knocking into another waiter, who I started to apologize to before I saw it was Bennie. I smiled sheepishly.

"Thought you were trying to be inconspicuous," he muttered, shaking his head, as he produced a brilliant smile, a new napkin, and somehow, a dish towel for the customers, whose ruffled feathers instantly began to settle.

I glanced around for Symphony and Jerome, and it took me a few moments to find them, huddled beside a giant potted palm in a corner, still talking. I considered the plant in its enormous blue-and-white porcelain vase. Would I fit behind it? How would I get back there without Symphony and Jerome noticing a full-size human trying to wedge between the plant and the wall?

The palm was near an open doorway that led to the hall where Bennie and I had entered. What if I parked myself just around the other side of that doorway? I set down my pitcher, leaving Bennie to finish mollifying the customers, and darted out a different door into the same hallway. No one was around, so I ran the twenty feet or so, afraid to miss any more of their conversation than I already had.

When I got to the doorway, I pressed my back against the wall and tried to slow down my loud breathing. All I could hear at first was a clarinet solo and the chattering crowd, but then I picked out Symphony's voice. I eased all the way up to the edge of the door and held my breath.

"You should slow down on the champagne, Jerome," Symphony said bitingly. "It wouldn't do to look drunk."

"I'm not trying to get drunk. It's just . . . to help me cope." His voice shook. "I can't stop seeing her there like that . . . Minty, I mean. Her face. Do you know what I mean?"

"I suppose I do," Symphony said more gently. "Let me have a sip of that then if it helps." Another moment passed; then she said, "Where's *Fitzroy* tonight?" The tone of her voice had gone acerbic again.

"His tuxedo is still being cleaned from New Year's Eve," Jerome said stiffly.

"Doesn't he have another?" I could picture her haughtily raised brows.

"Not everyone has a trust fund, Symphony. And from what I hear about the stock market, half the people here may soon face the torment of a one-tuxedo lifestyle."

"That may be true," she said, sounding unfazed by his sarcasm. "But it's beyond me how you can still defend him, after what he's done to you."

Jerome sighed. "I wish I'd never told you about that."

"He's a criminal, Jerome. He's using you."

A criminal? What was going on here? I shifted myself perpendicular to the wall to hear better, hoping neither of them decided to pop their head through the doorway and check for eavesdroppers.

"Please keep your voice down," Jerome said. "If anyone heard you say that, especially so soon after Minty—"

"Don't have an apoplexy, Jerome," Symphony said calmly. "No one said Fitzroy killed anyone. But if you don't want them to start, I wouldn't go around telling everyone that his tuxedo from that night needed cleaning."

"I didn't mean—Mine needed to be cleaned, too! And my coat was filthy!" Jerome's voice rose, and he made an effort to lower it. "The police already know who did it. They won't be bothering us, will they?"

"Perhaps not, but there's no sense in being foolish. Having suspicion of murder hanging over you could taint a lot of things. You have a future, Jerome. Isn't that the point of paying Fitzroy? I have a future, too. And Daphne wants to marry Philip Leveque and be a senator's wife. And Claude, well . . ."

"Is Claude."

They both laughed, sounding a little less tense. I wondered if they knew what a vile person their good pal Philip Leveque was.

"Did you hear Daphne arguing with Minty about Philip that night?" Jerome said.

Now, this was news. I edged closer and tried to focus on the sounds of their voices.

"Yes," Symphony said carefully. "I heard some of it. But I was too busy keeping an eye on Fitzroy. Why was he even there that night?"

"Minty invited him." Jerome's voice sounded pinched. "She told him she'd heard that place was a good party. And he . . . he's been wanting to get to know her better."

"I'm sure. Didn't you warn her about him?"

"No. We . . . weren't that close. And I already regretted telling you. Besides, I'm not certain—"

"Hey!" a voice behind me said, and firm fingers dug into my shoulder. I turned around, cringing, hoping Symphony and Jerome hadn't heard. The head waiter stood over me, glaring down into my face. "We're swamped in there. What are you lurking around out here for?"

He shoved me through the open doorway next to Symphony and Jerome. "You're one of the temps for tonight, aren't you? I'll make sure you're never hired back again. Get a move on!"

"Yes . . . yes, sir," I said, trying to keep my face turned away from Symphony and Jerome's corner. I hurried toward the more crowded part of the room, eager to make my exit before they saw me, but I'd only made it half a dozen feet when I felt fingers close around my arm.

"Were you *eavesdropping*?" Jerome said, jerking me toward him, but his angry eyes widened in surprise when he saw my face. "What . . . but . . . I *know* you! Aren't you a . . . a . . ."

"Girl?" I shook off his hand. He was holding a champagne flute, and his face was flushed with drink. I looked pointedly at the glass. "Had a lot to celebrate these days?"

Jerome's face reddened more, and he set down the glass on a passing waiter's tray.

Symphony glided up beside him, her face like marble, her eyes narrowed. "You were listening to us just now, weren't you?"

I opened my mouth and closed it. My first instinct was to lie, but maybe instead I should use what I'd heard to my advantage. I tried out a smile.

"I might've heard a thing or two."

"What did you hear?" Jerome said, his brown eyes overly bright. What was going on with him and Fitzroy that made him so anxious?

Symphony laid a hand on his sleeve. "It doesn't matter, Jerome," she said smoothly. "No one would believe a word *she* said anyway. You hold her here, and I'll go fetch someone to throw her out in the gutter where she belongs."

"You could do that," I said, skittering back out of Jerome's reach. "But while I'm on my way out, I might feel compelled to shout about some of the stuff I just heard. I can be very loud."

I hadn't really heard enough to shout about, but they didn't know exactly when I'd started listening. I could've missed more incriminating stuff.

Symphony studied my face carefully. "Why are you here? What do you want from us?"

"I came to get answers." I jutted out my chin. "To find out the truth about who's responsible for Arimentha's murder."

Jerome's eyes widened, and Symphony's narrowed.

"I don't understand," Jerome said. "Why do you care what happened to Minty?"

"She *doesn't,* Jerome." Symphony cut him a look as if he was a premium fool. "Don't you see? She is *friends* with that person who attacked our Minty. She only wants to clear his name."

Symphony was smart, and therefore the most dangerous to my efforts. I had to resist antagonizing her; wasn't that what Kitty had said? I had to be friendly.

"Listen," I tried in a less sarcastic voice. "People are starting to notice you're chitchatting with the *help,* so why don't we take this conversation somewhere more private?"

"Maybe we should go with her, Sym," Jerome said, glancing around and licking his lips nervously. "Just for a minute."

Symphony shook her head at him, but he looked pleadingly at her, and at last she sighed heavily.

"Fine," she said through her teeth. "A minute."

I led them out of the ballroom and around a corner into the servers' hallway. Jerome looked around curiously, as if he'd never seen a place so devoid of decoration, but Symphony kept her focus on me. I needed to do this quickly and get them out of here before any of the other workers came by and got suspicious.

I crossed my arms over my chest, then decided that wasn't friendly enough and let them fall to my sides. "So . . . Jerome, is it?"

He nodded warily.

"I gather you and Fitzroy have a bit of a thing going on."

Jerome's cheeks turned ruddy again, and he inspected his shoes.

I held up both hands. "No judgment from me. I'm more concerned about your financial arrangement."

He looked up again quickly. "Financial?" His voice cracked. "I don't recall saying anything about—"

"You didn't have to." I took a guess. "What's he got on you, Jerome?"

"I—he—" Jerome looked at Symphony as if for help, but she was watching me. "He doesn't—"

"Let me take a stab at it," I said. "The two of you *got together* and then he threatened to tell everyone if you didn't pay up?"

"You don't have to tell her anything, Jerome," Symphony said, still not taking her snake-green eyes off me.

"No." Jerome shook his head vigorously. "That's not—it was nothing like that. I wouldn't still be . . . seeing him if . . ."

Symphony rolled her eyes. "Wouldn't you, Jerome?"

"Of course not, this is different. It's only—" He looked at me, his shoulders sagging. "It's only about school stuff, all right? I paid him to write some essays for me, that's all."

"Seriously?" I narrowed my eyes. That couldn't be the whole thing. I was certain there was some kind of blackmail involved. "And then what? He threatened to turn you in for cheating?"

Jerome's mouth opened and closed. "You don't understand. Medical school is very important to me. It was only five hundred dollars."

I almost choked. *Only?* A person could buy a car with that. A nice car. "Let me get this straight," I said when I'd recovered from my shock. "He blackmailed you, and you still spend time with him?"

"He's very handsome," Symphony said dryly.

"It's not just that." Jerome sniffed defensively. "He can be very sweet. And I can afford it anyway. Fitzroy is always low on money and feels left out when we do things he can't afford, so I just . . . help him out."

I shook my head. "It sounds like you're getting the short end of the stick here."

"I . . . I know." Jerome swiped a hand over his face and looked at me beseechingly. "Please—you can't go shouting about this. You don't know what it would do to me if this got out."

"I have a pretty good idea," I said. "But don't worry—I'm not in the business of spilling secrets unless they pertain to this murder. Was Fitzroy targeting Arimentha for one of his schemes?"

"No." Jerome shook his head vigorously.

"Yes," Symphony hissed. "He was targeting everyone he could get his claws in."

I turned my focus to her. "You know about others?"

She adjusted the flower corsage pinned to her shoulder. "None that I would tell *you* about."

A door opened behind me, and Jerome froze. I looked over my shoulder and saw a maid backing out of the door holding a stack of linens.

"Evening," I said as she passed. She gave us a quick sideways glance and hurried off around the corner.

Jerome let out a sigh of relief. I noticed his hands were shaking and almost felt sorry for him. He probably wasn't a murderer. But maybe Fitzroy was.

"What about you, Jerome?" I said, trying to sound friendly. "Do you know any other people your buddy Fitzroy has had arrangements with?"

"Not . . . not for certain."

I took a step closer into his space. "But you've heard some things, right? Hints?"

"M-maybe."

"Don't tell her anything, Jerome," Symphony said. "She's not the police. You owe her nothing."

"Symphony's right." I reached out and straightened the flower pinned to Jerome's lapel. "You don't have to tell me. But I know a lot of important secrets about you now. And I'll never tell a soul, so long as you give me what I want to know."

Jerome cast an imploring look at Symphony. "It . . . it won't matter if I tell. It's only a rumor. I don't know anything concrete."

"We should go back to the party." Symphony hooked her arm through his and tried to tug him, but Jerome turned back to me.

"Leveque," he said, his dark eyes on mine. "Talk to Philip Leveque."

CHAPTER

15

I PERSUADED JEROME to point out Philip Leveque to me in the Blue Room, at a table near the stage, where the parade of white-ruffled debutantes were starting to be presented. Philip looked like a stiffer version of Marion, but also like any other swell—crisp black tuxedo jacket, clean-shaven jaw, dark brown hair neatly trimmed and slicked down, with a side part showing a perfect line of white scalp. He clapped politely for the debutante crossing the stage with her uncomfortable-looking escort, then returned to his conversation with a man who I recognized as the mayor of New Orleans.

Symphony attempted to drag Jerome away again, but he hesitated. "You're not going to tell anyone about . . . anything I said, right?" His eyes were hopeful as a puppy's, and I barely resisted patting him on the head.

"I won't tell anyone your secrets unless it turns out you've got a bigger one to hide." I gave him a significant look that clearly said *murder.*

Jerome nodded solemnly.

"Come on," Symphony said, taking him by the elbow. "Let's get away before anyone sees us with her and associates us with whatever she's about to do."

I didn't watch them go. My eyes were on Philip, the wheels in my mind already turning. Kitty had told me to take the indirect approach, and it had worked with Symphony and Jerome . . . until they'd caught me. But Philip wasn't likely to share his blackmail stories with an acquaintance across a banquet table, and the truth was, I couldn't wait to take a crack at him. I wanted to see what this man was made of who'd been so cruel to his own brother, my best friend. But I would have to be extra careful — now that Marion's picture had been printed in the newspaper, it was not only possible but likely that Philip had figured out what his brother had been up to all this time. The last thing Marion needed was me giving away his current location to an enemy nearly as dangerous as the police.

"How's it going?" Bennie's voice beside me made me startle like a skittish horse. I tugged down my white jacket sleeves to settle myself again before I turned to him.

"I need your help."

He smirked. "What else is new?"

I thumped him on the arm. "You're a good sport, Bennie. Now, I need to talk to that guy over there, left of the stage, dark hair, three people from the end."

"Okay," he said slowly.

"Alone."

"So, what's your plan? I can see on your face you've got one."

I grinned. "As a matter of fact, I do."

—·—

There is an inevitable moment when a man guzzling champagne must tend to certain needs.

I bribed the men's room attendant to take a hike, and Bennie and I took turns guarding the door from "customers" for half an hour, all while being forced to watch a cavalcade of overly privileged girls float across the stage in their white debutante dresses.

"Sorry, sir, there's been . . . an accident," I said over and over. "The restroom is being cleaned. Try the one in the lobby."

Some of the men grumbled, but most scurried away, looking disgusted. No one tried to go inside. Then at last Philip Leveque approached, and Bennie let him pass. I waited a minute, hoping he'd get his actual business finished, and then followed him inside, my nerves singing with anxious excitement, while Bennie stayed outside to block the door.

Philip was already washing his hands at the shiny black sink and barely glanced up as I took my post beside the basket of towels and pretended to be the bathroom attendant. His reflection in the oval mirror showed eyes the same striking blue-green as Marion's. His ears were the same shape, too, small and close to the head. I tried not to let it distract me.

He turned off the tap, rotated toward me, and looked at me expectantly. It took a beat for me to remember I was supposed to hand him a towel.

"Oh. Sorry. I was just thinking."

"Mmm?" he said vaguely, not really interested, as he dried his hands and avoided eye contact again.

"I was thinking you probably knew that girl. The one who died on New Year's Eve."

Philip looked up sharply, his jaw tightening.

"Everybody's talking about it," I plowed forward. "She would've been at this party tonight, wouldn't she?"

Philip's mouth twisted in a scowl. "How much is the newspaper paying you to harass me?" His voice was nothing like Marion's. It sounded older, rich with authority and full of disdain. The voice of a politician, not a singer. He tossed the towel back at me, and I caught it against my chest. "Which paper is it? Tell me now."

"I don't work for a newspaper, Mr. Leveque." I smiled tightly.

"Then who?" Philip smirked. "Senator Graham? Because you can tell him I won't be bullied out of this race, no matter how many—"

"I don't know any senators and don't care to."

This wasn't how this was supposed to go. I wasn't supposed to be this antagonistic, but Philip's immediate reaction had me all wrong-footed.

"Then we have nothing to discuss." He tried to move past me, but I stepped sideways into his path.

"Now, Mr. Leveque. Surely you aren't leaving so soon."

He stopped and studied me with narrowed eyes. I could almost see him assessing whether he could get past me by force. We were the same height, but he had broader shoulders and probably twenty pounds on me. I had to talk fast to keep him from pushing past me and avoiding the whole conversation. Deception hadn't worked on him so far, but maybe a bit of truth would grab his attention.

"I'm not a reporter," I said, trying to calm down, smooth out my voice. "But I do need to ask you some questions about Minty McDonough."

"Minty? How do you know her by that—ah . . . I see." A light came on in his eyes, and he looked me over again with a new expression, an odd smile forming on his lips. "You must be one of her unfortunate conquests."

"Her . . . conquests?"

"Yes, surely you can't have believed you were the only one she dallied with?" He looked at me with condescending pity.

I swallowed, taking a moment to think. Should I lean into his assumption and see where it took me? I started to run my hands through my hair but stopped, afraid to spoil my disguise. "I . . . I knew I wasn't the only one," I said tentatively. "But it's not right what happened to her. I'm just trying to find out who really did it."

"The police seem to believe they've already done that." I detected a hint of contempt in his voice. Did he believe Marion was a murderer, or was there some loyalty left in him for his brother?

"They're wrong," I said, watching Philip's face. "That singer . . . I've met him before, and he didn't seem like a killer to me."

Philip's gaze sharpened to a knifepoint, and he advanced a step toward me. "How well do you know him? Do you know where he is now?"

I coughed. "Not well. Just met him once or twice is all. Why did you and Minty break up anyway?"

Philip looked slightly surprised at the change in tack, or maybe by how much I knew about him.

"We . . . it didn't work out. That's all." He shook his head, like he was struggling to organize his thoughts. Was he still thinking about Marion?

"That's not very specific, Mr. Leveque. I get the impression you parted on ugly terms."

The bright alertness came back into his eyes. "Who have you been talking to?"

"Never mind about that. Did you still love Minty? Is that why she and your current girlfriend argued the night of her murder?"

Philip's hands tightened into fists at his sides. "My romantic feelings are none of your business, and I know nothing about an argument. But I can tell you Daphne has been very distraught since Minty's . . . death. She was one of the ones who found the"—he waved a hand— "you know."

"The body?" I enjoyed the way he flinched. "Where were you the night of New Year's Eve, Mr. Leveque? Why weren't you with your girlfriend?"

"I was out of the city on business."

"What kind of business?"

"That, I'm afraid, is none of your concern. And even if I had been in the city, which the police have already confirmed I wasn't, I would never patronize such a seedy dive as that one."

I clenched my right hand into a tight fist but tried to keep the expression on my face light. "I'm sure you've heard she was there with a date that night. Fitzroy DeCoursey. Did you ever meet him?"

Philip narrowed his eyes warily. "I don't believe I've had the pleasure."

"So, he's never contacted you, Mr. Leveque? About any *private* matters?"

His expression was inscrutable. "No one named DeCoursey ever contacted me about any matter, private or otherwise. There is little in the life of a politician that is private, but I have nothing to hide."

I rocked toward him on my toes and lowered my voice. "You mean to tell me you've never had one single skeleton *locked away*?"

Philip evaluated me coolly. When he spoke, his voice was softer, calmer, more dangerous. "What has this DeCoursey been saying to you?"

I hesitated. I could pretend to have already spoken to Fitzroy, and maybe trick Philip into admitting something. But with so little information, it seemed safest to veer close to the truth. "I haven't spoken to Mr. DeCoursey yet. I wanted to hear from you first."

His brows rose. "Then who *have* you been speaking to? It sounds as if someone has been making insinuations, and I would like to know who."

I waved a hand. "Oh, I can't reveal my sources."

For the first time, Philip looked rattled, his face flushed. "Surely, no one thinks *I* had anything to do with Miss Mc-Donough's murder."

I smiled. "I can't say what anyone else thinks, Mr. Leveque."

"Well, I can say what *I* think," he said hotly. "You're looking in the wrong place. Even if the killer is not R—" He paused, swallowed. "Not that singer, you should be looking for someone else from that so-called club. You should—" He stopped and shut his eyes for a moment, and the anger smoothed slowly out of his face, as if by sheer force of will. He opened his eyes and smiled at me with fresh malice. "I'd wager Miss McDonough's killer is from your part of the city. Sounds like the kind of violent display one finds there, don't you agree?"

I didn't say anything, but gripped my switchblade, Pearl, and contemplated how satisfying it would be to jab him with it. I'd show him a *violent display.*

Then it occurred to me—how did he know which part of the city I was from?

All traces of his flash of anger had disappeared. He smiled lazily, as if he knew just what I was thinking and was pleased by it. "Are you quite ready to let me out of here now?"

"I'm not holding you," I said, but my brain was still churning, trying to remember where I'd given myself away. Was he just assuming I was from the French Quarter because I'd admitted to meeting Marion before? Or did he notice something more?

Philip's brows rose into tidy right angles. "Is that so? Then why was that waiter guarding the door so studiously?"

My frown deepened. When had he put that together? I clutched the blade in my pocket, knowing I couldn't use it. "Go ahead and leave then."

"I will." Philip glanced in the mirror and straightened his already-straight bow tie. "But I advise you to take your leave as well. I don't believe for one moment you're in this hotel's employ, so *whoever* you are, when I leave this room, I will be going straight to the management to report an impostor."

He didn't wait for my reaction. He strode toward the heavy door and pushed it open. Bennie threw up his arms in surprise, but Philip merely brushed past him and walked away with purpose.

I shoved down my rage and grabbed Bennie by the sleeve.

"We've got to get out of here. Now."

—·—

Bennie and I hurried back to the waiters' dressing room and grabbed our clothes. We didn't have time to change since we could already hear the clatter of voices shouting about impostors from the other end of the hall.

Whoever you are. Philip's words rang in my head. He'd known I was from the French Quarter, but maybe he hadn't known I was from the Cloak and Dagger. Maybe he hadn't figured out the extent of my relationship with Marion. And if he had—what then? Would it make any difference? The cops already knew I was Marion's friend, and they had more resources to find me than Philip did. Probably.

Bennie and I dashed toward the exit door, shedding our white jackets and bow ties as we ran. The shirts and black pants we'd have to keep for now. I hoped nobody would connect Eddie to us and get him canned, but I couldn't do anything about it now. After this I'd owe him free drinks for a month, and it would all be for nothing if we ended up cooling our heels in jail.

"What did you find out?" Bennie said breathlessly as we bolted down a side street toward the river.

"I'm not sure." I still needed to fit all the little pieces of information into the big puzzle and see if the picture became any clearer.

"But did he tell you if Fitzroy has been trying to blackmail him? Or what Daphne and Minty were fighting about?"

I shook my head, clutching at a stitch in my side. "I don't know if he told me anything. He was a slippery one."

Bennie fell silent then, which I was grateful for. I needed my air for running, and I didn't slow down until we turned left and were across Canal Street and three blocks deep into our own neighborhood. I doubted the hotel people were so concerned about a couple of impostor waiters that they'd exert much effort looking for us, but I was glad to have left that place far behind and let the cool night air wash its perfumed stink away.

We finally stopped on the corner where I'd have to continue straight to go to my apartment, and Bennie would turn right to return to his room at the back of his parents' grocery.

"Thanks," I said, leaning against the nearest brick wall to catch my breath. "You really came through."

Bennie leaned beside me and stuck his hands in his pockets, as if he weren't also out of breath. He nudged my shoulder with his. "You going to tell me what all happened in there with that guy?"

He looked at me, and I looked at him, with the yellow glow of the streetlight shining on his dark eyes and hair. The air seemed caught between us, like a bubble I could choose to pop or not. I knew in my gut that if I kept looking much longer, he would kiss me, and that I would like it. And then what would I do with that? What would he expect? What would I?

I didn't know. Not yet. So, I pushed myself off the wall and took one step away from him, then another. The streetlight cast his face in too much contrast to read his expression.

"Tomorrow," I said, still backing away. "I'll tell you everything tomorrow."

CHAPTER

16

THE TRUTH WAS, the person I wanted to talk to now wasn't Bennie but Marion. I'd been in his old stomping grounds tonight. I'd met his brother. It had been like seeing the other side of a coin flip, the way things might have been. If Arimentha had never tried to kiss Marion, if they'd gone on as friends, maybe Philip would never have found out about Marion's proclivities. Maybe Marion would've been there at the Roosevelt Hotel tonight, hair sleekly combed, smelling of spiced cologne and sneaking off to button-shine with some handsome waiter in an empty room. Maybe Arimentha would be alive and there to laugh with him when he returned all mussed. They would still be best friends, and I never would have met Marion at all.

But that wasn't true. He couldn't have lived that life forever. He would've found us at the Cloak. He would've found me, and I would've found him. I believed that.

The smell of something spicy and delicious hit me as soon as I opened the front door of my building. At first, I thought it was coming from our downstairs neighbor's place, because the only

times anyone cooked in our household were the rare occasions
Rhoda came to stay with us.

But upstairs in our apartment, I found Marion's Bessie
Smith record playing and Marion himself standing clothed in
my mother's green dressing gown in our tiny kitchen, chopping
up onions with a giant knife. And beside him was Olive, sway-
ing a little to the music as she whisked something in a saucepan
on the stove. Her feet were shoeless and her legs bare of stockings, which were draped like two limp brown snakes over the
back of a chair next to her handbag.

"What you making?" I said, and Olive let out a little scream
of surprise. Her wide eyes darted from me to the chair, and she
snatched down the stockings and stuffed them into her handbag, her cheeks flushing.

Marion turned and laughed, wiping at his eyes with the
back of his hand. "She's seen stockings before, Ollie. Tell her,
Mill. This place is stocking central with Gladys around."

"I—yeah—" But I found myself staring at Olive's shapely
brown legs and feet and realizing I'd never seen *them* before.
Not really.

Marion rolled his eyes and scraped the minced onions into
the saucepan. "You're both hopeless."

Olive whirled, too, and started madly stirring again.

I cleared my throat and dropped into a different chair at the
table. "Where's everybody else?"

Marion waved his knife. "Gladys is God knows where. I suspect she went on a date. And Cal's still at the club."

"Did they know you were cooking? They might not have
left."

"I didn't mention it." His eyes twinkled. "I'm making it for you. Well, *we* are, now." He nudged Olive with an elbow. "She came over after work to see if you'd gotten back yet, and I recruited her. My arm needed a rest."

"Really?" I leaned over to see what Olive was stirring. It was thick and brown. "Is that a roux? Are you making . . . gumbo? Where'd you learn how to do that?"

"Must've learned from a black woman," Olive said. "Or else this roux wouldn't be right."

"You caught me." Marion laughed and brought a bell pepper and his knife to the table to chop beside me. "Enough about our business, Millie—what about yours? You going to spill or what?"

"Course." I fiddled with the saltshaker, which was shaped like a spaniel sitting up on its hind legs. I'd intended to tell him about everything in order, starting with Symphony and Jerome, but the news that I'd talked with his brother was highest in my mind.

I watched his face as I said it. "I met Philip Leveque tonight."

Marion sucked in a sharp breath. He let the air out of his lungs slowly and started chopping again, more vigorously. "Let me guess," he said, his tone acidic. "You found him delightful."

I snorted. "I found him . . ." I trailed off and Marion looked up, the oddest expression in his eyes, as if he expected me to have liked Philip and was bracing himself for the impact. "Repulsive. Snakelike. Satan on a stick?"

Olive chuckled, and Marion's shoulders relaxed. His smile returned. "He is horrid, isn't he? Did you learn anything useful from him?"

"Not exactly. He thought I was some spurned lover of Minty's."

Marion touched his chin with a finger and considered me. "You do look like her type tonight." He grinned and winked at me. "A boy with *big* secrets."

I laughed. "According to Philip, Minty had a lot of lovers floating around New Orleans."

"He give you any names?" Olive said, looking up from her stirring.

I shook my head. "Apparently, Minty was good at keeping secrets when she wanted to. She wouldn't tell anyone why she and Philip broke up either. And he sure wasn't telling."

The bell pepper bits got smaller and smaller under Marion's knife. Talking about his brother was clearly agitating him. I laid a hand over his. "I think you've chopped them enough."

Marion gave a little laugh and stood to scrape the peppers into Olive's saucepan.

"Speaking of potential lovers," Olive said, "I talked to Lo for you tonight."

I brightened. "What did she say?"

"She was there with her girlfriend. That's why we haven't seen her since New Year's Eve—she's been home in new-relationship bliss." Olive stirred in Marion's peppers, and I watched her shoulders move under the back of her modest dress. "Turns out she met this new girlfriend that night. Lo admits she tried to flirt with Minty, but when she got shot down, this other girl saw and teased her about it, and one thing led to another and now they're together."

"So, Lo has an alibi for the rest of that night?"

Olive winked over her shoulder at me. "And every night since."

I stood and leaned across the table to crack the window and let some of the steamy heat out. Down below, someone was hurrying across the courtyard from the club, toward the back door of our building. I turned to Marion and grinned. "Think we're about to have some more company. You might want to get out of that dressing gown."

His eyes went wide. "What? Who?"

"*Lew-is*," I singsonged, enjoying the tables turning. Olive and I both cackled as Marion scurried from the room, struggling with the knot of the dressing gown's belt.

"That Philip," Olive said when we'd calmed back down and she'd returned to the endless stirring. "Do you think *he* could've killed that girl?"

"I'd certainly believe it of him. What a creep. But he has an alibi—says the cops already confirmed he was out of the city that night."

"He could be lying."

"I'll check it out." I pushed the spaniel saltshaker up on its paws, testing how far it could tip without spilling any salt. The truth was, it would be highly convenient for me if Philip was the killer and got his comcuppance for what he'd done to Marion and Arimentha both. But if his alibi checked out, I'd have to strike him off the list.

Marion returned, looking a bit disheveled but attractively so, wearing a blue sweater and trousers instead of my mother's swanning-about-the-house garment. And not a moment too soon—a buzz at the downstairs bell announced Lewis had arrived.

"Millie, will you go let him in?"

I raised my brows. "Seriously?"

"Please?" He clasped his hands together and batted his lashes. "Just do it. For me."

I rolled my eyes and shoved myself up from the table. When I opened the downstairs door, Lewis stood there, wringing his hands and looking nervous as a stray cat.

"I . . . I just . . ." he began, but I decided to put him out of his misery and invite him upstairs without making him ask.

"Come on. Marion's making gumbo. You can have some in seventeen hours when he's finally done."

Lewis smiled gratefully and followed me upstairs.

The scene in the kitchen was a little different from when I'd left. Marion had his shoes on, for one, and the record had changed to one Lewis gave him for Christmas. Marion and Olive had traded places, so that he was the one stirring the pot, and she leaned over the table mincing garlic.

"Oh, hey!" Marion called with the utmost casualness, waving his spoon so that a drop of brown roux fell on the faded linoleum. "Come on in and sit down! Millie's been telling us about her adventures at the Roosevelt Hotel tonight."

Lewis squeezed between Olive and Marion to get to a chair on the opposite side of the table, his cheeks flaming red as his body brushed against Marion's. I glanced at Olive, and her mouth curved up in a conspiratorial grin over the cutting board.

"Did you find out anything that will help Marion?" Lewis said, once he was settled and his cheeks had started to cool.

"Well . . . maybe." I unbuttoned the collar of my shirt, tipped back my chair on two legs, and finished telling the three of them every detail of what I'd learned that evening, hoping they'd help me see some new thread I hadn't.

Marion went quiet and contemplative as he stirred the in-creasingly delicious-smelling roux. Lewis watched me intently across the table, and Olive asked good questions as she chopped first celery, then andouille sausage.

"So," I said when I'd finished, "who are our best suspects?"

Marion laid down his spoon and leaned back against the counter. "Okay, first we have Fitzroy DeCoursey, who's been blackmailing people and is clearly terrible."

"And Symphony Cornice," Lewis said. "She seems peeved you're snooping around."

"Jerome Rosenthal is an anxious mess, too," Marion said. "But he just needs to come to the Cloak and find some better boys to spend time with." He glanced at Lewis, and they shared shy smiles.

"What about Daphne Holiday?" Olive said, scraping the last of the sausage off her board into the saucepan. "She was fighting with Minty."

"And her younger brother, Claude," Marion said. "He's al-ways mentioned as an afterthought, so he could burst in at the last minute as the surprise killer."

I rolled my eyes. "You've had too much time with your de-tective novels lately."

"Okay, fine." He stuck out his tongue at me. "Really, my money's on Daphne."

I wrinkled my nose. "Why not Fitzroy?"

Marion shrugged and put another, larger pot on the stove. "Because blackmail is so boring. Thwarted love is so much more interesting as a motive."

I laughed. "I don't think murder is supposed to be *interesting*."

Marion cocked an eyebrow. "Then why do they make so many movies about it?"

"Okay, true. I still like Fitzroy for the murder, though. He was the one quickest to blame you."

"That's true," Lewis said, looking at Marion. "Reason enough for me to hate him."

Marion beamed at him but shook his head. "Fitzroy was also the one who heard me 'threaten' her, so it makes sense he'd bring that up to the cops."

"Fair," I said, tipping my chair so far I almost fell over and had to grab the table to right myself. Olive gave me an amused look that I pretended not to see. "But he's also broke, running with a spendy crowd, and a known blackmailer. I want to talk to him as soon as possible." I stood and retrieved the city directory from underneath the telephone in the hall outside the apartment.

I was already flipping to the D section as I walked back. "DeCottens, a bunch of DeCou, DeCoulode, De—" I frowned. "There's no DeCoursey. It skips straight to DeCuesta."

"See," Marion said smugly. "Told you it sounded like a stage name."

"Or he's unlisted because he doesn't want to be found. Now what?" I said. "How do I find him?"

"I have no idea." He smiled sweetly. "But I *do* know how to find Daphne."

I closed the city directory. "Okay, I'll bite. How?"

"Easy." Marion licked the spoon. "On the Magnolia Club tennis court."

CHAPTER

—·—

17

THERE WAS ONLY one tennis court where a girl like Daphne would play, especially a girl who reportedly played three hours every single morning, like clockwork. No public parks for her, oh no, she'd play at the private Magnolia Club. Luckily for me, Marion had been a member there in his previous life and knew exactly how to get me in.

I still thought Daphne was a long shot for the murderer, but eventually Marion had persuaded me that, as Philip Leveque's girlfriend, she might know more about Fitzroy blackmailing him—or attempting to. So, on Monday, I went to school as usual and suffered through the required Mass for Epiphany, the first day of the Carnival season, but then I slipped into the gymnasium, borrowed a tennis racket, and stuffed a uniform from the tennis team in my bag. I slipped right back out before anyone could make me go to Latin.

The Magnolia Club wasn't that far from Ursuline, just a streetcar ride and then a walk of a few blocks. On the walk, I stopped at a pay phone and called Philip's office to check on his alibi, but his secretary wouldn't give me any information. I'd have to try again later.

When I reached the club, I hesitated outside the columned antebellum mansion that served as its clubhouse. The property was surrounded on all sides by tall brick walls, but according to Marion, it wasn't as impenetrable as it looked. The maintenance entrance around back was easy enough to find, with Marion's directions. He'd said the door would probably be locked, and it was, but he'd also said to wait a bit for someone to come out and smoke an inevitable cigarette in peace without the swells watching him.

It only took five minutes for a black man in a white uniform to exit through the door and then stop short at the sight of me standing there in my schoolgirl clothes.

"Hi!" I said shyly. "I came out this way by accident and got locked—"

But I didn't even have to finish my lie. The man in white hid the cigarette behind his back and held open the door.

"Here you go, miss. Is there anything else I can do for you?"

He probably spent all day having to put aside his own needs and act unfailingly polite to these wealthy people. I wanted to tell him he didn't have to do that for me, that he could smoke his damn cigarette if he wanted to, but that would blow my cover. Instead, I just said, "Thank you," and moved past him inside the door.

I navigated the plain halls in the back of the clubhouse and entered the grand front rooms, trying to find the tennis courts without having to ask anyone. But in a room with a swear-to-God actual suit of armor, a guy with a gold name tag noticed me and approached.

"May I help you, miss?"

"Yes . . . I . . . ah . . . I'm looking for the tennis courts? And the changing room? I'm supposed to be meeting my friend Daphne Holiday?"

"Ah, of course. Right this way."

I followed the name-tag guy out of a side entrance and onto a shaded walkway next to a wide expanse of sunny court.

"I believe Miss Holiday is there, on the last court. Would you like me to summon her?"

"No," I said quickly. "I want to change first. I see her now, thank you."

He gave a little bow and retreated, leaving me alone outside a door marked LADIES CHANGING ROOM. Well, that was clear enough. I slipped inside and went to the far end behind a row of tall wood cabinets, and rapidly changed from my school jumper and cardigan into an equally scratchy pleated wool skirt and argyle sweater. This is what they wore to jump around and sweat in? Sweating I would do for sure.

I wadded up my own clothes into the bottom of my bag, took the tennis racket in hand so I'd look like I had a purpose there, and exited the changing room. I squinted out across the sunny courts and saw a girl and boy playing opposite each other on the far court. They were the only players out at the moment.

I approached slowly, staying under the shaded walkway alongside the courts while I could, and watched them. It was Daphne and her brother, Claude. The closer I got, the clearer it was she was beating him to a pulp. He was running ragged, sweaty hair flopping down into his eyes, while she was bouncing on her toes and smiling. She zinged a ball way out of his reach and laughed gaily.

"Can't we take a break yet, Daph?" he said, racket sagging.

"It's only ten, Claude!"

"But I need some water," he whined. "At least let me get some water. I feel a little sick."

"Not again." Daphne sighed heavily. "Go then, if you must. But be back in ten minutes or less."

Claude shuffle-ran off the court before she could change her mind.

"I'll be timing you!" she called after him.

I stepped out of the shadows onto the edge of their court. "Looks like you're in need of a partner."

Daphne turned to me and shaded her eyes. "Do I know you?"

"Not really," I said, and stepped into the sun. "But we've met."

I watched the realization dawn on her face. She glanced around quickly, as if afraid.

"How did you get in here?"

"I decided to pick up a new sport. Do you want to play or not?"

She took in my pleated skirt and argyle sweater. "*You* know how to play tennis?"

I bristled. "Of course."

True, I hadn't paid much attention in gym class, but I knew the rules and how the scoring worked. I knew you hit the ball with the racket and tried to make your opponent miss. It was right up my alley—if I wasn't wearing this ridiculous wool getup, that is.

"Fine then," she said. "Show me."

I skirted around the court and took up Claude's position opposite her. "I've got a few questions for you while we play."

Daphne served the ball directly at me, and I dodged a mere

instant before it would've hit me in the face. I glared at her, and she smirked. "Ask then. If you can."

I picked up the ball and whacked it back at her. She returned it easily, and I missed it again. I kept the ball in my hand this time.

"I heard you argued with Arimentha McDonough the night of her murder. About your boyfriend, who used to be her boyfriend. Why was that?"

"Serve the ball."

"Not until you answer the question."

Daphne blew out a frustrated breath. "It wasn't important. She'd tried to warn me away from him before but wouldn't even say why. So, I ignored her. *Serve.*"

I bounced the ball and hit it. It barely skimmed over the net, and Daphne ran forward and scooped it back over to me. I scurried to return it, and Daphne barely broke a sweat sailing it back to me and out of my reach. I'd lost a point, but the ball was in my hand again.

"Did Minty take you upstairs on New Year's Eve to continue the conversation?"

"No. God. I certainly didn't want to talk about it *more.*" Daphne scowled across the court at me. "Hit the ball."

I sent it back to her, and we had another round of volleys close to the net until I missed again and picked up the ball.

Daphne stomped her foot. "You're losing on purpose."

If only I was. "You didn't talk to Minty any more that night?"

"No! My brother and I stuck together and made the best of it." She set a hand on her hip. "If you're just going to ask questions, I'll wait for Claude."

I sighed and served the ball back to her. She eagerly resumed her pose and sent an easy one straight to me, so I wouldn't have an excuse to grab the ball again and stop the game. Okay. I'd just have to ask questions *while* we played.

"What do you think of Fitzroy DeCoursey?" I said as I darted forward to hit another ball.

Daphne's mouth curled in distaste, but she said nothing, just sent the ball hurtling toward the back corner of the court, forcing me to run for it.

"I've heard he has a habit of blackmailing people," I tried again, barely getting to the ball in time to clumsily hit it out of bounds. "Like maybe your boyfriend."

Daphne caught the ball on a bounce and came closer to the net. To my surprise, the expression in her eyes was fearful. "What do you know about it?"

"I know enough." I smiled. "Your boyfriend's political career is pretty important to him, huh?"

Daphne's chin rose. "Of course, it is. And to me."

I moved closer to the net, too, and lowered my voice. "If you told the police what Fitzroy's been doing, they'd have to look at him for the murder. And he'd be out of your hair, too."

Daphne Fitzroy glanced at me keenly. "Is this what you're doing—trying to find out who killed Arimentha?"

I nodded. "Did she ever tell you about people she was seeing? Romantically?"

Daphne shook her head. "She and I weren't close anymore since I started dating Philip." Her voice sounded regretful. "I only went that night because Claude wanted to go." She looked at her watch and away in the direction he'd gone.

"Then what about rumors? Did you hear anything about her love life in the months before she died?"

Daphne squeezed the ball in her hand tighter and gave me a hard look. "You want me to spread rumors about my dead friend?"

"I just want to know who was with her on the balcony that night." I stuck the racket under my arm and gripped the net with both hands. "I want to know why she died."

Daphne sighed and glanced away, as if hoping Claude would show up. "Have you talked to Symphony?"

"She wasn't much help."

Daphne made a face. "Then the only thing I can tell you is the same thing I told the cops."

I held my breath. "What's that?"

"That Minty kept a diary. If you want to know all about her life, I bet it was in there."

"Do the cops have this diary?"

Daphne shrugged. "I heard they looked for it but couldn't find it. Hey—where are you going? Don't you want to finish the game?"

"You win!" I called over my shoulder. I was already snatching up my bag and running toward the exit.

If anyone knew where Minty kept that diary, it was her former best friend.

—— · ——

"So . . ." I leaned against the bedroom doorframe and watched Marion organize my dresser drawers. "Were you ever going to mention this diary of Minty's?"

Marion stopped, bent over a drawer. "Diary?"

Pink tinted the back of his neck, and I knew I had him. I waved a hand. "Don't pretend you haven't heard about it. Why didn't you tell me? There could be a dozen potential murder suspects in there!"

Marion still wasn't looking at me. "One reason is because I didn't know if she still kept one."

"But you knew she used to."

Marion held up a white shirt with a blue blotch staining one shoulder, the shirt I'd been wearing under my cardigan when Virginia Baines "accidentally" spilled ink on me. "I tried to get this stain out, but it's stubborn. I think we should just throw it out."

I folded my arms across my chest. "That stain's not the only stubborn thing around here."

Marion whistled. "Look at the pot calling the kettle black."

"Tell me about the diary."

Marion sighed. "When I knew Minty, she was religious about writing in it. Always scribbling away."

"According to Daphne, she never stopped. What was the other reason you didn't mention it?"

Marion tossed the stained shirt on the floor and fiddled with the strap of one of my folded undershirts. "Because I knew you'd try to get it. I didn't want you putting yourself in danger. I hoped finding the killer would be easy and we wouldn't need it."

"But we do need it. Daphne said the cops couldn't find it, so Minty was obviously hiding it somewhere. You know where that is, don't you?"

I waited for Marion to say something, but he concentrated on unfolding, examining, and refolding a pair of my pajamas for a lot longer than necessary. "I need you to promise me," he said finally in the direction of the pajamas. "Promise you'll be careful."

"I will." I moved across the bedroom to his side. "I swear to you I won't do anything foolish, and I won't get caught."

"I know you won't." He tucked the pajamas in the drawer and looked up at me. "Because I'm going with you to make sure of it."

My eyes widened. "No. That's a bad idea."

"The cops won't be looking for me in the Garden District, will they? I'll wear my most manly outfit, and I've been letting my eyebrows grow in." He shuddered.

"You've been thinking about this, haven't you?"

Marion turned and shoved the drawer shut. "Say I can go, or I'm not telling you where the diary is."

"Okay." I resisted the impulse to throw a shoe at him. "Okay, you can go. Of course, you can."

"Good." A self-satisfied smile formed on Marion's lips. "But first, we'll need a costume and a crowbar."

CHATER

18

TURNED OUT MARION was only slightly exaggerating
about how little we'd need for this excursion. The crowbar I
borrowed from its hook behind the bar Monday night as I was
leaving work. We also needed dark clothes, so we wouldn't stand
out like sore thumbs at night, and we needed someone to drive
us to the Garden District in the wee hours after the streetcar
stopped running.

Most of the clothes, Marion scrounged up for us from Cal
and Mama's old vaudeville trunk while he waited for me to
come home. The ride required Bennie Altobello. Again.

Luckily for me, he came by the club with a delivery and
didn't ask too many questions when I asked if he could pick me
up at my place later and take me for a ride somewhere.

"I didn't realize Marion was coming, too," Bennie said
when both of us slid into the truck with him, looking like the cat
burglars we were apparently becoming.

"I mentioned it, didn't I?"

Bennie shook his head with certainty.

"Oh, well, he is. And I need to warn you now that you're going to be our getaway driver."

"Your *what?*" He looked up and down at our mostly black outfits. "Is that why you're dressed like that? Are you going to rob a bank or something? I don't think—"

"Geez, Bennie, calm down. We're going to sneak into a house, borrow a little old box with a diary in it, and pop right back out. No harm done."

His thick eyebrows looked skeptical. They were loud even in the dark. "*Whose* house?"

I bit my lip and pulled my school beret down farther over my hair.

Marion leaned up and looked across me at Bennie. "Arimentha McDonough's."

"*What?*"

"Millie," Marion said, giving me a chastising look, "you should've told him this when you asked him to drive us."

"We were in a public place, for crying out loud! I didn't want to shout it all over town." I didn't mention how Olive had been coming our way when I'd asked him, and I'd wanted to end the conversation before she heard me begging Bennie for yet another favor.

Marion sighed dramatically.

"You're telling me we're about to try to steal Arimentha McDonough's diary?" Bennie said. "Why don't the cops know about it?"

"They know it exists—" I said.

"They just don't know where it is," Marion finished.

"But don't you think this is too risky?"

"Probably it is," Marion said.

"But we've agreed it's the only way to get a jump on the police," I said. "This might give us some leads they don't even know about yet."

Bennie looked from me to Marion, then shook his head in defeat. "Why do I let you talk me into these things?" he muttered, but his hand moved to the gear shift, and soon we were chugging to a start.

"Not to look a gift horse in the mouth, Bennie," Marion said, "but why *do* you do these things?"

I elbowed him in the ribs hard enough to elicit an *oof.*

But Bennie laughed. "This one time when we were twelve or thirteen, some bigger kids had me surrounded in an alley, and I was about to be dead meat. Do you remember, Millie?"

I stiffened in surprise. I did remember. It had been the summer Mama dropped me off at Cal's and didn't show her face again for four and a half years.

"Then I saw this skinny black-haired girl barreling toward us," Bennie said, chuckling. "She was screaming and walloping those bigger kids in the head with—what was it?"

I laughed tightly. "Broken bicycle handlebars."

"That's right." Bennie laughed so hard he let the truck stall out at a stoplight. "Then you started in with your fists, and I couldn't let you show me up, so I fought back, too, and pretty soon they were running."

Marion looked from Bennie's face to mine, incredulous. "Why has no one ever told me this story?"

I shrugged. "You know me. Modest to a fault."

But the truth was, I'd spent that whole summer with blood-iced knuckles, and I wasn't always the one saving people from bullies. Sometimes I was the bully, hitting anything to make me forget the ache that filled my chest to bursting all the time.

The truck chugged to life again, and I shook myself, pushing thoughts of Mama back down where they belonged. I couldn't let her distract me now.

"On our way," I said with false cheer, rubbing my hands together. "Time to burgle some rich folks!"

Bennie and Marion glanced at each other across me, their expressions matching. Both of them looked like *What did we just get ourselves into?*

—·—

Marion directed Bennie to park the truck on the street behind the McDonough and Leveque residences, because the estates were so big they stretched all the way through to the next block. This street was little more than a cart path, with the backs of two rows of crushed-shell driveways and elegant carriage houses butting up to it.

"There," Marion said, pointing to a stretch of iron fence with a bunch of camellias crowding each other behind it. "They won't be able to see us from the house."

Bennie looked nervously at the backs of the houses across the street. "But what about them?"

Marion waved a hand. "The only people who come this far out back are the staff. A driver might spot us, but he'll think nothing of a delivery truck sitting here. If anyone asks—they won't, but just in case—tell them you're delivering groceries to the Leveques."

"Thought we were going to the McDonoughs'?"

"The Leveques are next door. Say Philip Leveque."

Bennie glanced at me, brows raised.

"Yes, the same Philip Leveque we cornered in a bathroom. Are we going to sit here jawing all day?" I tugged at the too-small gray gloves I'd worn, the closest thing to black in the vaudeville trunk.

"Fine, let's go." Marion took his sweet time about sliding out of the truck, checking left and right that the sound of the squeaking door hadn't brought out any lookers.

I jumped out right after him, holding the short crowbar, and shut the truck door behind me, gently. It still made an uncomfortably distinct clang. I looked at Bennie through the open window; his eyes were wide.

"You know, Bennie, you're awfully jumpy for a bootlegger."

He threw up his hands. "That's *why* I'm jumpy."

"Sit tight," I said. "We'll be back in a jiff."

I turned to find Marion had slunk toward an opening in the camellias. He waved a hand to me.

"This way," he whispered. "Over the fence."

"Why can't we go up the driveway?"

He pointed up at the nearly full moon. "Too visible."

I shot him a skeptical look, pretty sure we could stay out of sight just as easily if we kept to the bushes along the sides of the drive. But Marion was already vaulting over the low iron fence and ducking under the camellia in one smooth motion.

I dropped the crowbar over the fence and did the same, minus the smooth part. I fumbled my landing and crashed into a branch of the camellia, sending a shower of soft petals down on my head.

"Shhh!" Marion said, turning in his crouch to glare at me.

"Tell the camellia that," I muttered, kicking at the trunk

of the little tree. More petals floated down, and one landed on my nose. I huffed a breath and blew it away.

Marion gestured for me to come up next to him, so I crawled closer.

"There," he said, pointing at a large balcony that took up the entire rooftop of a side wing of the house. "Arimentha's bedroom is right through those double doors."

"I figured."

Marion gave me an irritated shake of his head. "See that trellis up against the house? With the vines growing on it?"

I could just make out the dark twisting vines against the white lattice. "I see it."

"That's where you climb up. I've done it before a million times."

I gave him a sly look and nudged his elbow. "A million times, huh? You and Minty were just *friends*, huh?"

Marion rolled his eyes. "If you're done being seven years old, we need to do this quickly and get out of here."

"I agree."

"Okay. We do it like we talked about—up the trellis, you pop the lock on the balcony doors, we pry up the floorboard, get the box, get out, voilà."

"Voilà," I said. "Except maybe you shouldn't go up."

"What do you mean? Of course I should. I'm the one who knows where the diary is. I'm the one who told you about it."

"You're also the one who's been accused of killing Minty. What happens if you get busted breaking into her room? You're going down for murder. The end. Curtains."

Marion's black-gloved fingers went instinctively to his neck, but then he stubbornly shook his head again. "You'll be my lookout. They won't catch us."

"If we're both upstairs, what good will a lookout do? Both of us won't be able to get down that lattice in time."

"Then I'll go alone and you look out from behind that clump of palmettos over there."

"Oh, you know how to jimmy door locks now?"

Marion's mouth opened and then closed. "How hard can it be?" he said, but his voice lost its certainty.

"Look, Marion. I'll be up and out quick. You look out from the palmettos, all right? Whistle if somebody's coming."

Marion met my eyes and reached for my hand in the semi-dark. "But what happens to *you* if you're caught, Millie? What if they start thinking you killed Arimentha? What if you go to jail for me? I couldn't live with that."

"Don't worry, I'm not planning on going to jail for any-body." I squeezed his hand and smiled. "Anyway, I got an alibi. A hundred people saw me in the club at the time she was mur-dered. Worst that could happen is they'd get me on breaking and entering."

Marion looked doubtful. "That's still pretty bad."

"Nah," I lied. "Let's go."

Then I was scurrying out of our hiding place and across open moonlit ground.

"Millie!" Marion hissed behind me, but I kept going and ducked into the shadow of the spiky palmettos. When I turned back to look, he was behind me.

"I still think—" he said.

"Shhh! We're too close to the house for a chat. I'm going up."

"Millie, can't you stop a second and listen to—"

I pressed my index finger over his lips. "See you in five minutes."

I released him and darted across the next open patch of ground, this time not stopping until I reached the deep, hard-angled shadow of the house. I pressed my back against the clapboards and caught my breath. Marion peeked from between the fronds of the palmetto and made a shooing gesture. Mouthed *hurry*.

I spun and faced the trellis. It looked sturdy enough, but Marion hadn't climbed it in at least a year and a half, if not more. That crisp paint could be hiding rotten patches and loose nails. It might peel off the wall with me on it and send me splatting flat on my back on the dried-up grass.

But I couldn't exactly turn back now and say, "Never mind, you go, Marion. It'll be fine. I was wrong about the cops probably hanging you." I stuck the crowbar through the back of my belt and found two fingerholds in the trellis, then one toehold, then another, until I was hanging on like a monkey. I looked up. Only fifteen or so more feet to go. Piece of cake.

Except the vines crawling up the trellis were roses. There were no flowers this time of year, but apparently thorns never went out of season. They tore at my black sweater and scratched at my hands through the gloves. I was going to look like I'd fallen off the back of a truck by the time I was done with this.

Finally, I reached the balcony and swung one arm over it. I grasped blindly for a foothold, afraid for one moment my arms would give out and I'd go crashing down and impale myself on the spikes propping up the rosebushes. But then my foot touched solid wood, and I hooked my other arm over the railing and hauled myself up and over.

I landed with a thud, on my hip instead of my feet. I scrambled into a crouch and stayed low behind the railing, watching the windows for a light to flicker on, listening for an unfamiliar voice to ring out. When nothing happened, I eased over to the French doors and tested the handle, in case it was unlocked.

No such luck.

Upstairs French doors typically had no keyholes, and this one was no exception. But I expected it would have multiple locks all the same, like the ones leading from our kitchen onto our wobbly iron balcony that I'd been practicing on: a simple horizontal bolt in the middle of the two doors, and four or more vertical sliding bolts to keep both doors from getting blown inward in a hurricane or an overly stiff breeze.

The horizontal bolt I dispatched easily enough by sticking my knife's blade through the crack between the doors and nudging the bolt slowly upward and out of my way.

The vertical bolts were another matter. I held my switchblade between my teeth and pushed on the left-hand door at the top and then the bottom. The bottom had plenty of give, but the top held solid—that meant only the top bolt was latched. One bolt to deal with wasn't so bad.

I took the knife out of my teeth and threw my weight against the door to widen the crack. I saw a sliver of the dark room beyond, and excitement and fear welled up in my chest, making me almost giddy.

I slid my knife into the crack and felt for the vertical bolt. I found it quickly, but I couldn't find the little knob to pull it down. I fiddled and fiddled, but the more I fiddled, the more my hands shook, and the worse it went. My heartbeat started playing double time. Maybe I'd overestimated my lock-picking skills. Maybe someone would look out a window and spot me here and call the police.

The crowbar's cold metallic weight against the center of my back tempted me to use it and hurry things along. Breaking in that way would be easy, but it would make more noise. I'd risk waking the house.

I raised up to glance over the railing at the clump of palmettos. Marion's hands flew up in a what's-taking-so-long? gesture. But at least he wasn't saying *Run for your life*. We were still okay, for now.

I turned back to the door and slipped the crowbar out of my belt, testing its weight in my hands. It might be my only option if I wanted to finish this job before sunrise.

Through the many glass panes of the French doors, Arimentha's bedroom was mostly hidden by gauzy curtains. A new thought occurred to me. What if someone was sleeping in there? Her distraught father, maybe, wanting to be where his daughter had been?

All I could do was try to open the door, as planned, and if someone was in the bed, take off the way I'd come.

I wedged the end of the crowbar into the door opening and glanced one more time at the dark windows down the side of the house. Then I shoved with all my might on the other end of the crowbar. The wood screeched and groaned, but I figured it was better to get all the sound over with quick and threw my weight behind the crowbar again and again until, with one last crack, the bolt came loose, and I was in.

I stopped and waited and listened, trying not to breathe too hard.

A slice of moonlight fell onto a thick rug, its colors washed silver and gray in the dark. The bed beyond it was like a black ship rising out of the night. I watched it, waiting for someone to stir, to sit up and point an accusing finger, to sound the alarm.

But nothing happened. No sound met my ears except a clock somewhere far away chiming twice for the hour.

I let out a heavy breath and stepped into the room. Shifted my grip on the crowbar and waited for my eyes to adjust to the deeper dark. The loose floorboard Marion had told me about was under the corner of the rug closest to the French doors, so some moonlight would reach me there.

I moved slowly, keeping to the soft cushion of the rug, and knelt near the spot. I flipped back the corner of the rug and studied the barely visible cracks between the floorboards. I ran my fingers flat over the surface, feeling for thicker cracks, a breath of air, something to indicate which board was the right one. A rough edge snagged the fabric of my glove, and I traced it for several inches. I pushed on the board, and it wiggled a bit. This was it. It had to be.

I eased the end of the crowbar into the crack and pushed. The board flipped up and landed flat on the wood behind it with a clatter.

Shit. I didn't have time to freeze and listen and wait again. Marion had said Arimentha's father's bedroom was two rooms away, but I couldn't guarantee he hadn't heard that. I ripped off my glove and reached into the dark opening, feeling with my fingers and hoping no spiders or rats had taken up residence in the past few days. On two sides I felt the rough wood of floor joists. On the third side, cool air and cobwebs. On the fourth, nothing but cool air.

That was my best bet. I set down the crowbar on the rug

and bent farther forward, shoving more of my arm into the hole until finally my fingertips touched something smooth and solid. The box.

I gentled my touch, afraid of pushing the box out of reach. I moved my fingers to the corner of the box to get the best grip and tugged.

"Come *on*," I whispered into the dark, and the box started sliding my way.

Something creaked behind me, like a footstep on floorboards. I spared a glance over my shoulder. Faint orange light shone under the crack of the bedroom door. My heart pounded faster, and I nearly lost my grasp on the box.

But I almost had it; Arimentha's darkest secrets were almost ours. I couldn't let them go now. I tightened my grip and pulled. The box wasn't deep, but it was wide and heavy, and it took both hands to ease it out of the narrow opening the floorboard created. I shoved the box under my arm, and the weight inside it shifted downward—the diary. Now I needed the key. It was supposed to be in an enameled bowl on Arimentha's dressing table.

But the floorboards outside the hall creaked again. The light under the door seemed brighter now, as if someone was carrying a lantern or a flashlight, and it was getting closer. I didn't have time for the key. We'd have to pick the lock at home. This kind of lock was usually easy.

"Is someone there?" A man's voice, tremulous, outside the door.

I looked at the loose floorboard. No time for that either. I stuffed my gray glove in my pocket, scrambled to my feet, and kicked the rug over the opening. Then I grabbed my crowbar and darted for the French doors.

The bedroom door creaked open behind me.

"A-Arimentha?" the man said. "Darling? Is that you?"

I stopped in the doorway for one instant, frozen by regret and pity. This was Arimentha's father, a man I hadn't spared much consideration for. Here he was in the dark, woken from fitful sleep, staring at the silhouette of a girl in his daughter's room and, for a moment, hoping it had all been a mistake, that his daughter had come home to him.

But she never would.

"I'm sorry," I said, and bolted out onto the balcony.

I tossed the crowbar and box over the railing onto the ground and swung myself over. I quickly shuffled along the edge of the balcony on my toes and grabbed for the trellis. There was no time for caution now, nor for any fear other than the fear of being caught.

Arimentha's father would recover from his doubt and shock quickly. He was a federal judge after all, known for his hard sentencing on Prohibition violations. He would be right behind me, and I had to get away before he saw my face, or worse, snatched me back into that room.

I shinnied down a few feet, much faster than I'd gone up. I missed a toehold and slid a foot, thorns scratching my cheek and snagging my sweater.

"Stop there!" The man's voice was stronger now. He might be leaning over the balcony, but I couldn't chance looking up at him and letting the moonlight shine on my face.

I climbed faster and finally, when the ground was a few feet away, let go and dropped. A branch of the rosebush jabbed into my shin, and I rolled away and into the crowbar. I snatched it up and shoved it against the ground to leverage myself up faster.

The box was a body's length away, in the wrong direction. I lunged for it, swept it up under my arm, and pivoted, my foot digging up dry grass and sliding.

"I said stop! I'm calling the police!"

I didn't stop. I ran headlong toward the palmettos and then past them, yelling as I went. "Go! Go!"

Marion fell in behind me and then overtook me. He dodged around the camellias this time and vaulted over the iron fence in one of the clearer areas. He turned back, eyes wide.

"Take them," I said breathlessly, and shoved the box and crowbar into his hands.

Then I launched over the fence myself, finally managing to land on my feet this time.

"The truck," I said, bent double.

Bennie was leaning out of the window, watching us with wide eyes. "What happened? Did you get it?"

We didn't have time or breath to answer. Marion flung open the passenger door of the truck and shoved me inside ahead of him. Then he got in and shut it with a loud clang that didn't matter now. The jig was up.

All that mattered was getting away.

CHAPTER

19

BACK AT THE apartment, nerves still jangling from the close call, we stared at the box where I'd set it in the middle of our kitchen table, under the single dangling bulb. The box was smooth, dark walnut, so well made that the line where the lid met the body was hardly a sliver.

All the tools we'd used to try to pick the lock or prize open the box lay scattered around it on the table—hairpins, a straightened paper clip, my switchblade, Bennie's pocket knife, a wire hanger, a letter opener, and a screwdriver. Bennie and Marion had taken cracks at it, too, but the box still sat there, sealed like a pharaoh's tomb. The lock was starting to look like a taunting mouth to me. The damn box was mocking us.

"What if we run over it with Bennie's truck?" I suggested.

"It would probably break the axle," Bennie said.

Marion ran a hand through his hair and blew out a frustrated sigh. "This was *supposed* to be the easy part." He shot a look at me. "You *said* you could crack the lock. 'Easy peasy,' you said."

"That was before I knew it was made by some fancy clock-maker in Switzerland!" I tossed a butter knife on the pile of tools. "You could've mentioned that part before I risked my ass breaking in and stealing the thing."

Marion crossed his arms over his chest. "I forgot, all right? I told you we needed the key!"

"Well, we don't have it. Why would anyone go to this much trouble for a lousy box to hide her diary?"

Marion groaned. "Her father bought it to keep her jewels in. But instead—"

"Her damn diary." I sank against the back of my chair.

"You think there are any jewels in there, too?" Bennie said.

I looked at him sharply. "Why? You hoping to take a cut?"

"No." He blinked in surprise. "I just wanna know how much trouble we could be in for stealing this thing."

He had a point. I picked up the box and shook it again. The sound was muffled by the thick walnut, but we all heard the book sliding from side to side.

"I could take it to my uncle," Bennie said. "He's a pawn-broker. Deals with this kind of stuff sometimes."

"Or a locksmith," Marion said.

"No." I shook my head and plunked down the box again. "I don't want anybody asking a bunch of questions about what this is and where we got it."

"Then what's *your* idea?" Marion said.

"Maybe I could go back tomorrow night and try for the key."

"No!" they both said in unison.

"But I'd be quicker this time. In and out."

"You're being an ass," Marion said bluntly. "You know perfectly well they're going to have the place locked up tighter now, cops watching it, the works. Judge McDonough is probably sitting in the room with a shotgun."

"But we need that key." I rubbed my thumb over the brass edge of the stubborn lock. And slowly, the nerves in my fingertip sent the message to my brain that they'd felt something like that recently. "Marion," I said urgently. "What did that key look like?"

He looked surprised. "Small. Size of my little finger, maybe. Brass."

I pounded my fist on the table, making the box—and the boys—jump. "I wouldn't have found that key in her room even if I'd had time to look. It was in her handbag, the night she was killed. I saw it."

Marion sat up straighter. "You have it?"

I chewed my lip and shook my head. "Wish to God I did. I took your picture out of the purse and left everything else. Handed it over to the cops."

"You're saying the *cops* have the key?" Bennie said.

"Looks that way."

"Great," Marion said. "That's perfect. Maybe we *should* try running over the box. Or throwing it off a building."

"Or," I said, looking from Marion to Bennie, "we could go get the key. I bet it's in Sabatier's office."

Bennie made a horrified face. "Just waltz into the police station and steal evidence?"

"*Borrow* evidence." I leaned back in my chair. "All we need is a distraction."

Marion frowned. "What kind of distraction?"

I rubbed the pad of my thumb over my lips. Nothing sprang to mind. The boys looked just as blank, and also aggravated and exhausted, with their usually neat hair sticking up at odd angles from running frustrated fingers through it. I figured that was about how I looked, too. We were all ready to launch this box into the Mississippi and give up.

"Let's get some shut-eye." I smacked a hand on each of their shoulders and forced a smile. "Maybe something will come to us in a dream."

"Maybe," Marion said wearily.

"Don't do anything without me," Bennie said.

"We won't," I promised, even though I wasn't sure I would follow through on it.

"See you tomorrow then," Bennie mumbled, and gathered up his jacket and pocketknife and left.

Marion and I changed into our pajamas, took our turns down the hall in the john, and dropped into bed, all without saying a word. I was too busy speculating, and his face said he was doing the same.

We lay side by side, not speaking, and it seemed like hours passed before I heard Marion's breathing slow.

A distraction. What kind of distraction?

All I knew was it had to be a good one.

—·—

The next morning, I told Cal about the locked box and the plan to get the key from Sabatier while I tugged on my school socks and shoes. I couldn't find my navy beret, so I stuffed a newsboy cap on my head instead.

Mama came swanning in from the bedroom in her dressing gown. "I know him, you know," she said lazily, draping herself across the sofa.

"Who?" I looked up from buckling my shoe.

"Larry." She waved a hand. "Your police detective."

"*My* police detective?"

"You know who I mean. Larry Sabatier." She smiled out the window in a self-satisfied way. "I think he had a bit of a thing for me way back when."

Cal was in the kitchen fiddling unsuccessfully with the lock. "You think everyone had a thing for you."

Mama shot her a glare. "He did. He brought me flowers after the show for a while."

I stared at her. How was she only now telling me this information?

"But then he stopped coming, right?" Cal said, giving me a significant look.

Mama focused on smoothing her dressing gown around her on the sofa. "Well, I left not long after that. With Millie's father."

I stuffed my foot into my other shoe and shook my head, watching our chance drain away. "You ditched Sabatier, didn't you? Made him think you liked him, let him buy you dinner a few times, and then ran off with someone else, right? He probably won't want anything to do with you now."

Mama shifted huffily on the sofa. "I wouldn't be so sure of that. I bet I could still distract him."

I focused on my other shoe buckle, trying not to look interested. "He's a grown man now. Seems pretty smart. Too smart to have his head turned by an old flame who did him wrong."

"I was eighteen years old, for Christ's sake." Mama pouted and tugged on a lock of her glossy hair. "So was Larry. Nobody does everything right when they're a kid—*you* should understand that."

I kept my face carefully impassive. She hadn't been a kid when she'd ditched me. She'd been thirty-two years old. But there was no point bringing that up now, not when I wanted—needed—something from her.

"Then you'd be willing to try it?" I said carefully.

"Well, I don't know," Mama said silkily, relaxing back into the sofa now. She had the power all of a sudden, and she liked it. "I don't like the idea of playing a trick on Larry."

"I don't either," I lied, because a not-small part of me really, really did. "But it's the only thing I can think of to get what we need for Marion."

"What do *you* think, Cal?" Mama called over her shoulder. She only asked her opinion when Cal was likely to agree with her.

Cal waved a screwdriver in a circle. "I like it even less than you do. Sounds like a good way to get thrown in jail."

I opened my mouth to protest, and Cal held up a hand to stop me. "I understand Marion's predicament, and we want to do everything we can to help him." She cast a glance toward my room, where he was still sleeping. "But you've already gone too far with the breaking and entering. What if you'd been caught? It won't do Marion any good for you to end up in jail."

"But I wasn't caught. And I won't be caught this time either. Sabatier won't notice the key is gone right away. And if he comes back while I'm in his office, I'll say I was coming to talk to him about the case, to ask him if he's found any new leads yet."

"Hm," Cal said, unimpressed, and bent back over the box with her screwdriver.

"*And*," I said, "if Mama's keeping him properly occupied, it won't be a problem at all."

"Properly occupied?" Mama said, a hand flying to her chest. "What exactly do you expect me to do, Millie?"

I wanted to roll my eyes at her innocent act and say it was nothing she hadn't done a million times before. But I had to keep making nice if I wanted her help. "He already had the eagers for you once," I said. "You'll hardly have to do a thing. Just keep him talking out in the lobby. Or better yet, talk him into going with you for coffee down the street. It's not even a trick if you actually did like him once. You're just old friends catching up."

"Well, I don't know." Mama fluffed her hair. "I do have a new dress."

"See there? Now you have an excuse to wear it."

"Gladys," Cal said, straightening. "You aren't seriously thinking of—"

"Oh, hush, Cal," Mama said, waving a hand. "You worry too much. Millie's a big girl. And so am I." She gave me an almost shy smile. "We can do this, can't we?"

Me and Mama hadn't been a "we" in a long time. I didn't know if I ever wanted to be again. But I made myself smile back.

"Sure we can."

———·———

After school that afternoon, I met up with Mama on the corner down the street from the police station. She wore a dress the deep green color of magnolia leaves, which contrasted prettily with her stylishly curled red hair. The dress had a low rounded neckline, and the skirt flared out when she walked, showing off her shapely calves. Gladys Coleman knew how to work her assets; I'd give her that.

She posed with a hand on her hip as if expecting a compliment, but she'd have to wait on Sabatier for that.

"You sure you can do this?" I said without preamble.

Mama pursed her lips and arched a single brow, a trick I hadn't managed to learn though I'd spent many an evening in front of the mirror trying. "Can *you?*"

I ignored the sense that I'd been checkmated. "Let's go."

We entered the police station's lobby and made our way up to the tall desk at the front. A jowly lady with an iron-gray bun glanced up at us from behind a pair of half glasses on a chain, then bent back over the papers on her desk.

"The position has been filled," she said in a monotone without looking at us again.

Mama smiled benignly at the top of the lady's head. "We're not here for a job. We just need a little help. See, I'm—"

The lady shoved a page across the desk. "Fill this out. Sit over there." She pointed to a wooden bench already full of people who looked like they'd been waiting since the early twenties. A couple of them were even asleep.

"I'm afraid you're misunderstanding me," Mama plowed forward, as if the old bird was actually listening. "I'm an old friend of Detective Laurence Sabatier. I was told he works here now, and I just wanted to stop by and say hello."

The lady sighed deeply and laid down her pen like it weighed forty pounds. "You do know this is a police station, not a society tea?"

I debated whether punching her would put a damper on our plans. Mama laid a hand on my arm like she knew what I was thinking, and I resisted the urge to shrug it off.

Mama batted her lashes and ducked her head, as if she

were embarrassed, but I knew she had no shame. "I'm so sorry, ma'am. I so respect what you folks do here. But Larry—I mean, Detective Sabatier—he's such a dear old friend, and I'd be ever so grateful if you could just tell him I'm here, and at least give him the chance to say whether he has time to pop out for a teensy little hello."

The woman at the desk sighed again and picked up the receiver of her candlestick telephone. "Sabatier," she barked into it. "Visitor for you."

"See now?" I said when she'd hung up. "That wasn't so hard, was it?"

The lady's stare could've frozen a sewer in August.

"We'll just be over here," Mama said, dragging me away toward the wooden bench.

I jerked my arm loose from her grasp when we were out of earshot from the front desk. "*I'm* going over there to watch which door he comes out of."

I slouched against the wall on the other side of the lobby, held a newspaper in front of my face, and peeked around it until Sabatier came out of a door on the left down the hall. Quickly, I ducked behind the paper and listened for the sounds of Sabatier's approaching footsteps, but the station had a tall ceiling and hard floors and too many people to discern one echo from another. Finally, though, I heard Mama's loud squeal of delight.

"Gladys . . . Coleman?" Sabatier spluttered. "You're . . . here. What are you doing here? That is, I'm—"

Mama trilled a laugh. "I'm in town for a bit, darling. Staying with my sister, just a visit while I'm between shows, and I thought I'd come catch up with an old friend."

"Friends." Sabatier's voice stiffened. "Is that what we were?"

"Oh, darling, I'll always consider you a friend." I peeped around the newspaper and saw her lay a hand on his sleeve and look up at him through her lashes.

"What . . . what brings you here today specifically?" Sabatier said. The mingled hope and doubt were plain in his voice, like mine every time Mama seemed too good to be true. She'd been right about him, though. He hadn't forgotten her.

"Well, I was shopping right over on Canal, so it wasn't so far to go. See what I found?" She showed him the contents of a shopping bag I hadn't noticed. The name in cursive on the side declared it was from a store that specialized in lingerie. Sabatier's cheeks reddened, and I suppressed a laugh. I'd forgotten how good Mama was at subterfuge, though I shouldn't have.

"My . . . goodness," Sabatier said. "And then you popped over to pay me a visit?" His voice had noticeably warmed. Back behind the paper, I rolled my eyes.

"It's been so long," Mama purred, dragging her fingertips down his sleeve. "We're all grown up now, aren't we? Wouldn't it be nice to have a real honest-to-goodness catchup?"

"It certainly would."

"Then what do you say we go for a coffee? There's a nice café right around the corner."

There was a pause. I peeked around the paper again; Sabatier was consulting an old-fashioned watch on a chain.

"I shouldn't go away for long. I'm in the middle of a murder case, you may have heard."

"Oh my! How fascinating! I wouldn't dare take you away from such important business. But you could spare just a few minutes, couldn't you? It's not good for a man to never take a break. You'll come back to it in ten minutes with fresh eyes. Won't that be nice?"

"All right, all right." Sabatier laughed. "How can I say no? Let me tell my partner I'm going."

I peeked out and watched Sabatier go in an office across the hall from his own. Craggy's, I assumed, which was good news. That meant they didn't share an office, a consideration I hadn't thought to worry about.

When Sabatier came back, Mama looped her arm through his, and they swept out through the front doors of the station. I tossed aside the newspaper and turned to watch through a window as they walked away up the street. *Yes.* I owed Mama one—well, she owed me one less.

Now, to get back to Sabatier's office without attracting attention. I looked around the busy lobby and waited for my moment, and when a pair of officers came through wrestling with a prisoner smelling heavily of booze, I decided this was it.

I hopped up and walked with purpose between the desks and toward the hall, not too fast and not too slow, keeping my chin up and my mouth ready with a smile in case I ran into someone and had to explain why I was wandering around the detectives' offices. Halfway down the hall, I spotted the door with a brass nameplate that read DETECTIVE LAURENCE SABATIER.

I glanced to the left and right, turned the knob, and slipped inside. My stomach lurched as I caught a glimpse of a man in the corner of the office, but then I realized it was Sabatier's coat hanging on a rack. I choked back a laugh and shook my head at myself. All this burgling was making me jumpy.

Now for the key. Where would someone like Sabatier keep

it? He seemed like the organized type, so he probably had it in a file somewhere.

I skipped over the corkboard covered with notes and slipped behind Sabatier's desk, a plain rectangle so scratched up it looked like it had been pushed down a flight of stairs twice. There was a shallow drawer in the front and two deeper ones down the right side. I shoved aside Sabatier's rolling chair and tried the top drawer, but it was locked. I'd brought along my hairpins, but my confidence in my lock-picking skills had worn a little thin, and I figured this drawer only contained pencil stubs and maybe a grooming kit for that luxurious mustache. I went for the deeper drawers and found the top one unlocked and filled with neat dark green folders labeled with names. That was more like it.

I pawed through the files in the top drawer. They were sorted alphabetically by last name, starting with A and ending with F. McDonough ought to be in the second drawer. I shoved the top drawer shut and yanked open the second. My fingers tripped along the folders until they hit the jackpot: *McDonough, Arimentha, deceased.*

I jerked the file upward and splayed it out on the desktop. On top was a picture of Arimentha I'd never seen before— her shoulders bare, her lips closed and serene, her eyes staring dreamily toward something in the distance. I leaned closer over it. She was wearing the same earrings she'd worn on New Year's Eve. The same ones that had winked up from her body in the moonlight. I shuddered and flipped the photo facedown on the other side of the file.

Below it were notes written in a neat, slanted hand. These looked like they'd been torn out of Sabatier's little black notebook. My own name jumped out at me, and I slid the note out of the scattered stack.

Coleman, Millie. 17 y.o. Uncooperative. Lying? Covering for her friend? Doesn't trust police.

I laughed. He had that right. I slapped the paper down on Arimentha's photograph and glanced at my wristwatch. It had already been four minutes. With luck, Mama would keep Sabatier busy for another fifteen or even twenty, but that wasn't guaranteed.

I flipped through the rest of the file quickly, checking a couple of envelopes that looked like they might contain the key, but there was nothing. I closed the file, pinched my fingers in the middle, and shook it a little, gently, to see if the heavier key would fall out. But the only thing that drifted down was a scrap of paper with Fitzroy DeCoursey's name on it—and what looked like his home address! I glanced at the still-closed door and stuffed the paper in my pocket.

I opened the file again and bent my head over the desk to look for more notes that could be useful. Underneath newspaper clippings of the stories I'd already read was a glossy photograph of Philip Leveque, looking serious and senatorial. Sabatier had scrawled across the top corner, *Alibi confirmed.* If Sabatier's detecting was to be trusted, that meant Philip was off the table as a murder suspect, though not necessarily as a victim of blackmail. I turned Philip's photograph over so I didn't have to look at his smarmy face anymore and shuffled through notes that said more of the same details I'd already figured out for myself.

Then a note with the name Altobello caught my eye, and I snatched it up.

Canvassed neighborhood with no results until I went
alone into Altobello's Grocery. The owner, Salvatore
Altobello, heard me ask the boy at the register about Mr.
Leslie and volunteered that someone by that name lived
next door in his mother's rooming house. The boy at the
register, who it appears was Mr. Altobello's son, became
distressed. Concerned they would warn the suspect,
I quickly retrieved my partner and knocked at the
rooming house next door.

I already knew what had happened next. So, it was Bennie's
father who'd given away Marion's whereabouts, albeit by accident. That explained why Bennie was so eager to help fetch
Marion's stuff for him after the cops came.

I glanced at my watch again. Eight minutes had passed. I
slid the Altobello note aside and flipped through the others until
another name caught my eye.

Symphony Cornice, age 18, neighbor and close friend of
the deceased. Interviewed at home, both in the company
of her parents and alone. She is adamant, as she was at
the scene of the crime, that Mr. Leslie is the culprit. My
personal feeling is that Miss C is hiding something—
possibly about Miss McD, to protect her friend's reputation
after death? When asked about the diary, she

"Miss Coleman!"

My head jerked up, and there was Sabatier, standing in his
office doorway. Mama was nowhere in sight.

"I—I was—" I promptly forgot all the excuses I'd come up
with.

Sabatier stalked closer, his cheeks flaming red. "What are you doing in my office, Miss Coleman?"

"I was coming to talk to you. See . . . see how the . . . if you had any new leads." I struggled to regain my footing. "See if you were ready to leave my friend alone yet."

Sabatier snatched the file off his desk and took his eyes off me long enough to read the name on it. "And when I wasn't here, you decided you'd get the answers for yourself, is that right?"

I eased around the desk in the direction of the door. "The drawer wasn't locked. I didn't see the harm."

"Miss Coleman," Sabatier said, his voice low and hard. "You think I'm a fool, don't you? You think I didn't see you standing there behind that newspaper?"

My eyes went wide, and I swallowed hard.

"You think I didn't know what Gladys was up to?" He dropped the file and grabbed my arm, stopping me from darting for the door. "You think I haven't seen what she looks like when she lies?"

I cocked my head in surprise. There was hurt in his eyes, but it wasn't fresh and sharp the way it would be if this was a new betrayal. It was an old hurt, and I recognized it. The hurt of being proved right about somebody, when all you wanted them to do was prove you wrong.

"What were you looking for in here, Miss Coleman?" he said. "And why couldn't you just ask me for it?"

I met his eyes and clamped my mouth shut.

"That's what I thought you'd say." The anger drained from his voice, replaced by weariness. His grip tightened on my arm. "Come with me, Miss Coleman. You're under arrest."

CHAPTER

20

THE WOMEN'S SIDE of the jail was sparsely populated on a Tuesday evening, though I had a feeling that would change before the night was over. Sabatier showed me into a dank, brick-walled cell and locked the door on me, then turned on his heel and left without another word.

I was supposed to be at the club in an hour. Tuesdays were slow, but both Duke and Olive were off tonight. They'd be short-handed without me, for sure, and when Cal came to get me—which I could only assume she'd do once my mother told her about this—she'd have to spend whatever they took in tonight bailing me out. Worse than that, the look in her eyes would say, *I told you so* and *What have you dragged me and my club into?*

That's *if* she bailed me out at all. Maybe she'd think this was a valuable lesson that would stop me from going off half-cocked next time I got a harebrained idea. Maybe she'd let me rot in here a few days. Maybe more.

I sat on a bench at the far end from the cell's other occupant, a drunk lady listing forward over her knees, arms swinging loose. The smell in here was something to write home about, and the letters would be long. Besides the charming aroma of the seatless toilet in the corner, I suspected the drunk lady had vomited down her blouse.

I slumped against the rough brick wall, nursing my hatred of cops in general, Sabatier in particular, Mama for not convincing him, and Arimentha for locking the stupid box in the first place. Who would try to steal a teenage girl's diary anyway? Besides me, that is.

By the time Sabatier came back three hours later, I was in a powerful funk. He stopped outside the bars and looked in at me, a pleased expression on his face. I refused to turn my head and acknowledge his arrival.

"Are you ready to have a conversation with me, Miss Coleman?"

I still didn't look at him. Kept my arms crossed over my chest. "I'm ready to eat a salami on rye. Unless you got one, you can go away."

Sabatier chuckled, his earlier anger obviously dissipated. This was the unflappable and smug Sabatier I remembered from the club. "I don't have a sandwich, Miss Coleman, but I do have something else to offer you."

The drunk lady's head lifted. "Did somebody say sandwich?"

"No," I said.

"Oh. Darn." Her head drooped back onto her chest.

"Don't you want to see what I have here, Miss Coleman?" Sabatier pulled something out of his pocket and held it up to the bars. I couldn't resist glancing at it, a wad of navy-blue wool.

"This was found on Arimentha McDonough's balcony last night. Someone broke into her room and dropped this."

He spun the thing carelessly on one finger, and I saw what it was. My school beret.

Shit. I swallowed hard, trying to keep the panic out of my eyes. How had I not noticed I dropped the damn beret?

"And that *someone*," Sabatier said, so close to the bars he was almost whispering, "would be in a whole lot of trouble. Unless he *or she* chose to cooperate with the police. With me. Now, I'll ask you again, Miss Coleman. What were you looking for in my office?"

I stared at him, my throat closing tighter and tighter. My brain spinning and spinning, trying to find a way out of or around this. I couldn't find one.

"A key." I gritted my teeth, gripped the edge of the bench.

Sabatier looked at me eagerly. "And what does it open? The thing you took from Miss McDonough's bedroom perhaps?"

I hesitated. If I told him about the diary, he'd be even more determined to get his hands on it. But maybe that could work in my favor.

"It's a box. With Arimentha's diary in it. At least we think so."

"We?"

"I. Just me. I think there's a diary in it. But I couldn't get it open. I need the key."

"I see." Sabatier's eyes went bright and contemplative. "Where is this box?"

"Somewhere safe."

Sabatier smoothed his mustache with one hand, his gaze unfocused. Thinking. Finally, he met my eyes again. "I have a proposal for you. If I let you out of here, you will go get that box and bring it to me. And after I have it, I'll conveniently lose track of this beret, and we'll pretend this little incident never happened."

"So, I'll have no arrest record? No bail money to get out?"

"That's correct."

I looked him up and down. He definitely had the upper hand; he had me behind bars, for Pete's sake. I could stay in here and martyr myself to keep the diary out of his hands, but then who would be out there trying to find out who really killed Arimentha? Who would be protecting Marion from this blood-hound?

And what if the diary contained information that cleared Marion's name?

The only way I could get that information was to share it with this cop.

I stood and grasped the bars in both hands. "I'll take your deal on one condition."

Sabatier's expression quickly shifted from surprised to wary. "What is it?"

"You let me out of this cell and meet me tomorrow after-noon. I'll bring the box. You'll bring the key. And we'll find out *together* what Minty wrote in that diary."

"Together?"

"Take it or leave it. That's the only way you're getting your hands on that diary." It was a gamble, considering our relative positions, but it was one I had to take.

Sabatier stared into my eyes, searching for signs of a bluff or a trick, and I met his gaze straight on. Didn't fidget, didn't twitch. He could never know with one-hundred-percent cer-tainty that I'd show up with that box, and I could never be sure he wouldn't bring a bunch of uniformed men to toss me back in the clink. But nobody won at poker by playing it safe.

"Okay," he said finally, rubbing a hand over his face. "You got a deal."

———·———

Maybe I should've gone to the club first, since I was supposed to be working, but the only place I could think about going was home to talk to Marion. I needed to check he was okay, to be sure he hadn't done anything drastic like gone and turned himself in to the police to get me out.

No sounds drifted down the stairs from the apartment, and my anxiety grew. But the moment I turned the key in the lock, Marion came barreling at me. He threw his arms around me. "I'm so sorry, Millie. I never should've let you do all this for me. I should've turned myself in to the police right from the beginning. This is all my fault."

"No, it's not," I said, peeling his arms off me. "Unless you killed Arimentha McDonough, in which case—yes, it's all your fault, and I'll never forgive you."

Marion swiped at his eyes with the back of his hand. It was clear he'd been crying.

"Oh, Mar. Geez. I'm okay. Look at me." I did a turn to show him. "Right as rain."

Marion's tears slowed, but his nose wrinkled. "You look all right, but what dead thing followed you home?"

I laughed and started stripping off my cardigan. "Never go to jail, Marion. You'd have to douse yourself in perfume to survive it."

"I might have to douse *you* in perfume."

I held up a warning finger. "Don't you dare."

Marion let out a giggle that bordered on hysteria. "Millie, I was *so* worried." His mouth crumpled again. "When Gladdie came home and told us what happened, I was beside myself!"

Gladdie? Now they had nicknames? I dropped onto Cal's green chair and bent to unbuckle my shoes.

"What exactly did my mother say?" *After she abandoned me to the wolves.*

"She said Sabatier was never fooled for a minute. That he spotted you in the lobby and figured out you two were up to something. He pretended to believe her and went along with it just long enough to give you a chance to incriminate yourself."

"Tricky bastard." I tossed one shoe and then the other over the sofa toward my bedroom. "He's too smart for Mama anyway."

Marion's brows rose. "I'm surprised to hear you say that about a cop."

"You haven't heard the half of it."

I filled Marion in on the notes I'd found before I got caught, the deal Sabatier had proposed, and what I'd had to give up in return. By the end, he'd had to sit down, too, in the midst of a pile of clothes on the sofa. *My* clothes, I finally noticed.

"What have you been doing?" I said.

He tossed a shirt at me. "Fixing all your junky clothes. I had to do something with myself while I waited."

I examined the shirt in the lamplight. He'd neatly repaired a hole under the pocket so that it was almost invisible. "Geez, you're a useful friend to have around."

"I could say the same about you."

"I don't feel so useful right now. I just got thrown in jail and had to give up our advantage to get my ass out of there."

"So," Marion said, his smile fading. His red-rimmed eyes focused on the rug beneath our feet. "Everything Arimentha wrote in that diary . . . all of it will become public knowledge?"

"Not public necessarily. But the cops will know."

"And before you can blink, the papers will, too." Marion buried his face in his hands. "The diary was supposed to *help* me. It wasn't supposed to do . . . this. Everyone . . . everyone will know I was in the asylum."

"No one who matters will care about that, Marion."

"But I do." He swept a hand down his body. "Marion Leslie is an illusion I'm selling up there on that stage. If everyone knows my past, how do I stand up there and pretend I'm glamorous and confident? When I look out there, all I'll see is pity in their eyes."

I touched his jaw and made him look at me. "Marion, the club is your home. It's my home. There's not a single regular at the Cloak who hasn't been thrown out of a home or beaten or ditched by their mother or been heckled on the street or just made to feel ashamed of who they are at some point in their lives. If anyone will understand, it's us. If anyone will know where the true blame lies, it's us."

Marion smiled weakly, his chin trembling.

"But if you really want to," I said slowly, "we still have one other choice. We destroy the box. Burn it. Then no one will ever know what the diary says about anyone."

Marion lowered his hands, and we both turned to look behind us at the box, where it still sat firmly shut on the kitchen table. In the courtyard where Arimentha died, there was a barrel where we could light a fire and turn the thing to ashes in half an hour. My heart panged at the prospect of never satisfying my curiosity about what was inside it, the possibility of never solving the mystery. But I'd do it if he asked me to.

Marion took a deep, shuddery breath. Slowly, he shook his head. "That diary . . . it might be the only way we find this killer. We can't destroy it just because I'm . . . I'm afraid." He swallowed, and then his voice sounded stronger. "The murderer is still out there, and we don't know why they killed her or whether they might do it again to someone else. If we can stop them, we've got to. If only for Minty's sake."

"Are you sure? I don't have to meet Sabatier tomorrow. All he's got is that key, and if we burn the box, we don't need it." I didn't bring up how he also had my beret and would probably throw me back in jail if I didn't show up with that diary.

Marion shook his head more firmly. "No." He squeezed my hand. "You two open the box tomorrow. And when you read it, remember . . ." His voice thickened. His eyes met mine, shining and dark. "Whatever that book says about me, remember you know who I truly am."

An anxious twist spiraled up in my chest like a wisp of smoke. "How could I forget?"

CHAPTER

21

THE NEXT DAY was the feast day of Our Lady of Prompt Succor, the patron saint of New Orleans, which meant sitting through yet another Mass, but also a half day off from school. Sabatier and I had arranged to meet at the K & B drugstore by the St. Charles and Napoleon streetcar stop, the one nearest Ursuline, at fifteen minutes past noon. I wasn't exactly thrilled to be seen in public with a cop, but I couldn't bring him to my apartment with Marion there.

Sabatier showed up looking more like a professor than a cop, in a tweed jacket with patched elbows and a gray porkpie hat.

"What's with you?" I said, gesturing to the getup.

"Day off. And you—" He gestured to my uniform. "This again? You really like navy blue, huh?"

I narrowed my eyes to slits. "This is my school's choice, not mine."

Sabatier sat back on his stool, blinking. "I didn't picture you going to school. You seem too—"

"Mature?"

"Independent," Sabatier said. I was pretty sure that wasn't the word he'd been thinking. I didn't care for the bemused expression on his face, and I wasn't there for chitchat.

"You got the key?"

His smile stiffened. "You got the box?"

It was resting on my lap, and I didn't offer it up. "Let me see the key first."

Sabatier reached into an inside pocket of his jacket and brought out the little brass key, pinched between his thumb and first finger. I made a move to snatch it, and he quickly folded it back inside his fist.

"Miss Coleman," he said warningly.

"Mr. Sabatier. How are we going to do this? You don't trust me, I don't trust you, and both of us have plenty of reasons not to."

Sabatier looked around the drugstore, smoothing his mustache, which I was learning he did when he was thinking. His eyes stopped on the soda jerk behind the counter. "What about him?"

I cocked an eyebrow. "What *about* him?"

"I give him the key. You give him the box. He unlocks it for us and sets the diary right here on the counter between us."

"How do I know you won't grab it and run out the door?"

Sabatier gave me a look that said he judged me more likely to pull a stunt like that. And he was probably right. "We'll *both* of us agree not to do that," he said.

I sighed. This could go round and round all day. Marion had said he was willing to take this chance. So I had to be willing, too. "Fine. I agree."

Sabatier looked pleased. He called the soda jerk over and told him what we wanted. The kid looked skeptical but consented to the job, so long as we ordered something and left a good tip.

"Done," Sabatier said. "I'd like a nectar ice cream soda."

"Me too." I hooked a thumb at Sabatier and grinned. "He's buying."

———·———

The drink was a little too light on the nectar syrup, but I didn't tell that to the soda jerk. He had the box in one hand and the key in the other, Marion's fate in both.

"What's so important in here anyway?" he said, setting the box on top of the ice cream bins. "Your rich granddad's last will and testament?"

"Sure," I said at the same time Sabatier said, "No."

The soda jerk rolled his eyes and twisted the key in that godforsaken lock. He lifted the lid, and I leaned sideways, trying to see around it.

"Huh," he said, clearly unimpressed. He picked up the book and studied it, a thick volume with brown leather covers worn at the corners and not a speck of gold in sight. Not what I'd pictured someone like Arimentha owning.

"Just give it to me," I said eagerly.

"To *us*," Sabatier corrected. "Put it down, please, right here on the counter."

He moved his soda to one side to make room.

The soda jerk did as he was told and retreated, shaking his head, as both Sabatier and I reached for the book.

"May I?" Sabatier said.

I hesitated, took a breath, and let go of the corner I'd managed to grasp.

He flipped open the cover, and we both stared. Someone had chopped out the first several pages with a sharp object, and only jagged edges remained. I ruffled the ends with my fingertips. More than several—the entire first quarter of the book.

"Did you do this?" Sabatier said, his voice rising.

"How? I couldn't even get the box open!"

"Maybe you were lying about that. It wouldn't be the first time."

"If I could get into the box, I wouldn't be here. I wouldn't be sharing it with you at all."

"You would if this was a setup. Maybe this isn't really her diary."

"Are you serious? What would be in it for me to plant a fake diary? Besides, I'm sure her room is chock-full of writing samples you could compare this with."

Sabatier's shoulders dropped a fraction. "That's true."

"Listen," I said. "I never saw this book until thirty seconds ago, same as you. I, for one, want to see what it says, but if you don't believe it's real, then hand it over. I'll be glad to take it home myself."

Sabatier clapped a hand flat on the remaining pages. "No."

"Then let's read it."

Sabatier nodded slowly and moved his hand back to the edge of the book. I dragged my stool closer and finally saw the words all this fuss had been about. The first intact entry was dated only eight months before, when Arimentha was still seventeen. There was no way of knowing how much time the missing pages had covered.

May 14, 1929
Dear Robbie,

Today I learned what really became of you. I came home—weeping, I admit—and in a fit of pique, I cut out every page I wrote in this diary before today and burned them to a sizzle in my bedroom fireplace. I wanted to erase what I'd done, but we both know nothing I ever do will be enough for that. I wish I could write you a letter, beg for your forgiveness, but I don't know your address, or even if you're still alive. So I'm writing you here.

"See?" I said. "She burned them up herself!"

"I see." Sabatier looked at me keenly. "Do you know who this Robbie is?"

It was fairly obvious to me who he was, though he'd never told me himself. I shook my head. "No idea."

Sabatier's brows rose. "Really? Because a friend of Miss McDonough's told me she went to your club that night to see an old friend named Robert Leveque. An old friend who now apparently goes by the alias Marion Leslie."

My mouth dropped open, and I quickly closed it into a scowl. Of course, one of the Uptowners had told him—probably that Symphony Cornice, who'd been more than happy to make Marion the bad guy. I'd stolen the photograph from Minty's purse and hidden the necklace, all to keep the police from finding out how Minty and Marion were connected, but it had been a waste of time. It was foolish of me to assume none of Minty's friends had known or recognized Marion. Of course, they had. Maybe they even hated him for leaving and breaking Minty's heart, because she couldn't have told them why he'd left without exposing him, and herself.

The corners of Sabatier's lips quirked as if he were trying not to smile. "I'm a better detective than you thought, Miss Coleman?"

"No," I said uncleverly. "Do you want to read the rest of this diary or what?"

Sabatier riffled through the pages that remained—a hundred or more, I guessed, with writing on front and back. We'd be here for hours reading if Minty had filled the whole diary with her overly flourished handwriting.

"Why don't we start at the back?" Sabatier said. "See what she's been up to the last couple of months."

If we found information about the murderer in the most recent entries, there would be no need to read the beginning. "Okay. Let's do it."

Sabatier flipped to the last third of the book and opened it flat, so I could see the page, too. We both leaned over the diary.

October 20, 1929
Dear Robbie,

You wouldn't believe what I've got myself into now. You would laugh yourself silly at the irony. I didn't think to begin it myself, but now that it's begun, I'm rather enjoying myself. Do you know how they say when it rains, it pours? I'm finding that is true for kisses, too.

October 24, 1929
Dear Robbie,

My Romeo and Juliette situation continues. To be <u>twice</u>
<u>enthralled</u> is such a delicious distraction from the way I've
been feeling lately—when I am dancing or kissing or lying
skin to skin, I can push away the doubts in my head telling
me my very existence in the world is pointless. That I was
somehow made wrong. How else would I have betrayed a
friend the way I did?

"Romeo and Juliette?" I said. "So she's falling for somebody she's supposed to hate?"

"A political rival of her father's, perhaps. Or she's merely using 'Romeo and Juliette' to refer to romance in a more general way. I wonder if there's a reason she's using this spelling of Juliette? It's usually J-u-l-i-e-t."

I didn't have the foggiest idea how the name was usually spelled, and I doubted it mattered—Minty probably hadn't known either. I tapped the page. "What does 'twice enthralled' mean? Double the . . . *enthrallment?*"

Sabatier smoothed his mustache again. "Maybe she's fallen back in love with someone from her past."

"Hmm." The only boyfriend I knew of from her past was Philip Leveque. It certainly hadn't sounded as if they were back together, but then again, that would've given her a reason to argue with Daphne the night of her murder. Also, a motive for Daphne or Philip to have killed her.

The soda jerk appeared in front of us again and gestured to my empty glass. "You want another nectar ice cream soda?"

"With more nectar this time."

"You, sir?"

Sabatier shook his head and shoved his glass aside, though it was only half drunk. He tugged the diary closer to him, but I smacked a hand on it and shot him a look.

"Don't get greedy, *Laurence.*"

"I wouldn't dream of it."

October 31, 1929
Dear Robbie,

I was lonely tonight, even strutting around in my peacock costume—what a laugh and no one there to laugh at it with me! Remember how we used to call them all peacocks and peahens at these parties—all flash and no brains?

Thinking of it put me in a melancholy mood, and I drank too much and, well . . . one thing and another happened, and before you know it, I'm sneaking home with my underpants wadded in my purse. Again.

Romeo. Juliette. Juliette. Romeo.

I believe I may be a terrible person. I'm sure you would agree. But this bottle of wine I sneaked up to my room <u>disagrees</u>, and the two of us shall soon be great friends!

November 4, 1929
Dear Robbie,

They say in Berlin and Paris all sorts of things go on in the clubs and cabarets. They say people of our age go there and enjoy themselves any way they please, then come home and ever after live the boring lives they've promised their parents. When I picture you, I picture you there.

I've even heard of a place like that here, though I haven't a clue where it is. Maybe I will try to find out.

November 10, 1929
Dear Robbie,

Romeo, Romeo . . . I won't finish that thought because I know exactly where he is and how he looks when he is very satisfied and perhaps I could fall for him if I was a person who still knew how to do that and also had no future to think of. Sorry I'm tipsy and forgot how to use commas. Good night.

November 16, 1929
Dear Robbie,

I don't believe I can be someone else's center of gravity, even a very nice someone's. I don't have enough mass. I feel as if I could float off the earth and disappear, and the moment I did, everyone here would forget me.

Does every relationship lead in this direction? Do kisses stolen on balconies and in broom closets always lead to one party wanting more and more from the other? Do they always lead to doom?

I should stop this, shouldn't I? Stop all of it. I wish I could ask you what to do.

November 26, 1929
Dear Robbie,

It's my birthday. I refused <u>both</u> of my invitations. I stayed in my room and sulked and drank every drop of a bottle of *gin, which is intolerable stuff and, as it turns out, not as good at inducing forgetfulness as I had hoped. I wonder if you remember it's my birthday. I remember yours.*

November 27, 1929
Dear Robbie,

I hope, wherever you are, that you never drink gin.

December 14, 1929
Dear Robbie,

I've been sucked back into the Romeo and Juliette dance. I tried to stop, on all counts, but failed, also on all counts. It is entirely my fault, as it usually is. It's just that my empty bedroom is the loudest place in the world, especially when I look across at the window that used to be yours and know I'm the reason it isn't yours anymore. So, I tiptoe down the hall and whisper into the telephone and find myself some company.

Tonight's result was the drawing tucked between these pages, a gift from Romeo. A sign his feelings are more invested than mine. I shouldn't call him again. I won't.

"Drawing?" I said. "Flip the page and see . . ."

Sabatier flipped the next page, but we saw no drawing, so he picked up the book and shook it gently. A rectangle of paper about the size of my palm floated out and landed on the bar. I snatched it up before Sabatier could.

It was indeed a drawing, in pencil, of a plump bird—a wren maybe? On the back were the words, *To my Little Bird, From your Romeo.*

"Can you get fingerprints off this?" I said.

"Besides *yours*," Sabatier said pointedly, and carefully grasped it by the edges. I let him take it, and he angled it toward the light. He sighed. "No, with this texture of paper, fingerprints would be nearly impossible, unless they're already smudged there in graphite from the artist's hands. But I see no prints like that."

"Maybe we can still find out who he is . . ." I tugged the book closer to me while his hands were busy carefully setting aside the drawing. There were only two dated pages left—we had reached the last entries before Minty's death. I looked at Sabatier.

"Last chance," he said.

I took a deep breath. "Let's see what we got."

December 26, 1929
Dear Robbie,

I called Romeo again. But this really was the last time. I told him about looking for a club like the ones in Berlin, about this faint hope I could find you there. He got the most eager look and said he knew exactly the place I meant. He said I should go with him to the Cloak and Dagger club on New Year's Eve because he had a feeling I'd find you there. I pressed him for more information, but he would tell me nothing, just begged me to go with him. I think it meant something to him, a symbol, an announcement—me and him out in public together, hand in hand on a night when half of New Orleans is out at the speakeasies.

I told Romeo I wouldn't go with him. While he is a beautiful boy, I don't love him or anyone. No Romeo, no Juliette. I can't fall in love while I have so much unfinished business in my heart.

> But that does not mean I won't go. I have plans to make and I feel energized. I hardly dared hope you could still be here in our city, right under my nose, and I swear to God I will find you if I can. I will see you in just a few days. I know it.

December 31, 1929
Dear Robbie,

See you tonight. I hope. I'm wearing your grandmother's necklace Philip gave me, for good luck. I hope she'll lead me to you. Fingers crossed.

Arimentha had written this with such hope, it made my heart ache to read it. Marion had rejected her peace offerings, and then someone had snuffed out her very life.

The girl whose voice lived in these diary pages was gone now. She'd floated away from the earth just as she'd feared she would, but she certainly wasn't forgotten. Marion remembered her, cared about her, whether he wanted to or not. Her father missed her, too, of course.

And me. I'd never forget her now.

But I glanced to my right at Sabatier's solemn face and knew his thoughts were less sentimental. He was staring hard at the words that piled more evidence on top of Marion.

I swallowed hard. I'd made a mistake trading this diary for my freedom. I'd made a mistake trying so carelessly to break into Sabatier's office in the first place. This was my fault.

I tried to keep my voice steady and my hand firmly on the diary. "What now, Detective Sabatier?"

He looked at me carefully, not letting go of the diary either.

"You tell me, Miss Coleman. Do you still believe your friend is innocent?"

"I don't 'believe' it, I know it. You should be focusing on figuring out who this Romeo person is."

"And I will. But there's no sense pretending the facts aren't the facts. It doesn't look good for Mr. Leveque."

"His name is Marion Leslie."

Sabatier inclined his head. "Mr. Leslie then. Witnesses say Miss McDonough came to the club that night to look for him; witnesses say the two argued and he threatened her; witnesses say she came back in the club alone to find him; she was found pushed off a balcony down the hall from his dressing room, during a period of time when no one saw him for twenty minutes. Her necklace, once owned by his grandmother, is the only piece of jewelry missing from her body. And now Miss McDonough says in her own words how eager she was to speak with him that night, and she's even provided a motive for the murder: whatever disagreement the two of them had in the past. I'm afraid your Mr. Leslie looks very guilty."

"But there's this, too." I jabbed a finger at the diary. "She broke up with this guy Romeo the night before the murder. And he'd invited her to go with him to the Cloak—maybe he went anyway, just in case she showed up. Then he saw her with Fitzroy and blew a gasket."

"It's possible. And I will pursue that possibility to its logical conclusion."

"Or maybe Fitzroy was blackmailing her."

Sabatier's brows rose gently. "The diary says nothing about blackmail."

"Then maybe she found out he was trying to blackmail

somebody she knew and the two of them argued about it."

"What makes you so interested in blackmail?"

I wanted to stab my drinking straw through his eye. "What makes you *not* interested? Maybe you should take a closer look at Minty's rich friends. Ask some more questions! They've got secrets, and I for one am going to uncover them all until I find the one that ended in her murder."

"I think you've done quite enough sleuthing, Miss Coleman." He stuck the bird drawing in the diary, shut it, and waggled it at me. "You're too close to the case to see it objectively. I'd advise you to keep your distance from Mr. Leslie; the closer you get to a killer, the more desperate he becomes, and therefore more dangerous. And enough breaking and entering. Leave the rest to the police. I would feel better if you stayed well back from this from now on."

I balled up my fists in my lap. "I just bet you would!"

Sabatier tucked the diary under his arm and plunked a quarter tip on the counter. "Tell your mother no hard feelings, and I'd like a rain check on that coffee."

My mouth dropped open. "What are you doing? We haven't read the beginning. There could be more. You can't just leave!"

"Yes, I can." He tipped his porkpie hat. "Good day, Miss Coleman."

I leaped from my seat and lunged for the diary. I got my fingers on it and it almost slid into my grasp, but Sabatier turned and gave me a stern look.

"Do not force me to return you to jail. Sit on your barstool and wait five minutes. I don't want to see you again tonight."

Then he turned and hurried toward the drugstore en-trance, ducking through a crowd of students. I snatched up the quarter he'd left and considered pinging it off the back of his head. But the soda jerk leaned across the counter and stared at me pointedly.

"I believe that's mine."

"Take it then." I shoved the quarter into his waiting palm and grabbed the now-empty wood box and useless key off the counter.

Then I saw it—the slip of paper facedown on the tile floor, its corner stuck under a kid's shoe. The words *From your Romeo* shone up at me.

The drawing. It must've fallen out when I'd grabbed at the diary. I swooped down, tapped on the kid's leg to get him to lift his foot, then snatched up the drawing.

I didn't have the diary, but I had this. It was something at least. Something to build on.

CHAPTER

22

MARION, BENNIE, AND Olive were all waiting when I
came through the apartment door. It looked like Marion had
moved on to patching Cal's clothes now, because one of her vests
dropped to the floor as he leaped to his feet.

"What are all of you doing here?" I said.

"We wanted to see if you got back all right," Olive said from
Cal's green chair.

"And we want to know what the diary said," Bennie said
with a wink, "after all that work we did to get it."

"You weren't the one thrown in jail over it," I reminded
him, and dropped onto the arm of Olive's chair.

"Did you get your beret back?" Marion said eagerly.

My smirk dropped away. In the fuss over the diary, I'd forgotten to ask about my beret. Before Sabatier let me out of jail,
he said if I handed over the diary, he'd "lose track" of my beret,
but I had no way of knowing if he'd really tossed it out or if he
planned to use it as leverage again.

"I'm sure it's all right," Marion said, correctly interpreting the expression on my face. "If Sabatier wanted to arrest you again, he could've today."

I nodded slowly. That was true, but it didn't ease my anxious feeling much. Sabatier was more slippery than I'd given him credit for.

Olive looked up at me, a crease between her brows. "But you got to read the diary, right?"

"Yeah. Some of it. The important parts." I tried to recapture the swagger I'd had a moment ago. "And I got this. We found it stuck in the diary."

I slipped the drawing of the bird out of my cardigan pocket and moved aside somebody's bowl of sliced apples on the coffee table to give it pride of place. Marion sat down on the sofa, and both he and Bennie leaned forward to look at the drawing.

"It's . . . a bird," Marion said.

"A magnolia warbler," Bennie said. "You can tell by the stripes on the . . ." He trailed off, noticing we were all staring at him.

My brows lifted. "You know birds?"

His cheeks reddened. "Me and my nonna used to bird-watch a little."

"Bennie and his nonna again." Olive snorted.

"Look what's on the back." I flipped it over, and as they all leaned in to read the message from Romeo, Olive's arm rested on my leg in a way that almost restored my mood.

"Whoever drew this was a boyfriend of Minty's?" she said, not retracting her arm.

"Yep." I reached forward and snagged a slice of apple from the bowl. "And she split up with him the day before she died."

Marion held up both hands. "Wait—let me write all this

down while the details are still fresh in your mind." He moved
to Cal's little desk in the corner of the room and rummaged in
the drawer for paper and a sharp pencil. "Okay, go. Don't leave
anything out."

I chomped down on the apple slice and told them every
word I could remember—the ripped-out pages, Minty's lingering melancholy about Marion, then how she'd addressed her
diary entries to him, how she'd been drinking a lot and that
she felt guilty about leading Romeo on when she wasn't capable
of love right now. I found myself avoiding Olive's and Bennie's
faces during that part. I told them Minty had written that she
was coming to the Cloak that night specifically to find Marion,
and because of that, Sabatier was convinced more than ever
that he was the killer.

When I'd finished and Marion's pencil had stopped scratching, he turned around and looked at the three of us, his eyes
tinged with red.

"I wish . . ." He looked up at the ceiling to stop himself from
crying. "If I'd only . . ."

"It isn't your fault," I said. "You're not obligated to forgive
her at all, let alone do it on her timetable. She sprung it on you
at work. How could you know it was your last chance?"

He took a handkerchief out of his pocket and dabbed under
his nose. "But she wouldn't have even been there if it weren't for
me."

"Maybe not." Olive leaned up in her chair to look around
at him. "But someone furious enough to shove a girl off a balcony probably had that anger brewing awhile. It was going to
explode sometime, somewhere. It was just bad luck it happened
at our club."

"Like this Romeo," I said. "If he was homicidal and hopped up on masculine pride, he'd go looking for Minty no matter where she was."

Olive's lips twisted. "This is why I don't date men."

I nudged her with an elbow. "Is that the only reason?"

Marion rolled his eyes, looking somewhat recovered. "One question—Minty wouldn't even go to the club with this Romeo, so why would she go upstairs with him?"

"And," Bennie said, "if she'd hurt his pride so much, why would he even ask her to?"

"Maybe he still hoped she'd change her mind." I grabbed another apple slice and punctuated my words with it. "She mentioned kissing him on a balcony before, so maybe he considered it the perfect place to rekindle their romance."

Olive watched me wave the apple and moved the bowl out of my reach. "And then when she said no thanks—"

"He didn't take it so well." I snatched at the bowl, and we tussled over it for a moment, laughing, until I let her win.

"How sure are we this Romeo is our murderer?" Marion said, still all business, flipping through the motley collection of paper he'd written my account on.

I coughed and tried to focus on the case instead of the cuteness of Olive's triumphant little grin. "I think he's a solid bet. But I'm still not ruling out Fitzroy."

Marion frowned down at the papers. "The diary didn't say anything about blackmail, did it? Or did I miss it?"

"No." My cheeks flushed with a sudden wave of either embarrassment or annoyance or both. I didn't want to admit it, but Sabatier had shaken my assumption that I could do this as well as the cops. It didn't help that he'd one-upped me with the beret.

"Did you mention your pet theory about Fitzroy to Sabatier?" Olive said, bumping me with her shoulder.

"He didn't want to talk about it, big surprise. He thinks he's already found his killer."

"But we know he's wrong about that," Bennie said. "He could be wrong about Fitzroy, too."

"I got Fitzroy's address from Sabatier's office," I said eagerly, sitting up straighter. "I could go talk to him."

"I think you should," Bennie said, scooting forward on the sofa. "I could come with you if—"

"Wait," Olive said. "Don't you think Romeo is the bigger lead right now?"

"I agree," Marion said. "Maybe we should try to find him first. Then see about Fitzroy."

I folded my arms, trying to decide what I wanted to say next and if it was worth arguing over. I was intrigued by Romeo, too, and I had to admit he seemed the most likely candidate for murder. Spurned ex-lovers often featured prominently in the detective novels Marion and I traded back and forth.

Olive picked up the bird drawing from the coffee table and studied both sides of it. "We know Romeo likes to draw, has decently neat handwriting, and knows the alphabet. Doesn't tell us much. Do we know where she met him?"

I shook my head. "But she sneaked off with him at least once after a rich-people's Halloween party. All we know is it was someone she wanted to keep secret."

"Could be a guy from the wrong side of Canal Street," Marion said. He flipped back a page in his notes and read from them. "She said she might love him if she wasn't worried about her future."

"Or maybe he's a friend's boyfriend?" Bennie said. "Maybe that's what she and Daphne really argued about that night."

"Or he's some creepy old married guy," I said. "Like that guy that used to come in the club. Remember, Mar? He always asked the Red Feathers if they liked to be tickled."

Marion's mouth curled into a moue of delicate disgust.

"You know," Olive said thoughtfully, "that friend of hers draws."

I straightened up on the arm of the chair. "Who? Fitzroy? Rosenthal? Claude Holiday?"

"No, no, Symphony. She was drawing on a scrap of paper at the table that night."

I vaguely remembered seeing one of the girls doodling during Marion's show, but at the time it hadn't seemed important.

"Did you see what she was drawing?"

"Marion. Onstage." She shrugged. "It was one of those weird modern portraits, but she kept glancing up at him as she drew, like artists do."

I rubbed my chin. "But what does it matter? Symphony can't be Romeo; Minty specifically referred to him as a he."

"Maybe that was code, too, like the name," Bennie said, leaning forward, his knee jiggling. "If she was having an affair with a girl, she could write 'he' to disguise the fact she was really seeing a 'she.'"

"That would explain why she was keeping Romeo a secret," I said. "But Duke said she didn't seem interested in the women who tried to pick her up at the club. And Kitty Sharpe never caught wind of her having an affair with a woman. Marion, did you ever notice hints she liked the ladies when you were friends?"

"No . . ." Marion twirled a curl around his finger the way he did when he was thinking. "But at the time, she mostly had a crush on me."

"I still think Romeo is a boy," Olive said. "She had this box locked and hidden under her floor, so why bother with changing Romeo's gender?"

"Then she wouldn't need the code name either," Bennie pointed out.

Olive rolled her eyes. "It sounds to me like she was doing all this 'Romeo and Juliette' code stuff for fun. She'd be in plenty of trouble if her father read this, names or no."

"But what if —" Bennie started.

"It doesn't matter right now," I said, getting to my feet. "We don't have to agree about the details, because we all know the next step is to interview Symphony Cornice again." I plucked the drawing from Olive's hand and waved it. "Either to find out if she drew this or to find out if she knows who did."

Marion and Olive nodded, but Bennie rubbed his jaw and frowned. "Remember how uncooperative Symphony was at the Roosevelt? Do you think she'd really agree to meet you again?"

"Meet *me*? No way." I grinned. "But she might just meet Kitty Sharpe."

—·—

I recruited my mother to call Symphony Cornice. Despite how she'd failed in our last escapade, I couldn't really blame her for it now that I'd cooled off. We'd both underestimated the detective. And the fact remained—when I considered all the women I knew, Gladys Coleman was the best liar by far, besides myself.

I couldn't call Symphony, in case she recognized my voice, so Gladys was it.

I hovered behind her as she used the telephone in the hall, the city directory flopped open in front of her. Mama put on a saccharine voice as she asked for Symphony. When I heard Symphony's voice respond a few moments later, I took a step forward but then stopped; I wanted to hear what Symphony said, but I somehow couldn't bring myself to squeeze right up next to Mama to listen.

Mama smiled into the phone. "Hellooo, Miss Cornice," she cooed. "This is Kitty Sharpe with the *New Orleans Item* society page?"

Even from a few feet away, I heard Symphony's tone go icy. I remembered her mother was one of the ones who'd complained to Kitty's editor.

"Ah yes, you've heard of me," Mama said. "I'm writing a profile of your dear departed friend Miss Arimentha Mc-Donough. A portrait of sorts, and I believe the clearest picture of her would come from her best friend."

Mama nodded along with whatever Symphony was saying.

"Yes, dear, but those other stories covered the bare facts of the case. I want to know who Miss McDonough *really* was. Her hopes, her dreams for the future. I want to know what the world has lost in her passing."

I took a step closer but could only catch incoherent sounds.

"I understand, I don't mean *now*, darling, of course. I mean at your convenience. I can stop by your house."

Mama kept a fake grin pasted on her face even though her audience couldn't see it. "Yes, well, I normally don't meet with the sources of my articles. I normally insist upon maintaining absolute anonymity. But in this case, with the sensitive nature of the subject, I decided to make an exception, just for you, to preserve your comfort."

Mama was silent for a long moment. I heard nothing from the other end of the phone either. Then Symphony said something, and my mother smiled.

"Fantastic, thank you so much for accommodating me, Miss Cornice. How is four o'clock tomorrow afternoon? . . . Excellent. I will see you then."

Mama hung the receiver back on the hook, looking pleased with herself.

"See? Nothing to it."

I grinned at her, then stopped myself. It was the least she could do, that was all.

Her smile faded. And I turned away to hide the unwelcome pang of guilt welling up inside me.

CHAPTER

23

COLISEUM STREET, WHERE Symphony Cornice lived and Arimentha used to, was lined with houses big enough to fit four of the Cloak and Dagger. Each garden could cover at least a block in the French Quarter, and the air was scented with camellias and wet leaves, not garbage or factory smoke or, for that matter, roasted pecans or marinara sauce or fresh beignets. Standing on that street felt like wearing a scratchy wool jacket one size too small. You couldn't throw a punch in a jacket like that. You couldn't breathe on a street like this.

Just the other night I'd been here with Marion and Bennie, breaking into Minty's house. My heart raced at the memory of her father's voice and our frantic retreat, and I tried to slow it back down as I stopped outside 3008 Coliseum and looked up, up, up at the house where Symphony lived. It was a huge blocky building with clapboards painted the color of fresh butter and surrounded by palms tall enough to brush against its eaves. There must have been enough rooms in there for an army, but the real Kitty Sharpe had informed me that Symphony, like Minty, was an only child.

A housekeeper answered my knock on the front door and showed me inside a foyer gleaming with polished wood and glass, golden from the light that streamed in from tall, westward-facing windows. It smelled golden in there, too, if that were possible, like lemons and honey.

The entryway of my building smelled like damp plaster and our neighbor's cigar smoke. I adjusted my cardigan, hoping the housekeeper didn't notice the place on the elbow where Marion had sewn up a hole.

She showed me into a room with way too many rugs and chairs and delicate tables covered in shiny doodads. I was told to have a seat and Miss Cornice would be with me in a moment, but I didn't feel like sitting. I lifted the lid of a crystal dish on a marble-topped table as soon as the housekeeper had left the room, hoping for a butterscotch candy, but there was nothing inside. What was the point of a bowl that held nothing?

"Miss . . . Sharpe?"

I jerked my hand back, letting the lid clatter back onto the dish, and turned slowly, delaying the moment when Symphony would realize who I was. But she'd figured it out long before my eyes met hers—that much was obvious from the furious expression on her face.

She picked up a bell from another little table at her elbow, but I lunged at her and closed both my hands over hers.

"Don't . . . please."

Symphony stared down at our hands in shock and disgust. She tried to wrench hers away, but I held tight. "How dare you? Let me go!" Her eyes narrowed. "Miss Sharpe was never coming here, was she? Who did I speak with on the phone? Another of your low-class friends?"

"Something like that. I need to talk to you."

She glared down her nose at me. "Tell me one reason I shouldn't call for the housekeeper and have you thrown out this instant?"

"Because I found something in Minty's diary. About you." It wasn't necessarily a lie. Minty hadn't mentioned her by name, but she could've mentioned her in code.

The tension went out of Symphony's arms, and I took the risk of letting go of her hands. She set down the brass bell. Her face looked as stunned as if I'd slapped her. "Her diary? But how did you—"

"Sit down and talk to me. Please."

Symphony hesitated. She glanced over her shoulder into the hallway and then pulled the pocket doors shut behind her. We were alone in the oversize room, and no one could hear us. What if Symphony was the killer?

She took an armchair in front of a warm, crackling fireplace and gestured toward a matching one across from it. She seemed to have recovered her composure as she looked at me with her customary shrewdness, taking in every speck of my uniform from my secondhand shoes to my borrowed beret.

"I wasn't aware you went to Ursuline, Miss Coleman." A chilly smile lifted the corner of her lips. "I'm surprised you can afford it."

Of course, she recognized the uniform. She probably knew some of my awful classmates. I chose to ignore her comment and looked around the room for any sign of art she might have done. There was a painting of a white crane at the edge of a pond over the mantel. "Did you paint that?"

Symphony looked taken aback. "No. What does this have to do with Minty?"

"It has to do with what I found." I slipped the drawing out of my pocket. "It was stuck between the pages of her diary. We—I hoped you might know something about who drew it."

She held out a hand for it. "May I?"

I hesitated. It was our only copy. What if she ripped it to shreds or tossed it on the fire?

"Be careful with it," I said as I released it into her hand, bracing myself to leap forward and snatch it back if she made a move to destroy it.

But Symphony brought it closer to her face, her fingers tracing just above the penciled lines. Unprompted, she turned the paper over and read the message on the back. Her mouth opened and then pinched tightly shut.

"Did you give that to Minty?" I said quietly, afraid to startle her while she held the drawing.

She looked up at me, her mouth curling in a sneer. "You think *I'm* this Romeo?"

"I think anyone can be a Romeo," I said evenly.

Her eyes roamed over me coldly again. "Not everyone is like you, Miss Coleman."

"I have no doubt of that, Miss Cornice." I struggled to keep the bite out of my voice. "But Minty said in her diary she was keeping this Romeo a secret, and there had to be a reason she'd go to so much trouble."

Symphony pressed her lips together, her eyes darkening to a deeper green. "I did not draw this."

I couldn't tell if she was lying, but I decided to play along. "Then who did? Do you recognize the style?"

Symphony surprised me with a harsh laugh. "There's no style at all. Unless you count 'amateur hour' as a style."

"What do you mean?"

She rolled her eyes. "See here? The way the lines are thick and clumsy? It's because the 'artist' was using a basic Number 2 pencil like the kind you'd use in school, and they don't know how to use even that properly. A trained artist would have an arsenal of skills and tools at his or her disposal."

"Or they just drew it on the fly with the materials available. Like you did in our club that night."

Symphony stared at me appraisingly, but I detected underneath the calm veneer that she was surprised again. She thrust the drawing back at me, went to a spindly-legged desk in the corner, and opened a drawer. When she returned, she was clutching a small piece of paper. She hesitated one moment, just as I'd done, and then handed it over to me. Now it was my turn to be astonished; it was the drawing Olive and I had seen her sketching on New Year's Eve. Marion, in profile, from the waist up. It was stark and unfinished, but it was good—like I was looking at a living, breathing him on the page.

"I drew this that night," Symphony said, with a hint of pride. "Tell me you can't tell the difference between these two drawings."

I was no art expert, but with the drawings side by side, they did seem very different. The bird was all tentative softness, while the portrait of Marion was made of sharp, bold strokes. I looked up at Symphony.

"Let's say I believe you." I passed the drawing of Marion

back to her, and she avoided touching my fingers as she accepted it. "Surely, Minty told you something about this Romeo person. No one's *that* good at keeping secrets."

"You'd be surprised."

"Then maybe you saw her sneaking off with someone?"

Symphony massaged her temple with one hand as if I were giving her a headache. "No. Never."

"Listen." I tried to keep my voice calm and hide my rising frustration. "I know you don't want to tell your friend's secrets. But she isn't alive to care anymore, and telling them might lead me to her killer. Don't you want to find that person? Don't you want Minty to get some justice?"

Symphony was silent a long moment, her face half hidden by her hand, so I couldn't read her expression. "She didn't . . ." Her voice came out pinched and rough. "Didn't tell me who he was. I asked, but she just laughed. Said he was no one important."

"But she definitely said 'he'?"

Symphony's other hand curled tightly around the arm of her chair. "Yes, I think—I don't know. I don't remember her exact words."

"Do you know why she was keeping him a secret?" I said quietly, trying not to scare Symphony into clamming up again.

"Why did Minty do anything?" Her voice rose and cracked. Her eyes met mine again, bright with unshed tears. "Did you know we were supposed to go to college together at Maryville in the fall? I have a gentleman friend there in St. Louis, and his mother was going to give Minty and me both a room to stay. But Minty fell behind in school and kept disappearing off to the

Vieux Carré. When I called her house, she was often gone and hadn't told anyone where."

"Do you think anyone else could've known about her romance?"

Symphony stiffened again. "If I didn't know, who else would?"

I sat back and met her gaze steadily. "Maybe someone who was looking for dirt on her. Someone with a reputation for blackmail."

Her brows rose. "You mean Fitzroy DeCoursey."

"Everyone seems to know him, and nobody seems to like him," I said, conjuring Kitty Sharpe's words. "How many of you Uptowners has he pulled his tricks on?"

Symphony's voice went hard. "I wouldn't know."

I studied her face for a long moment. The ice in her eyes could've chilled a roomful of drinks. "Did he ever try any of that stuff on you, Miss Cornice?"

"I have nothing to hide, Miss Coleman."

"Funny, that's the same thing Philip Leveque said when I asked him that question."

I stood and tucked the bird drawing away inside my bag. I smiled. "And *he* sounded like he was lying, too."

———·———

At the streetcar stop down the block from Symphony's house, I took out the scrap of paper I'd stolen from Detective Sabatier's office. I'd done things Marion's and Olive's way first, but now it was time for my way. The street Fitzroy DeCoursey lived on was about midway between Symphony's stop and mine, with a short walk beyond St. Charles Street on foot. I had plenty of time left before dark.

The cottages in Fitzroy's neighborhood were not as large or fine as the mansions in the Garden District, but they were pretty and freshly painted, with fences dividing small, neat lawns. I found the house with his number easily enough and hesitated only a moment before opening the little gate and mounting the steps onto the wide porch. The black mailbox hanging on the wall beside the front door was painted with the address 1660 Erato in white, below a name—Delacroix.

I frowned and checked the scrap of paper with the address again. This was the right place. I glanced around to see if anyone was watching and opened the lid of the mailbox. There were letters inside, and I slid them out and read the names. Mrs. Georges Delacroix was on two of them, and Mr. Roy Delacroix was printed on the third.

The front door creaked open, and there stood Fitzroy, managing to look perfectly put together even in a plain undershirt and trousers.

"I hear tampering with the mail is a federal offense," he said lightly, but his blue eyes were like stone.

I held the letters out to him and kept my gaze fastened on his. "I hear blackmail carries a hefty sentence, too."

Fitzroy let the letters hang there between us for a solid three seconds before he snatched them and tossed them on the floor inside the house.

"I know who you are," he said. "What are you doing here?"

The cadence of his voice was so different from what I'd heard him use at the Cloak. It sounded harder, older. Was he even really our age? Was Fitzroy even his name?

"I'm here to talk to you, *Roy*," I tried.

He didn't even flinch. "Yeah, that's my name. You want a cookie for figuring it out?"

"No thanks. But I'd like some answers."

Roy sneered, an expression that was far less attractive than his smile. "Why would I tell you anything?"

"Because I know what you've been doing, Roy. I know how you've been keeping up with those rich kids."

"So?"

"So, I don't care about that. You can take them for every dime for all I care."

Roy snorted, but his eyes showed a flicker of interest. I took a step closer, though it was the opposite of what I wanted to do, and lowered my voice. "All I care about is what happened that night on that balcony. Were you there with Arimentha when she died?"

Roy's expression changed to one of amusement. "It's cute you think I'd tell you if I was."

I smiled. "It's cute you think I won't tell the police what you've been up to. I've become very close with Detective Sabatier. I'm sure he'd be interested to know about your little escapades with other people's money."

Roy smiled back, looking vile even with one hundred watts of beauty shining out of his face. "First you'd have to persuade the rich folks to tell the cops about it. And then they'd have to admit all the scandalous things they've been up to. Somehow, I don't think they will."

He was too smooth, too venomous. I tried to change tack.

"What scandalous things did Arimentha McDonough get up to? I know you were watching her."

"You don't know anything."

"I do," I lied. "I know about Jerome Rosenthal, too. And Philip Leveque. And Symphony Cornice."

His brows raised, but he still looked bored.

"And Minty McDonough," I said. "I know you were looking for a way to blackmail her. And maybe you found it. Maybe you tried to spring the trap on her the night she died, and it backfired on you. She ended up dead."

"That's not what happened."

"Did you talk her into going up on that balcony? You're a smooth talker when you want to be, aren't you? And then what happened? She wouldn't give in and pay you the money to keep her secrets quiet?"

"No. That isn't—I didn't even know that place had a balcony."

"But you did find out some of her secrets, didn't you?"

"Not anything worth using."

"I told you I'm not interested in your petty crimes. What I need to know is what you found out about Arimentha. Where did she go? Who was she seeing?"

Roy glanced toward an older neighbor across the street who'd come out into her yard and was pretending to water her flowers, all while watching us intently. He rubbed his palm against the back of his neck and turned his hard gaze back at me. "Look, kid," he said in a lower voice, barely moving his lips. "I need you to get out of here."

"Why? Afraid your sweet old neighbor will find out you're a

criminal?" I raised my voice a little louder. "A murderer?"

"I'm not a murderer," he said through gritted teeth, glancing now at another neighbor who'd appeared. The two neighbors were chatting over their fence, both looking our way.

"But you did spy on Minty, right?" I said, drawing his attention back. "You did find some dirt on her?"

Roy hesitated a long moment, so long I lost patience.

"Tell me what you found, and I'll go right now, before your granny gets home and finds out what kind of boy she's raised."

The granny thing was a wild guess, but I could see its arrow hit home.

"I . . . I didn't find much, okay?" Roy sighed and flexed his hands like he'd like to throttle me. "And I didn't talk to her about it that night, or any night, because I hadn't found enough yet."

"What a shame. Now she's dead, and all your hard work is wasted."

"Hey!" he said sharply. "Don't talk about her like that. She was an all right kid. Just too rich for her own good. All of them are."

That I could agree with. But I'd found his weak spot and decided to dig in the knife.

"You're not all bad either, are you, Roy? Greedy, selfish, unprincipled, but not all bad, right?"

He crossed his arms over his muscled chest. "So?"

"So, tell me what you found out about Minty. Tell me and maybe you can do something good for once. You can help me catch her killer."

Roy glanced again at the neighbors, then at his grandmother's tidy bed of purple pansies and vivid pink dianthus along the fence. He ran a hand along his chiseled jaw and didn't look at me as he spoke.

"All I know is she'd been meeting up with somebody, but I don't know who."

"Where?" I said, anticipation percolating through my whole body.

Roy sighed heavily. "A speakeasy on the far side of the Quarter. A place called the Pelican."

CHAPTER

24

I'D BE LYING if I said Roy hadn't surprised me. I left his door-step as I'd promised, but on the way home I contemplated what he'd told me. The Pelican was a dive like ours, but its owners were black and so, mostly, were its customers. Minty would've stuck out like a sore thumb there, but that was good news—someone at the Pelican was likely to remember her and who she was meeting.

I was still mulling the possibilities when I finally walked into the apartment and found Marion climbing into our bedroom window, his feet bare and pale with cold. Cal stood by the door, casually fastening the buttons on her shirt cuffs, but there were pink spots high on her cheeks, the kind that only appeared when she was furious. Mama hovered by the radio, fiddling distract-edly with the knobs and looking flushed.

"Did something happen in here?" I said, and they all looked up at me.

"Cops," Cal said curtly.

"Detective Sabatier paid us a visit," Mama elaborated.

"What? How did he find us?"

A wide-eyed Marion came out of the bedroom, brushing a streak of rust off his sleeve.

"He found some ancient tax record that showed my address," Cal said. "I bribed a clerk a long time ago to get rid of everything, but *apparently* they missed one."

"But Sabatier didn't see Marion, right? How—" I closed the door behind me and waved a hand toward the open window.

Cal grimaced. "Gladys kept the cop busy while I sent Marion up the fire escape to the roof."

I looked at Marion, and he tried to hang a falsely modest expression over his terrified one.

"You're climbing out an awful lot of windows lately," I said, trying to make him smile. "Maybe if singing doesn't work out, you could be an acrobat."

Marion stuck his cold feet under a blanket on the sofa and made a face. "Maybe if being a smartass doesn't work out, you could be a jackass."

I stuck out my tongue. "Too late."

"*Anyway*," Cal said, sitting down to put on her shoes, "I think Marion could've danced the tango right in front of that cop's nose, and he wouldn't have noticed. All he did was look at Gladys."

"That's not true," Mama said, swatting at the air toward Cal, but she bit her bottom lip and her eyes twinkled. "He's an old friend is all."

"Right," I said, slicing coldly across their good humor. "Even murder is less important than Gladys Coleman."

"How did it go with Symphony?" Marion jumped in.

I rolled my eyes and flopped across the sofa next to him.

"She was a snob as usual. But she showed me the drawing she did of you that night at the club, Mar. It was really different from the bird one, and I got to admit it was pretty good. I should've stolen it to bring you."

"I think you've done enough stealing," Cal said, moving to the table behind the sofa and stuffing her keys in her trousers pocket.

"What about Romeo?" Marion said. "Did you get any more leads?"

"Just one. But I didn't get it from Symphony."

Marion frowned in confusion. "What do you mean?"

"I found Fitzroy DeCoursey. And it turns out you were right—it *is* a fake name."

"Knew it!" Despite his surprise, Marion managed to look smug. "Let me guess—his real name is Bob Jones."

I laughed and elbowed his side. "Roy Delacroix. It *rhymes*."

Cal rolled her eyes and slapped us both on the back of our heads. "Who cares what his name is? What's the *lead*?"

I ducked out of her reach and made myself settle down. "I found out where Minty had been meeting her Romeo—the Pelican Club."

Cal looked as surprised as I'd been when Roy told me. "Hard to picture a deb like her there."

"Hard to picture her at our club, too," I said, "but she was there."

"Maybe she went to the Pelican because she didn't want anyone she knew to see her," Mama said, taking the chair Cal had been sitting in. "If I met up with some guy I wanted to keep secret, I'd go to a place my friends didn't know about."

"Or she was seeing one of the patrons there," I said.

"Dating a black man certainly would've scandalized the Uptowners," Marion said. "They get upset if somebody wears the wrong color to a debutante ball."

"Whoever it was, we need to go to the Pelican and try to find out," I said. "You know anyone there, Cal?"

"Not well enough to do you any good." She jingled the keys in her pocket. "They're not going to be real welcoming to someone throwing around accusations."

"Then what do you recommend?" I said.

"Olive has mentioned going to the Pelican before," Marion said, sitting up straighter. "She told me and Lewis she has a friend who plays in the band there. You could ask her to go with you and make introductions."

"Good idea. Come ask her," Cal said. "I gotta be at the Cloak in five. And"—she gave me a pointed look—"so do you."

I'd missed a lot of work lately, and I was about to have to ask for another day off to go to the Pelican. I'd have to earn it.

I shoved myself up off the sofa but stopped and touched Marion's shoulder. "You going to be all right here tonight after that close call?"

"Of course." He faked a grin. "I'll keep one hand on the emergency bell."

I smiled back in a way I hoped was reassuring. "We'll be listening."

—·—

"Your friend will help me out, won't he?"

Olive kept stacking clean glasses under the bar. "I doubt it. He doesn't know you."

"But you could introduce me?" I propped my elbows on the bar and tried to look appealing.

Olive cocked an eyebrow at me. "If someone came in here and said, 'My friend needs to know something about one of your customers,' would you just roll over and give them all the information they wanted to know?"

Of course, I wouldn't. "But this is different. It's important."

Olive leaned on the bar, face-to-face with me. As she moved, a waft of jasmine scent floated toward me. Why did she have to smell so good? It was terribly distracting. A smile tickled the corner of her mouth, like she could read the thought in my eyes. I straightened and whirled around on my barstool.

"If you want me to take you out to the Pelican," she said behind me, "you could just say so."

I stopped the barstool and faced her again. She looked so smug I almost wanted to tell her never mind, I'll go on my own. But the prospect of a whole evening with Olive, with no dirty glasses or washrags or customers between us, didn't sound so bad. An image of her bare legs from the other night popped into my head, and I wondered suddenly what she would wear. At our club, she wore calf-length dresses buttoned up high to discourage grabby customers. But if we were out on the town . . .

I folded my arms across my chest. "Take me out to the Pelican tomorrow night. Please."

She looked at me slyly, as if she had to consider it, as if she hadn't just suggested I ask her. "What about work?"

"Aunt Cal will let you off."

Olive looked skeptical. "You ask her then."

"I will. Right now." I pushed myself off the barstool and

made to leave, but Olive reached out across the bar and laid her hand on mine.

"Millie."

Her eyes met mine, and I had to swallow to find my voice. "Yeah?"

Her smile spread like molasses. "I can't wait."

———

"Hold still! I'm trying—to—" Marion lunged at me with a hairpin, and I dodged.

"Go chase yourself! You're hurting me!"

"I'm improving you."

I rolled my eyes. "Improvement is in the eye of the beholder. I bet Olive isn't doing all this."

"I bet she is," Marion said. "And I'm not letting you show up to the Pelican looking like you just jumped off a boxcar."

"She hasn't changed a bit," Mama said, handing Marion another hairpin, which he jabbed at me, too. "Hated having her hair brushed as a little girl. Always went around with it sticking up every which way."

Marion laughed, but I glared at them both in the mirror. How dare Mama talk about when I was a little girl? How dare she act as if she'd never stopped being my mother?

Marion noticed the shift in my mood from cranky to volcanic and said, "Gladys, would you be a lamb and fetch me that little enamel box of bobby pins? I think I left it in the bathroom."

She glanced from his face to mine and didn't protest. "Sure, doll. Be right back."

I heard the front door click open and Mama's heels tapping down the hall to the bathroom.

Marion gave me a stern look in the mirror. "She's trying, Millie."

He guided a brush through the curls he'd created in my hair, softening them into waves. I was pretty sure they'd be stick straight again in half an hour, so all of this was a waste of time.

"She's not trying that hard. You only care because you're sick of hearing us bicker."

Marion's mouth tightened, but he didn't deny it. The tap-tap-tapping of Mama's feet returned.

"Found it!" she said brightly, avoiding my eyes as she set down the little box on the dresser.

I shoved back the stool and stood up, knocking Marion off balance. "You've curled and shellacked me all I can take. Can't I go now?"

Marion's hand gripped my shoulder like he was afraid I would bolt. "You don't even have the dress on yet."

"Oh, for Pete's sake." But I grudgingly let him and Mama help me into a pair of Mama's heeled T-straps that were a bit too pinchy in the toes and Marion's delicate silver-spangled dress, which we'd smuggled out of the Cloak. It skimmed close over my hips and floated around my calves. Rows of silver beads lined a deep V cut in the back.

"Cal! Come look at this!" Mama called, and Cal popped her head into the bedroom.

"Hot damn!" she said. "Who knew our Millie had legs for days?"

"Anybody with eyes, that's who." Marion beamed and nudged me with an elbow, but I wanted exactly none of their compliments.

"I feel half naked in this chandelier. You sure I can't just wear—"

"No," Marion said.

"Hell no," Mama said.

"I have an idea," Cal said, and disappeared into the living room. She reappeared moments later holding her black tuxedo jacket. "Try this."

She helped me shrug into the jacket. I turned to the full-length mirror on the door of the armoire, and for the first time since Marion had started dolling me up, I liked the reflection shining back at me. The silver dress and the V of skin at my collarbone peeked out from between the lapels of the jacket, and the strings of tiny beads swished below it. I imagined Olive's eyes on me in this outfit, and I wasn't displeased.

"I see you smiling," Marion said, nudging my hip with his.

"I'm not smiling," I lied. "I'm leaving."

I grabbed Marion's absurdly tiny silver handbag and lurched out of the bedroom in my impractical heels.

"Wait! You need earrings!" he said, chasing after me with bits of shine in his hands, but I didn't stop. I stuffed my switchblade in the pocket of Cal's tuxedo jacket and ran for it.

"Don't do anything I wouldn't do!" Mama said, leaning out of the apartment door.

"Don't do anything she *would* do!" Cal called. "And don't get that jacket dirty!"

—·—

Olive waited under the streetlamp outside the Pelican. Even in the harsh light, she was beautiful in a gold dress that contrasted with the burnished brown skin of her shoulders. Instantly, my earlier confidence drained away, and I felt too tall, gangly, ridiculous in this outfit.

My steps slowed, and I swallowed hard. I reminded myself the point of this date was to get information about Arimentha McDonough's romantic escapades. It didn't matter what I looked like, so long as I got into the Pelican and got the details I needed.

Olive turned, and the moment she spotted me, her mouth popped open in a pretty O. Her lips were painted a deep berry red, almost black in the light of the streetlamp.

"I hardly recognize you, Millie. You look so . . ."

"Uncomfortable?" I tried to smile. "Blame Marion. I do."

Olive laughed gently. "I just never dreamed I'd see you dolled up like this."

I wrapped Cal's tuxedo jacket tighter over the sparkly dress. "Is it such a bad thing to take a night off from being Millie Coleman?"

Olive grinned and offered me her arm. "I happen to like Millie Coleman."

Warmth rushed up from my belly, and I bit my lip to stop the smile creeping across my face. *I happen to like Millie Coleman.* I locked that one away in my memory to savor again later.

Olive led me into a walled courtyard off Esplanade and knocked five times in quick succession on a side door. The door was half hidden behind a giant camellia bush studded with hot-pink blooms, and the ground under our feet was littered with petals, their sweet scent wafting up with every step we took. It reminded me of the night we broke into Arimentha's house, and my blood sped even faster in my veins. I had to keep my mind focused on why I was here. Not on how Olive smelled or the way her hand was so warm in the crook of my arm, even through the tuxedo jacket.

The door opened inward a crack. The bouncer's broad face appeared and looked us up and down.

"Who's this?" he said to Olive.

"A friend."

He snorted and gestured to me. "Since when you friends with girls like her?"

Olive set her hands on her hips. "Since I felt like it. You the cops now?"

I stepped forward. "I know you let in white girls sometimes. In fact, that's why—"

Olive jabbed me in the ribs to shut me up. "Just let us in. She won't make trouble."

The bouncer looked me over with disdain again. "Looks like she's walking trouble."

Olive cracked a smile. "You're not wrong. But I got her. I promise."

The bouncer hesitated, then finally swung the door wider and stepped aside. "You better."

"Ready?" Olive said to me.

I grinned. "As I'll ever be."

We followed a narrow corridor and emerged into the din of the Pelican. Compared with the Cloak, it was like a kitchen instead of a train station—hotter, dimmer, and smaller but every bit as loud. Some of the customers turned to look at us, but most kept to their own business.

"Let's get a table," Olive said. "We can sit and watch everything for a bit."

I nodded, still feeling unsteady, out of my usual element.

Maybe it was the shoes, or the fact that I was the only white person in the room. I was happy to let Olive be in charge for a bit while I got my bearings back. She picked out a table with two chairs near the band.

"Which one's your friend?" I said.

"There. His name's Boots." Olive pointed to the guy playing the upright bass. He wore a gray fedora and a white shirt with the sleeves rolled up. Sweat shone on his forehead as he concentrated on making his bass thunk out a rhythm.

"He's good."

Olive crossed one leg over the other and kicked her foot in time with the music. "I know."

A waitress came to our table. "Hey, Ollie," she said, friendly enough, but her eyes slid warily over to me. "What do you and your friend here want?"

"Just bring us a couple of Coca-Colas," Olive said. The waitress raised her brows but left without comment.

"When that waitress comes back, you should ask her if she's seen Minty."

"Or you should." Olive slid a glance at me. "She won't bite."

I felt heat creeping into my cheeks and hoped she couldn't see me blushing in the darkened, smoky club. When the waitress returned with our two Coca-Colas in glasses, I shot a look at Olive and said, "You ever seen a blonde girl in here? About my age but rich looking?"

The waitress's brows lowered, eyes narrowed in distrust. "We don't get a lot of blonde folks in here."

"Maybe you'll remember her then. I've been told she came here at least a couple of times in the past month or so."

"I don't try to remember the folks who come in here."

I could respect that. It was our policy at the Cloak, too. But I couldn't let it rest. I had a murder to solve. "Is there someone else here who might remember?"

The waitress's mouth puckered. "I doubt it. But good luck."

"Swell. Thanks."

Olive hid a grin behind her hand, but I could still see it in her twinkling eyes as the waitress walked away. "Got all you need to know?"

I ignored that question. "Guess we've just got to hope your friend Boots is more chatty. When do you think his set will be over?"

"Sooner or later." Olive winked at me. "In the meantime, want to dance?"

"Me?" I stared at her in surprise. "And you? Here?"

"I wasn't planning to ask the waitress."

I bit my lip. I hadn't considered trying to dance in these shoes. Or trying not to make a fool of myself in front of Olive. But the band was playing a popular tune with a quick beat, and Olive was looking at me expectantly.

"Okay," I said. "Let's dance."

Olive stood up and offered me her hand. I took it, and she tucked it through the crook of her elbow and led me onto the dance floor. Being led anywhere was not something I was used to, but my body didn't seem to mind. Every nerve seemed to be urging me to get my skin closer to hers. Then Olive hooked one arm around my back, and I wished I wasn't wearing this jacket after all.

Our faces were inches apart, closer than we'd ever been. The entire room was reduced to the pressure of her arm and the warmth of her palm against mine, the invitation in her golden eyes and the smile that curled up one corner of her lips.

Our bodies started moving together without even trying to, like they were meant to do it. Like they'd know how to do it just as well without these pesky clothes in between us.

My cheeks flushed hot, and I told myself it was from the dancing. I tried to concentrate on making my feet flash, the way I'd learned back when Mama was still lugging me around the vaudeville circuit. For once, I was glad about something she'd taught me, because it kept me from tripping in her heels and falling on my backside in front of Olive.

The air whipped my hair against my face as we spun together around the floor, and the silver and gold beads of our dresses spun together, too. The waves Marion had sculpted in my hair were rapidly falling, and I didn't care. Olive reached up a hand to brush one of them out of my eyes, and I couldn't suppress a giggle at her touch. Her smile could have melted ice caps.

When the song was over, Olive's arm curled tighter around me instead of letting me go. For one moment, two, my body was pressed full-length against hers.

"You've been holding out on me," she said, chest heaving, her voice low. "Didn't know you could dance like that."

"There's a lot of things about me you don't know."

"I'd like to, if you'd let me."

I believed her. I wanted to let her. But a flicker of fear shot through me, like a flame racing up a curtain. Dancing with her, even kissing her I could do. But liking her, really liking her? Waiting, hoping she liked me the same way? Waiting, waiting for her to change her mind and leave?

"I'm thirsty," I said. "Want to sit the next one out?"

Olive blinked, like she was waking up from a spell. I didn't wait for her to answer. I spun away, and on the way back to the table, noticed we'd attracted more than a few curious stares. I didn't know anyone here, but Olive did, and I peeked back at her to see if she minded. As if she read my thoughts, she leaned closer and said, "*I* wasn't the one who wanted to quit dancing."

I reddened. "Olive, that isn't why—"

"Oh, look," she said abruptly. "My friend is coming."

I turned to see the band taking five and the bass player weaving his way through the crowd in our direction. "See?" I said. "We couldn't have danced another anyway."

Olive ignored me and moved to meet Boots halfway. They embraced, and I saw him whisper something in her ear. She glanced over her shoulder at me, then shook her head. She turned back toward me at last, towing her friend along by the sleeve.

"Boots, this is Millie. Millie, this is Boots."

I stuck out my hand. Boots shook it warmly, but his eyes were understandably wary. I was a stranger here, an intruder in a space that wasn't for me.

"I hear you need a favor," he said in a voice almost as deep as his upright bass.

"I do. Can you talk to us about a blonde girl my age who came in here a few times?"

"What for?"

"She was murdered a couple weeks ago."

Boots's stance changed to a defensive one and his head tipped back. "And you think somebody in here did it, huh?"

I held up my hands. "That's not what I'm saying. But she told people she was coming here and I'm trying to piece together what happened during her last days alive."

Boots snorted, looking like he wanted to tell me to get the

hell out—and I couldn't blame him when I'd want to do the same to anyone snooping around the Cloak—but Olive gave him a sharp dig in the ribs with her elbow. My ribs were still bruised from her earlier jab, so I felt a sympathetic ache.

"Ow!" he said, rubbing his side through his shirt. "Okay. Okay. For you, Olive. I'll tell you what I know. But not in here."

"Then where?" I said.

"Outside. Follow me."

CHAPTER

25

WE WERE IN front of the Pelican under the streetlight and the gnarled branches of live oaks, this time with Boots. The street was mostly deserted, but I heard the echoes of someone's laughter, and a scuffing sound like someone's shoes on pavement. I had the feeling we were being watched—and maybe we were. There were plenty of houses with windows overlooking this corner, plenty of massive trees to hide behind.

"You got a picture of this blonde girl?" Boots said.

I already had my notebook flipped to the photograph of Arimentha from the newspaper, and I handed it over. Boots pushed the fedora farther back on his head and angled the notebook toward the light.

"I heard about this. Somebody shoved her off the balcony, right?"

"At my aunt's speak, the Cloak and Dagger."

Boots whistled. "So, you're in bad shape."

"My friend's the one in hot water—the cops think he did it. That's why I'm here. Because he didn't do it."

"And you're hoping I'm just gonna hand over the dude who did, right? Let some friend of mine take the fall instead?"

He was saying everything I would say to a customer asking nosy questions. "I'm looking for the truth, that's all," I said. "I don't think the cops care about that enough."

Boots snorted. "You got that part right. But I'm not interested in putting a black man in their sights instead of your 'friend.'"

Olive laid a hand on his arm. "We don't want that either. You don't have to trust Millie, but you know me. If that was her thing, I wouldn't have brought her here."

"I promise you, nobody innocent is going down because of me," I said. "I'm just trying to find out who she's been sneaking around with. The guy might not even be responsible for anything, but he might know who did it. Please . . . can you tell me, Boots—have you seen this girl here before?"

Boots stared at Minty's photo in silence for so long I'd almost decided our goose was cooked. But then he handed the notebook back to me and sighed heavily. "Yeah, I've seen her. Came in maybe four, five times the last couple of months. Always alone. Sat right at the end of the bar, close to the band. Downed a couple drinks, looking at her watch. Then right at eleven o'clock, she'd take off, like she had an appointment to keep."

I leaned forward eagerly. "Did you ever see who she met?"

Boots shook his head. "She always went back out the way she'd come—alone. Way I figured it, someone was meeting her outside. Or maybe at the Felicity Inn over there. They rent rooms by the hour."

I whirled to look where he was pointing. There were nothing

but gnarled live oaks and tall, dark houses. "Where is it?"

"They don't splash it around that they're a hotel. If the city knew about them, they'd have to follow the city's rules, know what I mean?"

"So it's the kind of place you'd have to hear about from somebody else," I said, looking at Olive.

She nodded slowly. "And how would an Uptowner like Minty hear about it? Surely, they've got their own version of this kind of hotel on their end of town."

"That means she probably heard about it from the guy," I said.

"Maybe he's the one who told her about the Pelican, too."

"You're saying it's one of our customers," Boots said, shaking his head. "Just like I figured you would."

"Not necessarily," I said. Quickly, I flipped the notebook to Roy's picture and held it out to him, just in case. "What about him? Did you ever see him around here?"

Boots looked and shook his head. "Don't think so."

It was a long shot, but I showed him the pictures of Jerome Rosenthal, Claude Holiday, and Philip Leveque, too. Boots hadn't seen any of them either.

"Then did she ever talk to anyone when she was here?" I said, feeling nonplussed.

Boots rubbed a hand across his face. "Not that I saw. Tell you the truth, she looked like trouble waiting to happen, and nobody wanted a part of that." His gaze passed over me top to toe. "And you? You got that same look. I have to get back inside. My break's about over."

"But wait, what—"

"Let the man get back to work, Millie," Olive cut in and

flashed him a smile. "Thanks, Boots. I owe you one. If you think of anything else, call us at the Cloak and Dagger. Hemlock 5163."

Boots touched the brim of his hat and backed toward the courtyard. "Don't be surprised if you don't hear from me."

Olive nodded. "We won't."

———·———

When we were alone again outside the Pelican, I noticed a fog was rolling up, hazing the light around me and Olive. The air was turning damp and cold, too, like the night Arimentha died, and Olive tried to hide a little shiver.

"You're cold," I said, and took off Cal's tuxedo jacket. "Put this on."

She took a step back, shaking her head. "But then you'd be cold."

"Marion says I'm a human furnace." I held out the jacket. "You wear it."

Olive hesitated another moment, then finally let me help her put it on. It was a little bigger on her than it was on me, so the sleeves came almost down to her fingertips. She looked so cute I had to resist a strong urge to throw my arms around her and lift her off her feet.

"My switchblade's in the pocket," I said instead, "so if we get in mortal danger, it's all up to you to save us."

Olive smirked. "I've already got that covered—I have a knife in my garter."

If I hadn't already liked her, that would've sealed the deal. I liked her so much I couldn't think of a single witty thing to say in response.

"Want to try to find that Felicity hotel?" I said.

Olive raised her brows, her lips curving. "For business or pleasure?"

My cheeks heated, and I backed out of the circle of light under the streetlamp so she wouldn't see them turn red. "I just meant—"

Olive laughed and closed the distance between us. "I know what you meant, goose." She tugged gently on a lock of my hair. "We can look for it if you want to."

"Boots pointed that way, toward home," I said, trying to sound like my face wasn't still an inferno.

Olive smiled sweetly and offered me her arm. "Then let's go."

We started walking arm in arm down the dark banquette, looking for signs of life in the houses on our right, but it was hard to notice anything except the feeling of Olive pressing against my side, warm and alive and wanting to be there with me.

"Minty might not have even gone to the hotel," I said after we'd gone a block without spotting it. "Whoever she was meeting could've had a vehicle. She could've hopped in and driven off with them anywhere."

"Maybe. Or Romeo could live around here."

"Yeah, maybe he lives with his mom or at a rooming house with a strict landlady like Mrs. A. He'd wait until the coast was clear at eleven o'clock, and then slip downstairs and let Minty in the house the back way."

Olive's nose wrinkled. "I guess that's possible."

"We could knock on all the doors," I said, only half joking.

"It's the middle of the night," Olive said, seeing on my face that it wasn't fully a joke.

"We could do it tomorrow then."

She slid me a sly glance. "Millie Coleman, do you just want an excuse to see me again?"

"Of course not," I said, failing to hide a grin. "I just think it's a great plan. We'll say, 'Hey, were you having an affair with a girl named Minty, oh and by the way, did you murder her?' We'll solve the case by noon."

But Olive didn't laugh like I expected her to. She went stiff and quiet, and I noticed how the dense fog seemed to have dampened the sounds of car engines and drunken laughter and jazz that were common in the French Quarter, even late at night. It felt like Olive and I were far away from any other humans, even though we'd almost made it back to my apartment.

"At the Pelican," Olive said, her voice soft but still startling in the silence, "why didn't you want to dance with me anymore?"

My steps slowed. "I . . . I told you I was just thirsty."

"Please don't give me that old song again." She tipped her head to look up at my face. "Were you scared of people looking?"

"No."

"I know it's different there than at the Cloak. I forget sometimes that not everyone thinks the way we do."

"I forget that, too. But that's not why. I—"

Olive stopped abruptly under the last streetlight before my building and spun around in front of me, blocking my way. We stood in a halo of light, fog everywhere beyond it, so that the entire dark city disappeared. I wanted to avoid her eyes, but there they were, staring up into mine. Even swallowed up in Cal's jacket, everything about her looked soft and curvy and smooth. My hand moved to her waist under the jacket almost involuntarily, and a smile flitted across her lips, triumph in her eyes. Her small, pretty teeth bit her berry-painted lower lip.

"I could kiss you now," she murmured, close enough that I felt her breath on my cheek.

"You could," I whispered back.

She leaned in the rest of the way and closed the last small distance between us. My nerves trilled like violin strings; my fingers tightened on the rough beads of her dress. Her parted lips touched mine, and I tasted the warm sweetness of her breath. Her fingertips trailed up the back of my neck into my hair, and I regretted every minute that I'd wasted not kissing her, not touching her.

But then, uninvited, unwanted, an image appeared behind my closed eyes. My mother, the day she'd left me four years ago, wearing her favorite green dress, her eyes avoiding mine as she'd turned toward her man of the moment, turned to leave me behind.

The pleasure that had been zinging through my body transformed into something ugly, making my heart beat double time and sweat bead on my temples. I had time to think how funny it was that pleasure and panic almost felt the same, and then I opened my eyes to make the feeling go away. When that didn't work fast enough, I took a step backward, breaking the kiss.

Olive stood there looking at me, tenderness and confusion drawing her curved brows together. I made myself smile and pressed a hand to my chest like I needed to catch my breath. Come to think of it, I did. My heart was beating too fast, the old familiar pain surging through it sharper than I'd felt it in a while.

Where did that come from? I'd kissed other people before, some boys, some girls, and this had never happened. But Mama had still been gone then, and the pain of her leaving hadn't been all stirred up again like a hornet's nest. And, a voice whispered in my head, I hadn't cared about those people I'd kissed. I'd barely known their names.

Olive threw her arms up. "This again? No one's looking at us, Millie."

"It's not that."

"Then what? Explain it to me."

I could try to lie, but Olive always saw through me. "I . . . I'm trying to focus on this case," I said, fumbling to find my way between a lie and the truth. "I need to concentrate. I can't be distracted."

Olive stared at me. "You're saying that's all tonight was about? The case?"

I hesitated.

"You're trying to tell me you *really* needed me to get you into the Pelican?" Her voice rose. "*Really* needed me to introduce you to my friend?"

"Of course I did. Boots wouldn't have talked to me if you hadn't."

Olive shook her head. "I just thought . . ." Her lids dropped shut and she hugged her arms tighter around herself. She noticed Cal's jacket then and started taking it off. "Never mind."

"I did need your help," I said. "And . . . and I don't know what I'm doing. I don't know how I—"

Olive's head jerked up, her eyes gone fiery. "You don't know?" She thrust Cal's jacket into my arms. "Millie Coleman, I don't sit around waiting for somebody like you to throw me a bone."

"I don't expect you to sit around."

"You don't, huh? So, it won't bother you if I step out with someone else next weekend?" She started walking away from me.

Jealousy stabbing me sharply in the gut, but I moved to catch up with her. "Olive—"

"No." She held up a hand to cut me off. "I see how it is. You like me when I'm useful. Just like everybody else."

"That's not true, I—"

"See you at work, Millie."

"Olive, wait—"

But she was done waiting. She stalked off down the street, past my building and up another block, until the fog turned her into a shadow and then swallowed her whole.

Regret throbbed in my belly. Of course Olive felt like I was only using her; I'd done a terrible job of explaining. I only wished I knew how to tell her the truth.

But maybe this was for the best. Marion might go to jail, might even hang if I didn't find the right killer. I didn't have time to like anyone—not Olive and not Bennie—especially not with Mama back in my life.

Me and Marion—that's all that mattered right now.

Olive would just have to understand.

— . —

I'd hoped this evening would give me some answers, but it had mostly given me more questions. As I slipped off my wretched shoes and trudged up the stairs, suddenly aware of my sore feet, I was more confused than ever. And not only about the murder case.

Before I'd even reached the top of the stairs, Marion flung open the door. "I saw you down there," he singsonged, his voice echoing in the stairwell.

"Saw me what?"

"You know what."

I pushed past him through the doorway, draped Cal's jacket across the back of her favorite chair, and tossed my shoes in the general direction of our bedroom. Marion dogged my steps.

"Seriously, did you and Olive smooch or what? Is she a good kisser? You *have* to tell me. I'm cooped up in this apartment with no chance of kissing anyone until this murder is solved. It's only fair."

I had a perfect opening to tease him about Lewis, but I flopped flat on my back across our bed and flung an arm across my eyes. "Wouldn't you rather know if I found out who Minty was meeting at the Pelican?"

Marion grinned. "If you had, you would've run right up here to tell me instead of standing around in the fog like Ebenezer Scrooge."

"Maybe I was waiting for a ghost to tell me who did it."

"Or you were falling in loo-oove with Olive."

I felt around on the bed for the handbag he'd lent me and tossed it at him, but he dodged out of the way, laughing. He sat on the bed next to me and poked at my side.

"Come *on*," he whined. "You get to have all the fun, while I'm stuck here reading the same three detective novels over and over. The least you can do is tell me the details."

"There aren't any details," I muttered from behind my arm.

"You mean you didn't kiss her?" Marion sounded deeply disappointed.

"No," I lied. Maybe because if I told the truth, I'd have to tell him all of it, the stuff about the panic, too.

"But why not?"

"I'm trying to find a murderer. I don't have time for kissing."

Marion stretched out beside me and propped his head on his hand. "Kissing doesn't take that long, you know. Or at least it doesn't have to." He giggled, and I turned my head and peeked at him. He had long curly lashes and perfect Cupid's bow lips without even having to draw them on. I pictured him and Lewis together like this. Maybe it would be easy for Marion to cross the distance between them and turn wanting into a kiss and more kisses and more. But I couldn't imagine a way through that invisible barrier between me and Olive, between me and Bennie, between me and anyone.

"Later," I said out loud. "I'll kiss all the people later."

"All the people?" Marion said, nudging my side again. "Olive may be sad to hear that. Bennie, too, for that matter."

I grinned despite myself. "Maybe so. But the rest of the people won't."

Marion barked a laugh, and I socked him in the arm, and we laughed some more while he helped me out of the ridiculous beaded dress and showed me how to take off the makeup with cold cream.

But the whole time we were laughing and talking, a part of me was still thinking about that invisible barrier. And wondering if, once this murder was solved and my excuses were gone, I was ever going to get across it.

CHAPTER

26

A LOUD THUD woke me what seemed like fifteen seconds after I finally fell asleep. I pushed myself up on my elbow and checked the switchblade on my night table, lit by a shaft of moonlight coming through the shutters. A second thud followed the first, then a bump and a curse. I relaxed back into my pillow. It was only Mama, home from her date and probably drunk. I heard her soft steps as she padded barefoot across the floor into the kitchen, then the sound of a match striking. And then a little cry. I figured she'd burned herself with the matches, but she ran past my open bedroom door and burst through Cal's closed one.

"Cal!" she yelled, no longer even trying to be quiet. "There's someone in the club!"

"What?" Cal said blearily. It was still dark outside, not even a hint of morning yet. She hadn't been asleep much longer than me.

Marion still snored softly beside me, but I sat up straight, dragging the covers with me. I grabbed my switchblade and hurried across the cold floorboards into Cal's room.

"What's happening?" I said.

Mama tugged on Cal's arm, hauling her out of bed. "Come see," she said. "In the kitchen, quick before they're gone."

"You seeing ghosts, Gladys?" Cal said with a hint of amusement in her tone. I couldn't see the smirk on her lips but knew it was there.

"No! Someone's in the club! Maybe it's the cops!"

Cal shook off Mama's hands and stood up, amusement gone. "Show me."

Mama led her to the kitchen, and I followed behind. Marion stood in my bedroom doorway now, rubbing his eyes. "Why are we awake?"

Nobody answered him. We pressed ourselves around the kitchen table and looked out the window.

"I was going to smoke a cigarette, so I cracked the window, and I saw it *right there*." She pointed toward the single small window in the back hallway of the club. "A light, like a flashlight beam."

There was nothing but blackness in the window now.

"Are you sure about this, Gladys? You seem a little . . ." Cal wobbled her hand back and forth.

Mama pulled herself up straighter and aimed her unlit cigarette at Cal. "I can hold my liquor better than you, Caledonia. Don't you forget who's the older sister."

I stepped between them. "We don't have time for squabbling. Mama, are you sure you saw a flashlight?"

"Sure as sin."

"Okay, then there's only one thing for us to do."

"I'm going to check," Cal said, already turning to leave the kitchen.

"And I'm going with you," I said.

"Like hell you are."

"If there's somebody in there, it's not safe to go alone, and you know it." I held up my switchblade. "And I'll bring Pearl here."

Cal rolled her eyes, but she didn't protest anymore. We both threw on trousers, tucked in our nightshirts, and stuffed our feet into shoes. I dressed as quickly as I could, afraid if she got ready first, she'd leave without me. At the door, she checked the bullets in the small pistol she carried and stuck it in her pocket. She tossed me a flashlight.

"Let's go."

—·—

The fog was gone, but the air was still chilly and damp, with thick gray clouds blocking out patches of stars. I pulled my jacket tight as we crossed the courtyard and stopped beside the fountain where Arimentha's body had lain. I looked toward the balcony, uneasiness creeping up my spine. No one menacing stood up there, staring down with murder in their eyes. No one stood there at all, and I didn't believe in ghosts. But Mama had seen something in the club, I believed that.

"I go first," Cal whispered. "Keep the flashlight off until I say so."

I nodded.

The facing around the back door was cracked, the door open an inch. Mama was right; someone was in the club, someone who definitely wasn't supposed to be there. My body shivered, but one look at Cal's face steadied me. Her eyes might show a hint of fear, but her jaw was set. She was angry. This was *her* club. She slowly, silently pulled open the door.

We didn't need to turn on the hall light or the flashlight; we'd traveled this way so many times, we knew every step of it, every creak of the boards under our feet. We walked carefully, barely making a sound, but then up ahead, something crashed. My fingers curled tighter around Pearl. I didn't dare open the knife yet, in case I bumped into Cal in the dark, but I wanted it ready.

More crashing came from up ahead, glass shattering in the main room. I wanted to whisper something to Cal, but I didn't dare break her concentration. Who was in our club? It didn't seem like the feds—they didn't bother with sneaking around in the dark; they came loud and fast and padlocked your doors so you couldn't get back inside the next day. It could be the police detectives, trying to sneak around and find murder evidence they couldn't get a warrant for. I wouldn't put it past that Craggy. But when more glass shattered, I knew it couldn't be the cops either. Destroying the club wouldn't get them more evidence and definitely wouldn't get our cooperation. That left only the possibility of a thief or a vandal. Maybe more than one. I hoped Cal had that gun held at the ready now. I gripped my switchblade in one hand and the flashlight in the other, ready to use it as a cudgel if I needed to.

We stopped just short of the doorway to the main room. Cal could reach around the wall and press the push-button light switch, and we'd see our vandals. But we'd also reveal ourselves. Give them a warning.

My eyes had adjusted enough to the dark that I could see Cal's silhouette lean around the doorway and peek into the main room, then jerk her head back.

"One flashlight," she breathed over her shoulder. "I think it's just one."

"We can take him," I said.

"You stay here."

"No way."

"*Stay put.*"

Before I could argue again, Cal had stepped out into the doorway, her pistol arm raised, steady and straight. "Stop where you are, or I'll put an extra hole in your head."

Glass shattered again, as if the thief had dropped something. Cal moved slowly forward, and I peeked around the edge of the doorway behind her. The vandal had dropped his flashlight where he stood, somewhere near the bar, and its fractured beam sliced across a sea of glittering glass shards and overturned tables and lit up Cal's face from below. With the light pointing toward her, she'd have a hard time seeing the person who'd broken in. She'd never be able to aim properly. Meanwhile, the vandal could see her clear as day. What if he had a gun, too? He could be aiming it right now.

I had to do something to even the playing field. Cal had told me to keep our flashlight off until she said so, but she was too occupied now. I raised the flashlight in my hand, intending to shine it on the vandal, but nothing happened when I clicked the switch. I clicked it back and forth twice, beat it against my hand, but still no light. Okay, plan B. I moved behind Cal and said, "Distraction," in her ear. Then I hefted my flashlight and tossed it hard toward the stage, away from the bar where the vandal had frozen. My flashlight landed with a satisfying crash, and then we heard him moving. His feet kicked his flashlight, knocking its light away from Cal, but then he charged toward her, toward me. Cal jumped out of the way just in time, but then the vandal's hands were on my shoulders. I hardly had time to scream before he'd shoved me aside and kept running. I fell to the ground and caught myself with my hands on the glass-covered floor. Shards cut into my knuckles on the hand that held the switchblade and my palm on the empty one. Another shard tore the knee of my pants and carved a slice across my shin.

"Millie!" Cal crouched over me. "Are you all right?"

"Fine," I grunted. "Go get him."

Cal hesitated.

"Go."

—·—

Long minutes later, Cal came back breathless and red-faced with rage and frustration. I'd made my slow way to the light switch while she was gone, and she walked into a room that looked like it had been shaken up inside a snow globe. All the chairs were knocked off the tables and strewn on the floor. Most of the tables were overturned, too. The lights winked on shattered glass, scattered like confetti, all over the floor and on top of the bar. It looked like every glass under the bar had been broken, and the whole room reeked of hooch, so the vandal had broken those bottles, too.

"Who was it?" I said. "Did you see?"

Cal shook her head, barely looking at me. She looked hollow, as if whoever had broken into the club had broken directly into her body and pulled out her guts, too. The club was my home, far more than our apartment was, but it was Cal's baby, the culmination of everything she'd worked for, the place she'd made for all of us from sheer grit and determination and one very lucky hand of poker.

I watched her as her gaze shifted to the smoked mirror behind the bar, the one piece of glass in the place that hadn't been shattered.

In dripping red capitals, the vandal had painted a message for us. For me.

STOP LOOKING FOR THE KILLER OR NEXT TIME I'LL BREAK MORE THAN GLASS.

Cal looked back at me where I leaned heavily against the wall under the light switch, and now to my surprise, her eyes weren't angry. They were . . . frightened. For me. She shook herself. "You're bleeding. Are you—"

"I'm okay. Just sliced up a little."

She crunched across the broken glass on the floor, some of it stained now with my blood, and took my hands in hers. I was still clutching the switchblade. She studied my cuts, smearing her own hands with my blood.

"Can you walk?"

"Just about."

"Then let's get you home."

"What about the club? What about—"

"Later." She threw my arm over her shoulders and hoisted me up. "You first."

—·—

"Ouch!"

"Quit being a baby." Marion lifted a tiny shard of glass out of my palm with the tweezers he normally reserved for sculpting his eyebrows.

"You'd be yelling, too, if somebody was fishing around in your skin with a pointy object."

Marion glanced over his shoulder at Cal and Mama, who were hovering behind us in the kitchen. "Can somebody get her a drink?"

Cal didn't want me touching liquor, but Mama quickly handed over her own flask, ignoring the dirty look Cal gave her.

"It's medicinal," Mama said.

The piney smell of gin wafted up from the mouth of the flask, and I grimaced, remembering Minty's diary and her unfavorable opinion of the stuff. I had to agree.

"Just one," Cal said sternly.

"No problem." I held my nose and took a single swig of the strong clear liquor. It burned going down, and I coughed, earning me a glare from Marion, who was trying to extract another piece of glass.

"Be still."

I scowled at him. "Yes, Doctor."

Marion stuck his tongue between his teeth and slowly lifted out the glass. He dropped it in Mama's ashtray with the other shards. "There. Done. Go wash your hands in the sink—thoroughly, and with soap—then come back and I'll bandage you."

I obeyed, only limping a little where my leg had been sliced. Marion had already cleaned that up and wrapped it in a long strip of cloth torn from a towel. The cut had bled a lot, but it wasn't deep.

"So, you really didn't see who did this?" Marion said behind me.

"No." I tried to turn on the tap, but Cal leaped forward and turned the handle for me. "All we know is it was just one person. Probably a man, right, Cal?"

"Think so. All I saw was a silhouette."

"And I felt his hands on my shoulders. They seemed big. He tossed me aside pretty easy, too, though he would've had a tougher time if I could've seen what I was doing."

"I'm glad you couldn't see," Cal said, "or you might've got yourself in more trouble with that switchblade."

"I know how to use it," I said defensively, returning to my chair across from Marion. "Wish I'd gotten in a slice of my own with it."

Marion met Mama's eyes over my head, and I could tell he was trying not to roll his eyes.

"Just get to bandaging," I said.

"There's one other thing we know," Cal said slowly, meeting my eyes. The message on the mirror. Part of me had hoped to get away with not telling Marion about that at all. "The vandal had something to do with Arimentha McDonough's murder."

Marion stopped wrapping my hand in strips of pillowcase and blinked at Cal. "What do you mean?"

Cal glanced from him to Mama and back to me. "He left us a message on the mirror behind the bar."

Marion's eyes widened. "What kind of message?"

I looked down at my half-bandaged hands and forced a small laugh, trying to make it seem like no big deal. "Essentially stop looking for her killer or else. It must be Romeo. He must have followed me and Olive last night and saw we'd found their meeting spot. Guess we're getting pretty good at this detective thing, huh?"

"Millie, you have to do what he says." Marion's chin trembled, and his eyes filled rapidly with tears. "I can't let you put yourself in danger for me. This person has already ruined the club, who knows what they could do to you? What if—"

"Stop, Mar. I've already thought this through while I was waiting for Cal to get back. I'm not letting this guy scare me off."

"Maybe he's right," Cal said. "Mother Cecilia Marie called me yesterday. She's worried about you. Said you've been missing too much school. You're falling behind, and you're too smart for that. Now with this threat, maybe—"

"No," I said. "I don't care about school, and you know it. I care about Marion."

"So do I, but I also care about you." Cal jabbed a finger at my chest, her voice rising. "*Your* education and *your* safety. It's my job to make sure you get more of both than me and Gladys got."

Mama looked from Cal's face to mine, for once keeping her mouth shut.

I shook my head. "I can't believe you, Cal. You taught me not to sit back and take it when a bully messes with me. You taught me to punch back. How is this different?"

"I just . . ." Cal trailed off, the anger draining from her face. "I worry about you, kid." She looked at Marion and squeezed both of our shoulders. "I worry about you both. It's more dangerous out there than you know."

I pulled my switchblade out of my pocket and twirled it in my fingers. "You forget who raised me." I spared a glance for

Mama, who'd given me this knife and taught me how to use it when I was still in knee socks. The road wasn't a safe place for a girl, she'd said, and made sure I knew where to kick and stab. Made sure I knew how to scream loud and run fast.

Then I locked my eyes on Cal, who'd done the rest of the work when Mama quit. She'd showed me how to watch faces for a lie, how to slip a bribe under a table, how to know when a fight was about to start, and how to break it up before it began. How to win at cards with a losing hand.

"Millie," she said, but I could tell she was wavering.

Then Marion spoke up again. "No, I can't let you do it anymore, Millie. How can I call myself a friend if I let people put themselves in danger for me?"

"You're not letting me do anything, Marion." I leaned against Cal. "No one 'lets' a Coleman do anything, right?"

"At least call that detective!" Marion said. "Tell him what happened. Maybe he'll lay off me."

"I'll tell him, but I don't want to leave it up to him to decide if this is enough evidence. Your life is too important to put in his hands."

"But your club," Marion said, turning to Cal now. "It's ruined."

Cal set a hand on his shoulder. "This ain't the end, kid. I've come back from worse." She looked around at me and Mama. "We all have."

Cal was right. In this family, when we got knocked down, we learned to land on our feet like stray cats. If the world didn't give us a chance, we found a way to take one.

"Then let me help clean up," Marion said, conceding defeat. "I can do that at least."

"It's too risky," I said. "But there is one thing you can do.

We'll bring over your sewing machine from the club, and you can make yourself a new costume, the most beautiful one you've ever worn. And when the club reopens and we clear your name, you'll be there to welcome it back in style."

Marion bit his lip as if he was still hesitating, but I'd seen his eyes light up at the mention of that machine. He was talented at hand sewing, but the machine was his pride and joy. He'd nearly cried when Cal had found it at a pawn shop and presented it to him last year.

He lifted his chin. "I bet I can make a costume faster than you can fix up that club."

I grinned. "Bet you five bucks you can't."

Marion winked at me. "I'll be planning how to spend my five bucks."

CHAPTER

27

SATURDAY WAS SUPPOSED to be our best money-maker of the week, but Cal said there was no way we could open again for at least a few days. Even though we'd had almost zero sleep, we divided up the telephone numbers of the Cloak employees and started calling to tell them the bad news. All the ones who didn't have other jobs during the day came in to help fix the damage, and Rhoda showed up, too, with the passenger seat of her roadster full of extra brooms, mops, and cleaning supplies. Cal tried to make me wait to help until my hands and leg healed, but I lied and told her my cuts barely hurt. It was also a lie that I wasn't worried about what that vandal had written on the mirror. I was tempted to ask Cal to borrow her pistol to carry around with me, but there was not a chance she'd let me have it.

I was already at the club watching Rhoda photograph the wreckage when Olive arrived, looking pretty in a yellow dress. She carefully avoided meeting my eye, even when Cal assigned her to help me wipe the paint off the mirror. She just went to get the can of turpentine, some rags, and a stepladder from under the stairs, and I trailed behind her, not speaking, not sure what to say. I'd made a mistake, but I wasn't sure if the mistake was kissing her or stopping kissing her. Maybe I should be keeping my distance from everyone anyway, with a bird-drawing murderer around here threatening people. I hadn't considered Olive when I'd vowed to continue this investigation—I hadn't thought through what I'd do if the killer didn't come for me, but for people I cared about. Now that that prospect was here, it made something tighten and shrink inside my chest.

In front of the mirror, Olive set down the can of turpentine in the middle of the counter behind the bar and stood on the first step of her ladder while I reached what I could of the words without one. We took turns dampening our rags with turpentine, Olive still not looking at me. The sharp smell wafted up and stung my nose as I rubbed at the words *break more than glass*, the knot cinching tighter in my chest with every swipe. At least I was a little closer to finding out who Romeo was than I'd been a few days ago; I was pretty sure he was a man now, and I had somewhere to look next—the Felicity Inn. And Romeo must be afraid of what I'd find out there or he wouldn't have done all this damage to scare me off.

"You got hurt," Olive said gruffly, eyes still on the mirror.

I shrugged, trying to drag myself back from my worries, and hid the bloodier hand behind my back. The one holding the rag was only cut across the knuckles. "A little."

She gestured with her rag toward the message on the mirror. "Someone wants you to stop working on this case."

"Looks like."

She turned her head so that she was almost looking at me. "But you're not stopping?"

"Nope."

Olive shook her head and was silent for a long moment. "I hope you'll be more careful from now on."

"I can't really be any *less* careful, can I?" I faked a grin, trying to make her laugh, trying to hide how worried I was.

But Olive's rag stopped moving, and she finally looked at me with those searching eyes. "I hope you know what you're doing, Millie." There was still an edge of anger in her voice, but it was softer than before.

Part of me wanted to sink into her and say, "I don't know what I'm doing. When I started this, I didn't know what it meant—I didn't know what it would be like to have other lives depending on me." But I swallowed hard and forced a smile. "I just wish I knew who did this." I waved my rag at the damage in the room. "I'd like to teach him a lesson."

Olive turned to take in the rest of the room. "Speaking of that . . . there's something I've been thinking."

"Oh yeah?" The turpentine had gradually seeped from the rag into my bandage, stinging the cuts across my knuckles. I leaned my arm against the counter like I was just taking a break to listen.

"The damage in the club," Olive said, "it isn't really that bad."

"What do you mean? He broke nearly every piece of glass in the place. And dumped all the hooch."

"Yeah, but it could've been so much worse. He could've banged up the piano. Broken the chairs instead of just knocking them onto the floor. Could've taken a hatchet to the bar or even hacked up the dance floor."

"Maybe he was planning to do worse but got caught before he could."

Olive's brow furrowed. "Maybe."

"Or he's an amateur and didn't think of all that. Could be a rich kid who doesn't even know how to use an ax."

Olive still didn't crack a smile. "I don't think so. I'm getting more certain all the time that Romeo isn't one of them." Her face turned back to the mirror, and she lifted her rag, but she didn't move it over the smeared red words.

"What are you thinking, Olive?"

She shook her head and started wiping again. "Nothing."

I was going to press her on it, but then my mother's laughter trilled from the hallway, and it was the kind she made when she was hanging on some man's arm. I set my jaw and resolutely kept my eyes on the mirror.

"Millie," Mama said gaily, "why didn't you tell me your pal here is such a comedian?"

"Looks like you've figured that out for yourself," I said.

Bennie coughed and held the crate of hooch in his arms. "My dad heard what happened and sent this over."

"Good man," Cal said, bustling in behind him and clapping him on the back. "The hatch in the floor's got plenty of space now."

"Yes, ma'am," Bennie said.

I dropped my rag, eager for the excuse to rest my stinging hand, and crouched beside him to help unload the crate.

"Hey," he said, bumping a shoulder against mine.

"Hey," I said lightly, as if the sight of him laughing with my mother hadn't sent an icy wave crashing over me. He smelled of the hay packed in the crates, and oranges, and something else—shoe polish maybe? Then he moved, and a whiff of Mama's cheap perfume rose from his sleeve. I recoiled and nearly fell over backward.

"Steady there," he said, setting a hand on my shoulder. His eyes settled on mine, too, and the hand lingered. "Did you find out anything at the Pelican Club?"

I unwound the turpentine-tinged bandage from my hand and stuck it in my back pocket. "Not much, but Minty's definitely been there, and we have one new lead."

Bennie didn't respond. He was staring at the cuts on my knuckles. "Did that happen last night? In here?"

I tucked a bottle of rum into the hidey-hole and tried to sound casual. "Yeah, the guy knocked me over and I fell on some broken glass."

Bennie's mouth tightened. "Did you see who it was?"

I shook my head. "Nah. Cal didn't either. We're pretty sure it was a man, but that's all we know so far."

"How are you going to find out who did it?"

"He left that—" I turned to point to the message over my shoulder and found Olive staring at us. She quickly glanced away. I faltered, slowed. "He left that warning, so . . . I'm pretty sure whoever did this is also the killer."

Bennie's eyes widened. "Are you going to do what it says?"

"Quit? Not a chance."

Bennie chewed his lip, staring now at the bloody bandage on my other hand. "You're cut there, too?"

"And here." I hiked up my trousers to show him the other bandage on my leg. It was starting to throb, too, but I didn't mention that part.

Bennie looked incredulous. "You're all cut up and you got

that message and you still want to chase after this person?"

"I already had this conversation with Aunt Cal." I waved a hand in her direction, where she'd gone back to the other side of the room to boss somebody else. "It's already been decided."

But Bennie shook his head. "You don't have to take responsibility for everything. Maybe you should go home and let us work on the club today . . . Maybe leave this investigation to the cops."

"She said it's been decided." Olive stood over us suddenly.

Bennie rose to face her over my head. "Then maybe it's the wrong decision."

"Maybe so. Wouldn't be the first time." Olive crossed her arms over her chest. "But it's hers to make. Not yours."

Bennie motioned to the message on the mirror. "Tangling with a killer who's directly threatening you isn't a joke."

I stood up slowly, but they barely glanced at me. They kept staring daggers at each other.

"It's never been a joke," Olive said. "Threat or no threat. It was always dangerous."

"So, you think she should keep putting herself in danger?" Bennie grabbed my wounded hand and held it up. "She's already been hurt once. I thought you were her friend."

Olive narrowed her eyes. "Friend enough not to tell her what to do."

Bennie scowled. "I'm not telling her what to do, just asking her to think—"

"I'm right here." I snatched my hand out of Bennie's grasp. "And I've thought about it all I'm going to. I've discussed it all I'm going to. You two can duke it out without me."

Bennie and Olive gaped at me in stark surprise, but I turned on my heel toward the back door and tried not to limp as I flounced right out of it.

—·—

I didn't make it far. Just to the courtyard behind the club. My leg hurt, and both my hands hurt, and I couldn't even complain about it without the whole world telling me what to do.

The back door opened. Cal didn't say anything, just rested her back against the wall beside me and waited.

I rolled my head toward her. "You don't really think I should quit, do you?"

She stuck her hands in her pockets and stared out at the fountain where Arimentha had died. "I get where Bennie's coming from. He's worried about you. So am I. Part of me wants to wrap you up in cotton wool and hide you in a drawer, too."

"But—"

She held up a hand to stop me. "I know I can't do that. You're nearly grown. I have to trust you."

The wind blew a page of newspaper against my leg and I bent to pick it up. Of course, it was a story about the ongoing manhunt for Marion, with both his picture and Minty's four inches high. I folded it in half, hiding their faces. "So, you think Olive was right?"

Cal cocked one eyebrow at me. "What are you really asking me?"

"Just what I said." I folded the paper again. "Who do you think was right—Bennie or Olive?"

"They both care about you," she said carefully.

"But they were acting like jackasses."

Cal's shoulders lifted noncommittally. "People do that sometimes. You should know that."

"What's that supposed to mean?"

Cal blew out a heavy breath. "You're seventeen years old. Nobody's saying you have to pick your partner for life, or even see just one person. You can kiss a thousand people for all I care. But it's complicated when two of them are your friends. When they have to look each other in the eye and wonder which of them you're going to choose."

I pinched along the fold of the newspaper to crease it and peeked at Cal out of the corner of my eye. "What if I can't do this . . . romance or whatever? What if I don't know how?"

Cal smiled. "Nobody knows how. All you can do is try, and when you mess up, say you're sorry and try to do better next time."

"I think I already messed up last night." I bit my lip, debating whether to tell her. "Me and Olive . . . when we . . . you know." I turned the rectangle of newsprint in my hands, so I didn't have to look at Cal.

Her voice sounded amused. "It didn't go well?"

I shook my head. "For some reason, I started thinking about"—I glanced at her face—"about Mama. About that day she left."

She nodded slowly, her expression impassive. "And?"

My shoulders sagged against the wall. "And I messed it up."

"So, that's why Olive keeps glaring at you today. I don't suppose you explained what happened?"

I shook my head again.

"I see." Cal put an arm around my shoulders and pressed

me against her. "That's probably why she got so mad at Bennie, too. She probably thinks he's the reason you were acting funny last night."

My eyes widened. "But he wasn't!"

"Maybe you should tell Olive that."

I grimaced. "But . . . I don't want to tell her what it was really about either. It sounds . . . weak. Nobody understands why I'm so mad at Mama. Even I don't understand why she's still in my head."

Cal sighed. "Gladys cut you to the quick when she left, and plenty of times before that, too. But you got to let that go. I'm not saying you have to like her, or accept her. But hanging on to being mad at her is keeping all that pain stirred up. It's going to keep bursting out unless you find a way to heal it."

"But I stuck by her through all those boyfriends. I didn't even mind, or mostly didn't, because it was always me and her again after they left. But then she chose one of *them* and left *me*." The words almost didn't come out. "It . . . it wasn't fair."

"No, it wasn't. She's always had a knack for making the wrong choice. But sometimes, she makes the right one. Like the one she made for me."

"What?" I gave Cal a skeptical look. "When?"

"When we were just kids, younger than you. Did I ever tell you about the day I ran away from home?"

I swiveled my head and stared at her. I knew she and Mama had spent their early years somewhere in the Mississippi Delta, and that Cal had run away because of their father, but I didn't know the details. I'd long ago learned to steer clear of the topic of their childhood. It only made sharp tongues sharper.

Cal sighed. "Our daddy was a Holy Roller. Had me and

Gladys singing together on the tent revival circuit by the time I was ten and she was twelve."

I blinked, trying to make the pieces of the picture come together. "You're telling me the Captivating Coleman Sisters sang *gospel*?"

Cal laughed and covered her face at the memory. "There wasn't a thing captivating about us then. Just plain old Coleman Sisters."

"What went wrong?"

Cal looked away at some point across the courtyard, her fingers smoothing the hair at the back of her neck. When she turned back to me, a wistful look I'd never seen before tilted her lips.

"A girl happened. Her father was a preacher on the circuit. Real fire-and-brimstone type. Me and her got to be friends. Daddy didn't think nothing of it at first. Two Christian girls huddled up reading the Bible day and night—what could be wrong with that? But the way that girl looked at me over that Bible . . ." Cal bowed her head. "Mmm-mmm. Then one day Daddy found us . . . Well, I'll just say we were doing more than holding hands for prayer."

She smiled, but her eyes were far away.

"Then what happened?"

Cal sucked in a deep breath. "Daddy was madder than ten devils. He snatched me up and dragged me to the bus station. Sent a telegram to Mama, bought me a ticket, and said, 'Get yourself home. You're gonna learn to behave like a good Christian woman if it kills us—or you.'"

I rolled my eyes. "That didn't work out."

"Nope. The bus didn't leave for three hours, so he left me

there to wait. And when he lay down for a nap, Gladys sneaked off from the hotel and came back. She'd stolen forty dollars off Daddy and said, 'Trade in your ticket, Cal, and let's get outta here.' Without a second thought. The nearest big city was New Orleans, so we came here. Gladys changed up our costumes, threw on some sequins, and we added the 'Captivating' to our name. Started doing vaudeville. I cut my hair short years before everyone started doing it."

"But what happened to that girl?" I said. "Your friend?"

Cal's lips pressed together until they weren't smiling any-more. "Heard she got married. Has three or four kids now."

"Do you wish you went back for her? Asked her to come with you?"

"You know I wouldn't trade Rhoda for the world." Cal picked at a loose thread on the cuff of her jacket. She was silent for a moment. When she looked back up at me, her eyes were wet. "But all the same . . ." She picked up my bandaged hand and held it between both of hers. "I had a good thing, and my daddy spoiled it for me. Don't let your mama spoil this for you. Don't let her take up so much room in your heart that you don't have space for anybody else."

I thought about the memory of Mama popping up un-wanted when I'd kissed Olive. She'd taken up more than her fair share of my time and energy and space for a long time. It was like I froze solid when she left me, and I'd never been able to stop feeling as hurt and angry as I did in that moment.

I thought about Arimentha McDonough, how she'd let her pain about Marion wreck her plans to go to college and stop her from falling in love. I didn't want to do that, even if I was the one owed the apology, not the other way around.

"I think I understand what you're saying."

"Good." Cal took the newspaper from me and clucked her tongue at the way it had stained my bandages black. "Why don't you go let Marion bandage you up again? Maybe you can come back later if you're feeling better."

My hands were aching and my leg, too. I guessed I could give in this once. Cal started toward the club with the paper crumpled in her fist.

"Cal—"

She turned back. "Yeah, kid?"

"Did you ever go home to visit your folks?" I'd never met my grandparents, only seen their picture in a brass frame Mama kept on the dresser. Their faces were familiar, especially my grandmother's—wide at the cheekbones, like Mama's, like Cal's—but everything else about them was a mystery.

"I never did," Cal said. "Gladys did once or twice. But the welcome wasn't too nice, so she didn't go back. Wrote letters to Mama, though. Told her about you."

"She did?"

"Sure."

"Didn't they ever want to see me?"

Cal grabbed my shoulder and jostled me a little, how she liked to do. "That I don't know, kid, but if they didn't want to see you, they were fools."

I smiled, despite myself. "Are they still alive?"

Call shook her head. "They both died in a car accident a few years ago."

"Did you ever go visit their grave?"

"Yeah, once. I figure I had to go at least once, even if I mostly hated them. Said goodbye to the piece of them I loved before I knew any better." Cal gave my shoulder one last pat.

As she turned and went back into the club, I faced the fountain, where Arimentha had taken her final breath. Like my awful grandparents, she was resting now somewhere—that rich lady at the Roosevelt Hotel had said she was buried in a tomb in Lafayette Cemetery No. 1.

If Romeo was her killer, he'd been angry at her, maybe hated her. But he'd loved a piece of her, too, like Cal would always love a piece of her parents. And I would always love a piece of mine, even if I'd never admt it out loud.

Maybe Romeo had needed to see Minty's grave and say goodbye. And maybe, if he did, he left some clues behind.

CHAPTER

28

LAFAYETTE CEMETERY NO. 1 was only a few streetcar stops downtown from my stop for Ursuline. I'd intended to leave early for school on Monday and go to the cemetery first thing on my way, but I was too busy sleeping, so it would have to be in the afternoon.

At school, the other girls stared at my bandaged hands. Virginia Baines asked me if I had taken up boxing over the weekend, and the other girls giggled behind their own delicate hands. But when I put up my dukes and asked if they'd like a demonstration, they shrieked and ran away. Mother Cecilia Marie looked concerned and tried to call me into her office to talk at the end of the day, but I pretended to be in a hurry and promised I'd talk to her tomorrow, hoping she'd forget about it by then.

When I got to the cemetery after school, I expected a quiet, peaceful place, and was looking forward to the break. But once I entered the gates, I saw the cemetery was overrun with prim ladies decorating Confederate graves with flowers in preparation for Robert E. Lee's birthday next week. They tried to smile at me, assuming I was there to celebrate the glorious dead, too, but I wasn't interested in people who still clung to the Civil War like it was something to be proud of. I ignored them and kept going through row after row of tombs shaped like sad concrete houses, tripping on the live oak roots pushing up the walkways and checking the engraved names until I found the tomb labeled MCDONOUGH in capitals over the entrance.

There were only two names engraved on the marble tablet covering the opening where Minty's body had been stowed.

AURELIA SINCLAIR MCDONOUGH
APRIL 12, 1888—OCTOBER 21, 1918

ARIMENTHA SINCLAIR MCDONOUGH
NOVEMBER 26, 1911—DECEMBER 31, 1929

Two women struck down well before their time. Minty had lost her mother to the influenza epidemic when she was six years old. Would things have turned out differently for her if she hadn't?

Would things have turned out differently for me if my mother hadn't left me? Or if I'd had a different mother, who cared to be one?

A sense of heavy sadness descended over me like a curtain. Judge McDonough's hopeful voice the night I broke into Minty's room replayed in my head. *"Arimentha darling? Is that you?"*

At the bottom of the tomb was carved a message in the stone:

THERE IS NO DEATH! WHAT SEEMS SO IS TRANSITION.

Was that what Judge McDonough had been hoping for that night? That some part of his daughter lived on?

I didn't believe in ghosts or hell or anyplace, but those words on the tomb gave me the creeps. Minty's body was mere inches away, bricked up behind that marble slab, the bones of her mother below her. None of the Daughters of the Confederacy ladies were on this row with me, and their voices sounded far away, even though the whole cemetery took up only one city block. All these concrete tombs crammed together muffled and distorted the sounds. If someone came upon me here, and I screamed, no one would find me quick enough in this maze.

The warning on the mirror floated red in my mind. What if the killer was true to his word and came to hurt me next?

Shivers ran down my spine. What if he was watching me now? What if he was lurking behind one of these tombs?

I looked over my shoulder to reassure myself, but a man was standing there in the long shadows. I let out a strangled scream. The man stepped forward into the bright afternoon light.

It was no killer. It was Detective Sabatier. Relief surged through my body.

He held up his hands, to show he meant no harm, but he didn't apologize.

"That's Longfellow," he said.

"What?" I pressed a hand over my heart, which was still rocketing around in my chest.

"'There is no Death! What seems so is transition; this life of mortal breath is but a suburb of the life elysian, whose portal we call Death.'"

I glared at him. The last thing I wanted right now was a sneaky, poetry-quoting cop. "What are you doing here?"

"I come here twice a day most days, on my way to and from the police station."

"But . . . why?"

"For much the same reason you do, I expect. Because a remorseful killer might pay Miss McDonough a visit. I suggested the department assign a plainclothes officer to keep watch on the tomb around the clock, but my *superior* didn't think that was a good use of funds."

Craggy. That didn't surprise me a bit. "So, you come here yourself."

Sabatier smiled tightly, the bitterness still showing in his eyes. "I keep hoping I'll stumble on someone visiting. And now here I find you."

My brows rose. "You think I'm the killer just because I'm standing in front of her grave?"

"No, Miss Coleman." Sabatier studied me carefully in that unnerving way of his. "What happened to your hands? And is that a bandage on your leg?"

I bit my lip. I'd promised Marion I would tell the detective about the vandalism and the warning on the mirror, and it was essential information about the killer. But I dreaded having yet another conversation about how I should be leaving this investigation to the police.

Before I could decide how to phrase what I had to say, Sabatier spoke again. "I heard someone broke into your club. Is that how you got hurt?"

Surprised, I scowled and took a step toward him. "Heard from who?"

He hesitated, his gaze drifting back to Minty's tomb. "I have my sources. You really should've reported the incident to the police right away. We could've dusted for fingerprints."

I snorted. "Because that worked so well for you last time?"

"We could've taken photographs then."

"Already done." I looked at him steadily. "If you know about the vandalism and the warning, then you know the killer isn't Marion. That means you'll leave him alone now, right?"

Sabatier shifted his weight. "All I can say is I'm going to pursue all avenues, as I've always done." He nodded at Minty's tomb. "The only person I'm obligated to is her. I owe her justice."

"So the rest of the world can hang?"

He moved closer beside me and clasped his hands behind his back, still staring at Arimentha's name on the vertical slab. "I would feel the same way if it was you in there, or if it was Marion himself. She deserved a chance to make amends, to make her life what she wanted it to be. She was still so young, barely more than a child, like you."

I grimaced at him. "We were nothing alike."

"You both lost your mothers too soon."

"What do you know about it?"

He held up his hands again. "Nothing."

I turned away from him and looked at the two urns sitting on either side of the tomb's base, each filled with yellow flowers.

"Who brought those?" I said without looking at Sabatier.

"Her father has them sent over. He hasn't come himself since the funeral. Can't bear it, I'm told." Another stab of guilt sliced at my chest. I took a step closer to the tomb and ran my hand over the marble enclosure. It had only been here a decade, but the constant humid weather had already turned the marble as rough as sandpaper. This close, I noticed something I hadn't before—a tiny corner of paper poking out between the edge of the closure tablet and the wall of the tomb at about my knee height. Cautious excitement rose in my chest. Was this the clue I'd come here for? Or just something left behind when the cemetery workers closed up Arimentha's tomb?

The corner was too small to grab with my fingers and tug out quickly; it would require careful maneuvering, or else I'd push it in deeper and never be able to reach it. I glanced over my shoulder at Sabatier.

"Don't you have somewhere to be?"

His brows rose slightly. "Nope." He stepped up to the tomb right next to me. "Have you found something of interest?"

"Is there anyone else from their family buried in this cemetery?" I said, hoping to direct Sabatier's attention away from the McDonough tomb.

"Not that I know of," he said absently, eyes scanning the tomb where I'd been looking.

"What about her diary? Find anything else interesting in there?"

He didn't answer me. I saw on his face the moment he spotted the corner of paper.

"Miss Coleman," he said evenly, "do you happen to have a pair of tweezers with you?"

So much for losing him. "Why would I be carrying around tweezers?"

"Some people do."

I watched him staring at the paper, then sighed. Now that

he'd spotted it, he was going to get it with or without me. I'd rather make him share. "I do have a pointy knife."

I took my switchblade out of my bag, where I liked to keep it handy, even at school. I'd never used it on anyone, though was often tempted. Sabatier looked slightly alarmed when I clicked the button to open it, but then he held out a hand for it.

"It's my blade. I'll do it." I shouldered him out of the way and crouched in front of my new obstacle. The corner of paper was so tiny I could only use the tip of the blade. My hands would have to be steady.

"Be careful," Sabatier said unnecessarily.

"Don't talk. You'll interrupt my concentration."

Sabatier pressed his lips together into a flat line, which I took for grudging agreement. I held my blade over the corner of paper for a few seconds, wincing at the slight pain in my knuckles. I slowed my breathing to make sure my hand was steady, then stabbed the tiny bit of paper and began to tug. Bit by bit, it slid more into view until another corner was visible. I kept the first corner pinned with my knife and pinched the other with my fingers. I dragged the note the rest of the way, and it was mine.

Until Sabatier unceremoniously snatched it from my hand.

"Hey!" I shot straight up.

"It's evidence, Miss Coleman," he said, but without even bothering to gloat. He was already unfolding the paper, and there was another drawing, much like the one we'd found in the diary. Even I recognized this bird—a mourning dove. The paper was the same size and shape as the other drawing, probably taken from the same notebook; and since Symphony

Cornice had shown me the different styles of pencil strokes, I could recognize that the same artist had drawn this one. Quickly, Sabatier flipped it over and checked for a note, but this time there was none.

"Do you think the killer put this here?" I shivered, remembering that creepy feeling I'd had before Sabatier appeared. What if the killer really had been nearby watching me? He'd already watched me at least once, or he wouldn't have left that warning on the mirror. Between him and Sabatier's "sources," pretty soon I'd be tripping over stalkers every time I turned around.

"I don't know," Sabatier said, maddeningly averse to conjecture. "I believe this one matches the one from the diary." He gave me a pointed look. "The one I've mysteriously not laid eyes on since that day we found it together."

"Interesting."

"Miss Coleman," he said, turning stern, "these drawings may be the key to the case, and it's important I keep all the evidence safe and in police hands, so that I can get a conviction when we do catch this killer. If you have that other drawing—"

"All right, all right. I get it." I'd already gotten about all the use I could out of the drawing anyway, so I dug it out of my bag and handed it over. "For the record, I didn't steal it—you dropped it."

"Thank you, Miss Coleman." Sabatier held up the two drawings side by side. "Remarkable."

"Why do you think a killer would leave this here like a calling card?"

"I imagine he didn't think it would be noticed. It was only

a tiny white corner against white marble. Not everyone would have spotted it."

"That sounds dangerously close to a compliment, Detective Sabatier."

"Nothing dangerous about it, Miss Coleman. Your instincts are good. Your methods, however, leave much to be desired."

I rolled my eyes. "I'll stick to mine and you stick to yours."

"I will, Miss Coleman. We'll see in the end who prevails."

"Yes, we will."

CHAPTER

29

ON MY WAY out of the cemetery, I paid one of the maintenance workers two bucks and asked him to keep an eye on Minty's tomb and to call me if anybody came to visit. Another method of mine Detective Sabatier would probably disapprove of, but he'd be eating his hat if it paid off for me later.

On the way home, I tried to think of some other tricks I had that Sabatier didn't, and I remembered the Felicity Inn. Now was a perfect time to make a second attempt to find it.

The vivid blue sky of afternoon had faded to pale lavender by the time I'd made it back to Canal Street on the streetcar and walked to the far end, where the Pelican and the Felicity Inn were supposedly in close proximity. But there was still much more light to see by than there'd been the night I searched for the hotel with Olive.

I slowed my steps and studied each house as I passed it, looking for signs that it was anything other than a house. Then, about a block away from the Pelican, I spotted it—a literal sign. It was the size of an envelope and nailed up beside a purple front door. It read, ROOMS TO LET. SHORT TERM.

I stopped, heartbeat speeding up, and bounded up the steps. The faded pink paint of the house's clapboards was coated in coal dust, and the stained-glass sidelights around the front door were smudged and cobwebbed. I rang the doorbell once and waited, but no one came. I pressed the button again, longer this time, and heard the bell's chime echoing inside.

Just when I'd decided I had the wrong place, a woman opened the door halfway and looked out. She was tall, with plenty of natural insulation under her mulberry-colored dress and several rings on each plump hand.

"Is this the Felicity Inn?" I blurted.

She took in the sight of me in my school uniform, and her dark brows drew together. "Aren't you a little young for this place, honey?"

"I'm not here for a room. May I come in?"

The woman glanced to the left and right over my shoulder, then took a step back and waved me into an entrance hall that had been turned into a lobby. The signs of dust and neglect from the exterior of the house were absent in here. Everything was spotlessly clean, and a cushy orange chair stood behind a large desk in the middle of the floor, which was checkered in wide squares of black and white. The staircase to one side had worn dips in the middle of each step from so many feet over the past hundred years, but the wood was polished to a shine.

The woman sat down in the orange chair, her ring-bedecked hands perched on its arms like she was a queen and this was her throne. She said nothing but watched me expectantly, waiting for me to explain myself.

"Ma'am," I said, because she looked a couple of decades older than me, "I have a few questions to ask you. About one of your . . . guests."

Her eyes went flinty, and one hand moved protectively to a large ledger book on the desk. "I'm afraid I don't answer questions."

"I understand privacy is important in your line of work," I said, easing forward slowly. "It is in mine, too. What's your name? Can you answer that?"

The woman looked me over with an appraising eye. "You can call me Mrs. Felix. And just what is your business?"

"I'm Millie Coleman," I said. "My aunt owns the Cloak and Dagger club, and I work there, too."

Mrs. Felix shifted in her chair, her gaze sharpening. "You've had some trouble there recently, I heard."

I nodded, glad I didn't have to explain it all again. "That's what I'm here about." I studied Mrs. Felix and decided how to present my case. She wouldn't care if Marion was my best friend, or a nice person. I had to appeal to her as one business owner to another. "The cops want to pin the murder on our star performer, the one who brings in the big bucks. I'm trying to get him cleared, so he can get back on our stage."

"What does that have to do with me?" she said.

"We think the girl who was killed might've come here with someone in the past, maybe more than once. Her name was Arimentha McDonough. Maybe you can look for her in your ledger there."

"Nobody gives their real name here." Mrs. Felix laughed a smoky laugh that set her to coughing. "What else you got?"

I took out my notebook with Minty's picture pasted inside and laid it on top of her ledger. "You seen her?"

Mrs. Felix picked up the notebook and held it at arm's length to study Minty's face. She gave me a weaselly look. "I might've."

"What do you want? Money?"

She smirked. "You don't have the kind of money that would persuade me. But your customers . . ." She looked toward the staircase and rubbed her chin. When she looked back at me, her eyes were metallic bright. "You spread the word about this place at your aunt's club. Tell everybody this is the place to go for an hour or a night, and nowhere else. You promise to do that, and I'll tell you what I know."

I hesitated. Cal wouldn't like it. She made her own business deals, and for all I knew she could already have an arrangement with a different hotel.

"Take it or leave it," Mrs. Felix said, smiling.

"Fine." I clenched my fists, making the cuts on my hands protest. "I'll take it. What you got?"

Mrs. Felix looked pleased with herself and steepled her fingers together on top of the ledger. "I've seen your girl all right. She came here a few times."

"With someone?"

Mrs. Felix gave me a disdainful look. "Nobody comes here alone, sweetheart."

I clenched my teeth to stop myself from reacting to that. "Okay," I gritted out, "so who was her friend?"

"A kid, like her." Mrs. Felix waved a hand, her jewels gleaming. "Didn't dress or talk like her, though. Figured that's why they were here—a wrong-side-of-the-tracks Romeo-and-Juliet thing."

"What did he look like?" I said eagerly.

"About the same height as you. Black hair, too." She laughed. "He isn't your brother, is he?"

"No." I didn't have time for jokes when I was so close. "What else?"

"He wasn't as skinny as you. Looked like a strong boy. Big shoulders. Good-looking. Spanish or something like that. Couldn't blame the girl for slumming with that one."

"Got anything more specific? Scars? Tattoos? An accent? An eye patch?"

Mrs. Felix shook her head. "He was just a regular kid. He was even nice to her, not like a lot of folks I get in here. Looked at her like she was made of gold." She winked broadly. "Which I'm betting she was."

"Did she ever say his name?"

Mrs. Felix considered. "I don't think so. But he called her some kind of nickname."

"Maybe you wrote it in the ledger?"

"Come to think of it . . ." She started flipping pages. "Of course, they always used fake names, like everybody. And they were always different, but . . . ah." Her finger stopped on a line, and she spun the book around so I could see. "The girl's names were always birds."

I leaned over the book. The line said *Dove Jones and Romeo Catalano.*

Mrs. Felix flipped back another page and pointed again. *Sparrow Bells and Lorenzo Alto.* Another. *Fanny Cardinal and Sal*

Romeo. Another. *Robin LeJay and Romeo Benini.*

"Four times? Are you sure that's all?"

Mrs. Felix flipped a few more pages and shook her head. "Looks like it."

I listed off all the names again in my head. All Minty's names were for birds; all Romeo's names sounded Italian. Did that mean he was Italian? That narrowed down the selection somewhat, but not much. There were Italian families on every block of the French Quarter, not to mention the rest of the city.

"Oh," Mrs. Felix said, "and there's one more thing."

I looked up at her, mind spinning. "What?"

"That boy always had a smell about him, like he worked in a stable or something."

"He smelled like horses? Maybe an ice delivery guy? A truck farmer?"

"No, no." Mrs. Felix shook her head. "He smelled like hay."

I gaped at her blankly. My insides swayed as the dots connected in my brain. Dark hair, good-looking, broad shoulders, the same height as me, polite, smells like hay—like the hay packed around bottles of bootleg liquor.

Romeo could be lots of people. Could be anybody.

Or . . .

Suddenly, the names clicked into place.

Sparrow Bells and Lorenzo Alto. Sal. Benini.

He had been at the club that night. Had I even questioned him about where he was when Minty died? Or had I just assumed he was innocent? I backed toward the door. "I have to go."

Mrs. Felix laughed. "Figured it out, have you?"

I didn't answer. I couldn't.

I ran out the door and let it slam shut behind me.

—·—

I turned down Decatur, back into the heart of the French Quarter. Back toward Altobello's Grocery. My heart hammered. I told myself I was probably wrong. Bennie had tried to help me get out of the club the night of the murder. Bennie had gathered Marion's stuff from his grandmother's rooming house. Bennie had driven us to Arimentha's house and helped us try to break into the diary box.

But . . . what if he did those things because he was the murderer? What if he searched through Marion's things to find incriminating evidence against him? What if he wanted to see the diary in case his own name was in it?

If Bennie was the killer, then he was the one who vandalized the club and wrote that threat on the mirror.

If Bennie was the killer, he knew where Marion was, knew where my whole family was. All he had to do was knock on the door and they'd let him in.

What if they were all in danger?

My heart beat even faster, and I picked up my pace until I was running, ignoring the pain in my leg, dodging around pedestrians, even darting into the street to get more room. What if Bennie was there at the store now? What was I going to do? Would I be able to pretend everything was all right? Would I be able to trick him into confessing?

By the time I got close to the grocery, I knew I needed evidence. I'd never been inside Bennie's bedroom, but I knew where it was—in the back of the storage room, with its own entrance, so he could do late-night deliveries without disturbing the family. I was going in, if not now, then later tonight.

I slowed when I got to the corner across from the grocery.

I went around the block to the back, where they loaded the delivery truck, and peered around the corner. The truck was gone. Bennie was off making a delivery. I let out a breath. I had time, though there was no way of knowing if it was five minutes or an hour.

Mrs. Altobello's house loomed black against the deepening lavender sky over the muddy loading yard. Two upper windows faced this way, but no one stood at them. One of them was Marion's, and I knew his room hadn't been let again yet. Bennie had said Mrs. A was holding it for him. What would she think if her precious grandson turned out to be a murderer? What would Bennie's parents and sisters do? What would *I* do? I pushed that worry away for now. Two more windows in the apartment over the Altobellos' store looked down on the yard. White curtains covered them, and I could only hope no one in his family was peering through them at this very minute.

I stepped out from behind the corner and strolled casually across the dusky yard. Then I ducked under the little lean-to protecting Bennie's door from the elements. At least there, I wouldn't be visible while I picked Bennie's lock.

I took out my lock-picking tools but tested the doorknob first, and it turned easily under my hands. Maybe that was a good sign. People who had stuff to hide locked it up, didn't they?

I stopped thinking and slowly pushed open the door, still half expecting to see Bennie inside. But there was no one in the narrow room. Only a small, scarred desk and mismatched chair, a washstand with a ceramic pitcher and bowl, an old armoire, and a single bed along one wall, covered with a gray wool blanket and a pancake of a pillow. One window over the desk was open a crack, and a damp breeze twirled around me.

I went to the desk first and looked at the few objects there. There was a candlestick telephone and a lamp with a pull chain. The day's light was almost gone, and very little of it reached into the corners of this room, so I took a risk and turned on the lamp. It illuminated a cigar box containing a pen and a bottle of ink, a rubber eraser, a stubby pencil, and a short knife to sharpen it with. I picked up the knife, pushed the dull side against the pad of my thumb, and set it back down again in its place.

Underneath the desk was an old apple crate filled with papers. I crouched down and flipped through them one by one, but they were all receipts related to the business. Bennie must do the paperwork for his father. I didn't see a calendar anywhere and definitely no love letters or journals.

I straightened up and moved on to the washstand. The cabinet contained a stack of thin white towels and a glass jar with a two-inch layer of coins inside. The drawer contained a razor, shaving brush, box of extra blades, and a small bowl for the shaving cream.

Nothing.

Next, the armoire. I opened its double doors. One had an oval mirror on it, and the other had pictures pasted on the inside of beautiful movie stars cut from newspapers, not dissimilar to the ones Marion had stuck around his dressing room mirror, except I imagined Bennie had a different use for them. Inside was a hanging rod on one side and a stack of drawers on the other.

I cocked my head toward the door and stopped to listen. No voices, and I was certain I hadn't heard the truck pull up. Quickly, I pulled out each drawer, rifling through the contents, mostly Bennie's clothes. I managed to feel a little ashamed of myself when I got to the underwear drawer. I'd found nothing so far—maybe Bennie was innocent, and I'd jumped to conclusions and was violating his privacy for nothing. But if I hurried up and got out of here, he'd be none the wiser, and I wouldn't even have to be embarrassed about it. I emptied the pockets of Bennie's shirts and pants and his two suit jackets but came up with nothing more interesting than another nub of a pencil and a stray handkerchief.

I shut the armoire. Still nothing.

All nothing.

I turned around and looked at the narrow bed. It was the only place left, unless he had some secret hidey-holes in the walls or under the floorboards. I knelt on the bright rag rug next to Bennie's bed and peered under it. There weren't even any dust bunnies. The room was plain but neat, everything in its place, which fit what I knew of Bennie much more than his being a murderer. Maybe this long day had me jumping to conclusions.

I stood back up and looked under Bennie's pillow. I reached inside the pillowcase and found more nothing. I stopped and listened again. Still no truck engine or voices. Now for the mattress. I lifted it up at one corner and reached between it and the box springs, sweeping my arm back and forth. When I found nothing, I moved to the end of the bed and stuck my arm under there. A sliver of paper sliced into my finger. I yelped in shock, adrenaline pumping. I shoved my shoulder under the mattress and pushed it higher, not caring that the blankets were getting mussed. There on the box springs lay a thin stack of scattered papers of different sizes. Facedown.

My breath caught in my throat. Those papers could be anything—could be something he just didn't want his mother to see. Hell, they could be nudey pictures. But I had to know.

Hand shaking, finger bleeding, I reached for the papers and picked them up. They were drawings, all of them, done in hesitant gray strokes. I recognized the man on the corner behind his cart of oranges. Two girls walking arm in arm under a streetlight, their shadows stretched out long behind them, like me and Olive. Our cornetist with his lips pressed to the instrument and his cheeks puffed out. The river choked with boats.

And birds.

Lots of birds.

"What have you got there?"

My heart froze. Slowly, I turned my head.

Bennie stood in the open doorway, watching me.

CHAPTER

30

I SQUEEZED MY eyes shut. *No. No, no, no, no.* He'd sneaked up on me. How?

I opened my eyes and turned toward him, still holding the papers in my hand, a drop of blood from my finger blotching them.

I swallowed, tried to breathe. "I didn't hear the truck."

"I took it to the repair shop," Bennie said slowly. "Walked back."

I nodded, like this was a normal conversation, like he hadn't caught me literally red-handed in his room, snooping through his things. Finding evidence against him.

I was alone in a room with a murderer.

He stood in the doorway with his hand still on the knob. I could shove him, knock him off balance, slip past, hold tight to these drawings, take them to the police.

But the next moment, he came inside and shut the door behind him. Without turning his back on me, his fingers slid the bolt shut. The only light now came from the small lamp on the desk, and his face was in shadow.

I reached inside my pocket for my switchblade.

"Don't do that, Millie. Please."

I glanced at the window. It was big enough to jump through, but I'd have to waste time climbing over the desk and shoving up the sash. The only way that would work was if Bennie was down. Really down. And then I could just go through the door.

I swallowed hard again and slid out my knife, squeezing it so tightly the cuts on my knuckles stung. I didn't want to stab him, even now. I had never actually stabbed anyone, despite all my talk. Especially not someone I knew. Someone I'd worked with, laughed with, beat up bullies with, sat shoulder to shoulder with and plotted with.

"You," I said, and was surprised and annoyed to find my voice shaking. "You're Romeo. You killed her."

"No." He held up his hands but didn't advance toward me. He didn't pull out a weapon, but the pencil knife was still on the desk where I'd left it. The washstand drawer was full of razor blades. And he was bigger than me by at least thirty pounds.

I shook the drawings at him. "These . . . you . . . you did . . ." Where were my words? My lies? My best tools? They'd abandoned me.

"I didn't kill her, Millie. I swear."

I stuck out my chin. "I went to the Felicity Inn tonight."

Bennie ran a hand through his hair, rumpling it. His shoulders sagged. "You know then?" He looked pained. "About me and Minty?"

I gestured with the drawings. "These helped me put it together. How did you even meet her?"

"The Roosevelt Hotel, when I filled in for Eddie that time. She . . . she liked me. She . . ." His gaze drifted away from mine toward the window.

Anger flared, pushing down some of the fear. "She what? Seduced you? I'm sure it was somehow her fault, right? Then what? You fell in too deep, and she told you to get lost, and you pushed her off the balcony? Let Marion take the fall for it? Hung around with us, 'helped' us, all so you could save your own neck?"

"No. Yes . . . no, not all of it. I didn't kill her. I didn't even talk to her that night."

"I'm supposed to believe that? You're at the club and your lover—or ex-lover—walks in with another man, and you're just copacetic?"

"The last time I talked to her was the week before. She finally told me about the old friend she was looking for, and I realized he might be Marion. So I told her about the club, told her he'd be there, and I would take her. But she told me no. She said she wasn't looking to be my date, or anyone's. She said she was broken and wouldn't be fixed until she fixed something she'd done. She left me at the Felicity Inn, and I didn't see her again until that night at the club. But I didn't even talk to her, I swear. I let her be. I liked her a lot, maybe even could've loved her, but when she showed up with that rich kid, I figured she'd just been lying about being broken. I figured the real truth was she didn't want to be seen with some Italian bootlegger."

"And that made you mad."

"Yeah, I guess. Wounded my pride. But I was there with another date. And there are other people I liked, too." He rubbed the back of his neck, casting me a shy glance through his lashes. "I wouldn't throw everything away on Minty Mc-Donough. And I wouldn't have hurt her, or anyone. I . . . I won't hurt you, Millie. I swear. I just need you to give me back those drawings."

"What about the club? It was you who vandalized it, wasn't it? You wrote that threat on the mirror?"

Bennie's face turned positively mauve. He cleared his throat. "I didn't want to do that. I followed you and Olive that night you went to the Pelican. I was . . . afraid you were about to figure out I was with Minty, and I knew what you'd think. You might go to the police, to . . . to save Marion. I just wanted you to stop."

"So, you destroyed the place I work. Destroyed the place that my aunt loves and I love and Marion loves."

"I didn't destroy it! I didn't damage anything too expensive. And it wasn't really my father who sent that case of hooch—it was me, because I felt awful for how bad it looked in the day-time. I didn't want to really harm you, I just wanted to distract you. Slow you down."

"It didn't work."

Bennie's shoulders slumped even farther. "I see that. I should've known it wouldn't stop you. I panicked."

"Why go to all that trouble if you didn't even kill her?"

"The same reason Marion won't just turn himself in and hope the cops sort out the truth. Years ago a mob raided the jail and killed a bunch of innocent Italians because they got acquitted of murder. Nothing's changed. I have no reason to expect fairness from the police or the courts or even the people. They see *Italian* and think guilty."

I bit my lip. What he'd said wasn't wrong. Just like cops see *female impersonator* and they think guilty. "But you put that drawing in her tomb, didn't you?"

"Yeah, that was me." Bennie's eyes were mournful. "I couldn't keep it, could I? Too incriminating in case the cops ever came looking. I was going to burn it, but then . . . I couldn't bear to see another piece of her destroyed. So, I took it to her grave and gave it to her."

See another piece of her destroyed. Suddenly, I remembered something. "The night of the murder, I sent you and Eddie out the back way. Past the fountain. I told you not to look, but you . . . you saw her, didn't you?"

Bennie nodded sadly. "I can't stop seeing her like that. Her face . . . her eyes. She . . . always had so much life in her. Her laugh! And now . . ." The back of his hand quickly flicked at the corners of his eyes.

"I still see her, too," I said quietly. And I realized, somewhere along the way, I'd started believing him. I could see it right on his face. I knew it the way I knew Marion was innocent, even though so much evidence pointed at him. I knew it because I knew *him.* And he wasn't a murderer. The vandalism—that I could believe. Hadn't Olive pointed out how all the most expensive items had been left untouched? I remembered the contemplative look on her face then. Had she suspected this already?

I still clutched Pearl tightly in my hand, but the hammering of my heartbeat had begun to slow. "Okay. So. Let's say, for argument's sake, you're telling the truth."

Bennie looked up at me with bright hope in his eyes. "I am," he said urgently, and took a step toward me. "I swear I am."

I backed up, reclaiming my space. "If it's true you're Romeo and also *not* the killer, then who is?" I narrowed my eyes. "What else haven't you told us?"

"Nothing! I don't know who it is either! I—I would've told you if I knew."

I rolled my eyes. "You talked to Minty a lot the last months she was alive; you probably already knew half of this stuff I've found out, but you had me running around asking people like Symphony Cornice."

"I'm sorry." It was Bennie's turn to back up, shooting a fearful glance at my switchblade. "But I promise I didn't know much else."

"Much?" I took advantage of his fear and advanced, pushing him to retreat until his back bumped against the door. "Everything could matter, Bennie. Spill what you know."

He hesitated, his expression doing a complicated dance of emotions. "It's only—"

"Only?" I prompted.

"It seemed to me like I wasn't the only one she was . . . seeing. There were times she was secretive about why she couldn't meet me, and there was just this *tone* in her voice . . ."

I raised my brows. "A tone isn't much to go on. She didn't mention anyone else in her diary."

"That's just it. What if she did?" Bennie licked his lips, his eyes bright. "Remember how in the diary, she kept talking about Romeo *and* Juliette? I started wondering—what if Juliette wasn't code for Minty? What if it was code for another person? A girlfriend, maybe?"

Romeo and Juliette. Juliette and Romeo. Words from Minty's diary floated back to me.

"*To be* twice enthralled *is such a delicious distraction.*"

"*It's my birthday. I refused* both *of my invitations.*"

What if Bennie was right?

I frowned. "Did Minty ever actually say anything to you about liking girls?"

Bennie thought a moment, then brightened. "One time she made me take her to see *The Kiss* twice in a row, and she said Greta Garbo was to die for."

I rolled my eyes. "That's not exactly concrete proof. But Greta Garbo *is* to die for, so I can't fault her taste in ladies."

"What I was thinking," Bennie said eagerly, "is if there was a Juliette, Minty might've given her the brush-off, too. And maybe she wasn't so accepting of it as I was."

My thumb rubbed the hilt of my switchblade as I contemplated the options. Daphne, Symphony, every regular that had passed through the doors of the Cloak on New Year's Eve. I scrubbed a hand over my eyes, exhausted with the possibilities. There had to be a way to narrow them down. A way to find out Juliette's identity without tracking her all over the city like I had to do with Romeo.

Olive. She noticed everything that happened in the club. Knew everyone who'd been a regular since she started working there. We'd talked about the regulars a couple of times right after the murder, but so much had happened since then. Maybe if we talked again, something fresh would rise to the top.

"I'm leaving now, Bennie." I held up both hands, so the knife was pointed at the ceiling instead of at him, and the drawings fluttered in the slight breeze from the window. "I'm taking these with me as insurance."

"But—"

"And I want to see you at the club tomorrow with a broom in your hand."

He looked at me anxiously. "Are you going to tell Cal? That it was me?"

He was right to be scared. She would kill him, or at least he'd wish he was dead. She would cancel the contract with his father, too.

I wasn't sure what I would do. She deserved to know. He deserved to pay. But maybe not today. I had bigger fish to fry.

"I won't tell her."

Bennie sagged with relief. "Thank—"

"*Yet.* I won't tell her yet." Bennie visibly quaked, and my shoulders relaxed. "Now step aside, you criminal mastermind. I have a murderer to catch."

—·—

I went straight to the club, hoping to find Olive there working on repairing the damage Bennie had done. I wasn't ready to forgive him for that, and I knew Olive and Cal would be even slower to forgive, if they ever did. Olive never liked Bennie much, even when everyone else did, including rich debutantes. A picture flashed in my mind of Bennie and Minty in a room together at the Felicity Inn, and I had to squash down a twinge of jealousy. I'd been friends with Bennie for four years, and I could admit I'd been attracted to him lately. But if there'd been anything romantic between me and Bennie, it had to be over now. And I found I didn't really regret that. My feelings for Olive were bigger; that seemed obvious now, and I picked up the pace of my steps, eager to see her again.

As soon as I went in the back door, I heard the piano tinkling in a melancholy melody, the kind Lewis only got to play when no customers were in the club. Cal always said this club was for forgetting our troubles, forgetting how hard life could be for us in the world out there. In here, we could laugh and dance and feel sexy. Sadness was best left outside the door.

Of course, that was easier said than done. It certainly hadn't worked for Minty.

In the main room, Lewis paused his playing long enough to give me a wave. Olive was at a table unpacking a crate of glass tumblers. She looked up and saw me and didn't smile, but she didn't scowl either. I could work with that.

"Where did those come from?" I said, picking up a glass printed with the words KAYSER & CO—LOVELY FROCKS FOR ALL YOUR COSTUME NEEDS.

"One of the regulars brought them by. And another brought those over there." Olive gestured to a stack of two crates against the wall. "Said they wanted to help get the Cloak back up and running as fast as they could. Said the world's too bleak without us in it."

My heart swelled. There was nothing I wanted more than to give the club back to them, to give Marion back to them and let him do what he did best again.

But then I dropped back to earth. "There's something I've got to tell you."

Olive considered the expression on my face. "Should I sit down for this?"

"Maybe we both should."

We sat at the table, surrounded by the donated glasses, and I told her everything I'd learned at the Felicity Inn, and what I'd done next. What I'd found in Bennie's room and what happened when he caught me snooping. As I talked, she didn't interrupt, but her eyes went wide, and her hands trembled. Her knee jumped against mine under the table. But it stopped abruptly when I told her what Bennie had confessed to, and what he hadn't.

"And you believe him?" she said, her tone incredulous, angry even. "Just because he's Bennie Altobello."

I spread out my hands. "Well. Yeah. Not right away, of course, and I still kept the drawings just in case."

"Hmph."

I realized in her skeptical silence that the piano had stopped. Lewis was watching us now, listening. This mattered to him, too, of course. The club mattered, and even more than that, Marion mattered. They hadn't gotten to see much of each other while Marion was in hiding, and Lewis wanted this resolved as much as we did. I gestured for him to join us, and he pulled out a chair across the table and folded his long limbs into it. I looked from him to Olive and back.

"I believe Bennie because he's family. Just like Marion and both of you."

"Family, huh?" Olive said.

"Yes, and sometimes we want to punch family in the face.

God knows I want to punch Mama about six times a day. But she's not a murderer. And neither is Bennie."

"Then where *is* this paragon of virtue?" Olive said. "I'd like to have a little conversation with him myself."

"And you will. And so will Cal. But not now. Now we have to focus. Now I need your help."

She sat back in her seat and narrowed her eyes. "With what?"

"Ever since the club got vandalized—"

"By Bennie."

I ignored her. "We'd ruled out the killer being a woman."

"Remember how he knocked you down?" Olive said, eyes like slits. "Remember how your hands got all cut up?"

"I remember. But listen—Bennie suspects Minty was seeing someone else besides him. A female someone."

"How convenient for him," Lewis said, exchanging a skeptical look with Olive.

"Don't you think he's just trying to throw the blame off himself?" she said.

"I don't know. That's why I need your help, Olive. You've got the sharpest eyes I know. You know everyone that comes in or out of this club, and you notice things other people don't bother to see. Not to mention, you're always sober, unlike the rest of the clowns in here."

The tiniest of smiles crept across her lips. Despite rumors to the contrary, flattery got you somewhere with everybody, even Olive.

"So," I continued before she could bring up Bennie again, "I know we already talked about some of this, but maybe there's something you forgot about back then. Or that we didn't know was important. I need to know if you got any sense from Minty that she was interested in one of her female friends that night? Or if they had an interest in her? Or maybe you saw a regular looking at their group particularly hard?"

Olive held up both hands. "Slow down. Let me think." She fiddled with her earring, staring off across the club toward the place where the Uptowners had sat on New Year's Eve.

"It was so chaotic that night . . ." She shook her head. "I saw that girl Symphony drawing Marion, and Arimentha staring at him, too. Daphne was the kind who couldn't stop jiggling her leg and tapping her fingers. Like somebody else I know." I grinned and stopped pecking at the side of a glass with my fingernails. "Anyway, I didn't notice Daphne looking at Minty particularly much. If anything, she kept her back turned to her, like she was miffed at her."

"They did argue that night," I said. "Though Daphne could've lied to me about why. It could've been a lovers' spat."

"What about the regulars?" Lewis said, scooting closer to the table.

"Lo was the most vocal about her interest in Minty," Olive said. "But she has an alibi."

"And we never did figure out who that other girl was that Duke saw talking to Minty at the bar." I flipped my notebook back to that early page and read aloud: "'Kid with brownish-red hair. Maybe five foot eight. Femme. Hadn't seen her for a while before New Year's.' Does that ring any bells for either of you?"

Olive looked into the middle distance for a long moment,

as if she were flipping through a mental photograph album, but she finally shook her head. "Duke said he hadn't seen her in a while, so maybe she was a regular back before I started work."

"That's true . . ." I said slowly. "What brought her back to the club after months away?"

"Minty?" Lewis said.

"Bingo." I pointed at him, then lowered my finger. "Well, maybe. But how do we figure out who she is?"

"Question everybody at the club again?" Olive said. "Surely somebody knows her."

I huffed out a frustrated breath. The answer felt so close, but there could be another two weeks' work in rounding up all those regulars one by one, and then what if we ran into another dead end?

"Goddammit," I said. "We've found our Romeo. Now we need a Juliette."

"Romeo and Juliette?" Lewis said. "Like the symphony?"

"No, like the—" I glanced at Olive, and she was sitting up straighter, too. "Wait—the what?"

Lewis shrugged. "There's a symphony, based on the play. By Berlioz."

"A *symphony*," Olive breathed.

"Lewis," I said, grabbing his arm, "how does that Berlioz guy spell Juliette?"

He looked at my hand on his arm in surprise. "The French way, of course. J-u-l-i-e-t-t-e."

Olive and I looked at each other, eyes wide. "Could it be—" she said.

Lewis looked puzzled. "Yes, it's a symphony. I can play you a bit if—"

"But she claimed to have a 'gentleman friend' in St. Louis," I said.

Olive raised her brows at me. "Minty had a 'gentleman friend,' too, if you count Bennie as a gentleman."

"What's the significance here?" Lewis said.

"Symphony Cornice," I said quickly. "But the name could be a coincidence."

Olive tsked. "Maybe you just don't want to believe you overlooked her."

"I didn't overlook her—I was going on false information that we had only one artist in love with Minty. When she showed me her drawing next to Romeo's, I knew it couldn't be her."

"But now we know there's a Juliette—" Lewis said.

"And," I said slowly, trying to catch the idea trying to gather in my brain, "Symphony is pretty tall, almost my height. Red hair—that could've looked brownish to Duke in the dark bar. What if she used to come here to meet girls, but then she and Minty started fooling around and she stopped?"

"Until New Year's Eve," Olive said.

We all looked toward the stairs that led to the balcony.

"If it's her, we'll need proof," I said. "She's rich and well protected from the law. We could break into *her* house. Try to find her own diary."

Olive held up a hand. "Won't she have destroyed evidence like that?"

"Then we go talk to her head on," I said. "Try to trick her into confessing."

"Even if we manage that, her confession to us would be meaningless. The cops would never believe us."

She was right. Of course. It was infuriating. "Well, what do you suggest then, Olive?"

She opened her mouth to speak, and then the telephone rang. Lewis stood to answer it, and Olive leaned forward to whisper something to me, but then Lewis turned, eyes wide. "It's for you, Millie. He says it's about the cemetery."

I hurried to the telephone, a frown creasing my brow. Olive followed me and wedged herself beside me. "You're not leaving me out of anything this time, Millie Coleman."

I shuffled over and held the receiver between our ears. I was distracted by her arm curving around my back, her cheek so close to mine, but then the person on the telephone spoke.

"Miss Coleman? This is Harvey at the Lafayette Cemetery. You told me to call if I saw anyone at that tomb."

"Yes." My heart beat faster and not just from Olive being beside me. "Did you see anything?"

"Well, I sorta did. But I don't know if it's anything."

"Just tell me, and we'll see."

"Okay." Mr. Harvey hiccuped. "There was a girl this afternoon, right before five. I know because it was almost time to close the gates. I'd about forgotten what you said about watching that tomb, but then I noticed that's where that girl was heading. She was about the only one left in the cemetery."

"What did she look like?"

"Reddish hair. Young, maybe eighteen or twenty?"

I glanced at Olive out of the corner of my eye. She squeezed my arm just below the elbow. *Symphony.*

"And what did she do, Mr. Harvey?

"Wasn't nothing too unusual at first. Just crouched down there in front of the tomb and put some flowers in the vase. I figured she was just a girl, just a friend, and not the sort you were looking for, so I was going to leave her to mourn in peace, but then she started talking. I guess she thought nobody was around."

My breath caught in my throat. "What did she say?"

"It wasn't like she said anything bad, it just gave me a funny feeling I ought to call you."

"What was it, Mr. Harvey?" I asked again.

"Okay, well, she said something like, 'It was his fault, all of it. I know you could've loved me if you weren't so consumed with him. The police won't seem to do their job. That leaves only me.'"

"Did she say who she meant?"

"Somebody named Mary, I think? Which didn't make no sense with what she was saying, talking about a man and all."

I was suddenly itching to hang up, itching to go home. A bad feeling was creeping up my chest and down my limbs to my very fingertips.

"Did she say or do anything else, Mr. Harvey?"

"Not as I can recall. She just stood up and kissed her fingers and touched that girl's name on the marble tablet and left. I ducked back between the tombs and watched her go. She was the last one out, and I locked up the gates after her. I had to finish my rounds and all, and then I had a drink down at the . . ." He coughed. "I mean, I . . . just had a little break after work with some friends . . . and I kept remembering that red-haired girl and thinking maybe I ought to call you, and so now here I am."

That explained the hiccups. "Thank you, Mr. Harvey. You did the right thing."

"I don't know if—"

But I hung up the receiver before he could finish. I looked around at Olive and Lewis, their eyes wide.

"What is it?" Lewis said.

"Marion." The breath caught in my chest. "I think she's after Marion."

That's when the emergency bell rang overhead, loud and shrill as a scream.

CHAPTER

31

NIGHT HAD FALLEN, and a bright moon hung low over the buildings. Olive and I ran across the courtyard, Lewis trailing not far behind. Even from a few feet away, I saw that the back door of my apartment building had been tampered with. We always kept it shut tight and locked. Now it was open a few inches, and neither Cal nor our neighbors would ever leave it like that.

Up close, it was clear from the splintered wood that the door had been jimmied open. Olive and I looked at each other in escalated alarm. Behind us, Lewis's breaths came fast and shallow.

I took out my switchblade, and Olive reached into her dress pocket and produced one of her own. We pressed the levers at the same time, and our two blades popped out with a pleasing double snick.

"I knew I liked you," I whispered.

"You did?" Olive said, but I was already pushing the door open and creeping into the small, empty hallway, lit only by the orange light leaking out of the foyer up ahead. We hurried down the hallway into the foyer, and my gaze followed the staircase upward to our apartment, where Marion had rung the alarm.

I waved for Olive and Lewis to follow me up the stairs, and we crept upward slowly in single file. I skipped the third stair from the bottom, which always creaked, and held out an arm to stop Olive beside me on the landing, my favorite eavesdropping spot. Lewis stopped one step down from us. I pointed up to the transom window over our door. It was open an inch.

I held a finger over my lips. A female voice floated over the transom, and it wasn't Mama's or Cal's.

Symphony, I mouthed, and Olive adjusted her grip on her knife. Lewis's brown eyes were wide with terror and worry. I was scared and worried, too, somewhere deep in my mind, but I couldn't let those feelings rise to the surface. Not now.

We crept up the last six steps and listened again. Symphony was speaking.

"Now write this: 'I deeply regret my actions and can no longer live with the guilt. I must face the consequences.'"

There was a long pause, as I guessed Marion was obeying. Then he spoke, sounding defiant, angry. "Are you the one who vandalized the Cloak and Dagger?"

Symphony sneered. "I don't care about that club. I care about Arimentha. I'm the only one who really did."

"If that's true, why don't you want to find out who really killed her? Why do you want them to arrest an innocent man?"

"Because you're not innocent. Maybe you didn't push her off that balcony, but your actions led her there. You made her—"

"Made her what? How did I make her do anything?"

Paper rattled. Feet tapped across the floor. "Because she loved you. Because you're the only one she loved. She refused to move on with her life until she found you and fixed whatever was between you. I told her not to bother, I told her you were the one who left. To let you go. But she wouldn't listen."

I crept up the last few steps, with Olive and Lewis close behind me. I tested the doorknob. Symphony hadn't locked it behind her. Slowly, I turned the knob, eased the door open a crack, and peeked through it.

"Did she tell you why I left?" Marion said. I could see a sliver of him now, sitting at Cal's desk in the far corner of the living room.

"She said you two had a falling out." Symphony appeared in front of him and disappeared again. She was pacing. I saw the metallic flash of a gun in her hand under the single light bulb. "Arimentha was so intent on making up with you. It was ridiculous. And *you* made it happen. You're the reason we were even at that club. If you'd never—"

"Can I show you something?" Marion's chair scraped against the floor as he pushed it back. "I have it in my pocket. The note she wrote to me that night."

Symphony stopped pacing in front of him, hesitated. She was curious. So was I. Marion had never shown it to me, had hardly mentioned it since. "Read it to me."

Marion half stood and slid the note out of his back trousers pocket. He unfolded it on the desk, on top of the confession he was supposed to be writing, which no doubt would smear the fresh ink. Was this strategic on his part? He cleared his throat and started reading.

Dear Marion,

I address this to the name you've chosen, rather than the name I knew you by. I believe perhaps you are no longer the person I knew at all, but this new being I failed to know.

I wish you could've told me long ago the truth of who you are. I wish I knew for sure I would've accepted it and loved you anyway. I wish you'd had nothing to fear from me. But we saw that wasn't true.

I swear I didn't know what your brother would do to you. I didn't know he was so cruel. And when I found out about the asylum, much later, I stopped speaking with him.

Tonight, when I stood there staring at you on that stage, I knew I'd been a fool to ever try and make you into someone else, just for my own benefit. You looked beautiful up there, darling. I mean it, you did.

I love you still, my dear friend. I was a selfish fool, and I hope you can forgive me one day.

Much love,
Arimentha

There were tears in his voice by the end, and tears in my eyes, too. If she'd gotten the chance to give him this note, would he have forgiven her? Or would it still have been too late? She'd changed, she'd apologized, but sometimes it still wasn't enough to erase the damage done. And now she'd paid for her mistakes in spades.

"Let me see that," Symphony said, snatching up the note from the table.

"Do you honestly believe that after I read that note," Marion said quietly, "I would've thrown her off a balcony?"

"Maybe you didn't read it first." Her hand holding the note trembled. "Maybe"—she shook her head fiercely—"no, it doesn't matter anyway. She's dead, and it's your fault. Write it. Write that it's your fault."

"Writing it doesn't make it true, you know," Marion said. "Writing it doesn't erase what really happened."

"Do it," Symphony said, her voice wavering but her gun arm steady.

"What do you plan to do with me afterward?" Marion said. "Kill me and make it look like a suicide?"

"If need be."

That was it. I couldn't wait anymore. I slammed the door open, not caring that I was bringing a literal knife to a gun-fight.

"I'm sorry, Symphony. You're not killing anybody today."

Marion's mouth dropped open and eyes widened. Symphony swung halfway toward me, raising her gun, then seemed to realize she shouldn't turn her back on Marion. She retreated a step, keeping her eyes on us both, fingers fumbling to steady the gun.

Olive entered the room and stood just behind me to my right. Lewis didn't appear, but I couldn't spare a glance to see where he'd gone. I evaluated our situation. Two switchblades were no match for a gun, if Symphony knew how to shoot straight. And we had no way of knowing if she could until she shot at us and either hit or missed.

"Stop right where you are!" Symphony flung Minty's note back on the table and steadied her gun with her other hand. We stopped, our knife arms outstretched, and a frantic expression flashed in Symphony's eyes.

"Go away," she said. "This has to be done."

"I'm afraid we can't let you hurt Marion."

"I—I'm not going to hurt him. I want to see justice done. That's all."

"Justice? Oh, Symphony." I shook my head. "You know he didn't kill her. You know who did."

"I—I don't—" she spluttered. "It's his fault."

"His fault blah, blah, blah. You just want to find someone to blame, so you don't have to blame yourself. So you don't have to face what you did."

"No." She shook her head. "That isn't true. I loved Arimentha."

"Oh, we know you did. You really loved her, *Juliette*."

Symphony's shoulders twitched, wobbling the gun. "How?" She shook her head again. "No. I—I'm not—"

Marion's hand crept toward Cal's notoriously sharp letter opener. If he got it, we'd have three knives versus one wobbly gun. I liked those odds a little better.

I had to keep Symphony talking, distracted. "How did it happen? That night? You must've been angry, but why?"

"I don't know what you mean."

Marion's fingers closed over the letter opener. His eyes flicked up and met mine.

I took a step closer and slightly to the left.

Symphony stared at me, wild-eyed. "Stop there. Stop. I will shoot."

"Wouldn't be the first girl you killed, would it?"

Symphony blinked. "I didn't—it was . . ." She trailed off.

"An accident?"

She stiffened her shoulders, squared her jaw. Didn't answer.

"Was that it?" I said, gentling my voice as I eased another step closer. "You didn't mean to do it? Maybe you argued, and things got out of hand?"

"We . . ." The gun shook in her hand.

"Why were you on that balcony, Symphony? Did you take her there?"

"Stop."

"You'd been at the club before that night, hadn't you? You'd been there loads of times."

She looked at me, surprised. "How do you kn—" But she stopped herself from finishing the sentence.

"I know because you seemed to figure out right away the night of the murder that Marion was my friend. You'd seen us together before, hadn't you? And that made you suspect I was trying to protect him."

"That means nothing. You were behaving suspiciously. Anyone could see that."

"And our bartender saw someone who looks like you trying to pick up Minty that night. You knew just where to take her, too, once you persuaded her."

"I . . . I don't know what you mean."

"Sure you do. It must've been a while since you came there, since Olive didn't recognize you."

"Maybe not since before she started her fling with Minty," Marion suggested.

Symphony turned a sharp glare on him. "It wasn't a 'fling.' I loved her. And she . . . she would've loved me, but you ruined her. She couldn't think about anything else. All she wanted to do was go back and give you that stupid note. It was like she couldn't be whole again until she patched things up with you. She didn't have room in her heart for me."

"Or for Bennie either," I said.

"Bennie?" Marion said, looking up in surprise.

"Bennie?" Symphony said coldly, her expression turning haughty. "Is he the one she met at the Felicity all those times?"

"You're jealous of Marion but not him? Why?"

"I knew she didn't care about that boy at the Felicity. She was just having fun with him. Marion she loved. And yet he rejected her."

"How do you know she wasn't just having fun with you?"

"I—I—" Symphony faltered. "I just know."

"I know what that's like," Olive said, edging closer, too. "I know it's hard to find someone who seems perfect to you, who seems to like you, too, but they're always just out of reach. It can make you frustrated. Angry sometimes."

Marion eased himself out of his chair while Symphony's eyes were on Olive. I inched farther left.

"Maybe," Olive continued, "when she invited you to the club that night, and you knew what kind of club it was, you hoped this was a sign she was really ready to be with you. You took her upstairs, anticipating your Juliet and Juliette moment. But she was distracted, worried about giving that note to Marion. You kept going with the speech you'd planned anyway, hoping. But then she shot you down. Said she wasn't ready to love anyone. That she wasn't a whole person anymore and wouldn't be until she resolved this thing with Marion. And you got angry. Angry at yourself as much as at her. And you pushed."

Symphony's eyes brimmed with tears. I expected her to deny it again, but her shoulders sagged, the gun sagging, too, aiming more at my calves than my chest. "I . . . I was angry, but I didn't mean . . . it was only a little push, I swear it! But she tripped on the hem of her dress. She stumbled . . . I tried to grab her, but the momentum took her over, and all I had in my hands were the beads from her dress." Tears leaked down Symphony's cheeks. "I didn't want her to die. I . . . loved her. I . . ."

"Why didn't you tell that to the cops then?" Olive said, attracting her focus again so I could slip a little closer and switch my knife to my left hand. I clenched it tightly, ignoring the pain in my palm. "You're a rich white girl—they would've believed you."

"Because . . . because I was *angry*. Angry she was dead. And I wished it was him that went over that balcony instead of her." Her eyes went hot and swung to Marion again. "So I decided. I knew she had that note to him in her hand. I knew his dressing room was right down the hall. They'd blame him for her murder. And I'd let them. Then he'd get the punishment he deserved for ruining her life. And mine."

"You read Minty's letter, Symphony," Marion said. "I didn't ruin anything for her. She made a mistake that ruined mine. Or would have if I'd let it. But I left my old life behind and made a new one. Now you're trying to take it away because of your mistake. But I won't let you."

"Neither will I," Olive said.

I spoke with my knife. I lunged at Symphony and jabbed with my left hand under her ribs while I shoved up on her arms with my right. The gun went off, and Marion and Olive ducked. A bullet hole appeared in the ceiling, and plaster sprinkled down on Olive's hair like powdered sugar on a beignet.

The knife had been stopped by Symphony's sturdy wool

jacket, but I'd knocked her off balance, and I tackled her to the ground. Instead of fighting me off, she hung on to the gun with both hands.

"Stay back!" I yelled to Marion and Olive. Symphony had already shown she wasn't afraid to pull the trigger. I jabbed the point of my knife hard into her side so she could feel it even through the layers of wool. "Let go of the gun."

"No!" she grunted. "Get off me!"

She released her grip on the gun with one hand and used the other to bash me in the side of the head with it.

"Ow!" I yelled, and loosened my hold on her enough that she scrambled backward across the floor.

Symphony's arm swung from me to Marion and back. Her perfectly coiffed auburn hair was mussed now, and there was a gash in her wool jacket.

"Stop! I will shoot! I will shoot you all!"

"All?" I said. "Maybe you'll get one of us before we get you. But only one, and the rest of us will come for you, so you'd better choose wisely. Who do you think can do you the most damage?"

I knew, at least I hoped I knew, who she would choose. The loudmouth, the antagonizer, the one who wouldn't leave well enough alone and let an innocent man go to jail in her place. Not to mention, the one closest to her and easiest to hit.

Her arm shifted toward me.

"Don't let her get away!" I yelled, and tried to dive out of the way as she fired two shots in close succession. I'd gambled on her fumbling or hesitating, but time slowed and I could almost see the bullets carving a tunnel through the air toward my heart. Dying was not an option, but I couldn't find a way out of it, couldn't run fast enough this time.

"Millie! No!"

Someone knocked into me from the side, and we skidded together on the rug. I registered Marion's golden-brown curls scattered across my chest and shoved at him, but my hand slipped in something slick. "Marion?"

He didn't answer. My hand came away red. "Olive! Help!" I screamed, but she'd dived on top of Symphony and pinned the gun arm under her knee. A quick slice with Olive's switchblade across her thumb made her release the gun and scream like a devil on ice.

Then, like an angel, Lewis ran through the door, with my mother and Cal in tow, and then a man—Detective Sabatier? How? I didn't care right then. They helped Olive take charge of Symphony, and Lewis skidded to his knees beside me. He hauled Marion off me and laid him flat on the rug.

"I think he's been shot." I rolled to my knees and knelt over him, scanning his body for wounds. A flower of dark blood bloomed on the sleeve of his bright red sweater. His favorite color.

"Oh God," he moaned. And the very sound of it filled me with relief. He was alive. His eyes flickered open and squeezed shut again, and he clutched at his shoulder. "That witch shot me! Please tell me she's dead now."

A hysterical laugh bubbled up in my chest. "No, but she won't be shooting anyone else. Lewis—grab me something to make a tourniquet."

Lewis, his face stunned and stricken, bobbed his head and disappeared.

"Marion," I said, touching his hair. "You're gonna be okay. It's just your arm. We'll get you to Charity."

"But my new dress is sleeveless," he managed, trying to get a smile out of me. Then his pain-clouded eyes softened. "Are you okay?"

I swallowed down the sudden ache in my throat. "Thanks to you."

"It was nothing." He tried to shrug but winced.

"Don't start acting modest now," I said. "You still have to be our star."

"I know." He let his head sink back to the floor, and his eyes fell shut. "But not today, okay?"

I laughed and dropped onto the floor beside him, the coppery smell of blood filling my head. Tears filling my eyes. "You saved my life."

He smiled without opening his eyes. "Guess that makes us even."

CHAPTER

32

CHARITY HOSPITAL SMELLED of alcohol and sweat and positively rang with noise. Pretty much like a speakeasy, only with more nuns in giant white habits.

Marion sat upright in a narrow bed, tucked under a crisp white sheet, a bandage on his arm and his face pale. Everybody in our small universe had gathered around him like funeral attendees, though the sisters said he was going to be perfectly fine after a couple of weeks.

"Marion," my mother said from the foot of the bed, "next time you go to a shoot-out, do it in your own sweater." She held the stiff, bloodied sweater up to the light, so we could all see the small circular hole through the fabric.

"I'll be sure of that next time, Gladdie," Marion sniffed.

"Let's hope there won't be any more bullets," Cal said, patting Marion's leg through the sheet. "Detective Sabatier took that girl off to the jail, so at least she's out of our hair now."

"And so's he," I said.

"I wouldn't be so sure," Mama said, batting her lashes.

"What's that supposed to mean?"

Mama studied her fingernails. "Well . . . there's a reason Larry was there tonight. He and I have been seeing each other some, since that little incident at the police station. We've been keeping it low-key because of the case, but now that that's over . . . well." She wriggled a little, beaming.

"But what about the club?" Cal said. "You do know he's a cop, right?"

Mama waved a hand. "Oh, Larry doesn't care about *Prohibition*, only murderers."

"So he says until you break up with him," I said. "Then he'll want revenge."

Mama scowled at me. "Why you gotta be such a pessimist, Millie?"

"I'm not, I'm just—"

"Can you two hush?" Marion said peevishly. "You're making my head ache. I don't want to hear about Gladys and the cop's torrid romance. I want to know what *happened* tonight. How did you all get to the apartment? How did you know what was going on?"

Mama and Cal both looked at Lewis, who was standing by the bed, holding Marion's hand. He blushed. "It was me, I guess."

"You guess?" Cal said. "Don't be so modest, kid."

Lewis cleared his throat. "Well. I. Uh. I saw that Symphony person had a gun, and I didn't have a weapon, so I knew I'd be no use in there. So, I decided the best thing I could do was go call the police. I thought since Symphony was there waving a gun around, they'd figure out she was the bad guy and not Marion. I didn't notice there was a telephone in the hall; I just ran back to the place I knew had one—the club."

"But when he got there," Cal said, "we'd just arrived, and he told us what was happening instead of calling the cops. Gladys's new cop boyfriend was meeting her outside, so she went and rounded him up. And we got there as fast as we could."

"Could've been a little faster," I said, gesturing to Marion's bandaged arm.

"It was fast enough," Marion said, squeezing Lewis's hand. "Thanks for your quick thinking." He looked at me and Olive and grinned. "And for you two, diving in there with those little toothpicks you call knives."

"Toothpicks!" I cradled my knife and crooned, "Don't listen to him, Pearl."

Olive rolled her eyes.

"So, what happens now?" Mama said.

"I get my star back, I hope." Cal squeezed the toes of Marion's foot and beamed at him. "Didn't want to tell you, but even before it got busted up, the club was hurting without you. The Red Feather Boys keep asking when you'll be back."

"They do?"

"Course. And these days, Lewis plays the piano likes he's tickling a dead animal." She winked. "Needs his inspiration back, I say."

Lewis turned positively fuchsia. Marion laughed, color creeping up his neck, too.

"Well, Marion's free to come back now," I said. "He doesn't have anything to fear except a sleeveless dress."

Marion groaned, but he was still smiling. "And I'm free of that apartment. No offense, ladies, but I'm ready to luxuriate in the company of my own self for a while."

"And I'm ready to have my bed to myself," I said. "No more sharing covers!"

Amid the gentle razzing directed at Marion, I realized this meant I was free, too. Free to stop spending every waking hour hunting down leads and making up stories and getting in knife fights. Free to go back to cooking Cal's books and mopping floors and flirting with Olive and scrapping with Duke over who Cal left in charge.

Free. Huh. I'd never known freedom could feel so hollow.

But what else did I want?

———·———

The Cloak and Dagger club was still a grimy, low-ceilinged dive. Smoke still hung over the tables and clung to our clothes and our hair.

But here—here, at least—we were not outcasts or funny dressers, pickpockets or dope fiends or burglars or whatever the rest of the city believed of us. We were together. We were royalty.

Two weeks after Marion left Charity Hospital, Marion-the-glamorous took the stage at eleven sharp, clad in her new beaded costume, which Mama had added sleeves to so the bandage wouldn't show. The room full of loud talkers quieted down when the spotlight stopped and settled on her, turning her blue eyes translucent, her skin pale white under the dragonfly necklace resting against her collarbone. A whistle sailed up from the two tables packed full of Red Feather Boys at the front, and Marion's teeth flashed brighter than ever. Both versions of Marion were eighteen years old tonight, and they were free from the cops, and free of any chance Philip Leveque could control them again.

Lewis's fingers dragged music from the piano keys; his mouth smiled a secret smile at Marion. Cal perched on a barstool in her tuxedo and top hat with Rhoda behind her, arms around her, chin resting on her shoulder. Mama leaned against the bar next to Sabatier, their hands twined together. With her other hand, she held a long cigarette holder, from which she was vigorously smoking. Duke slid Sabatier a glass of something, and he lifted it in my direction. I raised my brows, and he chuckled and mouthed, *Water*.

I laughed out loud. He'd returned my beret the first night after arresting Symphony Cornice, and I figured that counted for enough to give him half a chance.

"What's so funny?" Bennie said, sidling up next to me like a stray dog.

I took a step away from him. "You've got some nerve coming in here."

"Millie, I'm—"

"A weasel? I know it."

Bennie looked down into his glass. "You didn't tell Cal what I did yet. I'd hoped that meant you forgave me."

I crossed my arms over my chest. "It means I've decided it's more useful for you to owe me one."

Bennie blinked, wide-eyed. "What do you—"

But Olive slid between us, cutting him off, and nudged me with the tray propped on her hip. "Birthday boy's about to start your favorite song. What do you say, Millie? Want to dance?"

I turned as if Bennie hadn't said anything at all and took Olive's hand. "I sure do."

Lewis played the intro to the first song Marion and I sang together, when he was still an Uptown kid and I was teaching him how to wring out the mop, how to swish it on the floor.

You wink, dear, and make me trip over my feet
You smile and I fall on my face
But falling is easy when you hold my hand
For you I'd fall anyplace

The Red Feather Boys stared up at Marion with devotion. But on every other line, Marion's gaze slipped toward stage right, toward Lewis, and Lewis's gaze met his, steady and true.

Maybe Marion *was* falling, like the song said. I hoped so. He deserved this kind of fall.

Olive set her tray on the bar and led me out onto the dance floor, and her eyes on mine made me forget there'd ever been any eyes but hers. Maybe this time, I wouldn't push her away. Maybe this time, I'd let myself fall, too.

As we swept around the floor together, a red hat bobbed through the crowd, and then a face appeared at the edge of the dance floor. The girl was wearing a purple dress and sparkling heels, but in her hand she held a notebook, and she'd tucked a pencil in that red confection of a hat.

Kitty Sharpe gave me a small wave. And after the song, when Olive had given me a lingering look that promised more dances later, I went and found Kitty.

I touched her arm, and she turned around, red lips smiling like a cat's. She leaned close to be heard over the jazz. "Congratulations, Miss Coleman."

"For what?"

"You solved the crime." She took the pencil out of her hat. "Now you owe me a story."

ACKNOWLEDGMENTS

OVER THE YEARS it took to write *The Boy in the Red Dress*, I fell in absolute love with these characters (even Gladys!) and had multiple false starts trying to find the story that felt like their truth and mine. But lucky for me, I didn't have to search for that truth alone.

A galaxy-size thank-you goes to the team of professionals who guided this book (and its anxious wreck of an author) to publication. Thank you to my agent Victoria Marini for fighting hard for me, and to her assistants Lee O'Brien and Maggie Kane for helping make it all happen.

Thank you to my editor Maggie Rosenthal, who has always understood this book and where it needed to go, and helped steer it there with a masterful hand.

Thank you to my brilliant copyeditors Janet Pascal, Krista Ahlberg, and absolute queen Anne Heausler, whose knowledge of New Orleans took the authenticity of *The Boy in the Red Dress* to a new level. Thank you to my sensitivity reader Jonah Mosher, whose insights brought this book closer to what I wanted it to be in so many vital ways, and to the team who made this book so pretty—jacket designer Kelley Brady, jacket artist Freya Betts, and interior designer Nancy Brennan.

My writer friends also deserve personalized trophies for putting up with my whining and middle-of-the-night brainstorming texts while I wrote (and rewrote) this book.

Thank you, Tia Bearden, for loving my characters as much

as I do, and never giving up on them or me. Thank you, Sasha Peyton Smith, for always being confident I could do it, especially when I was least confident.

Thank you, Kris Waldherr, for the insightful readings (both beta and tarot), and Heather Webb, for your generous advice. Thank you, Sarah Lyu, for being a trusted voice of reason, and Anna Birch, for commiserating as we travel this debut year together. Thank you, Amy Oliver, for boosting my mood even when I wanted to lay my head on the Panera table and give up writing forever.

Thank you to the Black Warrior Writers, who were the earliest readers of *The Boy in the Red Dress* and showed me I had something worth pursuing, and to the writers of Pitch Wars 2017 and Class of 2K20 Debuts, who gave me so much advice and sympathy. Thank you to my Pitch Wars mentors Heather Cashman and McKelle George; I was at a low point when you chose me, and your encouraging words made all the difference.

Thank you to my friends Amanda Mulkey, for helping me celebrate every milestone; Wendy Long, for being on my team since the actual '90s; and Kristen Mullins, for donating a little piece of your gorgeous smartassery to Millie's character. Thank you to my Egan's people; you were the inspiration for the Cloak and Dagger, a place where, even in 1929—or in Alabama— people outside the mainstream can find family.

Thank you most of all to my family for always believing I'd someday be a published author, even when it took longer than we expected. To my sister Kelly Lambert, thank you for sharing my vision for this book and always having my back, even when a trampoline fight turns ugly. Mom and Dad, thank you for giving my girls safe arms to snuggle in when Mama was busy writing. To my husband, thank you for acting out scenes with me, putting up with my crankiness when I'm stuck, and cooking all those dinners by yourself when I'm supposed to be helping but "just have to finish this scene."

To my two sweet girls, I'm not going to lie—you didn't make writing this book any easier! But you made me laugh even when I was stressed and refused to let me withdraw completely into my work cocoon, which was probably a good thing. Thank you for all the elaborate hairstyles, the pretty drawings, and most of all the hundreds of hugs and kisses you give me freely every day. I love you both so much.

To my dear, wonderful readers, the password is I LOVE YOU FOREVER. You're welcome in the Cloak and Dagger Club anytime.